GHOST PUNCH
NIGHT TERRORS

A. LAWRENCE

Night Terrors

Published by: Cloaked Press, LLC
PO Box 341
Suring, WI 54174
Cloakedpress.com

Cover Design by:
Carmilla M. Ravensworth
carmillacreates.carrd.co

ISBN: 978-1-952796-50-0

To Cindy. Thanks for reading
even when you were afraid.

CONTENTS

CHAPTER 1: LIVING THE DREAM

Shay's boots crunched on frozen blades of yellow grass. Trees stood sentinel around her, tall and solemn against a sky streaked bloody by the setting sun.

Ghosts walked with her.

Silent, pale, skeletal figures trailing thick clouds of glowing mist. Some distant part of her thought she should be afraid, should be running, but she kept trudging forward.

She stepped into a clearing.

An enormous moon glowed above, turning each blade of grass sharp and silver. It hung bloated and full above a circle of blue light that carved its way around the tree line.

Hundreds of ghosts crowded along its edge, washing up against it like waves. They pressed at her back and she had no choice but to step over, even though it was the last place she wanted to be.

It was the circle behind Holt Manor, where she'd fought Archibald. Where she'd nearly been lost to the void.

Where something worse had happened, so terrible that it gave a ghost without memories pause.

1

It wasn't until she crossed over that she saw him.

Archibald stood in the center of the circle, his back to her. She could barely tell it was him, a shriveled thing with gray skin and a whisp of white hair around the ring of his scalp, his clothes tattered and decayed.

When he turned to face her, he looked as he had in life. A tall, well groomed man with curly blonde hair swept away from his face, eyes glowing the same color as the circle.

He mouthed something at her.

"What?" Her own voice echoed, like it was coming from somewhere else.

He mouthed it again, more urgently.

"I can't—"

He was suddenly right in front of her, gripping her shoulders, his mouth moving but the wind whipping way the sound before it reached her. She recoiled, but he held her firmly in place. She shook her head, trying to say she couldn't hear him, to let her go, but she couldn't speak, her teeth clenched too tightly together.

One hand pulled away, but silver threads connected Archibald's fingers to her shoulder.

He looked up.

Shay followed his gaze and wished she hadn't.

The moon was closer, dropping slowly through thick lines of gossamer string.

It was a web.

It wasn't the moon.

It rotated just as she realized what it was and dropped to the ground with a shuddering thud. A pale, diseased thing that had too many arms, skin covered in puckered welts. Its face was a mass of scars.It crawled towards her and she tried to get away but her legs were stuck in thick webbing that covered the ground. Archibald was batted to the side like he was nothing, falling limp on the grass.

A massive hand with dark, serrated nails reached for her.

Shay jerked awake with a gasp.

Finnias was right above her and she shrieked, shoving him away. He sat back far too calmly, crossing his arms over his chest. "That's rude. I was trying to help you."

"You scared me!" She flopped back against her pillow. Pale, morning light wormed through the gaps in her new curtains, streaming across the ceiling. "I was...there was..."

"You were having a nightmare." Finnias sat on the chair she'd put next to her bed, his ankle on his knee, leaning against one hand. "I know. I kept you from falling off the bed. You're welcome."

"Oh." She put a hand over her chest. Her heartbeat so hard she was pretty sure she wasn't going to need coffee to wake up. "Right. Thanks."

"You're welcome." Finnias leaned back. He didn't need the chair, she'd only put it there after she'd woken up and found him looming over her in her sleep the first night he'd been anchored to her.

Max did not like the chair, but she was pretty sure they'd hate to find Finnias just standing there much more.

Shay sat up and pulled her braid over her shoulder. Most of her hair had escaped from its binding in her sleep, falling around her face. She untied the end and grabbed her brush from the nightstand. "Y'know, it's been like three weeks since I saw that death omen. I think I'm okay."

"Even if that was how death omens worked—"

"How do you know how they work?"

"-I'm not leaving it up to chance." Finnias ignored her question.

"Because if I die, you lose your anchor, and we have no idea what will happen, right?" She brushed through her hair methodically, starting at the bottom and working her way up. "We could always find you a nice potted plant to stick your ghost essence on."

"Conversations would certainly be more intelligent."

"Hey, rude." She pointed her hairbrush at him.

He ignored her again. "However, I doubt that's how it works."

"So you know how death omens work, but not how to imprint on something like a baby chick? You're the ghost here."

"Oh, is that the current theory?" Finnias arched one eyebrow. "That I'm some sort of baby bird?"

"Last I heard," Shay said.

It was at least something close to what Arlo had said. He and Jo had been debating what exactly Finnias was and how to handle him. Shay thought it was pretty obvious. Finnias had given up the echo of his death, his last memory, in order to save her life. In exchange, her presence was what kept him tied to the world of the living.

Either way, it was a necromancer thing, but finding out exactly what that meant proved harder than expected.

"Well, I suppose it's not the worst thing in the world," Finnias said.

"Aw, Finn, I knew you liked me," she joked.

Finnias smiled, just a bit. He'd become more and more expressive over the last few weeks, to the point that he almost showed affection. "On occasion I find your company tolerable."

He must have really been warming up to her. Like a really angry rescue cat.

"Thanks, I love you, too."

"This isn't going to distract me from your nightmare," Finnias said. "Was it the same?"

Shay put down her brush and started braiding her hair. "It's always the same, so we don't need to talk about it."

"It's been weeks."

"I'm aware." She tied her hair off. It wasn't the best braid in the world, but at least her hair wasn't left to roam wild and free. "I mean, I almost died, I think that's pretty normal."

"But the same dream?" Finnias's eyebrows pinched together. "I believe it's well past time that you talk to Jo."

"Why?" Shay stared at him.

"She may be able to help, or at least provide insight."

Shay snorted. "Yeah, okay. She'd just be like 'oh, Shay, you're super traumatized, of course you're having nightmares. Don't forget to restock the sandalwood incense. It smells like old ladies so I adore it'."

"Jo does not sound like that."

"I don't know what you're talking about, that was spot on, I even scared myself." Shay grabbed her phone off the charger. "Oh gross, it's only eight?"

At least she had a text from Max. Just a good morning, but she smiled as she replied that it was too early.

Finnias sighed, which was strange, since he didn't need to breathe. "Can you focus?"

"On Max? I try," Shay said.

"On Jo."

"What about her?"

Finnias looked ready to throttle her, so she was doing something right. "She's a witch that specializes in divination."

"Yeah, I know? What, is she going to divine my dreams?" Shay left the warmth of her covers, grabbing a sweater to pull on over her sleep shirt.

"Yes."

"It is freezing in here." Shay could ignore him, too. It was freezing outside of her blanket cocoon. The radiator ticked as it warmed up, but it never really seemed to warm up her room.

Problems with being haunted.

"I'm serious, dreams sometimes have meaning," Finnias said. "And repetitive dreams even more so. You should talk to her."

"Oh, so you don't know how to haunt plants, but you're a dream expert now." Shay pulled open her curtains.

Snow piled thick on the roof below her window and layered on the tree branches. Other than a handful of black tire tracks marring the street, a snowglobe could have been upended overnight, leaving the world pale and silent.

Shay sat on the window seat and drank in the quiet. There had been a few flurries earlier in the month, but this was the first real snowfall.

"It snowed like this, when I died." Finnias pressed a hand to the window. Vines of frost curled from his fingers across the glass.

"Do you…remember it?" Shay had seen it, herself. The snow on the ground, the circle laid bare. Her dream fluttered at the edges of her consciousness like cobwebs.

"No." He shook his head and seemed to come back to himself, the frost melting. "I only saw it with you and Duncan."

Shay pulled her feet up on the bench and patted the cushion next to her. Finnias sat down and she took his hand, lending him a solidness that made sitting almost necessary. "Do you…want to?"

They hadn't talked about it. His missing memories. She wasn't sure if it was something she was supposed to talk about, but it felt appropriate, with him kind of bringing it up.

"I don't know," he admitted. His fingers were cold in hers. "I've been considering it, these past few weeks. Even if it is possible, I'm not sure that I want them, not if I was keeping company with the likes of Archibald and Emmaline."

"I—"

A loud knock barely announced Duncan's presence before he burst into her room, making Shay jump hard enough to let go of Finnias's hand. "Good morning, Shay! Good to see you up and at 'em before sunset! You too, Finnias."

"Duncan," Finnias said in return. Duncan was the only other person who could reliably hear him. Probably because he'd been possessed by him more than once.

"What do you want?" Shay glared at him.

"I want what I've always wanted for my dear baby sister, for her to be up and about and seizing the day—"

"I will kick you down the stairs," she threatened.

"Yeah, fair." Duncan shrugged. "Actually, I'm here to tell you that you have a meeting. Right now."

Shay leaned her head against the cold window. "Ugh."

Duncan cackled. "Oh, I love that you have those now. It's so much fun being on the other side."

"You have work, too," Shay reminded him.

"I do, but it's in a nice, quiet, only mildly haunted library," Duncan said. "And I don't have any meetings today. I'm going to drink six gallons of coffee and attempt to vibrate myself into orbit."

"You do that." Shay accepted Finnias's hand up to get to her feet and followed Duncan down into the kitchen. Jo frowned at her tablet on the table. Arlo was going through the sidebar, pulling out jars.

Finnias drifted to the chair by the window, his gaze pulled to the snow outside.

"Morning!" Arlo said when he saw her. It was still a little weird, having him back. He wasn't home much, attempting to deal with Teton Falls increasingly worse ghost problem. "Glad you're up, we're heading out, need someone to man the counter."

"I could woman the counter," Shay said.

"Yeah." Jo didn't look up from her tablet but raised her hand to get a fist bump. Shay obliged.

"...Wait, that's it? The whole meeting?" Shay asked.

"Could have been an email." Duncan poured coffee into his thermos. "Or a text."

"Or a post-it note." Shay held out a mug for Duncan to fill for her. "Why don't I ever get to head out?"

"Like we said, need someone to watch the shop," Arlo said.

"Besides, I'm just doing some tarot readings and home cleansing for the holidays, you wouldn't enjoy it." Jo closed her tablet. "Now, the shop is going to be busy, so if we need to call someone in—"

"I can handle it, but I won't like minding the shop, either," Shay said. "What are you doing? I could help you."

Arlo shrugged. "Few hauntings."

"I could help with that," Shay said. "I should practice the whole punching thing, anyway, right?"

"You can when we figure out why you saw a death omen," Jo said. "Besides you...tend to...well, the thing is, when it comes to hauntings..."

"You make them worse," Duncan finished for her.

"Your face makes things worse," Shay shot back.

"That's so sweet, I'm going to cry." Duncan swung his bag over his shoulder. "Well, I'm off. Love working on a Saturday. Best part of the job. Call me if you need anything but try very hard to not need anything. I have a hot date tonight."

Jo grinned at him. "Is it a town meeting?"

"Ooh, you got me there, but this time it's an actual date. Gideon is taking me ice skating." Duncan pretended to swoon.

Shay frowned at him. "When did you learn to ice skate?""I never did, he's going to have to hold my hand the whole time, and then buy me hot chocolate," Duncan said. "He has been warned. Anyway, have a great day everyone. Enjoy the readings, and the ghosts, and…retail hell."Shay made a face at him, which he returned before he left the kitchen.

"Don't worry," Arlo said. "If I have trouble locating the ghosts I'll ask Jo if I can call you in."

"I'll say no," Jo snapped and he grinned at her.

"I don't actually need your permission to do anything," Shay reminded her.

"Yes, you do, I'm your boss," Jo said."Y'know, I'm fine, I can do that," Shay said. "I haven't seen any black dogs, or…magpies? Owls? Besides the house guardian, but she's not swooping in to predict my doom, so that's probably fine."

The new house guardian was carved to look like an owl. She was perched on the shelf above the cash register, where Shay could stand on the stool to give her loose change.

Jo sighed. "Shay—"

"And I have an attack ghost now," Shay reminded her. "I point and he takes care of the problem."

"No, I don't." Finnias finally looked away from the window.

"But you could."

"I won't."

"Boo on you, then." Shay finished doctoring her coffee the way she liked it, sitting next to Jo. "Boo on all of you."

"Look. We'll figure out the necromancer thing," Arlo said. "But for now, well, it's all new."

She sighed. "I know."

It wasn't that Shay wanted to throw herself into danger. Ghosts that weren't Finnias were terrifying, and more often than not trying to kill her.

But she wanted to be out and helping, doing something. Not just minding the counter.

"For now, we play it safe." Jo stood up. "I'd better get ready. And you'd better head out."

"Yup." Arlo finished getting his things together. "I'll see you guys tonight."

"I'll be here," Shay said.

Chapter 2:
Magical

Shay attempted to get up the willpower to make herself toast, or at least try to get Finnias to stop staring at the snow.

It was still a work in progress when Max walked through the door. Finnias vanished the moment that they did. He promised he didn't hate Max, that it was merely a conflict of energies, but Shay had her suspicions that he was lying. "I can't believe it, a wild Shay, really up before nine o'clock," they said.

"Wow, that's how you greet me?" Shay had no trouble getting to her feet to cross the room to them. "I am the epitome of a morning person, thanks."

"Sure." Max took off their jacket. The second it was off she hugged them, probably too tightly. Their sweater was soft and they smelled like coconuts and snow. They hung up their jacket with one hand, holding her with the other. "Good morning to you, too. Are you okay?"

"Just really glad you're here."

"Aww, you just want someone to help you with the counter." Max patted her head. "Which no amount of hug bribes will get me to do."

"Wow." Shay decided to let them believe that was the reason. "I can't believe you won't accept hugs as payment for violating labor laws. I'm hurt. It's like you don't even love me."

"I love no one that much."

"It's not like seeing your perfect face—" she smooshed their cheeks with her hands. Their skin was soft and still cold from being outside. "-isn't enough for me."

They sighed, but it was more fond than exasperated. "Yes, I'll keep you company."

"That's all I want." She smiled, patting their cheeks before stepping back. "You look nice. I like the sweater."

"Oh, thanks," Max said.

"What's the occasion?"

"Being seen in public?" Max shrugged. "No real occasion."

Shay was suddenly very, very aware that she was still in her pajamas. "I…should get ready for that. Probably. But really, I mean, the hoodies were great and fine, but you've been dressing nicer lately. And, y'know, seem more confident. Any reason? Are you dating? You'd tell me if you were dating, wouldn't you?"

The thought of Max dating someone made her feel sick, for some reason. Probably because they would have significantly less time for her.

"I'm not dating anyone, I would have told you." Max poured themself a cup of coffee. "I just…have been feeling more confident, I guess. More comfortable in my skin. I've been talking to Jo about gender stuff a lot, and it's really helped."

"…Why were you talking to Jo about gender stuff?" Shay frowned.

Max gave her a flat look. "You cannot be serious right now."

"Oh!" She felt a little stupid. "Cause…cause trans. And you're trans. Trans to trans communication. I got it."

"You forgot." They laughed.

"I did." She nodded. "But that's great! I'm really glad for you. I want you to be happy and comfy. The maximum amount, even."

"Really? You think that's funny?" They asked while she cackled at her own stupid pun.

It was a much slower day than she anticipated, probably because of the snow. Large, soft white flakes continued to tumble gently to the earth. It was pretty, but Max kept talking about how brutal the roads would be. Jo stopped by to give her a break and complained about it, too.

She was glad she didn't drive.

Near closing time Duncan blew through on his way from work to his date. He disappeared into the back and returned triumphant with his hair sticking up even more than usual, curled artfully above his forehead. The shop was empty of customers, voiding any safety measures she had against him. "Shay Shay! How do I look?"

"All that work and for what?" Shay asked.

"You're just jealous," Duncan said in a sing-song voice. "Because you don't have a hot date."

"Why would I be jealous of a hot date with Gideon?" Shay made a face. "Gross."

"I'm glad you're so against it, because if we had the same taste in guys that would get real weird, real fast."

"Real, real fast," Max agreed. They were sitting at the table in the corner, reading a fantasy book. At least she assumed it was, there was a dragon on the cover.

"You're weird enough for all of us." Shay leaned against the counter. Duncan gave her wide eyes. "You look fine. Shouldn't you get going?"

"He's picking me up, so you're stuck with me until he gets here." Duncan grinned at her.

"Wow, love that for me."

Duncan leaned in close, his voice dropping to a hushed whisper. "You know, if you're really jealous—"

"I'm not."

"-you could always just get those rocks out of your skull and ask Max to be your hot date."

She smacked at his shoulder but he jerked away with a laugh.

"Why do I have a feeling you're making fun of me?" Max narrowed their eyes.

"Maxi pad, I would never." Duncan put a hand to his chest, pretending to be hurt.

"Maxi pad?" Shay's voice tripped through a few octaves as she tried very, very hard not to laugh.

Max sighed, heavily. "You literally just called me maxi pad."

"It's because you keep us safe all night long," Duncan said.Shay did dissolve into giggles at that. Max gave her the most long suffering look she'd ever seen and she had to duck behind the counter, practically wheezing.

"It isn't that funny," Max told her.

"You're...helping me...during a difficult...period!" She managed to gasp out.

Duncan laughed with her. Max made a pained noise like a balloon deflating.

Gideon chose that moment to walk in, brushing snow from his hair and the shoulders of his dark coat. "...What are we laughing at?"

"The worst jokes anyone has ever told," Max said.

"Yeah, that tracks." Gideon nodded.

"Hey, you!" Duncan threw his arms around Gideon's neck, kissing him on the cheek. "Glad you made it. How bad is it out there?"

"Bad enough I think I'm going to insist on picking you up for work on Monday," Gideon said. "It's still coming down."

Duncan rocked back on his heels. "Are you saying something about my driving?"

"It's bad!" Shay told him.

"You don't have a license! You can't criticize me!" Duncan yelled back.

"I can because you suck!"

"You are pretty bad," Max agreed.

"At least I'm pretty." Duncan grabbed his coat from where he'd hung it next to the door, swinging it over his shoulders. "Shall we?"

"Yeah, get out, this is a place of business," Shay said.

Gideon reached behind him and turned over the open sign. "Yeah? What now?"

"Still going to have to ask you to leave," Shay said. "We're closed."

Gideon laughed, linking arms with Duncan. "See you guys later."

"Much, much, much later," Duncan agreed. The bell chimed merrily, accompanying a blast of cold air.

Max got up and locked the door for her. She supposed it was close enough to closing time. If someone knocked on the door she might open it.

Probably not.

"Give me a few minutes to close up," Shay said. "Then we can order pizza or something."

"Are you buying?" Max's eyebrows rose.

"Hey, you freeloaded all day, you can't give me those judgey eyebrows," Shay said. "But yes, I am paying. I have real money now."

Not a lot of money, but enough to buy pizza.

"I never thought I'd see the day." Max pretended to wipe a tear away. "Waking up early, buying your own food…you're all grown up now."

"I'm six months older than you," Shay reminded them, pulling the broom out of the tiny maintenance closet. "Go order whatever, I'll finish closing up."

"Whatever, huh?"

"I'm a human vacuum," Shay said. "I will eat anything."

Max looked out the window and grimaced. "I'll just…see if there's a frozen one. I am not going to be the reason some delivery kid is wrapped around a tree."

"Okay, yeah, fair point."

She closed down the till and swept up the shop. Finnias made an appearance, but just as a figure watching the snow. She greeted him, but he didn't reply.

He got like that, sometimes. She was starting to learn his moods and modes. There was very present Finnias, and this Finnias, who didn't even seem to be in the same room as her, like an echo of himself.

He'd once told her a ghost was like an empty house.

She turned off the inside lights. Spellbound was a small store, it never took very long to close up, even after a busy day. She headed back to the kitchen.

It smelled of baking pizza, and Max was just cutting it into slices. They ate while chatting about everything and nothing. "Now that we've consumed this entire pizza—"

"It was small," Shay said. "I think frozen pizzas used to be a lot bigger."

"Or maybe you're just hungrier," Max teased her. "Anyway, I have a surprise for you."

"A surprise?" She glanced at the calendar. It was the very last days of November. "I know you don't really do Christmas, but you're kind of early."

"It's not for Christmas, you goof," Max said. "C'mon."

They led her through the kitchen and out the back door. The motion light turned on, glinting off of the still falling snow.

"Is the surprise freezing to death?" She shivered when the cold air hit her, winding its way into her sweater.

"It's kind of the opposite," Max explained. They walked across the yard and Shay followed in their footsteps. At some point Arlo had shoveled the walkway back to the detached garage. It had filled up again, leaving a long indent in the snow.

Shay searched for ghostly glows, but saw nothing.

"Anything out here with us?" Max asked, as if sensing her nervousness.

"No," she said. "Not even Finnias."

"I figured. He hates me," Max said.

"He doesn't hate you," Shay reassured them, even though she was pretty sure she was lying. "He just…doesn't actually like anyone."

"He likes you," Max said.

Shay shrugged. "I mean, I guess. In his own weird little way."

"He does, I can tell," Max said. "Okay. Don't move."

"If you put snow down the back of my sweater—"

"How old do you think I am?" Max asked.

Shay decided to not tell them she'd had plans to do that exact thing to Duncan.

They were close to the back gate, their car parked on the other side of it. They grabbed the shovel from where Arlo had left it propped up against the fence and used the tip to draw a wide circle around her. The moment they completed it the line glowed, like liquid gold bubbled up from underneath the snow. Tiny globes of light rose from the ground to mingle with the falling snow.

It was breathtaking.

"How's it look?" Max set the shovel back.

It was a shame that they couldn't see their own magic. "It's incredible. You have the prettiest magic. Is this the surprise?"

"Of course not." Max smiled widely at the compliment. "Wait right here."

Shay folded her arms in an attempt to keep warm. If she looked back at the house she could see the warding. A glowing line around the perimeter of the house, and a faint shimmer in the air. No one else could see magic. It was all thought, intent, and direction of energy to them.

The gate closed and she turned back to Max, who was holding a package in their hands.

"Okay, so, this isn't much," they said, despite the fact that they were holding a rather large package in their hands. "But...well! Just open it."

"I don't have anything for you." Shay accepted the gift. It was soft, but heavy. She ripped the paper off and gawked, holding it up.

It was a jacket.

It was her jacket.

She'd thought Jo had thrown it out, after Archibald cut up the sleeve. It had saved her arm from being a mangled mess, but there had been enough cuts and blood she was sure she'd never see it again.

"Turns out, Nana knows how to get blood out of just about anything," Max said. "Slightly worrying, actually. And her fancy sewing machine can punch through leather, so..."

"Holy crap." She swung it on and zipped it up. The inside was lined with thick fleece and she instantly felt warmer. "This is amazing. I owe Nana like, the biggest hug. Like ten hugs."

"I'm sure she'll be glad to accept them, but for now, I will take her place." Max held out their arms and she hugged them, tightly. They held her there for a bit longer and she didn't really mind.

"You're the best."

"So you keep saying." Max's voice rumbled in their chest and she felt warm and safe. They stepped back, after a moment. "I just, y'know. I'm glad. You're in my life. And I'm going to do anything I can to keep it that way. Including fixing your ugly jacket."

"It's not ugly," Shay said. It was. It was too big for her and a weird shade of dark gray-brown, but it was a comfortable weight on her shoulders. "Besides, it saved my arm."

"It did," Max said. "And I'm infinitely grateful. Helping Nana fix it was the least I could do."

She could have made a sarcastic quip, but they were so earnest that she couldn't bring herself to. The light from the magic made everything soft, shining in their eyes and highlighting their hair and the snow during it.

"Well, I'm infinitely grateful you stick around," she said.

"Never getting rid of me," Max said. "We'll be the next generation Arlo and Jo when they die of old age, running spellbound."

"And fighting ghost crime," Shay said.

"Absolutely," Max said. "But I'm not much of a baker."

"I'm not much of an…Arlo," Shay said.

"You'd need to grow about three feet, for one," Max joked.

Shay pouted at them. "A short joke? That was low."

"You're right, low hanging fruit," Max agreed. "That you can't even reach."

"Oh, Mx. Patel, you are being so mean to me right now," Shay said. "Jerk. Big tall jerkface."

"I'm completely average height," Max said. "And you're a dork."

"Nerd."

"Four-eyes."

Shay laughed. "You wear glasses, too!"

"But I'm not right now." Max grinned at her. "Insult still stands. Now—"

Finnias was suddenly standing next to them and Shay shrieked, jerking her hands away from Max's.

"It's about time you noticed me," he said, calmly.

"Oh my god, you...you!" She pointed at him.

He nodded. "Me. Arlo is inside. He needs to speak with you."

"He's home?" She looked at the garage. "Why did he park out front? Can't he text me? Or...I don't know, we could get him a life alert?"

"I have no idea," Finnias said. "I am simply relaying the message. I was fine with giving you two...privacy."

"Don't say it like that or I'll shove snow in your face while you're solid," she said. "Mess up your perfect hair."

His hair wasn't perfect. It was slicked back, but a curl eternally fell over one eye.

He smirked, just a tiny bit. "I'd love to see you try."

"Don't test me," she warned him.

"I'll let him know you're on your way." Finnias disappeared.

"Ugh!" She kicked snow where he had been standing.

"Are you okay?" Max was clearly trying very hard not to laugh.

"I'm surprised he let me come all the way out here without hovering like a helicopter dad," she muttered. "He's so...ugh. He's worse than Duncan, y'know? At least Duncan has to largely respect the laws of physics."

"His hair." Max understood her so well. "Yeah, I guess…I can see that. He doesn't have to worry about walls….floors…"

"Boundaries," Shay muttered. "Let's just go see what Arlo wants before he comes back out here and drags me inside."

CHAPTER 3: FUDDY DUDDY

Shay was happy to have her jacket back, but the warmth of the inside washed over her like a balm. She kicked off her boots, barely getting them onto the boot mat next to the door.

Jo stood at the counter, placing cookie dough onto a baking sheet.

"When did you get back?" Shay asked. "Are we just not parking out back anymore?"

"I rode with Arlo," Jo said.

"Oh, makes sense." Shay looked around her to the cut out shapes on the sheet. "How stressed are we right now? What level?"

"I'm not stressed." Jo cut a reindeer out and slapped it onto the sheet. "It's Christmas. I'm baking Christmas cookies."

"It's not even December," Max reminded her.

"It's after Thanksgiving, so it's Christmas," Jo said, emphatically. "I see you got your jacket back."

"I did!" Shay twirled to show it off.

"It looks great," Jo said in the least sincere voice possible. Shay dropped her arms and gave her a look. "I'm sorry, I'm very happy for you. It looks very well repaired."

"Just say you think it's ugly," Shay said.

"It's so ugly."

"That's what I said," Max agreed.

"You guys just don't get sentimental value," Shay sniffed. "It saved my whole arm. You should be grateful. It would be much harder for me to sweep one armed."

"And yet, not impossible," Jo said.

Shay made a face at her. "I'm going to go see what Arlo wants, you two can be fashion snobs together."

Jo smacked the baking sheet against the grill inside the oven. "He's in the living room."

"Oh, we're mad at him," Shay said.

"I'm not mad. We are simply having a small…business partner disagreement," Jo said.

Shay nodded. "So you're pissed."

"Fine, yes, I'm beyond pissed," Jo admitted. "But…he unfortunately has made a few good points, and…anyway. Go talk to him."

Anxiety curled up in Shay's gut. She doubted anything that made Jo so mad she was going to make cookies she had to frost would be good for her. She headed to the living room, with its plethora of stuffed furniture. Arlo was getting a fire going, poking at fresh logs just barely catching alight, the smell of woodsmoke rolling through the room. Finnias stood near him, the fire reflecting oddly against him, like glass.

"Oh, hey, you got my message," Arlo said. "You guys have fun out there?"

"Maybe," Shay said. "Maybe next time don't use my friend as your own personal intercom system."

Finnias smirked a bit, which made it worth it. Sometimes he was distant, but most of the time it was like having another person in the room. If it weren't for the monochrome of blues and the hole in his chest, he could have just been a guy to Shay's eyes.

Only Duncan seemed to be able to see and hear him properly. Max said Finnias was just a vaguely person shaped cloud to them. Sometimes Jo couldn't see him at all.

"Well, I would love to, but you never answer your phone," Arlo said.

She dug her phone out of her pocket. At some point it had died, the screen completely unresponsive. "Okay, so, same friend is a ghost, and dead roommate means dead batteries."

"I did not drain your batteries," Finnias said.

"Intentionally, maybe."

"You wouldn't have answered, anyway," Max muttered, which was fair. She was terrible at remembering to check her phone, especially when Max was actively in the same building as her. Until a month ago, no one else texted her but Duncan.

"I think the problem here is that your phone is older than Finnias," Arlo said. "You should probably leave the antiques at home."

"Ha," Shay said. "Unless you're going to pay for a new phone—"

"I know what I'm getting you for Christmas," Max cut in.

"Nooo you got my jacket," Shay said. "Phones are expensive. Unless Arlo specifically is buying me a new phone, we can drop it. I wouldn't check a new one, anyway."

"It's true," Max agreed.

"Okay, fine, I'll think about it," Arlo said. "How about you two take a seat. We have business stuff to talk about."

Shay sat on the ottoman and Max on one of the arm chairs. Arlo finished poking the fire and straightened, dusting his hands off.

"The newest job is…a very large building," Arlo said. "It's definitely haunted, but I can't tell exactly where the spirits are. Makes it a little hard to clear it out. Jo and I discussed it, and we came to the conclusion that the best way to draw them out is to have you accompany me."

"…That's why Jo is mad," Shay said.

"You're using her as bait?" Max asked.

"Absolutely not," Finnias cut in.

"Hey, you don't get to tell me what to do," Shay said. "…But that does sound an awful lot like I'm bait. Or chum. Sounds more like chum. Here sharky sharky."

"I will be putting every precaution in place," Arlo said, confirming her chum status. "But we need this job, and we need to finish it, fast. There's an open air…well, not quite so open, but a Christmas market is being held at the old mall. It's a fun idea, but they've been plagued with cold spots, strange noises, shadow people, and whispers since it started two days ago. A few stalls were trashed overnight."

"That sounds like a poltergeist," Max said. "Have we heard anything about the spirit charmer?"

Shay shook her head. Emmaline disappeared the night they took down Archibald, but Finnias was convinced she was still out there, biding her time.

"I saw footage," Arlo said. "It didn't look like a poltergeist."

Jo came in with tea and cookies on her second-best tray. She set it on the coffee table and handed mugs to all of them. Shay learned to just go with it, even if she didn't really feel like tea. She wrapped her cold fingers around the mug. Jo sat next to her on the edge of the couch, her grip on her own mug turning her knuckles white.

"I believe the shadows and whispers are residual," Arlo continued. "The cold spots…well, it's a big open space with small space heaters, so…that's not really something I'm worried about. What I'm most concerned with is the vandalism. Stalls being overturned can quickly become people getting overturned."

"You didn't see anything?" Max asked.

"Second night there, and nothing," Arlo said. "Supposedly, a guard saw something, though I haven't had a chance to interview him."

"Right," Shay said. "So you want me to pull out the big mama ghost and tell her to get out of town."

"I want you to coax out the big bad ghost, so I know exactly what I'm dealing with," Arlo corrected her. "And then I will send you out and take care of the problem."

"This is too dangerous," Jo cut in.

"Shay will be in a salt circle the entire time," Arlo reminded her. "And we need this job. We can't afford to turn it down, and it has to get done fast."

"Things aren't that bad yet," Jo said.

"And I won't let them get that bad," Arlo shot back. "We are not losing the shop."

"What do you mean?" Shay asked.

Jo sighed. "Spellbound…is a passion project. It hasn't earned us a lot of money, and while the house is paid off, there are certain taxes and fees associated with running a business here, plus we're still paying off the renovations. It's not…critical, yet, but…"

"That sounds bad." Shay tried to remain calm, but that was her job and home they were talking about. "I've only worked here for like. A month."

"Of course, you'll have a place to stay, no matter what happens," Jo told her, gently. "I'm not kicking anyone out. Things just might change or be tight for a little bit."

"Less fancy tea," Arlo said.

"No, that will always be in the budget," Jo joked, weakly.

"Look, you've done a lot to help me," Shay said. "The least I can do is pull out the ghosties. Like bad teeth."

"Only if I'm coming with you," Max said. "I can help. You can pay me in food or something."

"I am going to be there, you know, the whole time," Arlo reminded them.

Shay wanted to make a quip about Max breaking labor laws for Jo but not her, but she felt a little too grateful to make fun of them.

"I'll be there, too," Finnias said, quietly.

"I still think there are other alternatives we should consider," Jo said. "I have been having dreams, and don't tell me they're just nightmares, I know when a dream means something."

Finnias gave Shay a significant look. She ignored him. Jo's dreams probably did mean something. Hers were definitely just nightmares. She was not a witch, and divination was so far out of her wheelhouse it had been outsourced to another country.

"Jo—" Arlo started.

"I'm just afraid you'll get a lot more than you bargained for if you go in there. Something is…off. Unbalanced. I know you feel like you have to fix things—"

"We're only in trouble because I was missing," Arlo said.

"That wasn't your fault." Jo sighed. "I just…I have a bad feeling. And it's not just anxiety, either. Unless you're going to study divination, you could listen to me."

"I saved the whole town, I think I'll be okay," Shay said. "And I've only kind of died once—"

"That's not funny," Jo and Max said at the same time.

"I'm just saying! I have a pretty good track record, and I want to help," Shay said. "Besides I was like. Born to do ghost stuff. Probably."

"You could do literally anything else," Finnias told her. She continued to ignore him.

"I know," Jo said. "I know you probably think I sound like an old fuddy duddy, but I just don't want you getting hurt any more than you already have."

"To be fair, saying things like 'fuddy duddy' is way more likely to make you sound like one," Shay said. Jo smiled thinly. "I know I can get hurt, I mean, I have gotten hurt."

Jo sighed. "All right, fine. As long as Max is with you—"

"Am I not here?" Arlo asked. "Am I still trapped in a basement?"

Jo smacked his arm. "You are also not allowed to joke about that. I know you'll do everything you can, but how about we have a little bit of ghost deterrent insurance. I'll talk to Rose, see if she's sensed anything. I just…I feel like something is wrong."

"I know," Arlo said. "But we're in the business, so…"

Jo sighed. "I know. As long as Shay's okay with it…"

"I am," Shay said. "I mean, I'll be in a salt circle and Max will be there, what can go wrong?"

"Why would you even say that?" Max glared at her.

"I like having famous last words." Shay shrugged.

"It'll be fine," Arlo said. "We should get going. The night is getting old and I'm already there. In and out, Jo, I swear."

"I am trusting you with her," Jo said.

"You guys know I'm an adult, right?" Shay asked. "I can drink and everything. I could go fight in a war."

Jo closed her eyes and let out a sigh. "I know you are. And I trust you, too. I know you won't do anything to needlessly endanger yourself."

"That makes one of us," Finnias muttered. Shay knocked her shoulder against his leg and all she got was cold on one side.

"I just worry, because I care about you."

"Awwww." Shay smooshed her hands to her cheeks. "Thanks mom, that's so sweet."

"Shut it." Jo was smiling, anyway. "Just…all of you, stay safe, don't take any risks. We'll be all right without this job, even if things get tight."

"Of course," Max said.

"And hey, if we're lucky, it was just some dumb kids tearing through the mall," Arlo said.

"Sure." Jo took a sip of her tea.

Arlo sighed. "You could sound slightly less like you think I'm a complete idiot."

"Why would I?" Jo's eyebrows rose. "When you are saying such stupid things?"

"Wow, thank you, I really appreciate that."

"I know."

"Well, now that Jo has her 'you're all stupid idiots and I'm the smartest person ever' speech out, how about we get going?" Arlo got up and clapped his hands.

"Why do old people always do that?" Shay asked Max.

"Herding us, like cattle," Max said.

"To the slaughter."

"Oh, definitely."

Arlo sighed. "You know what, I changed my mind, I'm going back alone, I don't need any of you."

Chapter 9:
Cool Chick

Shay leaned her head against the window of Arlo's beat up station wagon, watching the snow flurry through the amber of streetlamps, piling on the road, softening the lines of the sidewalk. Max talked quietly with Arlo. She let the noise mix with the rumble of the engine to wash over her.

Teton Falls was a long, narrow valley, situated between rolling hills full of cattle and wheat on one side and a mountain range on the other. It had been a farming community, back in the old days, but the fields went fallow, and industry moved in.

And back out again.

The Idaho National Laboratory was close enough that people still commuted out, and according to Duncan there was a pretty robust indie art movement, but downtown was nearly empty, and the mall had closed before Shay graduated. The bustling town she remembered eroded away into an empty shell of itself.

She picked at the new stitching in her jacket sleeve. She was grateful, of course she was. Max had put a lot of effort into getting her jacket back to her.

But the more she ran her fingers over the stitching, the more she remembered that night on top of the house, alone and scared. That sometimes she still looked in the mirror and for a brief instant saw a skull, or a woman with a thin face and a high-necked dress.

She wasn't sure if it was trauma or if it really was Emmaline, occasionally glancing through.

Maybe Finnias was right, and she should talk to someone.

"Shay?"

"Huh?" Shay looked up at Max. She really hadn't been paying attention. "We haven't fishtailed into a mailbox we're fine."

"What mailboxes," Arlo asked, which was fair. There weren't any houses around the abandoned mall.

"A metaphorical one," Shay said. "Anything can be a mailbox if you try hard enough."

"Sure," Max said. "Anyway, I was asking what wars you thought Arlo fought in."

"None," Arlo said. "When I called my knee the old war wound I was joking. There was no war."

Shay thought for a moment. "Well, besides the ongoing war between ghost and human, I think probably all of the world wars."

"All two of them?" Arlo asked.

"See, that's proof," Shay said. "Thank you for your service."

"I can't believe we get to work with such a decorated veteran," Max said.

Arlo sighed. "You two think you're so cute."

"Um, that's because we are so cute," Shay said.

Max nodded. "The cutest."

Arlo sighed again and turned into the mall parking lot. The car trundled through a pristine blanket of snow. Only a handful of lights flickered between orange and yellow like candlelight.

Only one other vehicle sat in the entire empty expanse parking lot, a white van with a green light on top and "Security Solutions" stenciled on the side. Arlo pulled up next to it. The back door was open, a tall white man probably a few years older than her sat inside, puffing on a vape like it was the only thing keeping him tethered to reality. Clouds of steam poured into the dark.

"Wow, he looks fun," Shay said.

"The security guard that saw something, he agreed to meet with me," Arlo explained, turning off the car. When he opened the door the cold swept away every bit of heat that he'd managed to coax out of the vents.

The guard scrambled to his feet, shoving his vape into his pocket like they weren't going to smell the artificial cotton candy from a mile away.

"Hi! Welcome!" He waved at them. "You're Mr. Hanson, right?"

"Mr. Gardner?" Arlo asked.

"Oh, uh, call me Nick," the guard said.

Arlo introduced her and Max as his associates. Finnias formed next to Shay, just out of sight behind the van door. He glared at the hulking darkness of the mall. Shay couldn't tell if that was a bad sign or not.

"So, you guys like, fight ghosts?" Nick asked. "Like…who you gonna call?"

"We assess potentially haunted properties and if there is an entity, we do our best to vacate it from the premises." Arlo was all business for a guy wearing a knitted hat with the biggest pompom Shay had ever seen. "Sometimes a haunting is just a plumbing problem or a carbon monoxide leak."

"Everything is up to code," Nick said, in a way that made Shay think that he'd been told to say it, which wasn't particularly comforting.

"I do believe that you have a legitimate haunting here," Arlo said, quickly.

"Yeah, we definitely do, I see things all the time," Nick said. Shay was sure that he did. "Even before they got things up and running, y'know? I've been night security for a while, even before this. Because they didn't want people breaking in, and shitty kids are always trying to spray paint the building or kick in the doors. Real pain."

Shay exchanged a quick glance with Max who gave her a look. At one point she'd almost become one of the shitty kids, before she left for college. In the end, Max wouldn't go with her, so she'd stayed home.

She supposed she was grateful.

"Yeah anyway, I'm supposed to do a walk through at least once a shift, and it's just the creepiest place," Nick continued. "There are still mannequins in there."

"No," Shay said.

"Yeah, you get it." Nick pointed at her. "Anyway, my partner and I, they called in sick tonight, but we were always hearing and seeing things. Whispers and weird shadows. See something dart behind the old photo booth. Creepy, but like…could ignore it, y'know?"

"What changed?" Arlo asked.

"So, they start this Christmas market, and it's fine or whatever. They want us to do rounds more. Sucks but it's an easy job, so it's fine. Then a few days ago we're heading down B Hall, the one that runs north to south, and we hear people talking. Like a whole group had broken in. So I ask Claire, that's my usual partner, she's cool, but anyway I ask her if she hears that and she said yeah. So we run over to the market to try and catch them. Lots of weird shadows that night…but there was this lady. Tall, pretty, had a…one of those big wand things with the cigarette."

"A cigarette holder?" Max asked.

"Yeah, one of those! Anyway, this lady looks like she's just standing there, but she was super pale, kind of washed out, y'know? And her dress was old fashioned and stuff," Nick said. "I tried to tell her she shouldn't be there. She smiled at me, blew smoke at me but it was…too much. Like way too much. And then I was suddenly in…well, it was a nightmare, because the next thing I knew I was waking up on the floor and my shift was almost over."

"You fell asleep?" Arlo asked.

"Yeah, man, I don't know, we both did," Nick said. "And Claire started calling in sick every day after that. Now the higher ups are saying you gotta clear the building? I dunno, feels bad man."

"That does sound like an apparition," Arlo said. "I came by earlier and checked around last night, but I'm hoping my visit tonight will be more fruitful."

"Yeah, it's like that. Like during the day and some nights it's like nothing, just a big, abandoned building," Nick said. "Creepy but it's fine. Then other nights it's like a whole other ballpark. I'll get you guys the key. We're not at the closest door to the market, but this is the easiest one to get through, y'know? Only have to unlock one door. Just don't wander around too much."

"We're just here to do a job," Arlo promised him. "Thank you for the time."

"No prob, man, it was nice chatting with you, gets lonely out here without Claire." Nick rummaged through the back of the van. "I'll get you a radio, too. So like, if you need something you can just holler. No one else is gonna be using it. I'll keep an eye on things out here."

"Thank you for your service," Shay said, and Max had to cough to disguise their laugh.

Nick passed along a radio and a ring of keys. "Thanks for checking it out, man. And for not thinking I'm just some crazy guy or something."

"Definitely not crazy," Shay said. "Ghosts are scary, I get it. We'll figure it out."

Nick's face split into a real smile. "Thanks, you're a cool chick."

"Uh, thank you." Shay tried not to grimace. She didn't want Nick to think they were even remotely on the same wavelength.

"Y'know, maybe I should get your number," Nick said. "Just in case like, I need to call someone about this."

Arlo coughed, that time, and Shay reminded herself to kick him later.

She smiled, somehow. "I don't have a phone."

"Oh." Nick looked like he didn't know if he should be upset or not. "That sucks?"

"Yeah, ghost hunting doesn't pay a lot," Shay said. "Thanks anyway, bye!"

"We'll call you if we need anything." Arlo lifted the radio.

"Yeah, all right," Nick nodded. "I'll just be out here. Doing my thing."

They walked towards the entrance, accompanied by the thunk of Nick closing the van doors. The green light on top glowed off of the snow before he pulled away.

"How does it feel to be a cool chick?" Max asked.

"Oh, Shay, maybe you should give him your number, just in case," Arlo added.

"I will kill both of you."

"You'd have to climb on something to reach," Max teased her.

"You like your kneecaps? Keep talking, see what happens to them."

Max outright cackled. "You know, you wouldn't have to be jealous of Duncan's hot date if you gave him a chance."

"Gross." Shay smacked their arm, which just made them laugh more. "Gross and disgusting. Absolutely not."

She tried to ignore that Duncan had said nearly the same thing earlier, regarding Max. She wasn't jealous, she didn't care, and she wasn't thinking about it.

"I don't like this." Finnias stared at the mall. "It feels…strange."

Shay was happy to change the subject, until she looked up at the looming darkness. It stood stark and black against the dull orange of the snowy sky filling her with trepidation, like ice cubes in her stomach. "…Well, we know it's haunted, right?"

"We sure do. Unless we need you, I think you should stay close to the doors." Arlo led them to the entrance. A large archway led to the doorway, so covered in graffiti it was impossible to make out what it said originally. "Man, I came to this place all the time growing up. It's kind of weird that it's closed. In Idaho Falls they turned their Sears into a charter school but what do we get? Big empty building, doing nothing."

"I used to go to the bookstore here, like, constantly," Shay said. "But I was a broke teenager with no money so…that's probably why they closed down."

"Yup, it was the two of us, entirely our fault," Max agreed. "We read so much for free they just couldn't keep going."

"Yeah, definitely wasn't the rising rent space or online shopping, all us." Shay nodded.

"Dang, can't believe you two killed the concept of the mall, that's brutal." Arlo unlocked the door and held it open for the two of them.

"We all have our own battles." Shay walked in.

It was marginally less cold inside, but Shay wouldn't call it warm. Other than the hollow echo of her boots squeaking on the tiles, it was completely silent. Arlo closed the door behind him, and the silence invaded.

"Haunted," Shay said.

Max nodded. "Definitely haunted."

"Case solved, let's go."

"No," Arlo said. "That's not the whole job. We have to get the ghosts out, too."

"Finnias, go stand outside," Shay said. He just looked at her, folding his arms.

"Hilarious," Arlo said, dryly. "Could you get serious, please?"

"Okay, grandpa, geez, keep your giant pompom on," Shay said.

She peered into the gloom. No spectral glows or hint of mist, just more shadows. It was just a cold, breathless tomb to consumerism. Arlo shone his flashlight over shuttered stalls. Between the empty planters were tables with chairs on top of them, like dead spiders with their legs curled up around their bodies.

"Wow, where will I sit?" Shay asked. "I don't see anything yet. Or feeling. I'm not a big feelings person, though. Max?"

"Just feels like the worst place I've ever been." Max stepped a little closer to her.

"What about the tunnels?"

Max thought for a moment. "No, this is worse."

"There's something here," Finnias told her. "Deeper in. You should stay here."

"Finn says there's something deeper in," Shay said.

"Then we'll set you up here," Arlo said. "But first let's take a moment. A training moment."

Both Max and Shay groaned.

"Don't be like that, this is an important learning opportunity," Arlo said. "I want you to close your eyes. Breathe. Try to ignore where you are, and focus on what you're really feeling, outside of how everything looks. It's hard, but it does get easier with practice."

Shay rolled her eyes even though Arlo couldn't see it but did as she was told. Nothing really changed.

"It's cold," Max said, after a moment. "But something…something is here. Something…it's like an echo, or a bad copy of something. It's there, but it's hard to figure out what it is."

"That's about what I'm getting, too," Arlo said. "You're good at this."

"Thanks," Max sounded pleased. "Shay?"

"It…" she tried to focus, but it was hard. "It feels…like its alive. Like it's going to pull us into the halls and hold us there."

Finnias touched her arm. The cold sank in through her sleeve, shaking her out of it.

"Sorry, I don't know why I said that," she admitted. "It's…it's empty. It's big and empty and sad."

"It's okay," Arlo said, but he was giving her a concerned look. "Like I said, it's going to get easier with practice, and this is good stuff. Let's set up a salt circle for you, I don't think you should go farther in."

"Yeah." She looked deeper into the mall and turned away with a shudder. Max patted her shoulder. It didn't help. "Good plan."

CHAPTER 8: WHISPERS

Shay dragged her heel across the floor, bouncing every time she met a new tile.

"I don't really feel like I'm helping." She hit the edge of the salt circle and moved her foot back to the beginning position.

Finnias sat on the table next to her. "Your presence should draw out anything that's not willing to show itself."

"Maybe."

"I cannot fathom why you are so determined to throw yourself into danger," Finnias said.

"I'm not." She looked up at him. His face was incredulous. "Really! I'm not."

"So much evidence points to the contrary," he said. "When we met, for instance."

"…In the old cafe?" Shay frowned. "I was dragged there.

"We met at the theater," Finnias said.

"We did?" Shay frowned. She was pretty sure she would have remembered that. "Oh yeah! When you possessed Duncan. I kind of forgot about that."

He rolled his eyes. "You were alone in a severely haunted building immediately after finding out you had dangerous abilities. I wouldn't say that I am exaggerating your lack of self-preservation instincts."

"...To be fair, there was free pizza," she reminded him.

"Oh yes, that definitely makes it worth your life."

"Hey, I made it out of there, and here I am." Shay spread her hands. "In the food court of an abandoned mall. Being useless."

"You do not have to be useful," Finnias said.

"I see where you're coming from, and that's kind of sweet, y'know, for you," Shay said. Finnias sighed, even though he didn't breathe. "What? It is. But...I don't like feeling like I'm just being coddled while my friends are in danger. You understand that, right?"

"I suppose," Finnias said. "Still....did you hear that?"

"No," Shay said, but even as she said it, she heard something, so sharp and sudden in the stillness that it made her press herself against the back of her chair.

A hiss of air, the sound of something moving and rustling.

For a moment she thought of rats, of the thing in the library basement, waiting to tell her what favor she owed it. She listened hard for the click of nails on the tiles, for the movement of a hundred little bodies scurrying through empty food stalls and overturned chairs.

It rose in volume, steadily, until she realized what she was hearing.

Whispering.

Like she was standing in a crowd, and everyone around her was whispering.

She gripped her flashlight, keeping it pointed at the tiles. There was hardly any light in the food court, just a faint glow coming from the doors.

In front of the doors were people.

Just the dark silhouettes, painted against the glass doors. She stood up, slowly and carefully so her chair wouldn't make a noise. The heads leaned against each other and the whispering grew louder, but not quite that she could make out what they were saying.

They moved closer.

She turned the flashlight up to shine on them.

The light for a very brief moment shone on a woman's face, the skin gray, her hair in a curled pouf tucked under a little hat.

Half of her face was missing, a dark eye socket staring out from nothing.

She moved to the side, shuffling just out of the light. Shay shone the light all around her. She was completely surrounded by people, standing in rows between tables and in front of food stalls, all of them the same washed out colors, all of them rotting with bones protruding from their flesh, skulls caved in, old fashioned clothes in tatters over their shoulders, each moving out of the way before she could get a really good look at them.

She didn't want to, pointing her light at the floor.

"Stay behind me," Finnias said, so quietly she could barely hear him when the whispered turned angry and loud, furious hissing like snakes.

"Should we leave?"

In response the whispers rose to a roar, so loud she could barely hear her own voice, but she still couldn't understand what they were saying. The middle of a crowded room full of angry people all whisper shouting at each other.

Finnias grabbed her wrist and whirled them around to face the doors, but they'd gathered the thickest there. Shay gripped the sachet Arlo had left her with. The salt circle would keep them out, for a while, but Shay had seen them fail before.

The shadows crowded around the edge. Her flashlight flickered and died, the darkness of the mall pressing in on all sides. She dropped the useless flashlight. The sound of it hitting the floor was lost to the sea of whispers. Shay crouched down, low, hoping to hide, hoping to not draw their attention. Despite her hands over her ears, she could hear the hiss of the voices around her. The salt circle was an island in a sea of malevolent snakes.

It felt like forever until the whispering stopped. By that time Shay was curled up on her side, back against the chair.

She hesitantly moved her hand. Nothing. The silence pressed tightly around her. The air was much colder than it had been. Her lip cracked and she tasted iron.

"Another guest," one voice whispered, out in the dark.

Shay started, badly, and probably only Finnias grabbing her shoulder kept her from upsetting the circle.

"Be careful," he said. "You should let Arlo know."

She nodded, sitting up very slowly, but the whispering didn't return. She couldn't see much by the light of Finnias's glow, but she knew the shadows were just outside of the salt circle, waiting for her.

Her phone was completely dead, and even plugging it into the external battery Jo had given her yielded zero results. The shadows had sucked everything dry.

"I can't contact them," Shay said. "Can you leave the circle?"

"No," Finnias said. "You'd have to make a break in the line for me."

"We need to check on them," Shay said. If Max was in the middle of something like this, she needed to find a way to help them. "Or at least let them know what's happening."

"Break the line and fix it," Finnias said. "I will be right back."

She took in a deep, cold breath. Her lungs burned all the way down. "Be careful."

He smiled, just a bit. "I don't have to be careful."

Shay crouched down again and made the tiniest break in the salt, the tile below just barely visible in Finnias's glow. The moment that glow was gone she fixed it as best as she could, fingers shaking, fear sour on her tongue. She must have done okay, nothing stepped into the circle with her.

She sat back against the chair again, pulling her knees up to her chest. The whispering started up again, but now she couldn't even see out the doors, as if the ghosts had blotted out every bit of light. She closed her eyes even though it made no difference.

The whispering faded and rose in volumes like waves.

"What are you doing?"

She screamed at the sudden voice, flinging herself back into the chair and knocking it over, scattering salt everywhere.

Nick stood between her and the doorway, holding a high powered flashlight. Shay threw up an arm to protect herself against it.

"Woah!" He hurried to help her up and even righted the chair. The whispering had stopped, the shadows a memory. "I didn't mean to freak you out! Were you doing like, meditation junk? With the uh...is this salt?"

Shay had been sitting for so long her foot had fallen asleep without her noticing, the pins and needles stabbing at her with a vengeance. She stomped her foot as discreetly as she could. "Um. Yes. I was. What are you doing in here?"

"It's been like, two hours, bro, I got worried and junk," Nick said.

All of the cold in the air froze in Shay's gut. She hadn't fallen asleep, she was fairly certain. She couldn't have been curled up on the ground, trying to avoid the whispering, for two whole hours. "…Are you sure?"

"Yeah." Nick showed her his phone. The background was a picture of him and some girl, but the time did read 10:02. "You guys got here at like eight, and it's past ten now."

"I can read," Shay snapped. It was rude, but she didn't care. Finnias still hadn't come back, and Max and Arlo hadn't even checked on her. She wanted to go tearing through the mall, but the thought of the shadows pressing around her without a salt circle made her hesitate.

"Oh. Yeah." Nick put the phone away. "Where are your friends?"

"They were walking the mall, seeing if they could find anything. I offered to hold down base," Shay said. It was more or less true.

"And they haven't checked on you?" Nick frowned. "Maybe something happened to them."

"Yeah we should go see," Shay said. Finnias was going to kill her himself, if Max didn't first. She tried her best to fix the salt circle, but it might have been a lost cause, the granules getting lost between the tiles and in the general dust and dirt. She realized exactly how dusty she was and grimaced.

"Why are you doing that?" Nick asked.

"Gotta be ready to meditate," she said. The circle was smaller, but it was at least whole, even if it lacked the beautiful geometric designs Arlo created. She stood up and brushed off her hands. It did not help. "Well, let's go."

She stepped carefully over the salt and followed Nick through the rest of the food court. The sweep of his flashlight made the shadows jump and bounce, but none of them were ghosts. She found where her flashlight had rolled across the floor. The batteries were very dead, rendering it a cold, cylinder of metal. She pocketed it. If Nick got weird, she could hit him, at the very least.

He hadn't called her a cool chick again. Hopefully the title had been rescinded when she wouldn't give him her number.

"Dead batteries?" he asked.

She nodded. "Ghosts. Y'know. Always doing that. Let's go, wouldn't want to keep you away from your…van."

"Oh, yeah, I'll need to check in with the big wigs soon," Nick said. "Stay behind me, I'll keep you safe."

"Oh, I have no doubt."

They walked down the first wide hallway towards the atrium. The stalls on either side were festooned with tattered and drooping Christmas decorations. Shay kept well away from them. At least there weren't any mannequins, though a few of the metal grates in front of old stores had shadows behind them that she thought must be old wares.

Nick's flashlight shone on the fountain at the end and for a moment she thought there were ghosts standing between them and the middle.

"Oh, hey, found em," Nick said.

It was Arlo and Max. They were both just standing there, looking at the large Christmas tree that had been set inside the fountain. It was listing slightly to one side, lights off.

Shay hurried forward. "You guys! You left me in the food court for two hours! What, were you going to fix the tree? I don't think that's part of our job."

They didn't move, or even acknowledge that she'd said anything at all.

"Max?"

Terror filled her to the brim, but she broke into a sprint, grabbing Max's shoulder when she was close enough.

No response.

"Are they okay?" Nick called after her.

"This isn't funny, you—" She got in front of them and stopped talking.

Max's eyes were closed. Their eyes moved rapidly under their eyelids, but they weren't moving and were barely breathing. She touched her hand to their cheek and was relieved beyond reason that their skin was still warm.

"Hey, are you...asleep?" Shay shook their shoulder a bit, but while they moved slightly, they didn't open their eyes. "C'mon, Max, wake up."

The temperature plunged from uncomfortable to unbearably cold. The flashlight went off, leaving her in near complete blackness.

"Nick?" she squeaked out. No answer from him, either.

Finnias's hand closed around hers, nearly jerking her heart out of her chest. His fingers were just a touch warmer than the air. "We have to go, Shay."

"Where were you?" She felt like she might cry.

"I was trying to wake them up," Finnias said. "And then...I don't know, you were here. We have to go, right now."

"Not without Max," she said. "And Arlo."

She was fine with leaving Nick there.

"We'll have to come back," Finnias siad.

"Max, please wake up," she shook them again. "Please—"

"That's not going to work, sugar."

Shay whipped around to the voice.

A woman stood in front of the tree, shining like moonlight on snow. She was very tall, wearing a flapper dress, the fringe at her knees moving slightly in a breeze despite the stillness of the air, the fabric shimmering with her own internal light. Her hair was curled and tightly pinned, painted lips pulled back from white teeth in a facsimile of a smile. The cigarette holder in her hand glittered when she moved.

Shay stood between her and Max. Ghosts didn't usually talk to her, but when they did, it tended to be a lot. She just had to distract her until she figured out how to wake Max up. "Who are you?"

"You're the guest here." She stalked forward, a predator eying prey she was confident she could dispatch of. "One more for the party.

"What?" Shay slipped her hand out of Finnias's. The woman hadn't even spared him a glance. Maybe she couldn't see him.

"And who is our guest today?" she drawled, her tone bored, her expressions kept flickering, from angry to scared, her hair uncoiling and then pinning itself back up, like she was moving through time with every step.

"Asked you first," Shay said.

She swung her hips like a weapon when she walked forward, towering over Shay. "You're right. I'm Delores. And you are?"

"Shay." She didn't see the point in not answering. Maybe she could keep her talking, figure out what she did to Max and Arlo.

"Shay, hm?" She tapped her cigarette. "Yes, that sounds right."

"What do you mean?" Shay was backed up against Max, she had nowhere she could go except maybe run screaming down the hall. Even as she thought about it, whispers filled the air all around her.

"One more for the party." Delores took a deep drag of her cigarette. The tip glowed blue.

She exhaled and a mist billowed out from her mouth, filling the hallway in an instant.

Shay coughed and staggered back. It smelled like death and decay, the cloying sweet of rot. Dizziness hit her like a truck, dragging her to her knees.

Finnias grabbed her arm and yanked her to the side just as the woman reached for her. He easily hauled her over one of the stalls and smashed through the metal covering of a storefront. Glass pattered on the carpet beyond. He dragged her through the store, so dark she could only see him.

Shay glanced back. Delores breezed through the metal entryway, strolling like it was a sunny afternoon.

Finnias got her to the back door, remarkably unlocked. He shouldered it open and dragged her inside.

It was a back room, bare except for a metal shelving unit at the back that caught in his light.

"The sachet," Finnias told her. He'd slammed the door shut. "Use it to seal the door."

She wanted to go back, but she was so dizzy she could barely even stand. Her fingers shook when she ripped open the sachet and spread its contents across the doorway.

She sat down against the wall. She was cold and clammy, her eyes still watering. Her throat and mouth burned, but it was fading, slowly, the dizziness draining out of her and leaving behind exhaustion.

Something banged on the door, making the shelving shake and rattle. The handle twisted violently. A horrible scratching filled the air. Shay covered her ears with her hands and screwed her eyes shut. It barely helped.

She couldn't take it after a moment, grabbing Finnias's pant leg. It didn't feel like cloth, but smooth and cold just like his hand did. "Finn."

He turned and his face was strange and cadaverous. He blinked, and it passed. He sat down between her and the door, taking her hand in his.

"It's going to be okay," he said.

"Our friends…"

"Just asleep," Finnias said. "They'll be fine. I'm more worried about you."

She couldn't say she was fine, stuck in the back room of an old store, still feeling sick from the mist. Finnias sitting with her made things a little easier to bear.

The banging slowed and finally stopped. Shay leaned her head against Finnias's shoulder and closed her eyes.

Chapter 6:
Out of the Closet

"And just when I thought I was out of the closet," Shay joked, weakly.

She had no idea how long they'd been sitting there. Finnias was the only light source, and it was so weak it was impossible to make much out about the old back room. Her phone was dead and she had no idea if her friends were okay. Nick had been out for a few hours, but she knew witches were at a much higher risk than the average person.

At least the nausea had passed.

Finnias gave her an unamused look. "This is not a closet."

"Okay, but, it might as well be," she said. "You know what it means, right?"

"I'm aware," Finnias said.

"Because of the whole Duncan mind meld thing?" Shay asked.

"Part, I'm sure, though a lot of that has faded," he admitted. "Mostly I believe it's the weeks I've spent with you."

Light flowed from under the door like someone was walking by with a flashlight, but the cold radiated from the fake wood like an ice chest. It slid to one side and disappeared again.

"I really wish she'd stop doing that," Shay murmured.

"She seems highly aware," Finnias said. "Especially of you. What a surprise. There's a reason I didn't want you here."

"You didn't know." Shay nudged her shoulder against his.

At least the salt was holding. She'd asked Jo why only covering the doorway worked, and she'd explained that ghosts were largely memory and symbolism. Blocking an entrance kept them from entering, despite the fact that there was plenty of ways for them to get into a room.

Shay shivered. "Maybe we should get you out of the closet."

Finnias gave her a flat look. "Shay, I'm dead."

"Not in…let's unpack that later, actually. What I meant was maybe you should be out there, at least scouting or distracting, not turning this into even more of a freezer than it already is."

"I doubt that would be helpful," Finnias said. "Isn't this normally the part where you come up with some insane plan and we all just have to go along with it?"

"Okay that was like, once. You weren't even there. And I'm too cold for insane plans," she said. Finnias just stared at her and she sighed. "Fine! I'll try. If we're lucky, which we never ever are, everyone will wake up in a few hours and come to find me. Pretty easy since you smashed in a window. I didn't know you could do that."

"Me, either," Finnias admitted.

"So…they come to find me and Delores knocks them out again, or does something like Archibald, or maybe even something worse," Shay said, too quickly, her thoughts spilling out of her in a dangerous torrent. "And this repeats until the roof caves in a few decades from now and daylight shines down on my bones."

"Shay—"

She held up her hands. "I'm just saying that I doubt I'm more resilient than a roof, since I'm already half frozen and you know, dehydration is always looming—"

Finnias took her hands. "Stop."

Her breathing had turned ragged, and she took a few minutes, trying to ignore the cold filling her chest. She exhaled, slowly, and it wasn't nearly as shaky. "Thanks."

"You're welcome." Finnias didn't let go of her hands, and she had to admit, she appreciated it.

"So, you can't possess me, right?" Shay looked down at their hands.

"No," Finnias said. "I have not attempted, if it puts you at ease, but I don't believe it would be possible for any ghost to possess you."

"No, I just…I realized I've never asked," Shay said. "But it's just me, right? You can possess other people? You haven't, since…I'm not saying you're the kind of ghost to just go around possessing people, just…"

"Duncan has asked me not to, and I'm respecting his wishes," Finnias said. "But as far as I'm aware, I do have the ability to possess just about anyone but you."

Shay could just make out the dusty old carpet through Finnias and she stared at it intently, thinking. "…What if they're asleep?"

"They would be particularly susceptible to…no," Finnias said.

"You haven't even heard my idea yet," Shay said.

"I'm preemptively calling it awful and dismissing it," Finnias said. "Not only would you need to break the salt line, but it might not work. Arlo will no doubt have taken precautions, and Max naturally repels me—"

"You've gotten close to them," Shay said.

"Because of you," Finnias said. "But you won't be there. You'll be here, at the mercy of a very powerful ghost that already made you sick."

"I can handle it, I'm ready for her now." Shay held up one fist.

She had no idea if that was true. She hadn't actually banished a ghost since Archibald, and they both knew that it didn't work on every ghost.

"I suppose if I had to, I could take over the security guard—"

"I don't think that's going to be very useful, no offense to him, I'm sure he's a nice person," Shay said. "What would it take for you to possess Max?"

"…I'd…have to take energy from you," Finnias said. "I am not in the habit of draining anything living, that leads to…well, it's not something I'm prone to."

"Take what you need," Shay said. She hoped that Max forgave her for what was about to happen. That she could forgive herself, if she survived it. At least they would be okay.

She hoped.

"If you get hurt…"

"I'll be okay," Shay said. Maybe not for much longer, judging by how cold she was. Dehydration would stop being an issue if she ended up with hypothermia. "I'd rather go out swinging than have my obituary say I froze to death in an abandoned mall."

"Shay—"

"I'm just saying!" She let out a long, slow breath. "I'll be quick and careful with the salt, and I know you'll be here soon. So just…do it, okay? You have my permission."

Finnias nodded.

Energy drained out of her like water, adding to Finnias's glow. She couldn't see the carpet through him anymore, and there was a hint of color to him, like a statue holding on to the very last bit of pigment. His hands didn't feel like smooth ice, more like the hands of someone who'd been standing out in the cold for a few months.

He let go of her hands and she had to lean back against the wall and just breathe.

"This was a bad idea," Finnias said.

"You keep talking like that and I'm going to get a complex." Shay sounded just as out of breath as she felt. "You were the one who wanted an insane plan. I just need a second, just got a little lightheaded."

"I should stay here."

"No, then this is pointless." Shay scooted forward. "Just hurry back."

"I'll bring reinforcements," he promised.

"Well, a reinforcement, but the best one, so we don't need more." She crouched in front of the door and made a break in the salt and herbs.

Finnias disappeared, leaving Shay in darkness so complete she couldn't even see her hands. She scrambled to get the line back together as best as she could by feel.

The sickly sweet scent hit her first, then the mist rolled in through a gap in the salt, burning away the dark. Shay coughed and scrambled to her feet, ignoring the dizziness that hit her and backing into the shelf. It swayed dangerously when her shoulders made contact.

Delores towered over her.

She didn't say anything, staring at her passively with hollow eyes. The mist lit up the room so brightly the lights could have been revived.

"One more for the party," Delores said, her voice hollow, devoid of any emotion. She stepped forward jerkily.

Shay balled her hand into a fist. Finnias had taken a lot out of her, but she could take out a ghost, probably.

He was coming back.

He had to be.

Shay punched Delores in the stomach, fire flaring around her knuckles.

It was like she hit a pillar of wet clay, her hand sinking into Delores's abdomen. She tried to yank herself free, but the ghost wrapped her arms around her in a parody of a hug, pulling her closer until she was submerged up to her shoulder.

The outside felt like wet clay, inside she felt like a hundred little strings. Shay tried to twist and yank them, but nothing happened except Delores's grip tightening on her ribs.

"One more for the party," she repeated, like a soft whisper of a breeze.

Shay struggled, but her arm was still stuck inside of Delores and the other was pinned to her side, the cold burning through her jacket. She tried to scream but it came out as a choked gasp.

A bright flash of light and Delores vanished. Shay dropped to the floor, gasping for breath, curling her hand up to her chest.

"Come on!" Max helped her to her feet.

"Max?" she asked, dazedly.

"Not quite," Finnias said. "They couldn't stay awake without me."

Finnias helped her out of the storage room, Max's fingers like brands against her hand.

They made it into the main hallway. Arlo was still standing there, Nick behind him. Whispering surrounded them and Finnias swung Max's candle, the flame leaving a bright streak against Shay's eyelids. The shadows receded.

"Arlo—"

"No time!" Finnias practically dragged her back to the food court.

A scream filled the mall, horrible and all consuming, tearing through every abandoned corridor and rattling the metal shudders, shaking dust from the high ceilings.

Finnias practically dragged Shay out of the doors. The glass cracked behind them.

Finnias jolted out of Max, hitting the pavement so hard Shay wouldn't be surprised if he felt it.

Max gasped for air, dropping the candle in the snow and leaning against their knees. "Ugh. Well. At least that was a ghost I knew. I need to…I need to get that door sealed up."

They pulled a bag of salt from their backpack.

"Max I'm so so so sorry," Shay said, immediately. She could barely stand, she was so tired, and her hand hurt from how cold it was. "I couldn't think of what else to do, and—"

"It's okay," Max said, pouring a line of salt in front of the door.

"But I—"

"Let's just get in Nick's van before we start throwing blame around." Max took her hand and led her to the van, still idling halfway up the curb. "You're freezing."

She couldn't argue with that.

"Is Finnias okay?"

Finnias was already on his feet, adjusting a sleeve that would be perfectly buttoned forever.

"He's fine," Shay said.

"Good." Max opened the passenger's side door for her and assisted her inside like she was a lady being led into a horse drawn carriage.

They got into the driver's side and turned the heat up all the way. Shay held her hands in front of the vents. Her right hand was so blue it was almost black. She attempted to rub life back into her fingers. It just felt cold, not injured. She saw a bulbous white spider on her sleeve and shrieked, jerking her arm.

"What?" Max winced at her hand. "That looks awful."

"There was a spider—"

"Where?" Max didn't immediately shunt away, but they did move their hand back.

"On my sleeve, it's gone," Shay said. "I guess that mall has been abandoned for a while. Still. Gross."

"So gross," Max agreed. "...How is it midnight?"

"Time kept...slipping," Shay said.

"Four hours?" Max's voice cracked. "I bet Jo is losing her mind."

They checked their phone, but it didn't even turn on.

"My phone died, too," Shay said. "Max, I really am sorry—"

"It's okay, I was aware the whole time, it...well, it wasn't great, but we had the same goal so...I'm not upset. I'm a little...I feel a little weird, but hey, if you're in danger and the only option is to have Finnias possess me, then by all means, he has my permission."

"How kind of you," Finnias said dryly from the back seat.

"I'm just glad it worked." Shay was exhausted. She leaned her head against Max's shoulder, closing her eyes, letting the warmth wash over her. "We left Arlo in there."

"He'll be okay," Max said. "Or at least...at least let us warm up and regroup a little bit."

"Yeah," Shay agreed.

A car pulled into the parking lot, headlights washing over the mall. Max sat up a bit. "Oh, thank god, I don't have to steal a smelly security van. Jo's here."

CHAPTER 7: DOMAIN

Shay was sorry to leave the warmth of the van, but not the stench of chemically induced cotton candy.

Jo pulled up next to the van in her ancient green sedan, fishtailing in the thick fresh snow, but she managed to not hit anything. To Shay's surprise, Rose got out of the driver's seat, Jo had been riding passenger.

"What happened?" Jo asked, pulling her hood up against the continuing onslaught of snow. "Where's Arlo?"

Shay explained what had happened, waiting for the "I told you so", but to her surprise it never came. Jo simply looked tired.

"Can we get Arlo out the same way?" Rose asked.

Finnias shook his head. "No. He's wearing too many protections, and I haven't spent as much time around him, I can't even get close."

"Right." Jo sighed when Shay relayed the bad news. "He should be safe, then. But this security guard...not so much."

"He's been put to sleep before," Max offered. "And woke up fine a few hours later."

"That was before…well, before Shay," Jo said. "Oh, I knew this was a bad idea."

There it was.

"Why don't you possess the security guard?" Rose suggested. "I doubt he has anything more protective than a stun gun."

"Honestly, I wouldn't give him that, either," Shay said.

"The risk of injuring him is fairly high," Finnias said.

"But when you possessed Duncan, he was a lot stronger." Shay frowned.

"That is not the type of injury I mean," Finnias explained. "The security guard is not a necromancer or a witch, and has extremely limited experience with ghosts. Possessing him has the potential to cause grave injury to his mind."

"…Okay, I'm slightly less willing to risk that." Shay felt a little sick. She was glad Finnias had specified witches, but she still grabbed Max's hand. "You sure you're okay?"

"Yeah, I'm good," Max said. "Why?"

"Just…making sure."

"Could Finnias possess me again?" Max asked.

"Shay has nothing left to give me without potential consequences, I don't want to risk it." Finnias gave her a very serious look. "No matter what you tell them I just said, I won't do it."

"I wasn't going to lie, geez." Shay was always careful when paraphrasing Finnias. Trust was a fragile thing, and she wasn't willing to lose his. And not just because they would still be stuck with each other after. "He says no. Bad idea."

"Extremely bad idea, you're practically swaying on your feet."

"I am not," she said, though she was feeling exhaustion dragging at her like a heavy net. "Definitely a no. What do we do?"

"I suppose we wait."

"No," Max said. "Shay needs to get somewhere warm."

"Is any part of the mall safe?" Rose asked.

Shay shook her head. "I don't think so. As far as I can tell, the whole place is her domain. Her and her shadows."

And she just wasn't willing to go back in there unless she had absolutely no other choice. She'd rather freeze to death.

"So we have a cluster haunting, a bad one," Jo said. "Made worse that it appears to be some kind of hive, with Delores acting as queen to all of those shadows, as far as I can tell. This is a huge area for a ghost to be ruling over. How could Arlo not find her for two nights?"

"I mean…I probably helped bring out the best in her," Shay said.

"That makes me think that she knew about you," Jo said. "You were pulled into the void."

"I didn't mean to."

"We know," Rose put a calming hand on Jo's arm. "No one here is blaming you, it was absolutely not your fault. But there are probably long reaching consequences. This haunting escalated insanely fast. This whole place looks like it's bathed in static, that's not a good sign."

"I no longer feel comfortable leaving Arlo in there," Jo admitted. "Finnias, is there anyone you would feel comfortable possessing?"

"One person," Finnias said. "I strongly believe I'd be able to get Arlo and the security guard out with his help."

"Don't say Donuts," Shay said.

"Fine, I won't."

"His date," Shay reminded him.

She knew Duncan had been looking forward to it. That he hated all of the ghost stuff, and was really only sticking around because of her. The guilt ate at her a little.

The moment she realized who Finnias meant, it became a ravenous beast, gnawing at her stomach lining.

"It's probably over," Max said. "It's after midnight…"

"Okay, I don't want to think about it not being over this late, so we'll say it's over." Shay slowly crouched down in the snow. She couldn't keep standing, but she didn't want to get wet. "Yeah. Call him. But I need to sit."

"I told you," Finnias said, but gently.

Max helped her into Jo's car, which smelled like lavender, miles better than the van. She closed the door on Jo's conversation with Duncan, she didn't want to hear it.

"You know he won't be mad at you, right?" Max asked, gently. "I mean, not really mad. Maybe surface mad. Petty catty mad. But not actually angry."

"You said he'd be mad three different ways just now," Shay said. She sighed and leaned against their shoulder, slumping there heavily. She was so tired, but Arlo was still in the building, there was no way she could doze off. "I know. Logically, I know that at worst he's going to be kind of miffed and annoying. But it's like my brain hates me. It keeps giving me doom scenarios, like he's going to tell me he hates me and is going to move out and be gone forever and he's annoying but…"

Max's face softened. "Shay, he loves you, he'll never do that."

"Gross."

"It's true, though."

"Still disgusting."

They chuckled. "Your gross brother loves you very much and would never abandon you."

"I know."

Duncan had been the one who came to get her from school, let her move into his apartment, and didn't even charge her rent. He'd always been there for her, no matter how tough things got.

He was still annoying and gross, but she had no idea who she would be without him.

Probably boring.

"I guess I love him, too," she said. "Wow, I didn't even feel icky saying that."

"Amazing, you are growing so much," Max said. "You're also falling asleep."

"No I'm not." She pressed her face against their shoulder.

"You are," Max said. "Nap. Please."

"How can I?" she asked, quietly.

"I'll be right here," Max said. "And I promise I'll wake you up when Duncan gets here."

That wasn't really what she meant. Arlo was still trapped in the mall, it was probably her fault, and they weren't sure what they were going to do about the ghost.

For the moment, there wasn't anything she could do.

She closed her eyes, too tired to keep them open, anyway.

It felt like no time at all passed before Max prodded her, though she remembered something about the moon. When she looked out the window the sky was still cloudy and close.

"Duncan is here," Max said.

"Right." Shay blinked, heavily. She thought she must have dreamed, flashes of a dull moon hanging too close to the earth, but the fragments scattered away from her the more she tried to hold onto them.

They got out of the car just as Duncan got out of Gideon's.

"I see why you called me in, considering my expertise." He peered up at the mall. "That looks bad. Really bad. We're right about at the end of my expertise."

Shay frowned and looked at the mall, and nearly slid in the snow.

The mall had always been a collection of boxy buildings all shoved together in a behemoth of dying dreams and even deader fashion.

Its silhouette, dark against the snowy sky, wasn't boxy at all. Tall, curving spires clawed at the clouds, the roof slanting sharply upwards in a series of bumps and knobs that looked almost organic.

"It didn't look like that earlier," Shay said.

"...Like what?" Gideon asked. "A mall?"

"I wish, it looks disgusting now, all...weird curves and...grossness. I'm pretty sure it's about to spout puss or something." Duncan shuddered. Shay couldn't really refute that. "You guys aren't seeing this?"

"Guess it's a necromancer special," Shay said.

"Awesome, love that for us." Duncan sighed. "Hey, Shay Shay, you look a little rough."

"So do you," she said.

Duncan's styling had wilted against the onslaught of snow, drooping low over his forehead. He flicked it back. "I look awesome."

"How was ice skating?" Max asked, politely.

"Got snowed out, which seems a little ironic," Duncan said.

"We had takeout and watched a movie," Gideon said. "It was very nice. I was about to take Duncan home when you called, so good timing."

"I can't believe you guys. I leave for one night and you...end up in this mess. Ridiculous." Duncan looked at her more carefully. "You're all right, aren't you? You better be all right or I'm going to be so mad. I'll throw a tantrum. I'll kick everyone."

"I'm fine, Dunc."

"Are you?" Duncan stepped closer and grabbed her shoulders, making her sway back and forth. "Hmm, you seem to have all your limbs. That hand looks pretty bad, though, that's just ghost marks, right? Not actual frost bite?"

"Yup, just ghost marks." She tucked her hand up against her chest again. It was so cold it hurt, which was better than being numb.

"Okay." Duncan let go of her shoulders. "You know I have to tell you that you're stupid, right? I have to tell you that you're a big old dummy dumb? Well, you're small, but your dumbness is quite large."

"Sorry I ruined your date," she said. "Can you get possessed already?"

"Wow, that's rude," Duncan said. "I'm just worried about my little baby—"

"I'll kick you," she warned him.

"Yeah, all right, where's Finn? Let's get this side show on the road."

Finnias appeared next to Shay and she didn't even jump. She couldn't tell if she was getting used to the suddenly appearing act or if she was just too tired to care.

"Shall we?" Duncan held out his hand.

Finnias took it and vanished, a glow settling briefly around Duncan. He shook himself a bit. "Stay here."

"I wasn't going to—"

"Stay. Here." Finnias repeated, very firmly.

"I'm staying, don't worry," Shay said. "Keep him safe."

"I will." He turned and marched towards the doors.

Shay's stomach churned, but she stayed put, just like she promised. Max wrapped an arm around her shoulders, though if it was to stave off the cold or because they thought they had to keep her from running in after her brother and Finnias, she couldn't actually say.

It was an agonizing wait. Every minute felt like an hour. She couldn't just stand there, watching the doors, so she pressed her face against Max's coat.

It was probably only fifteen minutes before she heard the doors open again and looked up. Finnias lead a very pale looking Arlo behind him, Nick bringing up the rear in silence.

"Run into any trouble?" Max asked.

"No, it was surprisingly quiet."

"Arlo, you idiot." Jo got to his other side, helping Finnias get him to her car.

"Yes, yes, you can tell me all about it later." Arlo sounded rough, like he'd been gargling sand. "I don't know what happened, one minute we were heading to the fountain the next…"

"We'll explain it as best as we can," Jo promised.

"I'm sorry about your date—"

"Duncan forgives you, this time," Finnias said. "He wants me to emphasize the this time."

"Who are all of these people?" Nick whispered to Shay.

"Oh, y'know, the whole team," she said. "Congrats on your ghosts."

"Thanks?" Nick didn't sound particularly happy about it, somehow. "Did you guys do anything to my van?"

"We sat in it for a minute to warm up," Shay said. "No grand theft van here, I promise."

"Well. Good." Nick nodded and winced. "I have the worst headache. Feels like a hangover. Can we like, talk about this tomorrow? I think I need to sleep this off."

"That sounds like a plan, yes," Arlo said. He fished out a card and started talking to Nick. Once it was obvious he wasn't needed, Finnias separated from Duncan, leaving him to stagger over to Gideon. Nick either didn't notice Finnias or couldn't see him at all.

"You okay?" Gideon rubbed Duncan's arm, holding him next to him.

"I'll live, probably," Duncan said. "It's not so bad. But I was very brave."

"You were." Gideon kissed the top of his head, product and all. Shay made a face and looked away.

To the edge of the parking lot.

Where an enormous black dog regarded her with shining eyes.

She froze, not even able to say anything. It was as enormous as it had been in her room, bigger, maybe. Glowing bones shone through its body, the little galaxies it contained glimmering and twinkling.

Finnias stepped in front of her and she realized she'd taken a step forward, away from Max.

The dog pawed the ground and turned away, disappearing into the night.

Chapter 8: A Tea For Everything

The ride home was quiet.

Shay rode with Max, driving Arlo's car after they interrupted him long enough to get the keys.

Shay stared at the spot where the church grim had walked away, expecting it to turn and come bounding across the parking lot as they left, but it was just darkness and swirling snow.

"It doesn't mean anything," Shay said after a few minutes of only the rumble of the station wagon's engine.

"We just had a near death experience and then you saw a death omen, but sure."

"Max—"

"Sorry." Max breathed out, slowly, their grip on the steering wheel making the ancient plastic creak. "I know it's not your fault, this isn't fair to you, but…why on earth did you go in that hallway? You knew how dangerous it was."

"Because it had been hours and I didn't know if you were okay or not," Shay said. "You were only there because of me, if something happened to you…"

"Nothing happened, I was just asleep."

"But I didn't know that," Shay reminded them. "Besides, I know…I know what ghosts can do. I can't…"

She sighed. Nothing she was saying was coming out right. She thought a few weeks between her and everything that happened at Holt Manor would provide the distance she needed to actually do her job, whatever it was.

"…I'm very sorry." Max rolled to a stop at a red light, even though no one was at the intersection. They reached over and took her hand. "I have been extremely unfair to you. Of course you were scared."

"I mean, I wouldn't say extremely, but maybe a little," Shay said. "A smidge."

"Just a smidge?" Max flashed her a smile. The light spilled into the car and bloodied the snow all around them.

It had been snowing when Finnias died.

Shay shook herself, a little bit. "Yes. Just a smidge. Smidgen. Smidgen pigeon. Wow it has been a long day, I was up before nine."

"I know." Max let go of her hand when the light switched to green. "And you worked so hard at the shop."

"So, so hard," Shay agreed. Her shift at the store felt like it happened weeks ago. "I need a pot of tea and seventeen hours of sleep. Minimum."

"I thought you didn't like tea," Max said, teasingly.

Shay shrugged. "Jo has made me a believer. And she has a tea for everything. Insomnia, nausea, random aches and pains, mortal wounds…"

Max laughed and the tension in the car finally dissipated.

When they got back to the house Shay wrapped herself in an afghan. The fireplace was dark and cold, so Max pulled over the radiator space heater.

"I'm going to check the wards, just in case," they told her. "Don't move."

"Where would I even move to?" Shay asked. "Why does everyone keep telling me that?"

"Why do you think?" Max asked.

Shay had to admit, that was probably a fair thing to ask of her, all things considered.

"I have a warden." Shay gestured to Finnias, perched on the arm of the couch. "He'll make sure I stay put."

"I will." Finnias nodded. "I'll sit on you, if I have to."

"I think that would have the opposite effect of warming me up, but sure." Shay leaned back into the couch. "I think the cushions have sucked me in, anyway. I'm done for. A goner."

"Yeah, all right." Max left her to her fate.

They were quiet, for a while, just the ticking of the radiator heating up. Shay's eyelids felt heavy, but she struggled to stay awake.

"You can go to sleep, if you want to," Finnias said, quietly. "I'll keep watch."

"Thought you weren't an attack ghost," Shay murmured.

"I'll allow it on special occasions."

"Yay." Shay tried to muster up some enthusiasm.

Finnias stared at the empty fireplace for a long moment. The heavy shades on the lamps made the room feel dim and close. Shay wondered if she took his hand if it would feel like ice or human, but she had no way to ask.

"It was tempting, you know," he said.

"What was?" Shay sat up a bit more.

"To…stay." Finnias frowned. "With Max, or Duncan. Either one. It was tempting."

"But you didn't give in," Shay reminded him. She wasn't surprised, exactly. She imagined that suddenly feeling alive was worth a lot to any ghost, no matter who they were. "That's what matters."

"But I was tempted," Finnias repeated. He put a hand to his chest, where the hole was. "I worry, sometimes, about my memories."

"About getting them back?" Shay asked.

"In a way, yes," Finnias said. "I...don't believe that I was a good person."

"I don't agree," Shay said.

"You are biased," Finnias reminded her. "I just told you that I was tempted to keep possessing your friend and your brother. You should be upset. You should be telling me to leave."

"But you didn't," Shay repeated. "That's what matters to me. Besides, I don't think Max would have let you—"

"They didn't kick me out," Finnias said. "When I realized I...I left."

"...Oh." Shay blinked. She'd assumed that Max had tossed Finnias out, not that he'd violently ejected himself. "Well. There you go. Look, I was wrapped up in my own junk, but you were amazing back there. A hero, even. So...maybe cut yourself some slack?"

"It was heavily implied that I was involved with a mass murderer," Finnias said. "...Two mass murderers."

"Oh, well, y'know, no one's perfect," Shay said. "Okay, fine, new plan. I promised to get your memories back. I promise to...not...do that. Unless you decide you want me to."

"That sounds an awful lot like doing nothing," Finnias said, but he was smiling.

"I love doing nothing, it's one of my favorite activities," Shay said. "I mean it, though. I want you to be, y'know, happy."

Finnias's eyebrows rose. "Happy?"

"Well, you're my friend, and stuff."

"What a rousing declaration," Finnias said.

"Shush." She waved him off. "I'm tired. Just…don't worry so much. I'm not worried."

"You're not the least bit concerned I'll turn out like Emmaline or Archibald?"

Shay tilted her head to one side, regarding him. Maybe she should have been. Finnias had been dead for over a century. Killing her would be easy for him.

She wasn't worried at all. "I think you'd need to grow a mustache, and I'm pretty sure that's impossible."

Finnias snorted.

"Oh my god, that was cute, do it again."

He frowned. "No."

"What was cute?" Max came into the room, holding two steaming mugs.

"Me," Shay said. "No, it was Finnias. Is that tea? If you took away Jo's tea making ritual she'll be so mad."

"Good thing it's hot chocolate, then." Max sat next to her, handing her a mug.

She wrapped her fingers around the ceramic, letting the warmth settle into her bones. Her right hand was still stiff and blue. She took a sip, nearly burning her tongue, but it was worth it for the chocolate and cinnamon. "I needed this. Thank you."

"Least I could do, considering you had to be stuck in the closet again." Max grinned at her.

"I wasn't all bi myself, at least," Shay said.

"Pretty sure you've used that one before."

"It's a classic." Shay took a much more careful sip of her chocolate. "It's fine, I'm good now. In fact, all aces."

"Admittedly been a while since I heard that one," Max said.

"It's okay, you can be jeal-ace of me."

They sighed. "Sure. I'm very enbious."

"Max!" Shay gasped. "You punned! That was beautiful, do it again."

"No, drink your hot chocolate." They were smiling, despite their words.

She did just that. "Are we, like, okay? I know we kind of had it out in the car but…"

"We're fine," Max said. "I promise. I'm even fine with Finnias, I meant that."

"I'm so relieved." Finnias sounded sarcastic, but Shay thought that secretly there was a little bit of sincerity in there, somewhere.

"You're not getting rid of me, stuck with me, for life," Max said.

"I dunno, I mean, eventually you'll get like…married or something." Shay's stomach felt sour and she stared at her hot chocolate. "Have a few little Maxes running around."

Max laughed. "I don't think that's in the cards for a long time. A really long time. If ever."

"What, are we just going to be a couple of besties forever?" Shay asked, feeling oddly nervous about their answer.

"Of course we are," Max said. "If that's what you want."

"Well, of course it's what I want," Shay said. "But really, you don't like anyone? Do we still call it a crush if we're over twenty?"

"I think you call it whatever you're comfortable with," Max said. "And maybe."

"Wait, seriously?" Shay stared at them. She couldn't imagine Max dating anyone, even though she knew they'd been on dates before, back when she was in college.

"It's not a big deal or anything," Max said. "Why do you want to know?"

"Just curious." Shay pretended like her stomach wasn't being eaten away by acid and her fingers didn't feel cold and clammy, despite the warmth of the mug. She glanced at Finnias but he was staring at the snow again, absolutely no help at all. "Have you told them?"

"Didn't see the point," Max admitted.

"What? Why not?" Shay frowned at them. "I can't imagine anyone not liking you back. Okay, that sounded much more grown up and mature in my head. I can't imagine anyone not reciprocating your feelings. Is that better?"

Max actually laughed at that. "You know I'm like…a mess, right? I'm fat and anxious, I don't have any ambition, I work at a day care and…well. Not exactly a catch."

"Um, first thing is a so what, just means you're the best for cuddles," Shay said. "And there's more of you! This is ideal. And you're good with kids! The anxiety, well, I wish I could help—"

"You help plenty," Max said. "Look, I don't really want to talk about this. I'm never going to say anything and…honestly, I don't want change. I like my life exactly how it is."

"Even the ghost stuff?" Shay's eyebrows rose.

"Even the ghost stuff," Max said. "I mean, c'mon, I've been obsessed with ghosts forever, this is actually sort of a dream come true. Or, it would be, if there was less screaming and getting thrown around. Anyway, the point is it doesn't matter, really. I'm happy."

"Well, good, I'm glad you're happy, despite all the screaming," Shay said. It calmed something inside of her, but she was still stupidly curious. "Can I have one more question?"

Max sighed. "Yes, fine, what is it?"

"You could have said that counted as a question," she teased them. "Do I know this mystery crush person you'll never confess to?"

Max was quiet for a moment, then nodded, looking directly at her. "Yeah. I'd say you know them pretty well."

Shay wracked her brain, trying to think of anyone she knew that Max would like but not tell her about. "...Is it Duncan."

Max spluttered. "What? Ew! No! I thought we were friends! I thought you respected me, honestly—"

"I'm sorry!" Shay laughed, putting down her hot chocolate before Max smacked her with one of the abundant throw pillows. "Stop! I didn't mean it!"

"Rude, honestly, the worst—"

Max's attack was cut short by the door opening. Jo and Arlo walked in through the kitchen, shedding snow covered coats.

"To bed, now," Jo said. "No arguments."

"I wasn't going to argue," Arlo promised. "But...maybe a mug of tea?"

"Fine, I'll bring it to you," Jo said. "You three, don't move. The four of us need to talk."

"I could—"Arlo started to say.

"No," Jo said, again. "Get to bed. I'll update you tomorrow."

"Fine," Arlo sighed, heading towards his room in the back. "Goodnight everyone!"

Jo pinned Shay and Max with one more look before she went back into the kitchen.

"Do you think we're in trouble?" Shay asked.

"I was abusing the throw pillow." Max put it on their other side, smoothing it out. "But uh...yeah. We're in trouble."

CHAPTER 9: DREAM JOURNAL

Shay finished her hot chocolate just as Jo sat down.

"So," Jo said.

"So…?" Shay couldn't tell if Jo was angry with her or not, sometimes it was hard to tell. Usually, she erred on the side of caution, since Jo paid the bills.

"You saw the black dog."

"Oh, right, that," Shay said. Jo gave her an incredulous look over her mug. "What? It's been a weird long night, and I'm really tired. I just saw it for a second, but it didn't do anything, just walked away. Maybe it's not a church grim or a black shuck or any of that. Maybe it's something else."

She knew she was grasping, but she didn't feel like it was malevolent, though it was hard to explain that and why she never could say whether she felt a place was haunted.

"Like what?" Max asked.

"I dunno, I'm more of a cat person," Shay said. "Don't really know dog breeds."

"Shay…" Jo started to say.

"I'm just saying, I've seen it twice and I'm still alive," Shay pointed out. "So, I'm kind of not really thinking it's a harbinger of doom."

Maybe that was just wishful thinking. The first time she'd seen it, there had been a mad scramble to update wards and make sure that Shay stayed safely within them, but as the weeks crawled by she was getting tired of cowering away in safety while everyone else took huge risks.

"You have volatile abilities that no one fully understands," Finnias reminded her. "Even if it's not a death omen, you need to be very, very careful."

"I've been careful." Shay pulled her feet up onto the couch. "Mostly. Largely. Not so much tonight."

"That was big of you to admit," Max said.

"Yeah." She didn't really have a rebuttal for that. "How about I don't go back to the mall? I mean, I can't do anything, anyway. That lady took my punch like a champ. Well, more like a wax statue, but you know."

She waved her hand at Jo. Her skin wasn't nearly as blue as it had been, but the ghost mark was slow to fade away.

"No one is going back to the mall," Jo said. "That's what Arlo and I were arguing about."

Shay stared at her. "But…I thought Spellbound needed the big pay day?"

"It would be helpful, I won't lie about that," Jo said. "However, Rose and I finally came to an agreement, and we're folding Spiritual Connections into our business. She'll be doing house calls, since we are clearly not set up to be calling spirits here, but I think we're going to be okay. We might have to go completely online, but you'll still have plenty to do. I'm not worried, and you don't have to be worried, either."

"Oh, okay." Shay definitely felt lighter. "Okay, yeah, that helps. Thanks, boss. I'm not like a huge burden or anything, right?"

"What gave you that idea?" Jo blinked at her.

"…The uh…mad scramble any time I breathe funny?" Shay reminded her. "Living here rent free? Causing problems?"

"I will admit, some things are slightly more difficult with you around, but they're things I'm more than willing to put up with," Jo explained. "You are wonderful to have around. I think this house would feel very empty without you."

"That's a nice way of saying I'm really loud." Shay felt warm in a way that had nothing to do with blankets or the hot cocoa.

"It's the perfect way of saying I enjoy having you here," Jo said. "Besides, I can't just turn you out onto the street. I'd feel awful and your brother would kill me."

"Yeah, he probably would." Shay could admit, sometimes, that Duncan was a good brother.

"I'd help," Max volunteered. "…Well, maybe not with the murder part, but I would provide him with a solid alibi."

Jo laughed at that.

"Well, I'll stick around, if only so you don't feel bad," Shay joked, but she was a little lighter when she leaned back into the couch again. "Also so Max doesn't go to jail."

"I would never get caught," Max said with absolute certainty.

"What about Duncan?" Jo asked.

"If he opens a can of worms, he can lie in it." Shay shrugged.

Jo laughed. "Well, I'll keep Max out of jail and Duncan out of worms."

"That's all I ask," Shay said. "So...we really aren't going back?"

"We are ill equipped to handle a haunting of that scale, and since the building is largely abandoned, I don't feel too terrible about leaving it be," Jo explained.

"And Arlo is okay with this?" Max leaned forward, frowning. "He seemed pretty set on wrapping it up."

"We had a...reasonable adult conversation about it, and agreed that it's not a job we can handle," Jo said. "Unfortunately, the Christmas market will just have to move to a better building."

"Y'know, it was kind of weird," Shay said. "There were stalls, sure, but they didn't have anything at them. They didn't even have banners and names and stuff."

"Really?" Jo frowned. "But there was a security guard."

"Sounds like Nick has worked there for a while," Max said.

"Yeah, he kept talking about it being an easy job," Shay agreed. "So he probably was working there before the market was even a thing. Who hired Arlo, anyway?"

"Um. Let me check the records." Jo set her mug down, but Max got to their feet to get her tablet from the front. They came back and handed it to her, sitting next to Shay again. Jo scrolled through a few things, a frown line appearing between her eyebrows. "A woman named Alyssa Paxton, she works for Security Solutions, according to her emails. Stuff about the market...information about the haunting..."

"Who's the owner?" Max asked.

"It looks like Miss Paxton only talked about Security Solutions." Jo frowned. "No mention of the owners."

"I'm gonna go ahead and guess the Stevens Realty group," Shay said. "Or hey, maybe their other one. The...fire one."

"Fireglass Innovations." Max nodded. "A pretty fair assumption to make, I think. We should talk to Taylor tomorrow, see if she knows anything."

"Yeah, cause this feels like a trap," Shay said. "I don't know why, though. It doesn't really make any sense, does it? I mean, obviously they're some sort of flavor of necromancer or witch."

"It would make sense," Finnias agreed. "Taylor has very few side effects from being possessed for so long."

"And why the manor was, y'know, like that," Shay said after paraphrasing for him. "We know they're dealing with ghost stuff, but…why trap Arlo again?"

"Because we panic and fall apart without him, I'm guessing," Jo said. "Maybe they hoped we'd return to Holt Manor, to that circle. Because whatever was there…"

"Was pushed back into the void," Shay said, quickly, a cold stealing over her. She'd had the same nightmare for weeks. The horrible moon, the bulbous creature it became. "We made sure of it."

She looked at Finnias, who nodded, but he was frowning.

"You did push it back, but it's still there," Jo said. "Whatever it is, it's old and extremely powerful. I don't use the term demon lightly, but I think it applies in this case. I'm afraid you only delayed things."

"I did my best," Shay argued.

"I'm not criticizing you," Jo said. "I'm sorry if it came across that way. I'm extremely grateful that you freed us, and for everything that you do."

"…Punching big ghosts?"

Jo smiled, slightly. "And sweeping the shop."

"Why do you think that thing is still a problem?" Max asked.

"I've been having dreams,'" Jo said. "They're always at the circle. It's active, and there's a great moon hanging in the sky, but it's not the moon—"

"It's the demon," Shay finished for her.

"I told you they meant something," Finnias said, quietly. "I told you that you should talk to her."

"Wait, I've had that dream, too," Max said. "And I'm not clairvoyant. Unless I am. I don't think I am. I'd probably know if I was, right?"

"…Well, I don't believe you are, but if we're all having the same dream, I doubt that's good." Jo's hands were shaking when she picked up her mug again. "There are so many things, and we're being pulled in so many directions. All of the displaced ghosts, the church grim, the thing in the mall…"

"Maybe I could punch the dog," Shay said.

Jo sighed. "You probably can't just punch a death omen in the face."

"Not with that attitude you can't," Shay said. Jo gave her a look over her glasses. "Okay, fine, I won't try to punch it. Do you think that nightmare…Archibald is there and he keeps trying to tell me something, but it's probably nonsense."

"How often are you having this dream?" Jo asked.

"Um…" Shay looked at Finnias, who glared very pointedly at her. "Almost every night?"

"Every night?" Max frowned. "That's…"

"Probably trauma related?" Shay suggested. "I mean, that's what I assume. I mean, that wasn't exactly a fun happy time I like remembering."

Max covered her hand with their own like they weren't quite sure what to say.

"It is a possibility. I have an idea." Jo got up and went into the shop. She came back with one of the fancy, hand bound journals that Arlo made in his spare time. It was purple with gold and silver stars. "Here. You should keep a dream journal."

"In the nice notebook?" Shay asked.

"A dream journal should be a little special." Jo smiled a bit. "I have Arlo make me a new notebook every time I fill one. It helps. Even if you don't think your dreams are relevant to the problem at hand, sometimes working out what our subconscious is trying to tell us can clear our minds. Even break the cycle of a repetitive nightmare."

"You're really smart," Shay said.

"I know."

Shay laughed. "Well, thank you. I'll do my best."

"Of course." Jo leaned over and gave her an only slightly awkward hug. "Now, you should both get to bed, you look exhausted. I'll hunt down a fancy pen for you."

"Because a special dream journal needs a special pen?" Shay asked.

"Exactly."

Maybe it was because they talked about it, or maybe it was because she was so tired, but Shay didn't have any dreams she remembered at all that night. She frowned at her journal, wondering if she should write down that nothing had happened.

"Just write that you were too tired to dream," Finnias told her.

"No, it's fancy, I don't want to ruin the fanciness with just…nothing," she said.

"Then don't write anything."

"But what if I'm supposed to?"

Duncan walked into the kitchen and poured himself a mug of coffee. He leaned over the table obnoxiously. "Ooh what's that?"

"Don't you have work?" Shay covered the page even though the lined paper was still blank.

"Budget cuts, library is closed on Sunday." Duncan sat across from her.

"What about a date?" Shay grasped for straws.

"We're going to hang out later, but for now, you're stuck with me." He grinned and she stuck her tongue out at him. "Wow, rude. Who raised you to be like this?"

"You," Shay said.

"You're right, that's on me." Duncan nodded. "So, what's the notebook for? Is it a journal? Are you writing secrets?"

"Dear Diary." Shay pretended to write, speaking in the most obnoxious valley girl accent she could muster. "Today my brother was soooo annoying. I took a knife and stabbed him. Teehee!"

"The spoken giggle really sells it, well done." Duncan saluted her with his coffee mug.

She gave a shallow mock bow. "Thank you, I try. It's a dream journal, Jo says I should keep one."

"Yeah?" Duncan nodded. "Makes sense. Shouldn't you write it down right after you wake up?"

"I didn't actually dream last night. It was a little weird." Shay closed the notebook, tracing a few of the stars. "I guess I write nothing."

She expected an "I already told you that" from Finnias, but he didn't say anything.

"Y'know, it's funny, it's like everyone is having bad dreams lately," Duncan said. "Gid and I were just talking about it last night."

"Yeah?" Shay asked.

"Yeah." Duncan shrugged. "You doing okay, though? Nightmares and all that aside? Last night was kind of a lot."

"I'm fine, see?" Shay showed him her hand, which looked perfectly normal. "No more ghost mark. And we dropped the job, so no worries there. You won't be called from any more dates."

"I tell you this because I know you won't abuse it, but you can call me any time, doesn't matter what I'm doing or with who," Duncan said, suddenly serious. "Whether it's to be possessed by a ghost or because you just need advice. This whole thing with Gideon, and I really hope it becomes a definite thing, it doesn't change that."

"Yeah, I know," Shay said. "Thanks. You're sometimes not the worst."

"Aw Shay Shay, I love you, too."

"Yeah, yeah. But you're okay too, right?"

"Oh, yeah, I'm great," Duncan said. "Finnias might not be, since he keeps vanishing every time I enter the room."

"He was…" Shay turned to where Finnias had been standing, but the spot wasn't even cold. "Hm."

"Eh, it's fine, he's like a skittish rescue cat. Someday, he'll learn to love again."

Shay did not want to admit she'd had the same thought literally the day before. "Maybe. Y'know, Max and I were going to play video games. Since you're not busy right now, you wanna join?"

"Oh, hell yes, I am there, dibs on Luigi."

CHAPTER 10:
SELF-REFLECTION

Shay stared into the circle.

She knew it was a dream. She still wore her flannel pajama bottoms and over-sized t-shirt. Frost coated grass speared up into her socks. The cold bit at her. She wrapped her arms around herself and shivered. The moon was gone, the purple sky ablaze with stars.

When she looked at the circle, Archibald stood at the edge of the circle, just inside the blue light. He held his hands loosely at his side, no knife or coat in sight, but she still approached him with caution.

"Hello, Shay."

She'd never been able to hear him before. She couldn't say if it was because she realized it was a dream, or the absence of the moon.

"Archie." She nodded at him.

"Come, we have a lot to talk about." Archibald gestured to the spot next to him. Shay was suddenly there, without any conscious effort of her own. She flinched away from him, but he made no move towards her.

"This is a dream," she said.

He looked up at the sky. "Dreams are just memories, all jumbled together. Just like ghosts."

"Are you trying to tell me you're really here?" Shay asked.

"Who can say?" he shrugged. "It might just be your memories of me. Or maybe every ghost you vanquish will haunt your dreams for the rest of your life."

"Either this is a terrible self reflection technique, or it's really you." Shay didn't know how to feel about either. "Gonna go with the latter. You kinda suck."

"That hurts." Archibald placed a hand on his chest, but he was smiling. "I only tried to kill you a handful of times. You ended up fine, in the end. More than fine, you can banish ghosts again. You could say I was crucial to your development."

"Shut up, Shay said.

"You can deny it, if you would like."

She shook her head. "It doesn't matter. You killed Finnias."

"Finnias." It came out as a growl that barely sounded human, his skull shining through his skin. Shay took a step back. He cleared his throat and adjusted his tie, gradually returning to normal. "It all comes back to him, doesn't it. If I hadn't killed him, you never would have met, and things could have been so much worse."

"Are you trying to tell me killing your friend—"

"Lover," Archibald corrected her.

Shay made a face, her stomach clenching. "Sure. That. But killing him was the lesser of two evils?"

"I am," Archibald said. "It needed to happen."

She couldn't imagine killing anyone she was close to, let alone trying to justify it. "I doubt that."

"You really don't know anything about him, do you?"

"I don't need to," Shay said. "He's my friend."

Archibald threw his head back and laughed. "Oh, that's rich! A necromancer with a pet ghost for a friend. The ghost of a murderer and a conman. You're so quick to condemn me for the same things that made him such a powerful necromancer. Even you naturally born ones tend to eventually kill a few people. It's in your nature, you can't help it. The power you get from it is too tempting."

"I'm not going to kill anyone."

The very thought made bile burn in the back of her throat.

"Oh, you will," Archibald said. "You will, and you'll have a very good reason, every time. And maybe eventually not very good reasons. Like I said, it's in your nature."

"I don't believe you."

Archibald ignored her. "Not that you needed to kill anyone to have a ghost under your thumb. Because you're special, aren't you, Shay?"

"He's not," Shay said.

"Oh, he is, don't be naive," Archibald said. "He would do anything to protect you, wouldn't he? He was like that in life, too. Never doing anything in halves. Especially for his sister, despite saying he wanted to stop her. He never really tried, in the end."

"Sister?"

She knew, in that moment, that she was probably talking to some form of the real Archibald. Everything else could have been her subconscious attempting to torture her, but this part was real. She took a step away from him, goosebumps raising on her arms.

"You really don't know anything," Archibald said. "It's actually sort of pathetic. I feel sorry for you. Finnias wasn't his real name, you know."

"Then what was it?" Shay asked. She knew Finnias was an alias, knew that he was a spiritualist active in the early 1900s, but she didn't have anything else to go on. No way to figure out who Finnias had been.

Archibald flickered. He was wearing different clothes, a brown travel coat and a rich green waistcoat, his hair less rigidly slicked back, curling around his ears under his bowler hat. He took an ornate gold pocket watch out and flipped it open. "It's time."

"Time for what?" She stepped forward, ignoring the radiating cold and the sense of danger screaming in the back of her mind. "What's his name?"

"The moon is rising."

Shay looked up.

The moon hung directly in the center of the circle, full and heavy.

"I wonder if you can outrun it." Archibald snapped the pocket watch shut.

Shay turned and ran to the other side of the circle, the grass cutting at her feet.

The ground shook when the demon fell to the earth.

She risked a glance over her shoulder.

It was huge, blotting out the horizon with its distended, bulbous body. It crawled towards her with hands that were far too human, jagged nails scoring the earth. The sores opened into red rimmed eyes, all the way up to the shoulder.

Shay put on a burst of speed, but the other side of the circle was too far away, stretched out impossibly. The air grew thick and her limbs heavy. She couldn't breathe.

A hand filled her vision, a single ruby red eye staring at her.

She woke up with Finnias's face inches above hers and screamed.

He jerked back, blinking at her.

"Whas happenin?" Max sat up, patting her side of the bed until they found her shoulder.

"Sorry." She sat up, still shaking. At least she hadn't started crying. "Bad dream. I'm fine."

"'Sokay." Max patted her shoulder clumsily, still clearly mostly asleep. "Sleep. We sleep again now."

"Yeah, I'll get there." She doubted it. She felt wide awake, along with the rest of the house. She was surprised no one was at the door asking her if she was dying. Duncan was just down the hall, but he'd slept through worse.

"Mmkay." Max flopped back down, stealing most of the blanket.

She needed to write in her dream journal, before she forgot anything. She grabbed it off of her nightstand.

The cold of the floorboards stung her feet. Orange light from the street lamps flooded through a gap in her curtains. She walked to the window seat and stared out at the street. It had stopped snowing, but the clouds stayed close, reflecting the city lights.

She half expected to see a black shape against the snow, but the street remained empty.

She closed the curtain.

"Are you okay?" Finnias put a cold hand on her arm.

"Yeah, just...wasn't expecting you to be so close," she said. "Sorry about that."

"I was trying to wake you up," Finnias said. "Was it the same nightmare?"

"About to write it down, right now." Shay glanced at the Max shaped lump on the bed. "In the bathroom."

She hurried down the dark hallway into the tiny bathroom and sat on the toilet. She scrawled out everything she could remember, taking absolutely illegible notes that she'd hopefully be able to decipher later.

The details felt fuzzy already, like she was looking at them through clouded glass, but she did her best.

She looked up to ask Finnias something and realized he hadn't followed her into the bathroom.

Well, she had asked him to not, but it was still a little unnerving to realize she was completely alone.

She closed her journal, hoping it all made sense in the morning. She wasn't tired, not exactly, but writing it all down had felt like pouring water out of a cup, leaving her hollow and empty.

She got to her feet and went to leave, but movement from the corner of her eye had her practically jumping into the wall.

Cobwebs fluttered at the edge of the mirror. Shay frowned, moving closer to inspect them.

It wasn't her face reflected at her, and she yelped and jumped back all over again, this time hitting the towel rack and knocking the towels to the floor.

"Oh, calm down," Emmaline said. She was in shades of blue, just like Finnias. A handsome woman with a long face, her hair pulled loosely into a large bun. "It's just me."

"Emmaline?" Shay blinked at her, surprised. "You're…I thought after the whole, y'know, thing with the mirror breaking—"

"Really? You thought that would stop me?" Emmaline asked. "Look, as much as I enjoy our little chats, we don't have time for this. You need to get downstairs, right now. You have to stop him."

"Stop who?" Shay was not used to Emmaline getting to the point right away, and it left her reeling.

"She has her hooks in Arlo," Emmaline said, leaning against the mirror's shimmering surface. "I won't be able to talk to you like this, I won't be able to help."

"When have you—"

"I told you we don't have time!" Emmaline snapped at her. "Go get him! You can't let him get back to the mall!"

"Wait, I still don't know what you mean." Shay was panicking, she knew she was, but all she seemed to be able to do was stand there and keep talking. "Arlo is downstairs? I mean he sleeps down there—"

"Exactly, he's sleeping, that's the problem." Emmaline glanced back, into the darkness that encroached on her. "It's too late. Ward the mirrors, you have to remember to tell them to—"

A snap like a gunshot almost made Shay scream again. The light went out, leaving her in the dark except for the dim glow of the mirror. It was covered in a thick layer of frost, ice layered in thin lines across the surface in the shape of a spiderweb.

Shay nearly fell out of the bathroom in her haste to get into the hallway. The night light at the end of the hall was out, too, and the air was icy, her breath a plume of smoke just barely visible by Finnias's light.

"What happened?" he asked. "You were talking, I thought—"

"Downstairs," Shay said, not sure if she really could explain why she was listening to Emmaline. She ran down the hall and stairs, nearly tripping on a carpet runner in her haste. She grabbed the railing at the bottom of the stairs to stop herself from falling, giving herself a moment to catch her breath.

The living room was a sea of dark shadows. The windows were bright, the reflected light on the snow making it a false daytime.

A whisper, somewhere in the dark, sounding almost like the rustle of cloth.

The shadows moved.

Shay pressed herself to the wall, clamping a hand to her mouth to keep herself from shouting, though she doubted her graceless entrance into the room left any doubt that she was there.

When she tried the light switch, nothing happened.

Probably not a human burglar.

Finnias's hand found hers, providing the tiniest amount of light. It took everything for her to move forward. Her foot hit the ottoman and her hip brushed against a table.

The whispering grew louder.

The same noise from the mall.

She froze in place, gripping Finnias's hand so tightly that if he had been alive, she would have pressed his bones together. His hand still felt human, like it had in the mall, but if she was hurting him, he made no sign.

"What is it?" he asked, quietly, though she doubted the other ghosts could hear him.

The whispering rose in volume, the voices all around her.

She took another step forward and ran into someone. She shrieked and hit them, before realizing it was Arlo.

"Oh my god, what the hell!" She smacked his arm more purposely. "What are you—"

There was just enough light that she could see that his eyes were closed, his hands held in front of him like he was being led forward to the kitchen.

CHAPTER 11: SLEEPWALKING

"Arlo!"

Shay didn't think it would work, but she tried anyway. He kept walking, slow and shuffling. She grabbed his arm, and he literally dragged her along even after she dug her heels in. Arlo was over a foot taller than her and very broad, she had no chance of stopping him with brute force.

Finnias grabbed her wrist and Arlo's shoulder, planting his feet. Arlo dragged them both into the kitchen, arms still held out in front of him, shadowy fingers gripping his wrists.

"Come on, wake up!" Shay hit his shoulder again, but she might as well have been smacking the couch for all the good it did her. She had a mean right hook, but she didn't dare use it on a person. "Wake! Up!"

Her yelling fell on deaf ears. She tried to get around him to grab the jar of salt in the kitchen, but icy cold fingers grabbed at her arms and clothes. She slapped at them, but they held firm. She twisted to punch, but missed and they dragged her to the ground, slamming her shoulder into the cold wood floor. Finnias tried to haul her up but there were too many, swarming over her. She struggled, fear clogging up her lungs and squeezing around her heart with a grip icier than the ghosts.

An incredibly bright light washed over them, and she was treated to a very close view of dry bones and flaking skin barely concealed by stained party dresses and ragged suits. The ghosts hissed and backed away, leaving her lying on the floor and Arlo standing in the kitchen.

"Yeah, that's right!" Duncan yelled, swinging a flashlight back and forth. "Get out of here!"

Finnias pulled Shay to her feet, and she tried her best to catch her breath, holding her fists up in case they came at her again. She could hear them whispering around the edges of the room, see the shape of them clear and sharp against the glow of the windows.

Duncan walked slowly down the last few stairs, wielding the flashlight like a sword. The bright light burned away the shadows, but by the time he'd reached the bottom step it was starting to flicker.

"C'mon, y'all, let's get upstairs," Duncan said.

"Arlo's sleepwalking," Shay told him. "I can't—"

The flashlight died, plunging them into a darkness much deeper than the one before. Shay blinked, hard, but her eyes took their time adjusting.

Duncan slapped it against his other hand a few times. It tried, feebly, to resurrect itself, but died completely after a few seconds. "Aw, beans."

The ghosts rushed in like a sharp, cold wind. Shay slammed her fist into the first one, igniting it in bright blue flames. It screamed as it burned away like a piece of old film left on the projector too long, exploding into a myriad of blue sparks, but there were more behind it, and a second and third punch had her swaying on her feet again.

"Stop!"

It was Max, but their voice held such power that Shay did exactly as they asked, freezing in place. Light rippled around the room, the glowing line of the wards shining gold and bright. The ghosts vanished in an instant, burned away by the intensity of Max's magic, leaving the living room dark again a moment later.

Shay sat down on the rug, despite Finnias's attempts to help her keep her feet.

The candle Max was holding blazed to life and they walked down the stairs. Arlo jerked awake a moment later, blinking in the sudden light.

"What in the hell…" He stared around the living room, absolutely confused. "Why am I in the kitchen…what are you all doing here?"

Shay rubbed her arms. There were marks all over her, little blue fingerprints from her wrists all the way up past her elbows, each one a cold point. "Delores's entourage was trying to pull you out of the house. I assume back to the mall."

"Quite the walk, do you think they know how to drive?" Duncan asked.

"I was having this dream…" Arlo rubbed the side of his head. He looked exhausted, his hair a wild mane when it wasn't tied back.

The lights flickered on and the fridge started back up, the hum obvious after the silence.

"C'mon, Shay, up on your feet," Duncan helped her up.

"How did you know I was down here?" Shay asked.

"Heard yelling," Duncan said. "Grabbed my handy dandy tactical flashlight. Expected it to last more than a minute, but there is a possibility I was very cheap when I bought it. Curse you, past Duncan and your frugal ways. Anyway, are we all good? Cause it's two in the morning and some of us have work tomorrow. It's me, I have work."

"How did they even get in?" Max asked. "I checked the wards literally yesterday, how could they—"

"The mirrors," Shay said. Everyone looked at her. "I had a little nighttime visitor, she said we needed to ward the mirrors. That's how—"

The lights went out again and something grabbed her braid, yanking her back, a sharp scream escaping her. Hands crawled across her face, fingers in her mouth, pulling her down.

Max lifted their candle and the flame let out a burst of brilliant light, burning away the shadows and leaving her kneeling on the ground, coughing.

"Mirrors." Max hurried down the stairs and helped her to her feet. She kept a hold of their hand, using her free hand to pull her braid back over her shoulder. "I can get the ones upstairs, Arlo, you take the downstairs."

"I'm coming with you," Shay said. "And someone needs to make sure Jo's okay—"

"I'm on it," Duncan said.

"No, you stay with Arlo," Max told him.

"Good plan," Duncan conceded. "But then who—"

"Finnias can," Shay said.

Finnias nodded and vanished.

"Great, we all have jobs." Arlo still sounded disoriented. "I'll um. First, we're going to need more candles if we're going to seal two active portals. Some incense. Maybe uh, maybe some oil…"

"I'll see what we're dealing with upstairs," Max said. "I'll let you know if I need anything."

Shay remembered Jo saying something about Arlo being very into rituals and props, while Max didn't seem to really need anything but salt and candles, but she didn't say anything.

Max held onto her shoulder before they headed up, looking her up and down. "You have marks…"

"I'll live," she said.

"You should have woken me up," Max told her.

"I know, I'm sorry, I kinda panicked," she admitted. Sticking close to Max and their candle seemed to keep the worst of it away, but she was very afraid of what would happen if Delores made an appearance.

"How did you even know?" Max asked.

"Uh, okay, so the thing is—"

"What the hell is going on?" Jo came down the hallway, dressing gown billowing around her like a cloak. "Finnias knocked an inkwell off my desk, it didn't break, but—"

"Oh hey, he's getting good at that," Shay said. Jo glared at her. She grinned sheepishly.

"There are ghosts in the house," Max cut her off. "They came through the mirrors. We need to ward them."

"...Right." Jo straightened, wrapping her robe around her. "Let's see what we're dealing with."

Ice still scrawled a spiderweb across the glass. Max frowned at it but wiped it away, moving Shay's hand soap so they could put the candle at the edge of the sink.

"I think they're more concentrated on the downstairs bathroom," Max said. "Do you have any mirrors in your room?"

"At my vanity," Jo said. "And any scrying tools, but those are warded. They won't be able to use them."

"Right." Max ran their fingers over the frame. "I can ward this, then the one in your room. Shay, any other mirrors?"

"Duncan has that full length one in his room," Shay said. "The one we moved out of my room."

It was a freestanding mirror and it had given her the creeps. When Duncan found out she had pointed it towards the wall he'd taken it to his room. She couldn't say if it was bravery, stupidity, or just plain old vanity.

"I'll watch that one," Jo offered. "Then we can do my room after. Do you need anything?"

"No, I don't think so," Max said. "But we'll need to get the ghosts out before we ward all of the mirrors, which one do you suggest we funnel them towards?"

"Downstairs, absolutely," Jo said. "The uh. The half bath."

"Dunc's hair shrine?" Shay asked.

"Yes, that one." Jo nodded. "Yes, I know, he won't forgive me if any of his product ends up haunted, but I think I can handle it."

"Right, I'll seal off this one, then," Max said. "And then you can go to your room where it's safe."

"But I—"

"I agree," Finnias cut her off. "There are too many, and you are…"

"Riling them up?" Shay finished for him.

"Not the words I was considering, but yes, essentially."

"Fine."

Light appeared under Max's fingers as they traced over the edge of the frame, but something snapped like electricity when they reached the cobwebs she'd noticed earlier. They jerked their hand back.

"Ow!" They shook their hand. "What the—"

A white spider crawled onto the frame. Max hit the wall behind them so fast they nearly knocked the towel rack off the wall entirely.

"It's just a little guy." Shay pretended she hadn't reacted the exact same way to a spider on her sleeve.

"It's the size of a quarter," Max said.

"Just a little orb weaver, they're the good guys," Shay said. "I'll go grab a cup."

"And put it where? It's snowing," Max reminded her.

"I was just gonna move it," she said. "Somewhere less dangerous."

"Nuh uh, I don't want to be in the house with a spider."

"You know, there are tons of spiders, eating bugs, all over the house, right now," Shay said. "But you want to kill this guy just because he's in the wrong place? That's so cruel."

Still, the more she looked at it, the more she didn't care for it. It was white with a red mark on its bloated abdomen, almost like an eye.

"Actually I don't want to get near him," she said. "Or her. Them."

"It can't share my pronouns."

"So stingy," she said, but she backed away. "Hey, Finn—"

"I'm not doing it," Finnias said.

"What is the point of having a ghost if you won't even take out spiders for me?" Shay huffed at him.

The spider crawled through the mirror and disappeared, leaving behind a silver line of thread.

"Oh, well, that's one way to deal with it." Max finished running their fingers over the frame. The entire surface flashed like it was reflecting sunlight, then returned to normal. "There. Completely warded. I'll let you know when it's safe, okay?"

"Right." Shay nodded. "Sure. Just…you stay safe."

"I will." Max patted her shoulder on the way out.

Shay retrieved her dream journal from where she'd left it on the rug and headed back to her room, sitting on the bed. The lamp flickered on a moment after she sat down. Max must have tried to turn it on before running downstairs.

She opened the journal and stared at her chicken scratch.

"What's wrong?" Finnias asked. He sat on the chair she'd pulled up for him.

"Archibald was in my dream," she said. "Not just…in my dream. It felt like he was really there. Like we were having a real conversation."

Finnias was quiet for a long while. When he finally spoke, it sounded a little more distant and echoing than the space between the bed and chair would allow. "Are you sure?"

"I think you were right, my dreams are important," she admitted. "They're always at the circle, do you think we should go there?"

"I don't know," Finnias admitted, sounding slightly more present and less like he was trying to communicate through a terrible radio. "You could say I'm right one more time."

"Ew, gross, no." She snapped her journal shut.

"I mean, I did tell you."

"Yes, yes, you told me so, I know." She flopped back onto the bed. "When you're ready to be mature about being right—"

"Never."

"Then we can talk about it."

She scoured the ceiling for spiders, but if there were any, they were hidden in the shadows stretching ominously across the textured white expanse.

CHAPTER 12:
GOOD SOUP

Shay thought she heard whispers, but when she looked up the steady glow of her lamp softened the edges of the dimness of her room. She checked outside, but there was no dog waiting for her. With little else to do, she wrote down what she remembered from the conversation with Emmaline, but it seemed very sparse when she read back over it.

A wind blew through the house, moaning as it whipped around the corners, and silence fell.

Max came in soon after that, looking tired.

"Did you get them out?" Shay sat up.

"Yup, ghost free as far as I can tell." They sat down on the bed.

"You should get some sleep, you have work tomorrow," Shay said. "I'm sorry, I should have let you go home—"

"I wanted to stay," Max said. "And I'm glad I did. I can't believe so many ghosts got through the wards."

"Well, the mirrors are all sealed up tight now." Shay patted their shoulder. "So…good job, team, and you should really get to bed."

"I think I'm going to stay tomorrow, too." Max ignored her. "Just to make sure it's safe."

"But you need sleep—"

"I'm not going to sleep if I don't know you're safe," Max snapped at her. She blinked in surprise and they sighed, pulling a hand through their already tousled hair. "Sorry. That wasn't...that wasn't the tone I was going for, I'm just tired and worried, and I am having a really hard time telling if you're taking this seriously."

"I literally have ghost mark in my mouth right now, so yeah, I'm taking it seriously." Shay scooted a little closer to them, even though she was a little upset with them at the moment. "Inside my mouth. I'd show you, but no one sees the inside of my mouth but me. And my dentist."

"And your doctor." Max smiled a bit.

"If I went to one that wasn't actually just a vet who's good at sutures, sure," Shay said.

"Shay."

"Max."

"The point is we're both really tired, and we're both going to say things we don't mean in a minute here, so let's just get some more sleep and we can talk about it all tomorrow."

Max sighed. "You're right."

"Say it again, it's so sexy," Shay said.

Max laughed. "You're right, we need sleep. But first, I really am sorry."

"Don't need to be, I have a track record." Shay leaned her head on their shoulder. She wasn't tired in a way that lent itself to sleep. She wasn't sure Max was, either. "We're okay."

"We're okay," Max agreed, wrapping an arm around her. She relaxed fully for the first time since she'd woken up, feeling safe and warm. She didn't know what she would do without them. "But how did you know Arlo was down there?"

"Emmaline, the spirit charmer, she talked to me," Shay said. "Through the mirror. I wrote down what I remembered. I think she won't be able to help that way anymore, not through the warded mirrors, anyway."

"Which is just about all of them," Max said. "So, she's still kicking around?"

"Guess so." Shay really didn't want to have to worry about her, too. "She warned me, though, so maybe she has ghost beef with Delores."

Max snorted. "Ghost beef."

"It's more potent than regular beef," Shay said. "She wants to kick her ghost ass. I assume. But you know what they say about assumptions."

"Asses and you and me," Max said, making it Shay's turn to snort. "Do you think she's going to be a problem?"

"She's never not been a problem, so…"

"There's a possibility she orchestrated all of this," Finnias said, breaking into their conversation. He was usually quiet when Max was around, but lately he'd been speaking up more. Maybe their brief possession encounter had forged some sort of bond. She hoped so. "But it's strange that she told you, and that she cautioned you to ward the mirrors. Didn't you make a promise to a certain ghost that you wouldn't do that?"

"Aw, man." Shay flopped back. "What if she's controlling everything again. I should have punched her when I had the chance."

"When did you have the chance?" Max laid down next to her with a little more dignity.

"…Could have punched that mirror," Shay said. She held up her left hand. The cuts had healed, after Archibald had sliced up her hand with an antique mirror. She'd needed eleven stitches, from cuts on the back of her hand all the way up to her elbow. The scars were still red and raw. Rahim and the internet reassured her that they'd fade overtime, but for now they still looked raw and ugly, even in the soft light of her lamp. "Maybe not."

"I'm glad you didn't punch the mirror." Max took her hand with their own. Their hand was so much bigger it engulfed hers, hiding the ugliness with perfectly smooth skin and bright blue nail polish. "Jo would have been so upset."

"Right? Probably original to the house," Shay said. She stared at their hands, still held above her. It wasn't like it was the first time Max had taken her hand, or even the first hundredth time, but something about their fingers intertwined made her heart beat a little faster. "And then we would have had to go antiquing with her. Well, you would. 'Oh, Shay, what if these things are haunted, you'd better stay home'."

Max laughed again. "Your impressions are terrible."

Their laugh made the same giddy warmth rise in her as their hands together and she had to drop them onto the bed between them, suddenly hyper aware of how wide the gap between them was.

"I think they're spot on, actually, the best impressions ever, I could take my show on the road." Shay sounded normal, to her surprise. She thought her voice would crack, at the very least, or maybe sound like she was going to cry, and she had no idea why.

"I don't think a traveling comedian is really the right career choice for you," Max said.

"Excuse you, I'm delightful."

"Of course you are," Max said. "But I'd miss you."

Her chest felt weird and tight. "Aww Max. You'd come with me. I don't know how I'd survive otherwise."

"You would be fine," Max said.

"No, I'm pretty sure I'd die," Shay said. "Just waste away. From sadness. And neglect."

If Max wasn't with her she was pretty sure she really wouldn't survive. She was secretly losing her mind over being six inches away from them, how could she handle any sort of distance or time? How had she handled it, back in college? She couldn't remember.

"Okay, fine, on the absolute slim chance I wasn't with you, Finnias would keep you alive, I'm sure." Max laughed, somehow oblivious to her complete and total inner meltdown.

Shay had forgotten he was in the room entirely. "Oh, no, I plan to utilize him on stage. When people don't laugh, he throws things at them."

"I'm not doing that," Finnias said.

"You always disagree with my ideas."

"Because they're terrible."

She laughed, turning onto her side. "C'mon, get in on this bed action, there's room for you."

And then maybe she'd regain at least an iota of her sanity.

"No," he said. "You should get to sleep. I'll keep watch."

"Aw fine, be that way." She sat up, dragging Max with her. "Finn is a major party pooper and says we have to go to bed."

"Boo," Max told him. "But…unfortunately he's right, and I do have work tomorrow, unlike you."

"I'm so glad we're closed on Mondays," Shay said. The shop was, anyway. Shay was sure Jo would have her doing inventory or checking on things while she was off running errands. "You could always play hooky and just stay in bed with me all day."

"Tempting, but I'm trying to save my sick days for actual world ending events," Max said.

Shay was pretty sure she was in the middle of a comparable sized crisis, but she didn't know how to say that. She wasn't even sure why she was thinking about it.

It took a long time for her to fall asleep, even as Max's breathing evened out next to her. When she finally dozed off her dreams were strange, the sound of whispers morphing into the scurrying of little claws against hardwood floors.

When she woke up, the sun was bright against her curtains and Max was gone. Even though it had happened a dozen times before, the disappointment was still bitter on her tongue. She smoothed her hand over their side, but the sheets were cold.

"They didn't want to wake you up." Finnias was still in his chair. "They left a few hours ago. Said to tell you goodbye and other things."

Shay wished, that for once, they hadn't been so considerate. "What other things?"

"I refuse to repeat them."

"Aww Finn c'monnnn." She pouted at him.

"No," Finnias said. "You can remember you have a phone you can use to contact people if you really want to know."

"Wow, if you're making fun of me, we're in dire straights," Shay said. "Were phones even invented when you were alive? I mean, probably, but geez."

"Geez indeed."

She flopped back against her pillows with a pout. She would have liked Max to wake her up before they left, even if it was just for a quick hug. Or a kiss on the forehead. Or...

Her cheeks burned and she flipped over, pressing her face against the pillow.

"Are you all right?" Finnias asked.

"Peachy." She didn't move at all. It was like her entire world's axis had shifted, and she had no idea how to tell anyone. She'd never really understood why people called it butterflies, or sparks, but at the moment it very much felt like insects that were on fire were squirming around in her stomach.

That was probably a gross way to think of it.

Max probably wouldn't appreciate the metaphor.

They liked someone else.

The metaphor would have to live and die inside of her.

Shay briefly considered rolling off of the bed and letting the hardwood floor jolt her out of whatever hell she'd landed herself in.

"Are you sure?" Finnias asked.

"I'm awesome," she said. "Totally and completely awesome."

Shay hoped for some hard-hitting task that would keep her mind completely occupied, but unfortunately she had been tasked with restocking a few things. It didn't take very long, and it wasn't distracting at all. She went over her dream journal notes again, like she was getting ready for a presentation, but it all seemed flat, scratched out by her shaky hand. She gave up, ran her phone battery down, playing a game, and made soup for everyone, one of the few cooking lessons Duncan had given her that stuck.

"Maybe I need to nap more," she told Finnias as she stirred potatoes and carrots together with an onion. "Then I'll have more dreams, right?"

And she wouldn't have to think about anything.

"Sure," Finnias said.

"Please pretend to be supportive, for my sake." Shay checked the recipe and pulled the celery out of the fridge.

"I don't think I will," he said.

She'd written down "control of Finnias?" and circled it, but she was already convinced that even if Archibald believed that it was utter nonsense. Finnias did whatever he wanted, it just happened that he wanted to keep her alive.

She wrote "my head might be full of rocks" and crossed it out with a thorough scribble, but she could still see the words in the lines, somehow.

"Rude." She chopped the celery, carefully. She had enough scars on her left hand, even uglier and rawer in the light of the kitchen. "You're so mean to me. I don't think you care at all."

Finnias sighed. "Take all the naps you want, if you think it will help."

"Thank you, that's all I wanted to hear." Shay slid the celery into the pot. "Y'know, it's too bad you can't eat, or smell, because this soup is going to be amazing."

"I'm pretty sure it's burning."

Shay stirred it quickly. A few potatoes stuck to the bottom, but she usually burned thing just a little bit. "Did that on purpose. It adds flavor."

"Uh huh."

"You're just sad you can't taste my amazing cooking, I know, it's okay."

"Let's go with that."

She nudged him with her elbow. It used to feel like trying to make contact with an ice statue. She wasn't sure if it was a good or bad thing that he felt more like a person every single day.

But Finnias had never been a normal ghost, not from the beginning, and certainly not after switching his anchor to her. Ghosts were memories, but he had none, just snippets. She glanced at the hole in his chest. Archibald had literally carved out his heart, she shouldn't even have listened to him at all. She considered ripping the pages out of her dream journal and tossing them into the fireplace. She doubted a single thing he said had been true.

Well, maybe the bit about Finnias having a sister, but she wasn't going to pry.

The sun had set, and she admittedly felt a bit nervous. Jo had left a big container of salt in every single room, just in case, but she said she wasn't expecting trouble that night. Not with the wards refreshed and the mirrors covered.

She still jumped when the door opened, freezing until Max walked in, carrying a large overnight bag and letting in the cold of the night.

"You're here!" She tossed the spoon into the pot and grabbed Max tightly around the middle, their coat crinkling under her grip. She felt like something clicked into place in her chest.

Max let out a rush of air, patting her on the back. "Wow. Okay. Hi. Yes, I'm here."

"Good." She stepped back so they could take off their coat and shoes. And she could attempt to be normal. "We had frozen meatballs so I'm making soup. Meatball soup."

"Aren't you supposed to make the meatballs from scratch?" Max sat down at the table.

"I cannot tell you how much I'm not doing that," Shay said. The conversation was so normal it almost hurt. She got the broth in and let the soup simmer. "I think everyone should just be happy I'm making food for them. How was work?"

"Oh, y'know, little kids crawling all over me," Max said. "Pretty average. How was…not work?"

"I restocked," Shay said. "Did some dusting. Hey, don't read that."

She closed her dream journal and slid it back to her.

"I wasn't going to," Max insisted, though she didn't really believe them. They couldn't know about her unfortunate idiocy. They'd ask why, and she wasn't ready to have that conversation. Maybe not ever. "Where's everyone else?"

"Jo has a meeting with Rose, apparently merging businesses isn't like going to the courthouse to get married," Shay said. "So they're working out details and stuff."

Why had she brought up marriage?

"I understand your analogy, but marriage should be about working out details, too," Max said. "Arlo?"

"He's been making more of these salt jars." Shay tapped the one he'd left on the table. "And I'm making soup and Finnias was…well, disagreeing with everything I've said. So, pretty average day here, too."

"Not everything," Finnias insisted.

Arlo wandered into the kitchen. "That smells good. Oh, Max, you're here. I wanted to talk to you about my ah…sleepwalking problem. Duncan is trying to find any information he can on Delores when she was alive, he said he didn't get a lot from the shadows, but he might have a window of time that she would have been alive."

"That's good," Max said. "The candle seemed to drive out the ghosts and wake you up, so I imagine her influence works a lot like her shadow puppets."

"Oh, that's a good one," Shay said.

"Right? Thought of it at work." Max grinned at her and maybe her heart stuttered in a completely medically inadvisable way. "Maybe if we leave a salt circle around your bed…?"

"Not a bad idea." Arlo put on a pair of reading glasses and sat next to Shay, taking notes on his phone.

Max and Arlo traded ideas, different protective spells, crystals, herbs, really strong warding, staying in an entirely different room…

Shay tuned them out after a bit, getting up to stir the soup on occasion, though once it was simmering it was mostly just waiting for the right time to throw everything else in. Her life felt a little bit like that. Like she was just waiting for the next event, stalled until something else happened.

She realized the conversation had stopped entirely while she'd been mulling over broth and looked back.

Max and Arlo were both slumped across the table.

Her heart lurched into her throat. She scrambled over to Max. They were breathing, at least, but their eyes were closed. She shook their shoulder to no avail. "Max? Hey, c'mon, I know Arlo is a little boring but—"

"Shay, the floor," Finnias said.

Mist eddied across the floorboards and pooled around her slippers.

CHAPTER 13: ASSAULTED

Shay snagged the jar off the table and laid lines of salt across all three doors. It hadn't stopped every ghost, and it certainly had never worked on Archibald, but she had to do something. "Okay. Okay okay okay. You're fine, Shay. You got this."

The lights flickered and died.

Shay dug into the drawer next to the sink, pulling out candles and matches. She nearly fumbling them with her shaky hands. It took her a moment to get a candle lit, setting it on the counter.

The temperature dropped steadily, until she could see her breath.

Arlo and Max had just redone the wards. She couldn't have possible worn them away that fast. She pressed her back to the cabinets, the edge of the counter digging into her spine, hugging the jar of salt tightly to her chest.

"Someone's coming." Finnias moved between her and the door.

"What?" Her voice cracked.

Max and Arlo were still asleep. The candle guttered dangerously low.

The doorknob rattled.

"Finn, move," she told him. He stepped out of the way, and she readied her jar of salt.

"Shay, wait—"

She hurled a handful of salt at the doorway.

"Hey!" Duncan yelled. "What the…Shay? Why are the lights out?"

"Oh my god, you scared me!" she shrieked back.

"Then maybe don't stand around in the dark!" Duncan brushed the salt off of his jacket. "I can't believe you assaulted me. How many times is this? Max, can you…oh. Oh, I just walked into a horror movie."

"Yeah you did, close the door," Shay said. She put another line of salt in front of the door, for all the good it would do if their assailant was sleepwalking like Arlo.

"Where's Jo?" Duncan pulled out his phone.

"In a meeting with Rose," Shay said.

"Nothing too important then." Duncan called her, but paused and stared at his phone. "Well. Hopefully she planned on having dinner at home. Smells good."

"That's the least of our worries right now," Shay hissed at him. "I can't get them to wake up, but the wards should be fine, I don't understand…"

"Break one of the salt lines, I'll find out what's happening outside," Finnias suggested. "Put the salt back immediately and stay together."

"Got it." Shay crouched down and made a gap in the line leading out into the shop. Finnias appeared on the other side, and she quickly repaired it. "Be safe."

He nodded and vanished.

Shay stood up and grabbed Duncan's hand.

"Hey, it's okay," he said. "I'm right here. I won't let anything hurt you."

"Yeah, somehow, not very reassuring," Shay said. "Mostly I'm hoping neither of us fall asleep."

"Oh, yeah, that too."

They stood in silence together in the kitchen. Duncan's hand was clammy, but Shay didn't dare let go. Outside the streetlights went out, one by one. Her candle flame burned low and small, barely shedding any light at all.

"Was that a pun?" Shay asked.

Duncan grinned. "Assaulted? Yeah. A-salted. I should have said that in the theater."

"When…you were pulled into the mirror?" Shay stared at him.

"When you threw salt at me the first time!" Duncan said. "Sure, I had a possibly literally splitting headache and I was kidnapped right after, but honestly, that's no excuse."

"Oh my god."

He shrugged. "You can be as punenthusiastic as you want, but it's true."

"I suddenly know how Max feels," she said.

They were quiet after that, watching the candle flame burn down, throwing strange shadows up onto the cabinets.

"So uh. How was work?" Shay asked.

"Seriously?" Duncan laughed, high pitched and nervous. "I shelved a lot. Sent some interlibrary loan stuff. Y'know, average day."

"Seems like everyone had one of those until now," Shay said. She looked over at Max, fast asleep as far as she could tell in the flickering light. "I hope they're okay."

"Me, too," Duncan said. "They're kind of like a second younger sibling, y'know?

"I mean, we have been together basically forever."

"But not together," Duncan said. "Unless you're planning on smooching that ghost, which I respect. Either way. Or both. Got two hands and all."

"Really? We're talking about this right now?" Shay hadn't even processed her own feelings.

"When else are we going to talk about it?" Duncan asked. "Anyway, it's okay, I get it, Finnias is really attractive in a smug pretty boy sort of way."

"Please don't ever say you find Finnias attractive again," she said.

Duncan shrugged. "I mean, if I had to have a dude inside me—"

"Gross." She swung their connected hands, hard. "I'm going to let go. Make sure you fall and hit the counter just right."

He laughed. "Love you, too, Shay Shay. Don't worry, he's all yours."

Arlo sat up.

"…Is he awake or sleepwalking again?" Duncan asked.

Arlo stood up, stiffly, knocking the chair over.

"Sleepwalking for sure." Shay backed up a step.

He stepped towards them.

"He just tried to leave last time, right?" Duncan asked.

"Yeah, but—"

Arlo swung a fist at Shay's head. Duncan yanked her out of the way and the blow connected with the cupboard behind her, splintering the wood.

"Hit him!" Duncan pulled her around and she went low, smashing her shoulder up into Arlo's soft, ample stomach He grunted and doubled over. Duncan yanked her back before he could grab for her, pulling too hard on Shay's shoulder.

"Ow!"

"Just trying to save our butts!" Duncan opened the door between the kitchen and the shop, and they both ran into the next room, slamming the door and locking it.

"We can't leave Max in there!" Shay tried to go for the door, but Duncan didn't let go. "Hey! Let me go!"

"Absolutely not, we have to get out of here, get someone who can do the whole…candle thing," Duncan said.

Finnias appeared next to them. "What are you doing out here? She's coming!"

There was too much happening, a whirl of adrenaline and movement, leaving Shay's head spinning. Glowing mist hugged the corners of the room and flowed around the shelves. The light made her eyes sting.

"Who's coming?" Duncan asked.

"Delores?" Shay asked, and Finnias nodded. "Of course she is."

The lock on the back door clicked open.

"Okay, Finn, time to suit up," Duncan said.

"But…" Shay wasn't sure what her protests were, but she was certain she had some.

"No time," Duncan gave her a grim smile and held out a hand to Finnias.

Finnias nodded and took it, disappearing. He straightened slightly and let go of her hand.

"We need to get up to your room," Finnias said. "That's the safest place in the house, and only Max and Jo have keys."

"Yeah, well, we either have to leave the house or get through him. You have any ideas?" Shay asked.

Finnias put a hand over his mouth, brow furrowed. "Duncan is faster and stronger than you are right now. I'll hold him off, you get around him and up the stairs. I promise I'll be right behind you."

"I hate this plan," she said.

"Now you know how everyone else feels."

"Lot of that going around," she said, without elaborating.

The door opened and Arlo stepped into the shop. He was clearly still asleep, his face relaxed. His eyes flickered rapidly beneath the lids.

Finnias braced himself and Shay readied herself to dash past them and up the stairs.

Arlo ignored them both, picking up a large chunk of quartz next to the door.

"That's one of the ward focuses!" Shay darted forward.

Arlo held it up and a wave of force knocked her back into Finnias, who barely kept her from hitting the floor. Symbols glowed brightly on the walls and exploded into showers of sparks that faded before they hit the mist. A line of light zipped around the room and went dark.

The front door burst open.

Delores strode in, followed by an entourage of shadows that gathered against the walls, whispering amongst themselves. Fog billowed around her and trailed at the ends of her dress.

"Grab her," she instructed Arlo. Shay yelped when Arlo dropped the quartz and grabbed her around the middle, hoisting her into the air. She kicked and fought, but he didn't even seem to notice.

Finnias lunged for them but Delores struck like a snake, grabbing the back of his neck. She twisted her wrist and yanked Finnias out of Duncan, shoving the latter to the floor and holding Finnias up by his neck like he was an unruly kitten.

"Let go of him!" she screamed, slamming her heel into Arlo's bad knee. He didn't even flinch.

Finnias struggled, but his glow faded, his color washing out, fading until he was almost a shadow.

"No!" She struggled harder, but Arlo was too big and too strong for her to twist out of his grip and she couldn't get a good enough angle to bite him. "Finnias!"

"Interesting." Delores looked strangely bored. "Usually, the dead have such delightful nightmares, but he's rather empty, isn't he?"

"Leave him alone," Shay said.

"Shay, I'm fine—" Finnias was cut off when Delores shook him.

"But you." Delores cast Finnias aside. He landed in a heap like a broken doll. Shay screamed but he didn't move at all.

Delores held up her free hand. Her fingers were too long, nearly invisible strings attached to the end of each one. She jerked her hand up, pulling Archibald from the mist. He hung like a puppet off of her hand, eyes closed and face slack. He was back in his vest, the coat over his arm bulging like a badly sewn on prop.

Shay froze.

"This pathetic thing still shows up, doesn't he?" Delores smirked. "I think he'd love to show you exactly how he feels about you, don't you?"

"No." She meant to sound defiant, but it was barely above a whisper, her throat going dry.

Delores took a deep drag on her cigarette and exhaled.

Arlo dropped Shay.

Frozen grass stabbed into her socks. The smoke pulled back, revealing the circle, the trees around it, and the ridge that hid the manor from view.

Archibald stalked forward, the coat falling away, bone-handled knife forming in his hand.

"You ruined everything!" he snarled. She turned to run but he was behind her when she did, grabbing her arm and yanking her up. His fingers were so cold it burned all the way to the bone.

She screamed and he shook her so hard her teeth rattled.

"I think I'll enjoy cutting out your heart." He lifted the knife. She tried to punch him and he shook her again, pain flaring through her entire body.

Someone slammed into him and she dropped into the grass. All she could do was lay there and breathe for a moment, trying to stop her head from spinning. She couldn't move her arm and the cold invaded her lungs.

"Shay." Finnias helped her sit up. He looked faded out, nearly a shadow himself. His hands regained some solidness where he touched her. She reached up with her good arm and touched his shoulder, coils of blue racing beneath her fingers.

"Are you okay?" she asked and he nodded, holding a hand over hers.

"That does raise an interesting point, doesn't it?" Archibald considered the glowing edge of the knife blade. "You're much more worried about the people around you than yourself."

"Get out of here," Shay told Finnias, her voice shaking. "Run."

"No." His grip on her hand tightened.

"Let's have a little change of scenery." Archibald snapped his fingers. Carpet spread beneath his feet, forming stairs behind him. Walls rose from the ground and the window opened up. Sunlight streamed through the glass.

The landing.

Finnias looked alive. Pale, his hair more rumpled than she'd ever seen it, but alive and breathing. His fingers were warm.

Archibald was in full color himself, from his blond curled hair to his shiny black shoes. "You've never been privy to how Finnias died, have you?"

"I'm not letting you." Shay hauled herself to her feet, somehow. Her right arm was a mass of black and deep blue, and in the relative warmth of the landing the feeling came back, throbbing pain all the way up to her neck.

"I don't think you have much of a choice." Archibald flicked his wrist and the banister wrapped around Shay's ribs, tight enough that she could barely breathe. She tried to move and it squeezed so hard for a horrible moment she thought it would crush her before it relented. "Come on, Finnias, you have a part to play."

"Finn—"

He was standing in the sun, looking like he always had on his landing. He turned to Archibald. His mouth was moving, but no sound escaped. Archibald didn't even bother with the pretense of the coat.

He stabbed Finnias in the chest with a wet thunk.

Finnias choked.

Shay screamed her throat raw.

Finnias turned to her, shaky, reaching out to her with a hand coated in blood like a glove. His voice was shaky, his breathing thready, red already on his lips, on his teeth. "It's okay."

She was crying and she wasn't sure when she'd started.

Archibald cut up and Finnias made a horrible, soft noise in the back of his throat. Bone crunched and muscle parted. Blood splattered on the already red carpet, dark on the front of Finnias's vest and staining the white of his shirt crimson.

"It's just a dream," Finnias whispered.

Shay pulled against the banister with everything she had, bruising her hands. She gave up with a frustrated sob and reached for Finnias's hand, their fingers just touching.

Something heavy landed on her shoulder.

CHAPTER 19: THE RAT KING

"It's just a dream," Shay whispered to herself, squeezing her eyes shut. "It's just a dream."

"We are very real, Shay O'Brannon," a hundred low, sibilant voices whispered. Sharp claws dug into her shoulder and teeth grazed the shell of her ear.

Her breath caught in her throat. She'd had nightmares, convinced herself more than once that she heard the sounds of rats.

And now it was sitting on her shoulder.

"We have a task for you, so you cannot die here. Not to this nightmare."

The banister unraveled and dropped her onto the carpet just as Finnias and Archibald both crumpled to the floor like their strings had been cut. She crawled over to Finnias, pulling him close. He was still warm. Blood soaked into her leggings and sweater. Finnias's head rolled against her shoulder. and she smoothed back his hair. "It's okay. It's okay, I've got you."

"Shay O'Brannon, you must focus." The rat dug their claws into her shoulder. She could just see it, out of the corner of her eye. A massive rat in shades of blue, it skull shining pale and white through its translucent fur. "That one is already dead. We do not have much time, and you must survive this nightmare. You must finish what you have begun."

"Is that your favor?" Shay's voice shook.

"It is not what we wish to ask you, but simply what you must do, if you want to save what is left of this one," the rat said. "The spider, from the void. The nightmare weaver. It is free. It hides and calls itself Delores, but it is not her."

She froze, still curled around Finnias. When she spoke, her words were rough. "The thing Archibald tried to summon?"

"Yes," the voices hissed together.

"How on earth can I finish that?" her voice cracked, horribly. She'd pushed it back into the void, but only with the help of Finnias and Duncan. Even then, it had been incredibly temporary. "Why can't you—"

"We can only assist. We cannot destroy," the rats said. "You are our champion in this fight, Shay O'Brannon. If you wish to save that one, to save yourself, then you have no choice."

"I don't even know what you are."

She was stalling, trying to process everything.

"Ah yes, we have not introduced ourselves." They let out a collective laugh, each voice slightly discordant with the next. "We are mischief. We are many. We are the Rat King."

They laughed again, hundreds of voices from shapes moving around her.

"Why me?" It came out so low and grating she could barely hear her own voice.

"There has not been a necromancer like you in so, so long," they said, full of longing. "And we have waited longer than you can imagine. They tried to hide you from us, the one whose house you live in, the one who shares your blood. But we found you. We were always going to find you. And you would always find us."

Shay turned to look at the rat on her shoulder, eyes wide, so many questions on her tongue she couldn't even fathom what to ask first.

There was nothing on her shoulder.

The dream unraveled at the corners of the landing, bright light piercing through the gaps. It split apart and she was back in the shop, still clutching Finnias, though he was cold and ghostly again.

Max stood in the shop entrance, holding a candle. Delores cowered back from them. Duncan held tightly to their hand.

"Get out."

The power that rippled off of them was incredible. Shay clung even harder to Finnias, terrified he'd get swept away.

When she looked up, Delores and her entourage were gone.

"Oh boy, that...that took a lot out of me." Max sat on the floor. "Is she gone?"

"She's gone," Duncan confirmed. "Shay?"

Shay looked down and Finnias was gone. Her breath hitched until she realized he was standing next to her, looking exactly how he always did.

He offered her a hand up. "Are you all right?"

She didn't know what to say, there wasn't anything she could say. He was acting like nothing had happened. Maybe he didn't remember it. No one had been there to witness it.

Her sweater was clean, not even a hint of blood.

She accepted Finnias's hand up and dragged him into a hug. It was cold, but she didn't care, burying her face into his shoulder. He didn't move for a minute, then very gingerly returned the hug.

"I'm all right," he murmured into her hair. "It was just a dream."

She wanted to say that she knew, but the words were all stuck inside of her and she was terrified if she released them it would unlock something in her chest and she'd start sobbing.

"I've been dead for a long time, Shay, it's all right."

She knew that. She knew he'd been dead for over a century. But knowing and seeing had been two very different things.

"I couldn't help," she finally managed to say something. Her voice was smaller than she thought it should be.

"It's all right."

"It's not, it's..." She took a breath and finally stepped back. She was vaguely aware of Max and Duncan's concern, of someone talking to Arlo, but she couldn't focus on them. "The thing from the tear is out, it's in Delores, and I have to stop it."

Having a focus, something to do, helped solidify the shakiness in her chest.

Finnias jerked, like he wanted to pull her into another hug, but he stepped back instead.

"What?" Duncan moved towards her. "Shay what on earth...you were just sitting there, like you were dreaming, we didn't know—"

"I need to fix the wards," Arlo said. Shay wasn't even sure when he'd recovered. "Max...you uh, stay here."

"Yup." Max sounded out of breath, pulling themself up by the door frame. "Just a little tired. I don't know how Duncan woke me up—"

"I'm a necromancer, too, in case everyone forgot, and I can do more than just have Finnias possess me," Duncan said. "I can't blame you, I have so many other talents and amazing traits that it's hard to remember them all. So, I figured I could probably get Max up if I tried hard enough. Anyway, none of what you said is…I'm going to need you to back up."

"I only want to explain it once." Shay could still feel the blood seeping through her clothes, the heaviness of Finnias's body, the weight on her shoulder.

She shuddered. She needed to go to Max, make sure they were okay. She needed to check on Duncan and assess the damage in the kitchen, but she was just standing there.

"Shay…" Finnias touched her shoulder. "It was just a dream."

"I know," she said. "I just…I know. I know it was."

"It wasn't real."

It was real enough, and the details weren't fading like they should have, and she didn't know how to handle it. What to do. Part of her wanted to sob for a few hours. Another part of her wanted to do anything to forget about it.

Neither of those things would help anyone.

She walked over to Max. She could do this. One thing at a time. "Are you okay?"

"I'm fine, I just put a lot of oomph into getting her out." Max looked at her, clearly very concerned. "…Are you okay?"

"I…" She wanted to lie, say she was fine, but every time she looked down, she expected her sweater to be soaked in blood, and she didn't know how to stop. "I dunno."

"Okay." Max took her hand. Their hands were very warm, and she realized that she was freezing. She held onto their hand too tightly. "Oh, you're like ice. Let's get you into the living room. Duncan, is one of your amazing abilities making a fire?"

"It is, actually," Duncan said.

Shay was bundled up on the couch. Time seemed to be moving strangely, in weird spurts. Tea was shoved on her, the fire was lit, a blanket wrapped around her. Finnias perched on the arm next to her, and it was so much like it always was that the dissonance made her head spin. Everyone was talking but it was like it was washing around her and she wasn't absorbing any of it.

She reached over and took his hand, even though it was probably a terrible idea with how cold she already was. He didn't move away.

"Did she hurt you?" Shay asked.

"No," Finnias said. "She tried to show me something, I think, but it didn't quite work."

"And then Archibald…"

Finnias put a hand to his chest, over the hole where his heart had been carved out. As a ghost it looked so clean, a perfect circle to the left of his sternum. "Yes."

"I'm sorry."

"It's not your fault," Finnias said.

It felt like her fault. Delores, the nightmare demon, whatever it was, had only done it to hurt her.

"What happened to my cabinets?!" Jo yelled from the other room.

It felt like it took too long to get everyone in the room, and so little time to explain. Max sat on her other side and held her other hand the entire time.

She glossed over the worst of it, focusing on what the Rat King had told her.

"So…that's it," she said.

"A rat king is just rats with their tails knotted together," Arlo said. "I've heard they're some kind of omen, but…"

"But none have ever been confirmed," Max said.

"I'm just repeating what it told me." Shay felt hollow, completely wrung out. She didn't want to talk anymore.

"It said it was waiting for me. That I was hidden, something about the one who lived here and blood…"

"I…may have an idea of what that is," Jo said. "But I would need to dig out my grandmother's journals. I packed them into storage bins and put them away and…well, until now I wasn't really quite ready to read them."

"I'll do it," Duncan said. "I mean, I'm pretty sure I'm the only one here who has actual training with old handwritten books."

"The blood…could that have been your um…" Max trailed off.

"My dad?" Shay asked. "I don't know. Probably. Just…hid me, whatever that means, and took off."

She was feeling so much that she couldn't even be bothered to dredge up the old anger she had towards her father.

"We'll figure it out," Duncan said. "For now…let's just make sure the wards in Shay's room are good."

"They're good," Arlo said. "I checked. Max did them, not me, so they weren't affected by…whatever I did. I didn't even know I could do that."

"Technically, you didn't," Jo reminded him.

"I'm really sorry about the cupboard—"

"That wasn't you, either." Jo sighed. "Let's worry about it tomorrow. Right now, we need to talk about this nightmare. Thing. Because if it's as bad as—"

"Actually, I think I'm going to go to bed." It wasn't late, but Shay really wanted to just not be around so many people. She didn't want to talk about what she had to do, or what it all meant. "I'm just…I'm tired."

Jo looked at her and frowned. "I think you should write everything down, get it out of your system. And it wouldn't hurt to have the notes for later."

"Sure." It was the last thing she wanted to do, but she found herself nodding.

"I'm not saying that to…I'm trying to give advice," Jo said. "It's always helped me."

"Oh." Shay blinked. "Right. Thank you."

"Max, those calming techniques I showed you—"

"I can teach her." Max nodded. "You go ahead, I'll grab your journal."

She nodded and took the stairs to her room. She needed to wash her face, at the very least, but she found herself sitting on her bed, staring at her hands. It felt like a lifetime ago she hadn't wanted to get up because of her own stupid feelings.

Finnias was fine.

For the moment.

She wasn't sure what the Rat King meant about saving him. Why they had been waiting for her. It scared her, more than she was willing to let on.

A knock on her door made her jump. She expected Max, but it was Duncan.

"Hey, Shay Shay." He sat on the bed next to her. "Jo wanted me to apologize for going full war council on you back there. And I wanted to let you know I packed up your soup. There for you any time you want it."

"Oh. Right. The soup." She'd completely forgotten about it. She thought about eating it and her stomach clenched. "Maybe later."

"You got it." Duncan was quiet for a moment. "I get not wanting to talk about things right now, but when you're ready, you can talk to me. Not just Max. I think I have a pretty similar perspective on things."

"I know."

"And I've had the same dream."

She stared at him. He hadn't mentioned it before. "The…circle one?"

"No," he said. "The one you just had. I've had it, too. And it's pretty brutal, so…heck, I avoided him for a little while, thought it might be the whole memory thing."

Finnias looked away from the window, staring at him. "Dunc…" She hadn't even realized.

"The thing is, I realized something today," Duncan said. "I can't just…keep on letting this control me. Any of it. And…I think that's advice you need, too. Anyway, let's not talk about that right now. Just…when you're ready, let's talk, yeah?"

"And not be super obnoxious to each other?"

"Oh, no, that's like asking me to move the moon. Or to stop breathing." Duncan grinned at her and for the first time since the nightmare she felt just a little bit better.

"You're right, I would never ask you to move the moon," she said. "The breathing part, on the other hand…"

"Yeah, yeah." He stood up and gave her an obnoxious smooch on top of her head. "Mwah."

"Gross," she said, more out of habit than anything else.

"Gotta be, sometimes," he said. "Wuv you, Shay Shay."

"Yeah, yeah, I wuv you, too."

Chapter 18: Journaling

Shay held up her journal. The dream was detailed in dry bullet points, her chicken scratch so erratic even she could barely read it.

"You know, I don't think I'm cut out for having a fancy pen and a fancy journal," she said. "Maybe just one of those college ruled ones for ten cents or whatever. That's all my handwriting is worth."

Max leaned over to take a look at her work. "I can read it."

"I'm glad one of us can." She leaned back against the headboard. "I hate that Jo was right and this helped."

Writing had felt like leeching poison onto the pages instead of ink, her thoughts pouring out onto the pages. Writing it helped it feel distant.

"You hate it?" Max laughed, a little bit.

"Yes, I hate that journaling helps, it makes me feel like a grandma," Shay said. "Is journaling a word?"

"Sure," Max said. "Taking nouns and adding 'ing' to the end makes everything a verb."

"No, that's terrible." She found herself smiling despite herself.

Max nodded. "Sad but true. Journaling, adulting..."

"No."

"Mugging."

"You're going to mug someone?" It was her turn to laugh.

"I was thinking more in terms of tea, but realized a second to late that it's already a word," Max said. "No, sadly, I am not cut out for mugging. Not the least bit intimidating."

"I cannot reassure you in this, because it's true, you're like a teddy bear." Shay patted their hand.

"Wow."

"You are! Except to ghosts, they're terrified of you," Shay said. "You knocked her right out of the house."

"It helped that there was some residual energy from the old wards, but yeah, I guess I'll take it."

"Yeah, you will." Shay nudged their shoulder with her own. "How did Duncan get you up, anyway?"

"I have no idea, I was having this dream…and then it changed? I think it might have been him." Max frowned. "I don't really remember the details, but the shift was jarring enough I woke up."

"I didn't know he could do that," Shay said.

"To be fair, he probably didn't, either, since when I woke up he said 'oh damn that actually worked, sick'." Max shrugged. It did sound exactly like something Duncan would do. And say. "I'm glad it did. I wish it had sooner."

"You were awesome," Shay said.

"No, I was asleep for most of it," Max corrected her. "I think I've figured out how to stop it, though. So, there's this branch of magic called sigils. If I design one and keep it on me, then there's a higher chance of me staying awake."

"Yeah?" Shay asked.

"Arlo knows more than I do, but I think this will work," Max said. "I'll get it tattooed on me, if I have to."

Shay frowned. "…You're afraid of needles."

"I can look away and you can hold my hand," Max said. "I'm serious, Shay. I'm not doing that again. I can't do that again."

A sudden stillness fell over her. The sense of something about to change. About to break. And all she could do was push forward. "Max—"

"No. I mean it." They put their hands on her shoulders. Sitting on her bed felt a little too informal for a conversation where Max was so serious. Where it felt like the world was about to teeter in one direction or the other, and she didn't know which one it was. "I'm not leaving it up to Finnias next time. I'm going to be right beside you. I don't care what it takes. I'll be there."

"But I do," she said. The room was quiet. It was snowing again. She needed to close her curtains or Jo would complain about the heating bill again, like she hadn't been the one to burn her old curtains in the fire pit out back.

"…What do you mean?" Max finally asked, their voice cracking slightly.

"I care what it takes," she said. "I don't…I don't want you to do something that will permanently mess your life up—"

"It's a tattoo, like, on my shoulder."

"You know what I mean."

"Don't."

"Max, we can…we can joke and I can give you affirmations but we both know I'm just blowing smoke—"

They shook their head. "No."

"Max." She slammed her journal against the bed. It didn't make much noise, but Max jumped a little. She felt bad, but she pressed on anyway. "I...this is so big. It's so much. And we have to...we have to...I have to kill a demon. A nightmare demon that's gunning for me, and we have to acknowledge that there's a possibility I can't punch my way out of this one."

"I know," Max said, quietly. "I know it's a possibility."

She didn't know what to say. They carefully removed her hands from her dream journal, where she had been gripping it so hard her fingers were sore without her even realizing it. Their own hands were shaking but they held hers like they were her lifeline.

"I…" they sighed and tried again. "Shay, I know that...I know this is big, and that everything has been turned upside down on us, and I know...I know what could happen. I really do. This is...so much bigger than either of us. But I can't...I could never, ever live with myself if I didn't do everything in my power to keep you alive. So, whatever it takes, I'm there."

"Max—"

"Shay, I love you." They pressed their forehead against hers and she closed her eyes. Her heart pounded. "I love you so much, and I can't...I don't want to live without you. I know how that sounds and I'm just not saying things well but I—"

"Okay." Something resolved inside of her, the storm of emotions solidifying into something that she could use. "Then I simply won't die."

Max cracked a smile. "Yeah?"

"Yeah," she said. "I'll beat up a nightmare spider demon and tell a swarming rat demon to get pipered into a river. For me. And for you. Because I love you, too."

More than they could ever know.

Platonic, romantic, it didn't really matter. As long as Max was with her, she really did believe she could do anything.

"You're my favorite person in the world," Max said.

"You're mine, too," Shay said. "The best friend anyone could ever ask for. I can say with absolute certainty that you'd never carve out my heart with a knife."

"Never," Max said.

"Even if I deserve it," she tried to joke, but it fell flat.

"Never ever," Max said, a little too firmly for a joke. "Not for anything. I'd let the moon implode first."

"Wow, you feel very strong about this," Shay said.

"You could say my heart's really in it," Max said.

She snorted. "As long as mine isn't."

They laughed. "Don't worry, I won't have a change of heart."

"Aww. My heart is so full."

"Please stop," Finnias said, but he didn't sound like he really meant it. At least he wasn't staring out of the window anymore.

"Yeah, all right." She leaned back, letting out a shuddering sigh. "Okay, I think that's enough heavy stuff for me tonight."

"Same." Max nodded. "Oh. Hi Finnias. Sorry about your um. All that."

"I don't need your pity," Finnias said.

"He says thanks," Shay said. Finnias looked so offended she burst out laughing.

"He didn't, but I'll accept it, anyway," Max said. "Feeling a little better?"

"Well…" She took stock of her own emotions. She still felt like there was a heavy weight on her shoulders, and anxious dread filled her chest, but it wasn't as overwhelming as it had been. "I think the complete meltdown has been avoided for the moment, so yeah. I guess so."

"You're the toughest person I know."

"I mean, I've met your Nana, and I'm pretty sure she's the toughest lady on the planet," Shay said. "I'm actually kind of concerned about her knowledge of getting blood out of things. I think she might have murdered someone."

"Oh, probably," Max said. "I mean it, though. If that happened to me...I'd still be in the shop. Full on crying. Just big sobs. Nothing would be able to move me for hours. Maybe days."

"I could lift you," Shay said.

"Let's spare your back and not test that," Max said. "I just...think you're awesome. I guess. Is my point."

"Aww I think you're awesome, too," Shay said. "And I super appreciate you and everything you do. Especially putting up with me."

"I am happy to," Max said. "And no talking about ruining my life. I will look awesome with a tattoo."

"I just...it's so permanent," Shay said.

"And you're permanently stuck with me, so..."

She smiled a bit. "Yeah, all right. Just don't get it on your face or something."

"It wouldn't work at all with getting bloodthirsty done on my forehead."

"Oh yeah, that's the ticket," Shay said. "Just make sure you get it prison style for extra sexiness."

"You know it."

Shay cracked up. It was a little hysterical.

"There we go." Max looked very pleased with themself. "Are you good to be alone for a minute? I wanted to check on those wards. I trust Arlo I just...well, I want to make sure."

"I'm never alone." Shay gestured to Finnias, who shrugged. "But are you sure? You kinda wore yourself out earlier..."

"I'm going to be honest, this is entirely for my peace of mind," Max said. "Keep an eye on her, Finnias."

"Don't tell me what to do," Finnias said.

Max slipped off of the bed and closed the door behind them.

"So are you not going to keep an eye on me, just to be contrary?" Shay asked.

Finnias huffed. "I'm not doing this because they asked me. I want that on the record."

"I thought you guys were doing better," Shay said. "After the whole possession bonding thing."

"I suppose I'm grateful they can reassure you," Finnias said in a way that did not sound sincere at all.

Shay smirked. "Ah, I see."

"See what?" Finnias's eyes narrowed.

"Are you jealous of Max?" Her grin widened.

"No."

"You are jealous!" She tried very hard not to laugh. "That's adorable."

"I am not adorable," he said. "I meant it. I'm grateful."

"Yeah." She got up from the bed. Finnias was acting completely normal, and some of the worry dropped off of her. "You know I really rely on you, too, right?"

"I don't need your reassurances."

"I know." She nodded. "But I wanted to tell you, anyway."

"Oh." Finnias looked mildly pleased, at least. "You need someone to rely on."

"I know, I'm a disaster."

"You are."

"Could disagree with me a tiny bit," Shay told him.

"Why would I?" He raised one eyebrow.

"Rude." Shay moved to the window to close her curtains. The cold radiating from her window felt intense, and she probably already kept the heating bill incredibly high. Jo had already yelled at her twice to keep the curtains closed once she replaced them.

She grabbed the edge of the curtain and paused.

Two lantern-like eyes stared up at her from the shadows across the street, the outline of a great, black dog visible against the paleness of the snow.

"No." She yanked the curtain closed.

Her hand came down in the snow.

She was outside.

"What?" She glanced back. She could see her room, the light barely visible at the edges of the curtains. The snow as cold and wet, sinking into the knees of her pajama pants and socks.

A warm rush of air stirred her hair.

She froze like a small, frightened animal. A huff.

It took everything she had to look up.

The black dog rose above her, containing galaxies, its bones glowing through its own darkness.

CHAPTER 16: LEAD

Shay climbed to her feet as slowly as she dared.

The dog was huge when it wasn't constrained by the size of her room, at least twice her height.

Finnias shoved her back, standing between her and the dog, one arm raised up. "Get back to the house."

She grabbed his arm, not sure what else she could do. She couldn't let him get hurt. Not for her. Not for anything.

"I'll be fine." He glanced back at her. "Get back to the house."

The dog didn't growl, didn't even move, just stood there regarding them with eyes that glowed an even, soft yellow.

"What do you want?" she asked.

"Please don't provoke it," Finnias hissed back at her.

"No." Shay stepped up. She couldn't keep hiding behind him, or in the house. Clearly that didn't work, anyway. "What do you want? Are you a death omen? Are you…some sort of harbinger of doom? If you're going to kill me then get it over with already."

"Shay." Finnias looked at her like she had lost her mind. Maybe she had, but she was too angry and tired to be afraid.

The dog cocked its head to the side, ears flopping with the motion. It made no move towards her.

"…Okay?" Shay glanced at Finnias. "I don't think it's going to hurt me?"

"I don't think I'm willing to take that chance," Finnias retorted.

"Fair." She took another step forward, despite the noise of protest Finnias made. Warmth rolled off of the dog, shimmering in the cold air. "Okay, if you're not here to kill me, what do you want?"

The dog leaned forward, snuffling at her hand, and it took everything in her not to jerk back. It shrunk in size until its head was even with hers and nosed at her hip. She kept her hands up and stood absolutely still, waiting to feel teeth sink into her side.

"Are you just some kind of ghost dog?" Shay guessed. It snorted in response. "Guess not."

"I am begging you to please stop talking to the death omen," Finnias said.

"I don't think that's what it is," Shay said. She'd told that to Jo before, but she hadn't really believed it until that moment, standing in the snow, shivering while the dog investigated her. "So um. Girl. What are you, then? What do you want? Why do you keep showing up?"

The dog huffed and backed up, looking down the street. Shay followed its gaze, but she didn't see anything.

"I don't get it," she said.

The dog let out a sigh that was surprisingly human and stepped forward, pressing its forehead against chest. Shay still had her arms up, not quite sure what to do, if she was allowed to pet the probably not a death omen.

She slowly lowered her hands and scratched the dog behind the ears.

"Shay are you serious right now?" Finnias asked.

"She's a doggy," Shay told him.

"She is big enough to rip you in half."

"Big puppy," she said. The dogs fur was soft and thick. "I'm going to name you Beans."

"Beans." Finnias sounded like it caused him physical pain to repeat her.

"Yes. Her name is Beans, and I love her." Shay knew she sounded absolutely insane. Giddiness fizzed in her chest, hot and electric, almost painful.

A flash and they were surrounded by blue flames in a perfect circle.

"Look what you did," Finnias said.

"No, I…I know this," Shay said. She'd seen it in her dreams every night for weeks, it would be hard to not recognize it. "It's the circle. The one at Holt Manor."

The dog stepped back, huffed again, and took off down the street in the direction it had looked in before.

Just as the door burst open.

"Shay!" Max ran over, Duncan close on their heels. The flames died down, leaving a melted line in the snow. "Oh my god, how did you even…what was…was that the dog?"

"Uh. Yeah?" Shay realized how cold she was with the dog gone. "Probably definitely not a death omen?"

"She pet it," Finnias said.

"Are you serious right now?" Duncan asked.

"That's what I said," Finnias muttered.

Max had Shay by the shoulders, checking her over for injuries, but clearly she had none.

Duncan slipped his cardigan off and wrapped it around her shoulders. "C'mon, let's get you inside before you freeze."

"Wait, I know something, I think," Shay said. "I think we need to go to the circle."

"...The one where Archibald had you pulled into the void?" Duncan asked.

"Okay, yeah, not the best memories, but I think Beans was trying to tell me something," Shay said.

"Beans," Duncan repeated. Max mouthed it, face scandalized.

"Yeah, so, Beans wants me to go to the circle, and I think I have to," Shay explained. "And I think—"

"Inside, you're shaking," Max cut her off, leading her across the street. The only footprints were Duncan and Max's. "How did you get out here? Why are you out here?"

"I just...was."

And if the dog had been able to do that the whole time, then she was pretty sure it wasn't going to kill her.

"That doesn't make sense," Duncan insisted. "With...physics and stuff."

"When did you start caring about physics?" Shay looked pointedly at his hair.

"Got a point there, I'm more of a liberal arts kind of queer," Duncan said. "And it's not like physics cares about us. Clearly."

"Clearly."

"You're being awfully calm about this," Finnias said as they headed back into the house.

"I don't know how else to be about it." Shay was still buzzing from not getting ripped into little pieces. "Sorry I scared you."

"Are you?" Finnias glared at her. She shrugged sheepishly in return.

They went inside before she could answer. The shop wasn't warm, but it was miles away from the chill of outside. She looked at the spot where Delores had pulled her into the nightmare and ripped her gaze away. The shop seemed almost unfamiliar, the shadows slanting strangely.

She needed to get used to it. She worked the next morning. "Ugh, that was cold. How did you know I was out there?"

"Finn let me know," Duncan said. "And we were both in the kitchen."

"Go get changed. I'm insisting on a bowl of soup," Max said. "Upstairs, right now."

"Okay, fine." She was a little hungry, somewhere around the anxious twist of her stomach. "I mean, yes, okay, I'll be right down."

She headed through the living room. The fire was still going, burning low over mottled embers. She frowned. It was weird that Jo and Arlo weren't in the room, usually they spent their evenings in front of the fireplace like the old people they were. She realized she actually had no idea what time it was, and she hadn't even glanced at the old grandfather clock in the shop.

"Do you know what time it is?" She looked at Finnias.

"No," he said.

"Oh, c'mon, Finn, are you mad at me?" Shay asked. "It's not like I asked the dog thing to drag me down there."

"I'm not mad," Finnias lied. "I also don't know how late it is. Time doesn't have much meaning to me."

"I guess so." Shay wondered what the world looked like to Finnias, but she wasn't sure how to ask. "Me, either, before I got a job. Duncan coming and going and Max's hours were just about the extent of my time keeping abilities. So, I kind of get it."

She'd been haunting her own life, plagued by horrible migraines and trying her best to find a job with half a college degree and no car. Drifting from day to day, really only present when someone else was around.

Maybe that was what it was like for Finnias, but unlike her, there was no end in sight.

They started up the stairs and something brushed against her arm. She yelped and jumped straight into Finnias.

"What?" he asked.

"Something touched me." She rubbed the spot. Her skin was colder than it should have been. She checked the wall, hoping it wasn't another spider.

The wallpaper distorted and a hand reached through it like it was cloth. She shrieked and batted it away, but another hand took its place along with the vague impression of a screaming mouth and hollow eyes.

She ran up the stairs, the hands reaching for her, faces with their mouths open as if in agony pressing in on all sides.

Mist boiled up from the bottom of the stairs.

"Run!" Finnias grabbed her wrist.

They ran together, but the hall was longer than it should have been, stretched out and dark like a throat. Shay grabbed at a doorknob, but it didn't even budge under her hand.

"Hurry!" Finnias urged her. She glanced back and a wall of mist was hurling at them, something writhing within it.

They dashed to the end of the hall and hit a door she'd never seen, but the handle twisted, and she flung it open.

They tumbled out into snow and sunlight.

"What the…" Shay's exclamation died in her throat.

Finnias looked alive.

More than that, he didn't even look like she'd always seen him, in a dark gray pinstripe waistcoat and a snowy white shirt. His hair was loose, falling over his forehead.

His dark brown travel coat was open over a blue waistcoat.

"Finn?" She was shaking, and it had nothing to do with the cold. She slowly got to her feet and helped him to his. His hands were warm.

"Where are we?" He seemed oblivious to his current state. "The circle?"

That was exactly where they were, in the forest behind Holt Manor. It looked like it had a century before, when she'd seen it in Finnias's death loop. Young trees stabbed their naked branches to the sky. Snow covered the circle, reaching up to Shay's knees. Her teeth started chattering. At some point she'd lost Duncan's cardigan.

Finnias pulled off his coat and wrapped it around her shoulders. It was heavy and warm.

"Finally."

A familiar voice, right next to her. Shay started away from Emmaline who was suddenly standing there. She had been in washed out blues the few times Shay had seen her, but here she looked just as alive as Finnias, wearing a dark green riding habit with a severe neckline, her hair pulled back into a bun.

"What are—"

"I've been trying to contact you for ages," Emmaline said. "My usual methods were cut off, but I figured if Delores could use my methods, then hers shouldn't be too hard."

"...This is a dream?" Shay's voice cracked.

"Technically, yes," Emmaline said. "But also technically no, I really am here. I have a lot to tell you. Delores is—"

"The nightmare demon," Shay said.

"Oh." Emmaline looked a little disappointed. "Well, glad you know."

"You can control ghosts. Can't you control her?" Shay asked.

Emmaline winced. "Well, see, the thing is, even if I could, it's impossible right now."

"What does that mean?" Finnias asked. He'd stepped in front of Shay.

Emmaline looked surprisingly hurt, but her face smoothed out a moment later. "Do you know how powerful a necromancer's heart is? Why Archibald took Finnias's? Why he tried to take yours?"

"It has something to do with our abilities, right?" Shay asked.

"Anyone who is in possession of a necromancer's heart, the physical heart, takes control of their abilities," Emmaline explained. Shay had known that, in a vague sense, but hearing it out loud made her feel sick. "The trade off being that any of their descendants become necromancers themselves. Delores has my heart, so she has my abilities, and…well, my power is greatly diminished."

"But you could before—"

"Because she was trapped in the void, I was technically sort of kind of still alive until very recently, do try to keep up, Shay," Emmaline said. "That's why I tried to use you, to retrieve my heart, but sadly it didn't work out, and here we are. So, now I'm all but powerless, good job."

"You tried to kill me," Shay said.

"In my defense, I'm sure I wasn't the first, and I definitely wont' be the last." Emmaline shrugged. "Keep up, Shay, this is time sensitive. You can make it up to me if we team up and you help me get my heart back. Then I'm in charge of my own destiny or whatever and Delores the Dream Demon wont' have a chance."

"And then you actually kill me," Shay said.

"No," Emmaline said. She glanced up. The sun was sinking towards the horizon. The sky blazed orange, reflecting on the snow like fire. "We're running out of time, and I have so much to tell you."

"If you're missing your heart, why do you remember everything?" Shay asked.

"Probably because I was dead the moment I hit the void," Emmaline said. "My major organ removal was postmortem. Believe me, if I knew how to return Finnias's memories, I would. Help me get my heart back, and I can tell you who had his last."

"Why would you want to do that for me?" Finnias asked, still standing between Emmaline and Shay.

"Oh, you sweet, simple little boy," Emmaline said. "I'd do just about anything for my baby brother."

CHAPTER 17:
GOOD ENOUGH

"What?" Shay's voice cracked.

Finnias looked at her. For answers? So she could tell him it wasn't true? His face had gone as pale as his corpse.

"There, you have my motivation or whatever," Emmaline said. "Can we focus? If you don't get my heart back, you won't stand a chance again Delores. Do you understand? Or should I write it down for you. Maybe using big, bright colorful letters!"

"You're lying," Finnias said.

"You can think that if it really makes you feel better," Emmaline said. "I have no reason to lie about it. Your real name is Silas Breckenridge, but since that was our father's name, you rarely used it."

Finnias flinched at the name.

"Yeah, I didn't like him, either," Emmaline continued. "The least of his sins was murdering some hapless necromancer before we were born. Be glad you don't remember him. If it helps, we toured as the Woodrow Twins. And you always used the name Finnias. And there you go, a little bit of your history. But believe whatever you want, I don't care."

She crossed her arms, the fabric of her sleeve bunching where she gripped it. She had gone pale, too, gray against the snow.

"Why Finnias?" he asked, voice hoarse.

"It was the name of a favorite uncle, you took it after he died," Emmaline said. "You were always so sentimental. I got my alias from a book."

"Finn…" Shay touched his shoulder, a little surprised when he didn't wrench away from her.

Emmaline sighed, loudly. "We do not have time for this."

"You're hurting him," Shay told her.

"That was not my intention, but it doesn't matter." She put her hands on her hips. "The plan. Shay gets my heart back. I help her take care of the demon. Do we have a deal or not?"

"Fine, your stupid plan. So, what, we do get your heart back, and get rid of Delores, and you…go on a killing spree?" Shay asked. "I need the details."

Finnias gave her a wild-eyed look. She didn't know how to respond so she kept looking at Emmaline.

"Oh, please, you act like I'm some sort of notorious old timey serial killer," Emmaline said. "I'm not, thank you very much. I have plenty of ghosts I can control, I don't need to make more. What I can do is help you get Finnias's heart back. Believe me, you're going to need me at full strength."

The shadows of the trees stretched long and blue. A wisp of smoke curled above the ridge.

"We're out of time," Emmaline said. "The moon has risen."

Shay looked up. The moon hung above them, too close, too large.

Emmaline moved so quickly Shay didn't see it, directly in front of Finnias. She shoved him, hard, and he vanished. Before Shay could react, Emmaline's shoulders were on her hands and she fell back.

She sat up in bed, gasping for air.

"Woah, hey, are you okay?" Max put a hand on her shoulder, right where Emmaline had just touched her. "Shay? You're freezing—"

"…It…it was a dream?" She stared up at them. The room looked exactly as it had before, she'd been pulled into the snow. The warm light of the lamp spilled across the comforter, leaving lines of shadows in the wrinkles.

"Yes?" Max looked confused.

"All of it?" She couldn't remember when she'd fallen asleep, what had been real and what had been a dream. The grim? The shop? She needed to look outside. She threw off her covers and stared.

Her pajama pants were soaked up to the knees.

"Holy crap." Max pulled the blanket the rest of the way away. Her sheets were filthy from her extremely dirty socks. "You were asleep when I got back from checking the wards, I thought…did you go outside?"

"No? Not on purpose." She stared at her pajama pants and started shivering, the cold hitting her. "There was this…I don't know. Am I awake now?"

Max pinched her arm.

She smacked their hand away. "Ow!"

"Sorry! I thought that would be the fastest way—"

"No, it's fine." She rubbed the spot, her skin aching. "…Where's Finn?"

He wasn't in his normal chair or at the window.

Shay scrambled out of bed, pulling off her socks after the first very squishy step. She dashed into the hallway. When he wasn't there, she hurried down the stairs.

The living room was empty, and so was the kitchen. Shay looked at the shop door and for the first time since her mad dash out of her room she paused, biting her lip a little too hard, the sting doing nothing to bring her courage.

Max nearly ran into her.

"Sorry!" They held up their hands when she whipped around. "I thought you knew I was right behind you. What's going on?"

"Something…something happened," she said. "I had a dream, and Finn was there, and I think he was really there, and it was…it doesn't matter. I have to find him."

"Okay, okay, let's just breathe for a second." Max put their hands on her shoulders. She'd started shaking, hard. "He can't have gone far. It's not a big house. Well, it is a big house, but he has a limited number of rooms he uses."

"What if he sank into the space between?" Shay asked. "The…ghost world place he goes to sometimes? I don't know how to pull him from that, I mean Archibald thought I was controlling him but of course I'm not, I'd never do that, and he never agrees with me on anything and…"

A little sob escaped her. More bubbled up in her chest and it took everything she had to keep them there.

"If he did, he'll come back eventually, he always has," Max said, quietly.

"I don't know what to do without him," Shay admitted. She'd watched him die, right on the other side of the door, just a few hours ago. She'd held him in her arms while he went cold.

He'd only been with her for a few weeks, but she was so used to it. She'd even forgive him coming through walls and floors if she could just find him.

"I promise, you won't have to," Max said, gently, calmly. "He would never do that to you. Do you think he's in the shop?"

"It's the only room he's been in a lot that I haven't checked," she admitted.

"Okay, I'll do it." Max touched the handle and flinched back. "It's freezing."

"Must be him." Shay tried very hard not to cry, but her eyes stung, and her vision had gone watery. She blinked hard, biting her lip again, hoping the pain would ground her.

Max opened the door.

"He's at the window," Max whispered. "Do you want me to—"

"No, I've got this."

"Are you sure?" Max asked. "I'm not...I just want to make sure you're okay."

"Yeah. I...I can do it. I'll be okay." Shay patted their shoulder. "Thanks."

"I'll be here," Max promised her.

She nodded and stepped into the room.

The quartz had been replaced, and the shop picked up and swept. It looked like it always did at night — a little creepy, but mostly just a dark place of business, ready for opening the next morning.

Finnias stood in front of the window, staring out intently.

Shay motioned Max back. Closing the door took more courage than she thought she had. The click of the latch was impossibly loud, a gunshot over the thunder of her pulse in her ears.

She leaned against the door for a moment, just breathing. The room was cold, the chill invading her lungs. She hadn't put on her glasses. Without them everything was soft and blurred.

Finnias turned to look at her. She couldn't tell what expression he wore.

"Hey," she said, awkwardly.

"I believe Arlo should be able to break whatever...attachment I have to you," Finnias said, voice almost robotic it was so flat. Like everything that had made him Finnias had seeped out.

"Why would I want him to…what are you even…" She closed her eyes and took a breath, trying to center herself. "I don't want that."

"You heard her," Finnias said. "You were there. You know it was her. And you believed her."

"So what?" Shay walked over, one terrible step at a time, until she was at the window with him. She reached over and took his hand. It was like holding onto frozen metal. It burned her fingers, but she didn't dare let go.

"She tried to kill you," Finnias reminded her. "She almost…she hurt so many people, and yet…"

"And she's not you," Shay said.

"She's a horrible person, and I'm her brother," Finnias snapped. "Shouldn't you be having some meeting with all of your little friends? How to deal with me? What to do about me?"

At least he didn't seem emotionless, but the anger was painful in its own way.

"You're my friend."

Finnias looked down at their hands. "But I…"

"And I won't tell anyone if you don't want me to," Shay said. "I'll take a vow of silence. About only this, though, don't get too excited."

She glanced at him, and he had his free hand over his mouth, and she couldn't read the rest of his expression.

"I don't care about who she is, or who you were, I don't care about any of it," she continued. "All I care about is the Finnias I have right now, with me. I said that before and I meant it, and I'll say it a thousand times if I have to. I care about you. The you right now. And I want you here, if that's where you want to be."

She meant every word, saying them with everything she had.

"Any good deeds I've done have been entirely in my own self-interest," Finnias reminded her. "After all, we don't know what will happen to me if something were to befall you."

"I know," Shay said.

"And originally, I was influenced by Duncan's thoughts and emotions, after possessing him," he said.

"I know," she repeated. "But I still care about you. No influence. Your sister? Doesn't change that. Your past? In the past. So...so there."

"Oh."

His hand softened, in degrees, until it was like holding a slightly colder than average hand. She squeezed his fingers, and he held her hand tightly back.

When she looked at him again, he appeared more like himself. She practically sagged with relief. The tears that had threatened before spilled over onto her cheeks and she sniffed, hard.

"...I didn't mean to make you cry," he said, wiping a few of her tears away with his starchy feeling sleeve. She laughed a bit, even if it was choked.

"Of course I'm going to cry, you big dummy," she said. "You...you huge drama queen."

"For someone who just claimed they cared about me so much..."

"Just shut up and hug me?" Shay suggested.

Finnias blinked in surprise but gave her a very quick hug. "I'm sorry, for the worry I caused."

"It's okay." Shay attempted to mop up her tears with her sleeve. She was freezing cold, and her sleeves were already wet. "I'm just having a really bad night. Can we go to bed?"

"Of course," Finnias said, not reminding her that he didn't sleep, and that he would be perched in an armchair all night, not in bed. She appreciated that he didn't correct her.

When they got back to the kitchen Max was gone, but Duncan was there, and Shay was reminded of the dream, or not dream, with the black dog.

"Hey, Shay Shay, you all right?" He gave her a one-armed hug. He was wearing the cardigan he'd had in her dream. He took it off and draped it over her shoulders. It felt exactly the same. "You are freezing cold."

"It's not that bad," she lied.

"It is, actually," Duncan said. "Did you go outside? Was Finn out there? Finnias, if you dragged my sister out in this cold I am very disappointed—"

"I didn't," Finnias said.

"He didn't," Shay said, at the same time.

"Oh. Well. Good, I'm glad you're still with us, I understand that was a concern?" Duncan looked at Shay. "Is this one of those secret things that you're not going to tell me about?"

Shay looked at Finnias, who shook his head. "I took a vow of silence. About only this."

"Fair," Duncan said. "Anyway, I insisted that iMax Theater gets you to bed, right this instant. They said something about clean sheets…anyway, I promised to wait for you."

"Why are you up?" Shay asked.

"Surprisingly, I actually do get two days off a week, and tomorrow is one of them," Duncan said. "So I was bumming around and heard a lot of yelling. You need sleep."

"…Yeah." She wasn't sure she ever wanted to sleep again.

"Good. Anyway, I'll see if Jo will give you the day off, too. Maybe call Gideon in to work the counter, he never minds."

"I'm sure he minds more than he lets you know," Shay said, but the thought of working in the shop the next day made her stomach clench.

"He won't say it to my face and that's good enough for me," Duncan admitted. "Besides, we have journals to go through tomorrow. You can help me dig them out of the basement."

"Eugh, the basement." Shay made a face. "It's so creepy down there."

"Slightly less creepy with the wire reindeer and Santa out on the lawn instead," Duncan said. "To bed. Now. Both of us, actually. Maybe we'll figure some things out tomorrow, yeah? I hear Jo's inviting the gang over."

"Is Taylor coming?" Shay asked.

"Not sure, why—"

"I need to ask her about something," Shay said. "About the circle, behind Holt Manor."

"Why would you want to ask her about that?" Duncan walked her through the living room and up the stairs. She half expected a hand to reach out and grab her, but the wallpaper remained the same flowery pattern as always.

"Because I think it's important," Shay said. "I need to go write in my dream journal."

A lot of it was fading away, but she did remember the circle.

"You go do that." Duncan headed to his own room. "I'm going to attempt to get some sleep."

CHAPTER 18: GLOVES OFF

Shay dug through the bottom shelf in the basement, looking for a clear, plastic tote full of old journals.

"Why am I on the ladder again?" Duncan asked from above her.

"I have a bad knee." Arlo checked the shelf next to hers.

"I'm basically a gnome." Shay shrugged. "If it makes you feel better, Arlo is probably going to send me scampering back behind things soon."

"I am," Arlo said.

"I do feel marginally happier, yes."

Jo's basement was crowded with boxes, bins, and bags, all stacked together on shelves that stretched the entire length of the room. When she'd converted the attic into her room she'd moved years worth of stuff down to the basement shelves next to the world's oldest washer and dryer. It was otherwise a cement box with bare bulbs hanging down from the ceiling.

Shay absolutely hated it. She'd already bribed Max to do her laundry twice since moving in.

"Can Finn catch me if I fall?" Duncan asked.

"No," Finnias said.

"Wow, that's cold."

"I can't even begin to break your fall unless Shay is holding my hand, and then I doubt that I'll be particularly helpful." Finnias leaned against the shelf next to Shay, leaving her to fall prey to any spiders or non-ghost rats that had taken up residence. So far, she had found none, but she knew they had to be there, lurking in some dark space, waiting for her to put her hand on them.

Duncan shrugged. "Fine. You train Shay on having better reflexes and in the meantime, I'll just smash my head open on the concrete."

"You are up two whole steps." Shay thought about reaching over and shaking the step stool, but the fall out complaining would be more annoying than the brief satisfaction was worth.

"Two steps up from solid concrete."

"You'll be fine," Arlo said.

"I'm falling on you," Duncan threatened him.

Arlo patted his middle. "I'd make a good cushion, great choice."

Shay laughed and moved to the next shelf. All she'd found so far were decorations and even more doilies, which considering the living room looked like it had been snowed on, she found herself impressed and mildly afraid. She dug out a box that seemed to be all old pots and pans.

"I think Jo might have a problem with throwing things out." She shoved the box to the side with some difficulty.

"She was really close with her grandma," Arlo explained. "When she died I think she just stuck everything she didn't need down here, couldn't look at it. She renovated pretty soon after that. I think she needed the change."

"That's fair." Shay found a box of shoes and thought maybe it was slightly not fair, but she wasn't sure how she would react if someone she was close to died and she had to go through their things, either. She saw the glint of a plastic box and dove halfway into the shelf, surprised at how deep they were, yanking it out. "I think I found it!"

"Wait, seriously?" Duncan turned so quickly that the step stool went up on two legs and he had to grab the shelf for support, eyes wide. Arlo offered him a hand and he took it, allowing himself to be led down to the ground. "Oh my god, no more."

"You lived, though! Good job." Arlo patted his shoulder.

"Can someone help me with this, it's bigger than I am." Shay was still trying to yank the box out. Arlo and Duncan quickly shoved the boxes on either side away, helping her yank a huge plastic tote out from behind everything.

It was definitely full of journals, but there were a lot more than she was expecting. There were at least thirty, stacked on top of loose papers and thick envelopes.

"…Who else thought there would be like…four?" Duncan asked. "I was looking for one of those little shoe box deals. I never would have found it."

"It's going to take forever to go through this," Shay said.

"Nah, we just need to find the journals that belonged to Jo's grandma," Duncan said. "But let's do that upstairs."

"You got it." Arlo hefted the box up easily. Then again, he'd lifted her like she weighed nothing, and only seemed to be limping because she'd kicked him. "Good job, guys."

They headed back up to the hallway that led from the living room to Arlo's bedroom.

"Get that to the living room, I'm going to clear off the coffee table," Duncan said. "No one touch those, they're old."

"Do we need gloves?" Arlo asked.

"Oh no you asked the question," Shay whispered and Finnias looked away, covering his mouth with one hand so she knew he must be smiling.

"That is a common misconception, but it's better to just wash our hands thoroughly," Duncan said. "Gloves can catch on the pages and tear them, or even carry more dirt than clean hands. So. Now you know. Don't ever ask me that again."

"Okay, noted, no gloves," Arlo hauled the box into the living room.

"What can I do?" Shay asked.

"Go to my room and get my laptop," Duncan said. "I want a record of everything in here before Gideon gets here to transcribe for me."

"Do you...need that?" Shay asked.

"More than I've ever needed anything in my life." He sounded completely serious.

"But if we just need—"

"Shay, I need to know everything that's in this box, or I will die," Duncan said. "I will drop dead, right here, and then you'll be an only child."

"I'd say dreams fulfilled, but I don't really want that responsibility," she said.

"And possibly wanted for murder, since I'm mostly healthy and in my late twenties. Do you want that? Do you want my corpse on your conscience and record?"

"Calm down, nerd, I'll get your laptop."

"Thank you." Duncan started clearing off the coffee table.

Shay headed up the stairs to Duncan's room. It was smaller than hers, tucked into the back of the house and wedged above the kitchen. It really only had room for a bed, desk, the mirror he'd stolen from her room, and some shelves full of books from the last library rummage sale and salvaged from the apartment. Only a handful of his action figures had survived the fire, posed carefully on his shelves.

He'd insisted on taking the smaller room, explaining he'd probably be out of the house a lot more than Shay was, but she still felt a little guilty. He'd given her the bigger bedroom in the apartment, too.

"Laptop laptop…" Shay murmured to herself in a sing song voice. It was closed and set in the exact middle of the desk, but Shay was immediately distracted by a perfectly round black spot on Duncan's neatly made bed. "Aww it's Becky! Becky Becky Becky."

She smooched the little black cat between the ears. Becky stretched and made a noise between a purr and a meow. Shay occasionally convinced her to come down to the shop during her shift, but she spent the majority of her time in Duncan's room.

"Aww I wuv you." Shay pet her a few times. "Why don't you ever come hang out with me anymore? Is my room too haunted?"

"If you want me to apologize, I won't." Finnias leaned against the door frame behind her. Becky hissed at him. He hissed back.

"That was adorable," Shay told him. "But stop encouraging her."

"She started it," Finnias pointed out, like he was being reasonable.

"She's an eight-pound ball of fuzz with a brain the size of a marble, so that's not really going to fly with me," Shay said. "But Becks, you gotta get used to him. You have to live in the same house now. It's not up for debate."

Becky hissed again and dove under the bed.

"Rude." Shay stood back up, snagging the laptop this time. "Guess you're too spooky."

"I could be spookier," Finnias offered.

"Really?"

He shrugged. "Sure."

"What does that mean?" Shay headed back down to the living room.

Finnias did not elaborate, just kept her from sliding down a few stairs by grabbing her arm. Duncan had cleared off the coffee table in the meantime and was carefully laying everything out.

"I'll wash my hands," she offered.

"Nope, I got this," Duncan said.

"But—"

"I am in the middle of creating a system," Duncan said. "I am shifting into archivist mode. Do not take this from me."

"Okay, fine. I have more important things to do, anyway." Shay sat down on the couch and checked her phone. Max had texted her, asking how her day was. She smiled and gave them an update, pulling the afghan from the back and wrapped it around herself. There was a fire going and the room was warm enough it made her feel drowsy.

"Take a nap," Duncan suggested.

"I'm keeping you company," she said. Arlo had already wandered off to the kitchen to assess the damage to the cupboards, closing the door behind him.

"Just having you in the room is company," Duncan said. "You barely got any sleep last night."

"He's right," Finnias said.

"Okay, but if I have another nightmare someone has to wake me up," Shay said. They both nodded, which was good enough for her, curling up on her side, nestling into the plethora of throw pillows. She placed her glasses on the table next to her before she forgot and slept with them on her face again. "If we ever move out we're stealing this couch. And all the pillows."

"You got it," Duncan said. "We'll arrive in the dead of night and squirrel it away with our impressive upper body strength and the truck we definitely own."

Duncan's ancient car, a compact he affectionately called Sandra, was half rusted and definitely could not haul a couch of any size.

"As long as our house has lots of windows," Shay said. "Big ones."

"Sounds nice," Duncan agreed. "Lots of spots for Finnias to look out onto the world and get random photos of our house all over the internet. Photoshop or real? Ghost spotted in small Idaho town."

"I mean, I think there are already hundreds of those at this point," Shay said.

"Got a point there." Duncan shrugged. "Could be funny."

"I wouldn't," Finnias muttered.

"What do you want in our hypothetical future house, Finn?" Duncan asked.

"I don't care," Finnias said.

"Oh, c'mon, I would want a big kitchen," Shay said. "And a tower, so I can live in it. Let's just stay here, actually."

"Done, I hate moving," Duncan said.

"Do you think you'll move in with Gideon?" Shay asked.

"Guess that answers the question if I blur the line between a gay man and a butch lesbian," Duncan said. Shay would have thrown a pillow at him if he hadn't been sorting documents. "I don't know, too soon to tell. Maybe, but not for a very, very, very long time. You're stuck with me for a while, don't worry."

"I wasn't worried," Shay said.

"Sure," Duncan said. "Even if I did, I'd just be across town. Just a call away. Always."

"I know, don't be dumb," Shay tossed the doily from the arm of the couch at his head. It landed on the floor a few inches away from the couch.

"Wow, what an arm you have." Duncan grinned at her. "I have to say, this doesn't sound a whole lot like napping."

"I'm working on it, I'm getting comfy, I'm nesting." She snuggled further down into the pillows. "How goes sorting?"

"Well, we have a lot of stuff from Jo's grandma, Geraldine." Duncan gestured to two stacks of leatherbound journals in various states of binding. "Looks like some of these are from her great grandma, Josephine, who was a witch, too. Must be a family thing."

"Better than our family thing," Shay said.

"…Yeah."

They hadn't talked about it. She'd told him, what Emmaline had told her about necromancers, but there hadn't been time to sit down and discuss it. She'd been avoiding thinking about it, when she could, but it made her feel sick.

"Do you think he was the one who…?"

"I don't know," Duncan admitted. "Maybe. I mean, either way, we're descended from a murderer, so that's neat and fun. I can't imagine doing that. I mean, murder in general, very against that, but dooming your kids and future generations just for some power?"

"I don't get it, either."

"Some people are very short sighted," Finnias said. "That has no bearing on either of you."

It sounded a lot like what she had told him the night before. She reached over and squeezed his hand, briefly. "That's sweet, Finn, thanks. So…what about the loose stuff."

"Right." Duncan grabbed the change of subject with both hands. "Look like a lot of these loose things are letters and important documents. At least they were important circa 1954 or so. Probably not so much, now. Don't think Jo even looked at these when she shoved them in here. Gonna be fun to get them in order."

"You're such a nerd," Shay said.

"Proudly," Duncan said.

Their conversation lulled after that, and Shay drifted off to the hissing sound of old papers being sorted.

CHAPTER 19: STORYTIME

Shay woke up to the sound of soft voices and the clacking staccato of someone typing quickly.

She sat up and rubbed the side of her head where it had pressed into the throw pillows. Duncan and Gideon were talking quietly while Gideon typed things up. She rummaged through her blanket, trying to find her phone, but realized it had fallen to the floor. She snagged it up.

It was just after five, and Max had just let her know they'd be on their way soon.

"I didn't think you had any nightmares, so I didn't disturb you," Finnias told her, quietly.

"I didn't, thanks, Finn," Shay said.

"Good morning, sleepyhead," Duncan said. "Did you have a good nap?"

She considered for a moment. She didn't feel rested, exactly, but not fully tired. Just dull and with an aching head. "I feel like someone knocked me out with a shovel."

"Ah, yes, well, naps do that," Duncan said. "Gideon and I have been searching tirelessly through these journals."

"I brought him an iced coffee, that seemed to help," Gideon said.

"Look, I can do things without my little gay iced coffee, but why would I want to?" Duncan asked.

"That sounds right." Shay sat up completely, pulling the blanket around her shoulders. "Did you find anything?"

"I found a passage about us," Duncan said. "Which was really weird. I was waiting for Jo to get back here, I think she needs to hear it."

"Okay, sounds good," Shay said. The weird headache was fading, leaving her hungry. "I'm starving."

"I'll heat up some soup, I need a break," Gideon volunteered, hopping to his feet.

"Amateur!" Duncan called after him, clearly teasing. He had everything sorted into perfect piles, but he still adjusted them a little bit, like he needed something to do with his hands.

"Did you find out anything about the circle?" Shay asked.

"So that was Josephine, the great grandma." Duncan flopped back against the armchair. "And she said it was too horrible to comprehend and much too terrible to put into words. So that was useless, unfortunately."

"Are you okay?" Shay asked. He seemed jittery, constantly lifting his hand to fiddle with his hair, then seeming to remember he'd have to wash his hands and dropping it again. He'd been picking at his nail polish, big flakes of sparkly blue missing.

Duncan shook himself. "Yes. No? I don't know. Jo invited Rose, Taylor, and Rahim over. So. Whole gang will be here. And all I have is something that's actually pretty personal to the two of us. I've found nothing particularly useful about necromancers, and it's not like we can cite Emmaline as a credible source. I'm supposed to be good at this. This was supposed to be, y'know, the thing that I did to contribute."

"You contribute all the time," Shay said. She was going to make a quip, but he didn't seem to really be in the mood for it.

"Yes, I know, I always have a witty comment or a great pun, but I really wanted this to work." Duncan sighed. "It's okay. It's fine. I haven't looked through everything yet. I did find out that before she built this house, Jo's great grandma lived in a witch commune, so that was kind of cool. It sounds like it disbanded right around the time of the incident, though, so who knows what happened there."

"Maybe it's all connected," Shay suggested.

"I thought that, and I'd love it to be, but I don't know." Duncan picked up one of the envelopes. He flipped it over and set it back down in its pile with a sigh.

After Shay had soup Max came in and checked on her, but the ghost marks she'd accumulated had faded.

"What about you?" Shay asked.

"I'm feeling a lot better today, despite the children," Max said.

"Oh, you love the children, you're not fooling me," Shay said.

Max nodded. "I do. They're fun. Today we did finger painting, that's why I'm late. There was so much blue in my hair."

"I bet you pulled it off," Shay said.

"I definitely did, but I think it works better with actual hair dye and not the cheapest finger paint money can buy." They shrugged. "But who knows, maybe it'll end up being super moisturizing. Anyway, I'm triple checking the wards. On the mirrors, on the doors and windows, on the whole building."

"Good plan," Shay agreed. "I'll tag along."

She was pretty sure if she tried to stay in the same room as Duncan for more than a few minutes, she was going to snap and say something mean. Or strangle him. Or at least mess up his hair.

It took less time than she expected, but by the time they were back in the living room Jo was there, talking to Duncan and Gideon.

"Oh, good, you're here," Jo said. "I had an idea I wanted to run by you and Duncan before everyone else got here, but it's a little dangerous."

"Dangerous how, exactly?" Duncan asked. "Because I promised my boyfriend here, Gideon, you might have met him, handsomest man on the planet."

"Oh, you." Gideon looked more amused than embarrassed.

"You're right, goes without saying." Duncan nodded. "Anyway I told him that safe- is my middle name, and I am standing by it. For boyfriend reasons, and not coward ones."

"Safe and careful," Max reminded him.

"That's right. Duncan Safe Careful O'Brannon," Duncan said. "It's still deeply unsexy, but this is the cross I bear."

"They're sexier than his actual middle names," Shay said. She grinned as he made strangling motions at her. "Well, I don't have a significant other to tell me no, you can tell me."

"You have me," Finnias said.

Max cut in at the same time. "Okay, but you have me, and I'm very concerned about your safety."

"Aww you two are sweet." Shay batted her eyes at them. Max and Finnias gave her the exact same expression from both sides, and she barely kept herself from laughing at them.

Jo ignored all of them. "I think we need to go to the circle. Or at least, you need to."

"How is it dangerous?" Max frowned. "Archibald is gone and so is the...demon thing."

"We don't know that the entire demon is gone, part of it could still reside within the circle, or something else could be happening there," Jo said. "And I think that we can get a much clearer picture of what's happening if we go. I was going to ask Taylor for permission tonight."

"I think it's a good idea," Shay said.

"I don't." Duncan folded his arms. "I think it's a terrible idea. Unfortunately, I don't have better ideas, so I guess that's the plan."

"Good," Jo said. "Now that we have that out of the way, I think you wanted to read something for us?"

"I did!" Duncan immediately looked happier. "It's about Shay and I, and your grandma, so apparently we have some interesting entwined history. The interesting part is about us, though. It's kind of big personal family stuff, but I'm going to let y'all in on it because I'm so kind and charitable. Also it provides some much needed context for why we are the way we are without having to go to an actual therapist."

"Are you going to read it or not?" Jo asked.

"I'm just providing background, disclaimers, and entertainment," Duncan said. "Gid, you want to read it for us?"

"Yeah, I can do that." Gideon scrolled on the laptop. "Okay, here it is. 'I was visited by a necromancer today. He tried to hide his nature, but the stench of death magic was heavy around him. He would only give me the name Walter, and if it weren't for the children, I never would have even spoken to him. The boy is about seven and the girl must be barely one, but she's already seeing spirits, and in the last day acquired blue marks from the touch of one. The boy knows things that he shouldn't'."

"It's like nothing has changed," Duncan said. "But she did leave out the part where we're very adorable."

"I'm sure it's implied," Jo said, dryly. "Continue?"

"If you're done?" Gideon looked at Duncan, who shrugged and made a noncommittal noise. "So, no. Um, where was I… 'They've clearly inherited the curse that I hoped had passed out of this area, and I am confident their father murdered for his own power.'"

Shay felt cold and sick. She'd thought that maybe her father was a natural born necromancer, like her and Duncan, but Geraldine seemed very sure of her assessment.

"'He wanted the powers sealed. I referred him to several people who would be happy to take the children in if he was not willing to own up to his mistakes, people who would gladly train them in their abilities and keep them safe.'"

"Your grandma tried to get us adopted out?" Shay asked, slightly horrified. Maybe she hadn't had the best childhood, but she couldn't imagine growing up without Duncan.

"Hey, this is news to me, too." Jo held up her hands. "Maybe…I don't know, she thought it would be better. I wasn't even here."

Duncan shuddered. "Can you imagine if we didn't grow up together? We are a pair. Do not separate."

"Yeah!" Shay agreed.

"There might be a few less puns," Max said, quietly.

"You secretly enjoy the puntiful harvest," Duncan said. "Don't rye to me, Max."

"Wheat would you do with-oat us?" Shay asked.

They sighed. "Not question my life choices, for one."

"That's not very rice." Shay nudged her elbow at them.

"We've barley begun," Duncan agreed.

"Are we done?" Gideon asked.

"We're bread-y to be," Shay said. "This is the yeast of our puns."

"Don't get mad that we're rising to the occasion." Duncan patted his knee.

"I'm going to go against the grain and ban further puns until this story is done," Jo said.

"All right, putting my pun bans in the oven." Duncan said. Jo threw a pillow at him, and he laughed. "Okay, I'm done, for real."

"Great," Gideon said. "Continuing. 'He refused my suggestions, and only wanted their abilities to be sealed. I called in some favors and was able to perform the ritual, but I warned him that the girl especially is very powerful, and the seals won't hold forever. I do not want anyone to be involved with necromancers, so I'm hoping the seals will hold and the children will lead normal lives, but the cards tell me otherwise. I will have to prepare.'"

"I kind of remember that," Duncan said. "Dad took us to this old house, guess it was this one, but I only saw the front room and it's obviously very different. A lot of it is fuzzy, but there was this old lady and she kept being mean to him. Must have been her."

"A few days later he had to bring Shay back in." Gideon scrolled a bit more. "Here. 'The girl is just a baby, but she's already trying to break through the seals. She has been crying nonstop, according to the father. I imagine she's in a lot of pain. I called a favor in that I did not want to. I did not want to see Vera again, but her help was necessary. I'm afraid I have set her up for pain later on, but I was careful to never divulge her name or the identity of her father. If we are lucky, they'll all move very far away, and that will be the end of it.' That's pretty much the last mention of you two."

"So that's why I haven't been getting headaches," Shay said. "I was wondering. I haven't had a migraine since I started seeing ghosts."

"And that's a good thing," Duncan agreed. "I guess it's a mixed bag on us staying in the area. But what I'm interested in is this Vera person, because if we cross reference to Josephine's journals, she also talks about a Vera breaking the lesbian commune coven apart."

"But the entries are almost a hundred years apart," Gideon pointed out. "There's no way it's the same Vera, unless the first one was a baby."

"I mean, exhibit A." Duncan gestured to Finnias, who started. He'd been very quiet, there were too many people who couldn't hear him. "Over a hundred years old."

"Got a point there," Gideon said. "Well, I don't know. I think that's all we've found out so far."

"So if we want more information, we'll have to go to the circle." Jo frowned. "We'll come up with a plan for that tonight, but this is a very powerful demon. She can control people, put people to sleep, and if she gets more powerful I don't think that Shay and Duncan will be exempt from that for much longer."

"Could you guys do some witchy stuff to her?" Duncan asked.

"Honestly, there are limits to what we can do already." Max sighed, scratching their head. "We have a few options. We could trap her in the mall, which is not ideal but it's not like anyone is going there. We could trap her outside, but since she's not sitebound that would do very little good."

"And even those things are relatively shaky," Jo admitted. "For now, we can keep her out of the house, but even then, she's proven she can get past our defenses. I'm afraid nowhere is truly safe."

"So…we get out of town," Duncan said. "Go start a life in, I don't know, Oregon."

"Do you really want to move to Oregon?" Shay asked.

Duncan sighed. "Ask me eight years ago and yeah, in a heartbeat. Now? Not really. I've put so much work into the library and the community here. I know it's just a dinky, shitty little town, but it's my dinky, shitty little town. Still, would be nice to live somewhere less…I don't know, cursed? I think the whole place is cursed."

"Probably because they changed the name to Teton Falls," Max said.

"You have a point, Ravenscroft was much cooler," Duncan agreed.

A knock echoed from the back door.

"That must be Taylor." Jo got to her feet. "I'll make tea, and we'll figure out what we're doing."

CHAPTER 20: GROUP PROJECT

Shay wasn't surprised that Finnias made himself scarce before Taylor came into the room. He never seemed to know what to make of her and having so many people around seemed to conflict his energies. She imagined it was like sensory overload, but for ghosts.

She wished she could follow him. Being around people felt like sitting on a coal.

Taylor got a hug from Gideon before she sat down.

"No Finnias?" She asked, like she did every time.

"Wasn't feeling the crowd." Shay answered, the same way she always did.

"That's too bad."

Shay knew it wasn't, that Taylor was secretly relieved. Her only other extended acquaintance with a ghost was Emmaline, and Shay couldn't blame her for hating her.

Rose came in next, exchanging pleasantries.

"Nightmares?" She asked Shay. Rose was gorgeous and had a way of making Shay feel like she was the only person in the room that she was paying attention to. It was a little flattering in a "probably her big sister's ex" sort of way.

"Oh, y'know, I think we're all having them," Shay replied.

"I imagine that's what this meeting is about?" Rose turned to Jo.

"We have a lot to discuss," Jo said.

Shay wasn't so sure that was true, since it really just boiled down to "point Shay at a nightmare demon like a cannon and hope for the best". No one else had voiced a single plan that sounded plausible, and Jo wanting to go to the circle felt like she was stalling.

Rahim came in last, and Shay braced herself, but no calming numb rolled off of him, as far as she could tell. He greeted her pleasantly enough, considering the last time she'd seen him he'd been taking out her stitches. The time before that, she'd blown up at him.

In her defense, it had been an incredibly stressful night.

"Sorry I'm late." He placed an attaché case on the coffee table. "Had a late surgery. Dog hit by a car."

"Oh no, not the puppy," Shay said.

"She's going to be fine, don't worry," Rahim said. "I've been getting quite a few emergencies along those lines. I'd like to attribute it to the weather, but…"

"Traffic has been insane," Taylor agreed.

"'Tis the season." Duncan shrugged. "I haven't really noticed anything, but my trips have been limited between here and the library."

"And you drive like evil is tailgating you," Max said.

"Maximo, I will have you know I'm an excellent driver," Duncan huffed. "It's everyone else in this town that is absolutely awful."

"Sure, babe, whatever makes you feel better." Gideon patted his knee.

Duncan scoffed. "Wow, alright, Brutus, just stab me again."

"Okay, now that we're all here, there's a lot we need to discuss." Jo sat in her armchair, like a queen presiding over her court. Which probably made Shay her sad little jester.

Shay tuned out, for the most part. It was just Jo rehashing her encounter at the mall, her failure at the circle, and every terrible thing since. She leaned against Max's shoulder and not so subtly stared into the fire, the flames leaping and crackling across the logs, slowly reducing them to ash and cinders.

She was half dozing when Jo saying her name shook her out of it.

"Present," she said, automatically. "I mean. What? Yes?"

Everyone was looking at her expectantly. The light from the fire played over their features, turning their eyes dark and hollow.

"I was asking you if you had any further insight on your dreams," Jo said.

"Oh, uh, I don't know." Anxiety spiked through her. It felt like she'd been called on in class and had no idea what the answer was, or even the subject. "Nothing new? I haven't really…I mean, just the same dream, as always."

She couldn't say anything about Finnias, and that was the last dream she'd had.

"How disappointing," Jo said. The shadows made her expression completely unreadable.

"Uh, I'm sorry about that?" Shay shrugged, not sure what else she could possibly say. "I've tried to write them all down."

To the best of her ability, all things considered.

"Hm." Jo turned and started whispering to Rose, her tone harsh but the words an unintelligible hiss.

Everyone started whispering, their tone similar to Jo's, all of them glancing at her. Even Max had moved to the other end of the couch to talk to Taylor.

"Okay, that's about my creep quota for the day, I'm going upstairs." Shay climbed off of the couch and stumbled, landing on her knees in the grass just outside the circle.

Blue fire showed its edges, reflecting off of the frozen blades all around her. The shadows were long and blue, the sun hovering on the horizon, red and pink.

"What are you doing here?"

Shay jerked her head up.

Duncan was standing just a few feet away, just inside the circle like she was.

"What am I...what are you doing here?" she pointed at him. "This is my dream! Aren't you supposed to be Archibald or Emmaline or..."

"Why would I be either of those two freaks?" Duncan folded his arms. He was in his flannel pajama bottoms and a t-shirt for a local band Shay had never heard of. Those were definitely his pajamas, but he'd been wearing jeans and a cardigan just minutes before, whispering harshly with Gideon. "But this isn't exactly my normal dream."

"I don't think I want to know." Shay accepted his hand up. "Did I fall asleep on the couch?"

"I think so," Duncan said. "All kind of fuzzy, really. This is weird, right? As far as I'm aware, lucid dreaming is not a group project."

"Not usually," Shay said. "You could be a figment of my subconscious."

"Or you could be of mine."

"No, this is my dream, I'm pretty sure you're the figment," Shay said.

Duncan reached over and tugged on her braid. "Would a figment of your subconscious do that?"

"Yes, because it looks like you, and you're a brat." Shay swung her braid over her shoulder.

"Yeah, that's fair." Duncan shrugged.

"You two need to get out of here." Finnias was on her other side, wearing what he had been in the dream with Emmaline, his hair rumpled. "She's coming."

A huge, pale moon hung in the sky above them, suspended in a sparkling purple sky.

Something rushed past Shay, a figure made of smoke. A scream echoed through the clearing, distant and distorted. Garbled words emanated from nowhere, like a badly tuned radio. Mist bubbled up from the center of the circle, forming the shape of a person.

Emmaline's old mirror burst out of the ground like a grave. It was shattered from a central point, cracks spiraling outward like a spiderweb. It teetered and fell to the earth, the corroded reflective surface facing the sky, reflecting the bulbous moon.

The figure rushed past Shay again and was yanked into the mirror with a short, sharp scream.

"Definitely not my dream," Duncan said.

"This has never happened before," Shay admitted, backing away to the very edge of the circle. She squinted, trying to make out details, but every time she thought she caught something, the details bled away.

The loop began again, the figure rushing past her, the scream, the person standing behind it. Something rushed next to her head, so fast and close it rippled her hair.

"We need to go," Finnias took her hand. "We need to get out of the circle."

The actions repeated, just as quickly, snatches of conversation flowing past her like the howling wind.

A scream cut short. Something flying past her. Finnias tugged on her hand, but she felt frozen to the spot, like she was encased in the same ice that covered the grass beneath her feet.

The figure behind the mirror moved differently, turning towards her, a flash of gold.

Eyes like a wolf.

"Shay!" Finnias shook her. "Wake up! Wake up right now!"

She couldn't move, couldn't say anything, even as the figure stalked towards her like she was some sort of prey animal.

A glint of teeth, the gleam of golden eyes, the vague shape of a woman reaching for her.

Duncan grabbed her hand and the scene shifted, melting like water and paint. They were standing on the ever-familiar landing. Finnias's clothes changed to his normal attire. He adjusted his bowtie.

"You don't understand," he said, turning around, but Archibald wasn't there. He was speaking to an empty staircase. "I have to at least try."

"Try what?" Duncan asked, but the scene melted again, and they were in front of Spellbound, but it wasn't the shop. The house wasn't even red, painted a dull and flaking gray, the porch stairs sagging inward.

A woman who looked an awful lot like Jo stood on the steps, staring down at them. She was wearing a long, flowered dress and a thick cardigan, despite the green, warm stillness of the air.

"I can help you," she said. "But I know what you are, Walter, and what they'll become. That's something you can't hide forever."

Everything faded again and she was standing in a dark room, cracked tile beneath her feet.

"Duncan?" she called out, looking around. "Dunc?"

No answer. Light filled the area immediately around her, like she was under a spotlight, but the light didn't seem to have any source that she could see, squinting at the ceiling.

"Finnias?" She tried, quietly.

"There you are." Delores stalked out of the darkness and Shay jerked back. "We expected you hours ago."

The ghost grabbed her by the arm and hauled her forward. A mirror loomed up out of the dark. It was covered in cobwebs, but her reflection was just visible in the corroded surface. Shay wasn't wearing her pajamas in her reflection. She was in a suit jacket and dark pants, tucked into knee high boots.

"What a shame," Delores said. "It looks like you already belong to them."

A mask covered her face, black and silver, shaped like a rat's skull. Shay jerked back in horror, but Delores held her fast.

"One more for the party," Delores said. "But I'm afraid it won't be you."

Something heavy landed on her shoulder.

Shay woke up with a gasp.

She was downstairs still, curled up on the couch. The only light was from the fire, just a collection of dying embers, some of them far too close to the edge of the grate.

Shay got to her feet, pulling her blanket around her shoulders like a cape. She grabbed the poker and pushed back the embers before they got close. Stirring the fire made it glow a little brighter.

Someone was standing right next to her.

It wasn't Finnias.

"Sorry, I didn't know someone was—"

She turned and slapped her free hand over her mouth to stop herself from shrieking. Whoever it was, they were covered head to toe in spider webbing, welding them to the wall. The fire glowed a little brighter, showing similar figures, in chairs, against the wall, even one on the stairs.

The one nearest to her jerked free of the wall and reached for her with cobwebbed fingers. She tried to move but there was webbing crawling up her legs, holding her to the floor.

Shay sat up in her bed with a shriek, almost punching Finnias in the face, but he whipped away from her just in time. Max wasn't quite so lucky, but she hit them in the shoulder.

"Woah!" They grabbed her hands. She hadn't realized she was flailing until they did. "Woah, hey, you're awake, I'm right here."

"Max?" Her voiced cracked, horribly.

"Hey, I got you." Max kept a hold of her hands. "You were breathing pretty badly—"

"Just a nightmare," she said, reaching up with a shaky hand to brush back her hair. A dark blue ghost mark formed a hand on her forearm. "Oh, yeah, that tracks."

"Shay!" Duncan nearly hit the doorframe in his haste to get into her room, sliding on his socks. "Oh, oh good. You're here. I thought…you were gone and I woke up and—"

"Yeah, I'm here," she said, in a small voice. "Someone want to bring me my dream journal? I think I have some homework to do."

CHAPTER 21:
CRIMES

Shay gripped her knees in anxious anticipation, staring out the car window.

The snow blanketed the hills starkly against the dark gray of the sky and the long, dark ribbon of empty road.

It could have been the entire world - the snow, the road, and the heavy sky looming overhead, threatening to crush down on the roof of the car.

"Music." Duncan leaned over the middle console to fiddle with the radio.

"Wait—" Taylor tried to warn him. Garbled static and a voice that Shay could almost make out spat out of the speakers. Duncan turned the radio back off. "It's still broken."

"So, what, you just drive in silence and you don't go crazy?" Duncan asked.

"Sometimes I hook up my phone to a speaker," Taylor said. "I just thought that we were going to be, y'know, talking. Planning."

They hadn't said much since leaving the house.

"Well, admittedly, Jo and Arlo getting called away on a job did throw a bit of a wrench in my plans." Duncan leaned back against the seat next to Shay with a soft thump. "They weren't great plans, but still, kind of heavily involved the mega witch and the clairvoyant lady."

"I mean, it is their livelihood." Shay shrugged.

Jo insisted they go ahead, to make sure they had plenty of daylight.

"So what, saving the world is a side gig?" Duncan asked.

Shay shrugged. "Unpaid internship?"

"All work and no play makes you a dull Shay Shay," Duncan told her.

"Let's focus," Max suggested. They were sitting in the front seat, looking through their spell kit. "It's just the four of us, so we will have to make do."

"Right." Duncan sighed. "All that talk about calling us all in. 'Oh Duncan, it's a weekday, I can't get the day off. Oh, I had prior commitments. Ohhhh.' Whatever."

"You done sulking yet?" Shay grinned at him.

He poked her in the side, and she slapped his hand. "Now I am. Okay, so, we get there, we check it out...it's hard to plan when we don't know what we're going to find, honestly."

"Well, presumably you two can figure out what happened there a hundred years ago," Taylor said. "Do your wonder twins thing."

"We're not even close to being twins," Duncan said. "I am seven years older than her."

"Whatever, book boy."

Duncan gasped, and it didn't even sound sarcastic. "Book boy?! I am a librarian. I went to college for years to be a librarian. You do not get to call me book boy."

Taylor smiled, glancing at him in the rear-view mirror. "What are you going to do about it, book boy?"

"Max, grab the wheel," Duncan said, urgently. "Run us off the road. I promise it's worth it."

They sighed. "No."

"Fine, but know that we will not be trapped in this car forever, and when we reach our destination, my retribution will be swift and terrible." Duncan crossed his arms.

Shay patted his shoulder. "There there, we all know you're very smart and educated, book boy."

"You're my sister, and I love you," Duncan said. "So, when we get out of the car, you get a five second head start."

"Aww what a sweet donut you are today." She leaned back quickly to avoid a swipe, cackling.

"I'm feeling more savory by the second."

"I think that's a bagel," Max said.

"No, not quite, it's all in how you cook them. Bagels are boiled and baked, donuts are fried. They're totally different things," Duncan explained. "Just a similar shape. It's like convergent evolution but with dough."

"Do you bake?" Taylor changed the subject, which was probably wise of her, since Shay had been on the verge of calling him a nerd, which would have probably devolved into name calling and elbowing.

"I do, actually," Duncan said. "I'm not like, Jo level or anything, but I make pretty good bread. It's nice living in the house. I actually want to be in the kitchen so I've actually been baking and cooking."

"He's a very good cook," Max said.

"Yeah, you should come by sometime when it's Duncan's turn to cook," Shay said. "Not me, though. I only know four recipes."

"We'll fix that," Duncan said. "Y'know, after….all of this is over. I learned from grandma, you can learn from me."

Shay had never expected him to offer. He never had before, but she supposed there had never been a good time before she went to college. "Aw, thanks, Dunc. I'd like that."

"I wish my older siblings were as nice as you," Taylor said.

"He's not nice," Shay said.

"I'm not nice," Duncan chimed in at the exact same time. "How many do you have?"

"Two, my brother and sister," Taylor said. "They're...well, we have a big age gap."

"We do, too," Shay said. Duncan was seven years older than her, but they'd always been close, even though they'd deny it.

"My brother is closest to me, and he's eleven years older," Taylor said. "Anyway, you've seen them. They're on every real estate sign in Teton Falls and Doveton."

"Oh yeah, your sister was selling the house where we ran into our first mirror!" Max said.

"But someone carved her eyes out on the sign, sorry for your loss," Shay said.

"Wait, really? My sister was selling the house with the first mirror?" Taylor asked.

"Oh yeah, it was super creepy. Everything upstairs was just...left," Max said.

"I can't believe you broke into an empty house for your ghost show." Taylor laughed.

Max shook their head. "We didn't break in. Totally legal entry. Had the key and everything."

"What, you think I would have called the cops on you?" Taylor sounded happier, at least. "Break into any house they're selling for all I care. Tag it up. Could be a fun group activity. Let's forget the circle and just go mess up some houses."

"I cannot do that," Max said, and it was Shay's turn to laugh. "Don't make fun of me. We can't all be delinquents like you."

"Oh, please, name like, three laws I've broken," Shay said.

"Breaking and entering into the cemetery—"

"There was a gap in the fence, it wasn't breaking, just entering," Shay corrected them. "And you came along for that adventure."

"We broke into that thrift shop," Duncan said.

"That was an emergency, and if I recall, you did the breaking part, I just followed you," Shay said. "But that's the same law so it doesn't count, anyway."

"You stole that lip balm from the craft fair in our sophomore year," Max said.

Shay felt her face heat up. "That was an accident. I went back and left money on the counter. Doesn't count."

"Fine, we won't count that one," Max said. "But I am confident you have committed at least two other crimes."

"Good luck, you'll never take me alive." Shay grinned.

The car crested a hill and they headed down into the forest, a few trees at first, then they were growing right up to the road. Shay was pretty sure at least part of the land was federally owned. A lot of land in that direction was one national forest or another.

Shay watched the tree trunks flash past. The dark pines speared the sky into place above them. A deer leaped through the trees, but no one else said anything. A secret to keep between her and the forest.

"Have you murdered anyone." Duncan dragged her attention back into the car.

"No," Shay said. "Nothing you can prove, anyway."

"You liked that…that one band," Max said. "The boy band. You liked them in middle school."

"I've liked several bands?" Shay stared at them. "I don't see how that's—"

"No, they're right, that was a crime against humanity, and more specifically my ears," Duncan said. "You used to blast them in your room."

"I don't—"

"The bubblegum band, they were like Swedish or something, probably literally made in a lab," Max said.

"Chewy Pink!" Duncan clapped his hands.

"Oh my god I forgot about that," Shay admitted.

"You liked Chewy Pink?" Taylor outright cackled.

Chewy Pink had been a one hit wonder Europop boy band that became incredibly and suddenly popular very briefly while she was in middle school. Every girl in their grade had picked a member to have a crush on, and she'd played along. She'd been desperate to fit in more, to have something to talk about with the other girls, but it didn't take long for the band to fade into obscurity, and she didn't try chasing the next big thing.

"I was twelve. It was a phase! I'm normal now. But I was annoying about it, so I'll allow it as one of my crimes. That's two."

"Driving without a license," Duncan said.

Shay mock gasped and shoved his shoulder. "You said that was our secret."

"That's three," Max said. "Sorry, Shay, you were a delinquent."

"Were! I'm reformed," Shay said. "I haven't listened to the Chewy boys for years. I changed my mind, you can't hold that one against me, I was twelve."

"Too late, you've broken so many laws." Duncan patted her head. "I'll visit you in prison."

"Please don't," Shay said.

The farther they drove the more snow there was, drifting across the asphalt in huge white masses.

"Here's our turn off," Taylor said, slowing down. The sudden change in speed caused the car to slide across the ice, throwing Shay against her seatbelt, her stomach lurching. Taylor turned the wheel sharply and the car fishtailed, swung the other way, and stopped violently, facing the way they came. Silence filled the car for a moment. Taylor's knuckles were white from her grip on the wheel. "…Everyone okay?"

"I think I bruised my collar bone," Duncan said, shakily.

"Sorry, sorry, it was a lot slicker than I thought, they don't plow out here very much," Taylor said. "We're lucky we can get out here at all."

"The drive definitely hasn't been plowed," Max pointed out. "I don't think your car will make it. Even if it would, it'd be pretty obvious we'd been here to anyone who decided to check."

"You really think someone is going to come all the way out here just to see if there's tire marks in the drive?" Duncan asked.

"We just talked about how Taylor's sister was selling the house we got attacked by ghosts in," Max reminded him. "So, an abundance of caution is more than appropriate. There was a turn off back there. I think our best bet is to park there and walk to the circle."

"Okay, but I really don't want to do that," Duncan said. "These woods are haunted. In case you forgot."

"I mean, I don't see anything yet, but…" Shay gestured to the side of the road. The trees grew so closely together it was impossible to see far.

"Max is right." Taylor pulled forward, slowly. They didn't slide this time.

She parked the car in a pull off that was still full of snow. Everyone piled out and pulled on all of their winter gear. A biting cold had settled into the hills.

"Is that Arlo's hat?" Max asked.

"I couldn't find mine," Shay said. "Jo said I could borrow it. Could do without the mega pompom. It feels like I have a head stacked on top of mine."

She wiggled her head, the hat moving along with her.

"Like a little snow person." Max grinned, patting the pompom like it was a living thing. "I've been wanting to do that since I saw it."

"Dork," she said.

Finnias appeared next to her.

"You're not very close," he said.

"I dunno, I guess we could be closer." Shay took a micro step closer to Max.

Finnias sighed. "You know what I mean."

"We're trying to be sneaky," Shay wrapped her scarf snuggly around her neck. "We're hiking in."

"I am really glad I wore my boots," Duncan said, pulling on his own gloves. "Wish we had some skis. Could just slide on over."

"Sadly, I'm not a fan of skiing, cross country or downhill," Taylor said.

"Cross country is way better than downhill," Duncan said. "There's only the terrifying fear of the wildlife, not of crashing into a tree. Much more palatable."

"I'll take your word for it."

"Let me make sure we're all protected before we head out there, we have no idea what we're going to be facing," Max said.

They pulled out a bottle and put a tiny dab of oil onto Shay's forehead. It smelled like lavender, but more importantly she felt a warmth cascade over her, like she was being enveloped in a protective film. The feeling faded, but her forehead still tingled. When Max did the same to Taylor and Duncan, light shimmered over them.

Max passed out sachets and gave them each a bracelet, just a twist of embroidery thread with a few beads on it.

"Keep these on, they're not anything amazing, but they can only help. I have plenty of salt, we should be fine."

"Right, just have to find the place now," Duncan said. "Anyone know where exactly we need to go through the trees?"

"...I think we have a guide," Shay said.

Up ahead, standing in the middle of the road, stood the black dog.

Chapter 22: Teamwork Makes the Dream Work

The dog's back was even with the tops of the trees, an imposing being of bone, smoke, and stars. Shay held her breath, not quite sure what would happen. If her dream about the dog had just been that - a dream.

Finnias stepped in front of her.

"What is it?" Duncan asked.

"I don't see anything," Taylor said.

"It's the black dog, isn't it?" Max stood next to her, taking hold of her hand, like it would keep her safe. Maybe it would. She didn't imagine it could hurt. They were the most reassuring presence in the world.

The dog regarded her for a moment, cocking its head to one side, before it turned and walked into the trees, shaking the snow from their branches.

"Are those trees moving?" Duncan was on her other side. "Is that the dog? Holy crap."

"Yeah, that's Beans," Shay said.

"...Beans?" Duncan asked. "You named the possible death omen Beans?"

Shay shrugged. "What else do you name a death omen?"

"Anything else?" Max suggested.

"No, I'm with Shay, that's a solid point," Duncan said. "All right. Well. Is Beans leading us to the circle? Isn't that bad? I think that's probably bad. We should leave, right? Try again on a day that's not full of big black dogs and when we have more experienced witches with us? No offense."

"None taken, I agree," Max said.

Duncan blinked, clearly surprised. "Well, first time for everything. I love you too, Maximus Prime."

"You've used that one before," Max said, quietly.

"Oh, I'm sorry, I didn't know I had to be original every time," Duncan said. "I'm very stressed right now, Maximum Occupancy."

"See, that one sounds rude."

"You're both very pretty and funny." Taylor put her hands on their shoulders. "Can we focus on the big death omen dog thing that only Shay can see? Are we leaving or not?"

"Finnias can see it," Shay said. Her insides were all twisted in on themselves, like snakes, but she knew that walking away would be a mistake. "We came this far. I think we need to see it through."

"Oh, so, we're just willingly going to our dooms because we already used so much gas," Duncan said.

"Gas is very expensive," Taylor said.

"I'll spot you some dollars," Duncan offered.

"Well, I'm going." Shay let go of Max's hand and stepped into the trees. The snow had drifted up against the trunks, but Beans led her around the worst of it. It was the size of a large wolf, moving silently and effortlessly through the thick trees, leaving no tracks in the snow.

She almost didn't want to glance back, but when she did, everyone was behind her, following her through the trees. She slowed down just enough so she could take Max's hand again, just so she knew they were there without looking. She wished Duncan would make a quip about everyone holding hands, but he stayed quiet for once.

The only sound for a long time was the crunch of their boots in the snow.

"We're nearly there," Finnias said, his voice barely a whisper.

The trees opened up into the clearing.

The circle glowed just as brilliantly as it did in her dreams, the bright blue light spearing up through the snow.

Inside it was an enormous spiderweb.

It was a delicate looking thing of lacy silver, beads of moisture frozen in little crystal spheres on every strand. Beans walked right up to the circle and sniffed the edge. The line looked a little thinner in spots, like it was eroding away from the inside.

"Oh, that cannot good," Max said. Their voice made her jump. They tightened their grip on her hand.

"Bit of a sticky situation," Duncan agreed.

"Spiders," Taylor said. "...Sorry, I have nothing to add just...eugh eugh ugh eugh."

"No, that about sums it up." Shay's stomach was full of acid. "The circle is glowing but it's...getting worn away."

"I can try to shore it up." Max let go of her hand to walk over to the edge, standing close to Beans, who only huffed at their presence.

"What about you two?" Taylor asked.

"Wonder twin powers?" Shay took off her mitten and offered her hand to Duncan.

"I'm serious, we are finding a better catch phrase," Duncan said. "I'm so much older than you."

"Six years, eight months, and three days," Shay said. "But who's counting?"

"I think you might be counting on me." He took her hand.

There was still snow on the ground, the sky still heavy with clouds, but the trees were smaller and younger.

The circle was clear, dark earth, and a woman with long red hair kneeled at the center in a dark green dress. Her hands brushing over the black surface of a familiar mirror, her fingers forming ripples of light.

"Who is that?" Duncan asked.

"Why would I know?"

Duncan shrugged. "I don't know, you hang out with a ghost all the time, I don't know who you know anymore."

"Stop being dramatic," Shay said. "He has no memories, why would he randomly remember this person?"

Something about her seemed familiar, but Shay couldn't place it.

Finnias was suddenly next to them, outside the circle, his eyes fixed on the woman at the center. He looked like he had in the dream, rumpled hair and blue waistcoat.

Archibald, Emmaline, and a woman that looked a lot like Jo stood with him. Emmaline looked like Finnias, the same serious gray eyes, the same narrow and pale face. Her dark hair was the same shade, pulled back into a bun. A few strands had come loose to frame her face.

The woman that must have been Josephine stepped forward and slammed her hands to the outside of the circle. The blue line, glowing more vibrantly than Shay had ever seen it, snaked out from under her hands and surrounded the woman at the center.

"Oh, please, did you really think that would work?" the woman sounded bored. She didn't look up from her ministrations over the mirror. "You're just a witch, Josephine."

"So are you, Vera," Josephine said. "I'm going to stop you."

"Oh, you're welcome to try," Vera said. "I don't think you're going to enjoy your odds."

"Kill her," Emmaline said.

"Wait—" Finnias held up a hand, but the poltergeist raced forward, a shimmering blur.

Vera didn't even look up. She made a backhanding motion and the poltergeist shattered with a scream.

"No!" Emmaline started forward and Finnias had to drag her back by the elbow.

"It'll be fine, Em, it'll reform," he reminded her.

"I am allowed to be upset." Emmaline shook him off. A wind started blowing around the edge of the clearing, tossing the branches of the trees until they clattered together. "Are you going to just stand there or are you going to make yourself useful?"

"Calm down," Finnias told her. Emmaline made a spluttering noise and hit him in the shoulder. He ignored her, holding one hand out.

The earth cracked open.

Skeletons crawled out of the earth, some still had flesh and fur clinging to them. Most of them were deer, a few were smaller animals, one was a wolf. Ghostly flesh wrapped around them, sinew and tendons made of glowing blue light snaking through their bones.

Vera finally looked up. Even at the distance, Shay could see her eyes were golden, like a wolf. She made the same motion she had with the poltergeist and one of the deer exploded into shards of bone and globs of ectoplasm, but the rest rushed forward. She grabbed the antlers of the first deer to reach her, sliding back. It stepped onto the mirror and the front half of its body fell into the darkness, the back half collapsing with a hollow sound, leaving Vera holding the skull. She threw it at a deer coming from the side and stomped down on the skull of a rabbit.

"I'll admit, this is very annoying, but you're far too late," Vera said.

A huge, pale hand rose from the mirror, grabbing at the earth. Dark, ragged fingernails cut grooves into the dirt. Red eyes opened all across the arm, flicking back and forth.

Shay took a step back, even though they were safely on the outside of the circle, even though it couldn't touch her. Bile burned at the back of her throat. Duncan's grip on her hand was too tight, but she couldn't let go herself, couldn't look away.

It dragged itself out of the mirror, each arm covered in a dozen eyes, and its face…

It had four eyes, like pits of tar.

Ghosts rushed past Emmaline, but Vera swatted them away with the same motion, exploding each one into blue smoke. Archibald pulled out a pistol and fired, but the bullet slowed down long before it reached her, metal peeling away and turning into flower petals until there was nothing left but a scattering of pink on the ground.

"Damn." Archibald struggled to reload.

The circle sparked and flickered. Josephine strained against it, her face going pale.

Emmaline drew a sword out from her skirts, a rapier with a black blade.

"No." Finnias grabbed her arm again. "Archibald, help Josephine."

"Right." He kneeled next to her in his nice suit, his hands on the circle next to hers. The glow strengthened, but the wind was stronger, the sky immediately above them darkening.

"You really think that will stop it?" Emmaline yelled.

The demon had already dragged itself halfway out of the mirror and pulled itself to the edge of the circle. Finnias put one hand to the ground and tree roots exploded from the earth, wrapping around the arms. It tore free with ease.

The circle faltered.

The demon grabbed Finnias.

"No!" Emmaline stabbed its wrist and it let out a roar. It snagged her instead, dragging her into the circle.

"Em!" Finnias dashed forward but Archibald launched himself to his feet and grabbed him around the middle. "No! Let me go!"

Emmaline slashed the nightmare across the face. Pale fire erupted from its tar pit eyes, viscera dripping hot onto the ground, leaving welts in the dirt. It screamed, a horrible, all-encompassing sound. Emmaline stabbed at it again and again until it swatted at her, and the sword went sailing right past Shay, so close she felt it pass, flying into the trees.

Shay had seen this before.

Vera made eye contact with her, she was sure of it, between the flailing limbs of the demon. Her smile was wide and manic, her eyes gleaming.

And she was gone.

The nightmare dragged Emmaline down into the mirror and the wind stopped abruptly.

"Archibald!" Josephine yelled. He let go of Finnias to slam his hands back down on the circle. It glowed brightly, blue light swirling and spiraling across the entire clearing. It pulsed, and when Shay could see again, Vera had disappeared.

The circle faded.

Finnias made it to the mirror, but it only reflected the dark clouds above them.

"Open it back up," Finnias said. "We have to get her out of there."

"I can't do that." Josephine stood, brushing her hands off on her skirts.

"Your underling—"

"Vera was a powerful witch in her own right, but there is no way she was acting alone," Josphine explained. "Even if I wanted to, and I do not have any wish to free that thing, I cannot open the portal back up. She's gone, Finnias. I'm sorry."

"But with Archibald—"

"No, I'm not risking that thing getting out again." Archibald reached for his hand. "I'm sorry about your sister, love, but—"

"Sister?" Duncan hissed. Shay had forgotten he didn't know. She had respected Finnias's wishes and hadn't told him.

"Dunc—"

He shook his head, sharply.

Finnias snatched his hand away. "Just…help me get this mirror inside. I don't want it to break, if it's the only way…"

"All right," Archibald agreed, a little too easily. "I believe they're expecting us at the manor, anyway."

"You two go ahead, I need to disband the coven," Josephine said. "Vera is still out there, and she clearly wasn't working alone. I can't trust any of them anymore. Thank you, for your assistance today. And once again…I'm sorry."

"Right." Finnias looked younger than he ever had, scared and lost. "…Take care of yourself, then."

"I'll see you again, soon." Josephine put a hand on his shoulder. "Don't lose hope, we'll find another way. I swear we will."

Finnias nodded and they walked to the tree line.

Something waited for them.

It was impossibly tall, a dark, thin shape with a pale face. She couldn't understand why Finnias and Josephine weren't reacting to it.

It turned its head, slowly, and made eye contact with her.

The memory broke apart, fading to sepia tones and shattering into pieces until they were left standing in the snow in the present day.

CHAPTER 23: SWORD EXPERT

Shay let go of Duncan's hand and fell to her knees, crunching into the snow. A few snowflakes landed on the back of her hand, melting quickly.

"Oh, thank god, you're back." Max helped her back up to her feet. They rubbed her arms and then pulled her close. They weren't really warm, the outside of their jacket a cold shell. "You are shaking."

"How long were we gone?" her voice trembled.

"A while." Finnias attempted to sound bored and annoyed, but an undercurrent of worry tugged at his words.

"About two hours." Taylor handed her a thermos. "It's hot chocolate. Should still be hot."

"That long?" Shay stared at the thermos. It had a red plaid pattern, shiny and bright. Hard and metal and out of place.

"What the hell?" Duncan asked.

"I don't know," Shay said. "I've never—"

"That was…that was her, wasn't it? She's his sister?!" He jabbed a finger in Finnias's direction.

She blinked, heavily. "Oh, right."

"Shay are you serious right now—"

"I asked her to not say anything," Finnias said, quickly.

"It doesn't matter, right? He doesn't remember, and—"

Duncan threw his hands up in the air. "Doesn't matter? Again, are you serious right now?"

"Okay, let's calm down," Max said.

"Do not tell me to be calm." Duncan took a few steps back. "Finnias's sister is the spirit charmer."

"What?" Taylor backed away, too, wrapping her arms around herself protectively.

"He's not her, he's just—"

"Her brother," Duncan snapped. "She possessed Taylor for months. She tried to kill you. It's kind of a big deal! Why are you being so nonchalant about her? About him?"

"I trust him." Shay didn't know what else she could possibly say.

"Perhaps I should go?" Finnias suggested.

"Go where? You're stuck to her." Duncan motioned to Shay. "Because she's an idiot who got herself yanked into the void—"

"That was not my fault," Shay said.

"And almost died!"

"Still not my fault!"

"And now supposedly you're directly haunting Shay and allegedly you have her best interests at…some part of you, but the truth is we don't know anything about it," Duncan said. "And we don't know anything about you, either."

"Dunc, it's Finnias," Shay said, weakly. She knew it wasn't a good argument, but she didn't have anything else to say. "He helped us close the tear. He saved me."

"Maybe." Duncan held out his hand. "Make him solid and let me take a little trip down memory lane."

Shay hesitated. "I mean, do you even know how to do that?"

"I'm winging it!" Duncan yelled. "I'm trying my best, Shay! I didn't ask to wake up as an…evil death version of a witch, all right? Neither one of us asked for this, and it's not fair, and I'm just…"

"Necromancers aren't evil," Finnias said, quietly.

Shay ignored him. "I know, Dunc, it's a lot. Trust me, I've been stuck in the house for like a month. No one knows better than me how hard this is."

"I know that! And it pisses me off!" Duncan held out his hand. "Now make him solid."

"No one else is on board with this right?"

"Well…" Max had the decency to look sheepish.

"Do it," Taylor urged Duncan. "Make sure."

"He's fine!" Shay's eyes stung and she bit her lip to keep herself from crying.

"Everyone agrees with me. Now, give me your hand." Duncan shook his hand for emphasis.

"Shay, it's all right." Finnias held out his own hand. "If what he sees doesn't put him at ease, I will gladly leave."

"But I won't be glad," Shay muttered. She tried to ignore the way everyone was looking at her, taking Finnias's hand.

And he took Duncan's.

She saw flashes, but nothing specific. A small house. A field of grass covered in dew, mist hugging the ground even with the sun dazzling everything, a barefoot girl running, the moisture captured on the hem of her dress.

Fuzzy, grainy shots of a stage, a ferris wheel, hotel rooms.

She knew Duncan was pushing too hard, but she had no idea how to stop him.

An empty field of brown grass rippling like water in the wind, covered by a sky the color of iron.

Something appeared in the middle of the field, the same tall, thin dark figure from the tree line. It was closer in a blink.

Shay yanked her hand away.

With a sound like cloth ripping her and Duncan were tossed back into the snow. Shay lay there for a second, staring at the sky.

Finnias reeled back, clutching his chest.

"...Ow." Duncan sat up. Blood trickled from his nose. "So. That's clearly not how that works."

"You idiot." She smacked his shoulder, clambering to her feet. "You're all idiots, actually. Finn, are you okay?"

"I...I'm fine." He straightened. He looked a little more transparent than usual, the blue faded out. She frowned in worry. "Merely a shock."

"Looked like more than that." Shay didn't help Duncan to his feet. "Are you all satisfied now? Fine. Yeah. His sister is the worst. Taylor's whole family sucks and we still hang out with her."

Taylor's face matched the snow, but she nodded, a little too tightly. "That's...that's true."

"And you're a big butthead, but Max still hangs out with me," Shay said to Duncan.

"I can't argue with that." Max helped Duncan to his feet. "Sorry, Shay's right—"

"Wait, really?" Shay had been too indignant on Finnias's behalf to consider whether she actually had any sort of moral high ground.

Max sighed. "Yes, Shay, you were right. We were...well. Are you okay? I have some tissues...let's see..."

They dug through their bag until they found one.

"Fine, I'm a big enough person to also admit that I was wrong," Duncan said.

"Incredible," Shay said.

"I mean, I'm almost always right, but in this one specific and incredibly rare instance, you were right, and I was in the wrong." Duncan sighed, shoving a hand through his hair. His styling products were holding up surprisingly well to his fingers and the snow. "I overreacted. I freaked out. I'm sorry. And sorry, Finnias."

"It's all right," Finnias said. Shay couldn't really read him, she had no idea if it was actually okay, but she thought that eventually it might be. "I understand, but know I would never hurt Shay."

"Yeah, I know that," Duncan said. "What was that thing?"

"What thing?" Shay really hoped he wasn't about to say what she thought he was.

"In the field...the tall thing. What was it?" Duncan asked. "Oh, who am I kidding, Finnias won't remember, and you obviously don't know, so I might as well not add it to my current list of worries because it's already really, really long. Moving on! Tay, you cool?"

Shay wanted to talk about it, but realized maybe Duncan was right.

"...I think so." Taylor didn't step closer, but she didn't run screaming through the trees, either. "So, you...really saw her?"

"Saw how she died," Duncan said. "The mirror thing makes sense. There was this witch, Vera, she was using it to summon the demon, and then the demon dragged Emmaline through the mirror. Her sword definitely did not help her."

"A sword?" Max asked.

"...Wait, the sword did hurt it, though," Shay said. "Permanently. It still has, y'know, no...face eyes."

"Ew." Taylor made a face.

"It is extremely ick, yeah," Duncan agreed.

"It flew out of the circle," Shay said. She found the spot where she had been standing, her boot prints deep in the snow. "And it…went that way…"

She pointed towards a thick strand of trees.

"Okay, yes, she had a sword, and it did hurt it, kind of," Duncan said. "But even if it's still there, which is a big if, and we can find it, another big if, it's probably more rust than sword by now."

"But it doesn't hurt to try," Shay argued. She knew, deep in her gut, that the sword was still there. She couldn't explain it, so she didn't try. "Maybe that's why we were supposed to come here, maybe—"

She turned around and the black dog was standing directly behind her.

Duncan held up his hands. "Don't…don't make any sudden moves."

"How did it…?" Taylor sounded like she was rethinking running away screaming.

"Shay, back up, slowly, put your hands up," Max coached her, quietly, their voice shaking.

Shay held up her hands. Her heart pounded in her ears. She'd given it a silly name, but it was still a huge supernatural black wolf that possibly had been leading her to that very moment.

It pressed its nose against her forehead.

It didn't convey what it needed to in images, just feelings, but somehow she understood. Like she'd always known, and it was simply falling into place.

"It's the house guardian," she said.

"What?" Max asked. "Shay—"

"No, it is. When I went into the circle the first time, I had Jo's house guardian in my pocket," Shay said. "It…manifested, because of the void. And me. It's been trying to get me to come back here. To make sure the circle is still strong."

"So it's not a death omen?" Taylor asked.

"Nope, it's a doggy." Shay pet its head and it leaned its whole body against her. If Finnias hadn't been right behind her she would have fallen. "Woah, okay, you're a little big for that."

Beans huffed, warm breath stirring Shay's hair.

"Thank god," Max breathed.

"Okay, so, not dangerous, just horrifying in every way." Duncan's voice shook. "Glad we…solved that. But if the demon is already gone, why does the circle matter?"

"Because it's not all the way out, that's why the spiderweb is there," Max explained. "I'm the witch here, so I'll work on fixing it. Did you guys see it formed or…?"

"We did, wow, I did not explain what we saw very well," Duncan said.

"Or at all," Max said.

"You got a point. Okay, so…"

While he talked, Beans turned away from Shay and led her to the edge of the trees, its paws not leaving any impression in the snow. She followed.

One tree stood shorter than the rest, twisted and dark, its branches bare.

And still stabbed into its bark was the sword, the entire tree had curled itself around it and it had rotted out a dark hollow deep into the trunk.

The silver wire basket was completely untarnished. It looked like stems covered in thorns, twisted back in on itself. The hilt was wrapped in soft looking black cloth, but the pommel made it obvious that the entire handle was bone, just like Archibald's knife.

The blade was black, absorbing the light and drawing the eye.

Shay steeled herself and stepped forward, wrapping her hand around the grip. The cloth was silky and oddly warm to the touch. It didn't even take a yank for her to free the blade. The sword was lighter than she had expected, and the grip seemed to be made for her hand.

The sense of wrongness hit her a moment later and she almost dropped it. Everything in her told her to leave the sword, that it wasn't for her.

She barely managed to carry it back to everyone else before she dropped it in the snow.

"Holy crap, you found it," Duncan said.

"I don't like it," Shay admitted, wiping her hand on her jeans like it would stop the crawling sensation on her palm.

"I'm gonna call Gid." Duncan pulled out his phone.

"…Why?" Shay asked.

"Because he likes swords," Duncan said.

"Why didn't I know this?" Shay asked.

"Because you haven't been to his house, where he apparently thinks that swords are wall art," Duncan said. "Though he insists he's more of a bow guy, he's still as close to a sword expert as we have right now. C'mon, one bar. Just one measly bar."

"We're in the middle of nowhere," Taylor said. "And yeah, he's serious about archery. He's won like medals and stuff."

"I saw!" Duncan grinned. "He's at practice right now, that's why he couldn't come. Too bad, I could have gone and watched, but instead I'm here, no cell service, crying…"

"Are you telling me Gideon has secretly been interesting this entire time?" Shay asked.

"I thought you liked Gideon." Duncan held his phone up in the air.

"Liking him and thinking he's boring are two different things—"

"Didn't you go through a sword phase when you were a kid?" Max cut her off.

"You remember that?" Shay laughed. "Yeah, about the same time I really liked pirates. And I mean, really liked pirates. But my mom unfortunately remembered the time she bought me a plastic pirate sword and I tried to jab Duncan's eye out."

"Ah, memories." Duncan pretended to wipe a tear away. "Well, Shay, take a stab at it. What can you tell us about this sword?"

Shay considered it, carefully. The shadow of the blade was incredibly dark against the snow. "Well. It's a rapier."

"Wow, that is an in-depth analysis," Duncan said. "Stunning use of your rapier wit—"

"I wasn't exactly a sword expert back then, and I'm definitely not now," Shay said. She'd wanted to take fencing, but she'd never gotten the chance. "I can tell you it's a rapier, it has a bone handle like Archibald's knife which is probably significant in some awful way, and it gives me the creeps. The heebie jeebies, even."

"Straight to the point," Duncan said.

"Are you out of sword puns yet?" Taylor asked.

"Do not doubt my s-word play abilities," Duncan said. "Just because you don't appreciate my cutting sense of humor doesn't mean you can make slashing remarks. Now I'm out. For the moment."

"Yeah, all right, it's freaking me out, too," Taylor admitted. "Let's just take it back to the woods and leave it there."

"We can't just leave it here, it hurt the stupid demon, we have to at least consider putting it in your car," Duncan said.

"Nope, no, absolutely not, that's my car and I say we don't consider it."

A whisper came from the sword, faint and just low enough Shay couldn't make out the words. A hiss that sounded just a little too human. She frowned and took a step closer, trying to understand. The whisper got louder, but it still didn't make any sense. Shay kneeled next to it, heedless of the snow that immediately melted and soaked into her jeans, reaching for the sword. It was like having a word she'd forgotten right on the tip of her tongue, some understanding that was just outside of her reach, if she could just get a little bit closer, she would know something important.

That she had to take the sword, that it was a part of something bigger, something important. It longed to be used, and she could wield it, and it would bring terrible ruin to the world.

"Are you going to take it?"

Duncan's voice cut through her focus and the whispering stopped.

Chapter 29:
Needs and Wants

"What?" Shay blinked at Duncan.

He sighed. "The sword. Are you going to take it back or…?"

"…Yes?" The question didn't make sense, like Duncan had said the words in the wrong order and she was left to puzzle them together without a corner piece. "No?"

"I'm no sword expert, but I think we should maybe stay away from the creepy black blade, just a thought." Max helped her to her feet and her head cleared, just enough that she realized she'd been listening to a sword whisper.

"If the spirit charmer used it, then it's no good to us," Taylor agreed. "Let's just leave it here."

"I don't believe that is wise," Finnias said.

"Why not?" Taylor asked after translations were made. "It's just an ugly sword."

"There's something wrong with it," Shay said.

Duncan nodded. "Yeah. I mean, besides the obvious bone handle and wire…stuff."

"Hilt and basket," Shay corrected him.

"Aw look at you, a little sword genius for real," Duncan said.

"This is old magic." Finnias looked down in it with utter distaste. "I don't know its exact purpose, but I do know that we are lucky it hasn't been found. If it falls into the wrong hands, it could be devastating."

"It was in a tree," Shay said. "Can we just…put it back?"

Finnias shook his head. "No. The tree may have protected it, but now that the sword is removed, I doubt that will remain the case."

"He's right," Max said. "That tree was probably covered in protections. I bet Josephine put something to keep the sword in place. They were probably already wearing thin, and that's why Shay was able to find the sword."

"Don't forget I'm special and awesome," Shay said.

They nodded. "Yes, how could I have forgotten that."

Finnias sighed. "Please, focus."

Shay wanted to ask Finnias why he sighed if he didn't need to breathe, but she figured that was not what he wanted her to focus on and kept herself quiet, for the moment.

"I really don't want that thing in my car," Taylor said. "But if it's the only option…"

"Let me strengthen the circle and I can see about it," Max said. "I might be able to renew the protections, or at least figure out how to make new ones."

"Or we could wrap it up using Shay's giant pompom." Duncan flicked it and she swatted at him.

"That's optimistic, but unfortunately it's not going to work."

Shay stepped back from the voice. Of course she recognized it, she'd heard it often enough, trying to coerce or threaten her.

Emmaline.

She stood just outside of the circle. Her skirt ruffled in a breeze that didn't touch Shay at all. Blue prisms glittering in the snow around her.

Taylor recoiled, taking several steps back and ending up behind Duncan. "You."

"Me," Emmaline said.

"What are you doing here?" Finnias stepped between her and Shay. Max pulled her close, holding a little too tightly.

"Oh, Finn, please, stop being so dramatic," she said. "You don't even remember you're supposed to be ridiculous. It's embarrassing, actually."

"I'm glad I don't remember you," Finnias hissed at her. "You used me, controlled me, and you think you can just…get out of here. Leave."

Emmaline might have looked briefly hurt, but it smoothed over so quickly Shay was almost sure she imagined it. Emmaline waved Finnias's concerns away. "Oh, barely. You should be thanking me. Without my help, you would still be trapped in that stupid manor."

"What is she doing here?" Taylor asked, her voice barely above a whisper and full of venom.

"Can't hear me, I see, pity, I would have loved to catch up." Emmaline waved at her.

"You're actually here." Shay gaped openly at her. "Not in a mirror or possessing another ghost or—"

"Yes, it's me, in the…well, not flesh, exactly." Emmaline looked down at herself and clicked her tongue. "No matter, we are quite short on time. Your plan won't work."

"You have a really bad habit of eavesdropping," Shay said.

Emmaline laughed. "And a good thing, too, or you'd be doing some very stupid things. Or have you not looked at your hand?"

Shay looked down at the hand she'd used to grab the sword.

Her palm was stained black.

"Oh, that looks…does it hurt?" Max asked.

She wiped her hand on her jeans again, but it didn't make any difference. "No, just…yucky."

"Here." Max got out tissues and hand sanitizer, but scrubbing did nothing to remove the color, like ink had soaked into her skin.

"You can feel it, right?" Duncan reached over to poke her palm. She slapped his hand away. "Well?"

"Yes, it's fine." Shay flexed her fingers. Her hand didn't feel any different.

"Wielding that sword requires…a certain amount of finesse," Emmaline said. "And your abilities don't exactly lend themselves to a delicate touch, now do they?"

"What do you want?" Shay repeated.

"To help you, isn't that obvious?" Emmaline asked.

"No," Finnias and Shay said at the same time.

"Oh, well, since I have to be incredibly blunt, I'm here to provide assistance," Emmaline said.

"Why?" Shay asked.

"As…riveting as this conversation is, I need to patch that circle, it's not going to hold," Max cut in. "Shay, stay away from the sword. I mean it."

"I wasn't going to touch it," she said. They gave her a look. "I wasn't!"

"Uh huh, make sure you don't."

"They're right, you shouldn't," Emmaline said.

"Yeah, the big black mark on my hand kind of clued me into that," Shay said. "This is going to fade, right?"

"Yes, with time," Emmaline said, which was not as reassuring as she probably thought it was.

"How about you just tell us why you're here and then you can leave," Duncan said.

A blink and Emmaline was suddenly directly in front of Shay, grabbing her wrist and holding up her hand to Duncan. Shay was frozen, for a moment, too scared to move while the cold burned into her wrist from Emmaline's grip, nothing like Finnias's slightly cold fingers. "This is why I'm here, isn't it obvious? The sword can hurt that demon, and obviously she can't wield it, and I don't trust the rest of you with it."

Finnias grabbed for her, but she was a few feet away before he reached her.

"You want to possess someone," Duncan said.

"No." Taylor called from the tree line.

"Incredible, one of you is intelligent," Emmaline said. "Yes. You need me, and you need the sword. Otherwise, you're out of luck, and I don't think your little witch is going to keep that circle from failing."

"Stay the hell away from her," Duncan said.

"Oh, Taylor is lovely, but I actually had a different host in mind," Emmaline said.

Duncan blinked, then pulled Shay another step back. "Me?"

"I'm unaware of any other willing subjects in the vicinity, and here I thought you were the smart one."

"I am not a willing subject," Duncan snapped at her. "You can go to hell."

"There's no such thing, as far as I'm aware," Emmaline said. "You're either a ghost or you're not. But you should be begging for my help. How do you expect to defeat a demon without me? You need me, whether you want to admit it or not. Besides, there are other ways I could help."

"I doubt it would be worth the cost," Finnias said.

"Oh, don't worry, I want that bitch ripped apart and scattered to the wind just as much as you do," Emmaline said. "I have a vested interest, to get my own abilities back, and murder the thing that killed me. And what about you, Finnias? Even after this, what will you do?"

"Stay with me," Shay said.

Emmaline laughed. "Ghosts are memories, my dear, and he has none. But I could tell him. About his life. About his death. Even who killed him."

"It was Archibald, everyone knows that," Duncan said.

"Oh, sure, he sunk the knife in, but the real question is, where did he get it?" Emmaline smiled, slyly. Shay did not like that look on her. "Who gave it to him? And who has your heart now? I could tell you."

"And what would you want in return?" Finnias asked.

"Can't I just want to make sure my brother is all right?" Emmaline asked. "After all, I don't know how long you'll last. You were just a death echo until I pulled you out. Until Shay saved you. Everything that is special about you is because of me. What do you think is going to happen to you?"

"You're lying," Finnias said.

Shay knew Emmaline was a liar, but she felt the hint of truth in her words, making her sick.

"And what if something does happen to you, who says it won't hurt Shay?"

"I..." Finnias glanced at Shay, uncertain.

"Um, guys?" Max sounded scared and Shay's focus snapped to them. "I don't think this is working."

Shay hurried over. The circle was thinner than ever, the lines snapping and breaking apart, sparks scattering into the snow and flickering out. No matter how much Max tried to shore it up with new lines, they kept fading.

"We should leave," Emmaline said, conversationally.

Power thrummed inside the circle like someone plucking a giant guitar string. The sound and pressure reverberated in Shay's chest.

"Now would be good," Emmaline continued.

"Okay, normally, I don't agree with her on principle, but we gotta go," Duncan said.

"Agreed." Finnias nodded.

"We can't just leave," Max said. "If I stop, then the circle is going to fall, and we are not going to be very far away from it."

"Then we should probably move fast." Shay offered them a hand up. She realized it was the hand that was painted black and switched, quickly.

They stared at her hand, blue lines forming and fading underneath their fingers, then sighed and swept everything back into their kit, shouldering it and accepting her help up.

"What do we do about the sword?" Shay asked.

"I don't know," Duncan admitted. "Or about her."

"Leave her here!" Taylor yelled. "Just leave it, we'll come back!"

Sticky webbing shot from the circle and ensnared Max's leg, yanking them off of their feet. Shay grabbed their arm, digging her heels in.

The edge loomed close.

She grabbed for the sword, missed the pommel by inches. The webbing dragged her across the ground. Her fingers drew furrows in the snow but there was nothing to hold onto, nothing to get any purchase.

The black dog leaped out of the trees and snapped at the webbing, but more webbing snagged at it, dragging it towards the circle with them."

They stopped just short of the lines. Max looked at her with wide eyes and she tightened her grip, trying to scoot backwards in the snow and drag them with her, but it was an exercise in futility.

"Shay…"

She wanted to tell them to keep that thought to themself, but she couldn't spare the breath.

"Don't let go!" Finnias grabbed onto her and managed to pull them back an inch, a monumental effort that left her seeing stars. Her arms hurt and her chest was on fire, but she couldn't let go. Not for anything.

The webbing pulled again, harder, and she pulled back with as much force as she could muster. She wasn't losing Max. Not to a stupid spiderweb.

Taylor grabbed her around the middle and yanked, her boots sliding in the snow. "Hold on!"

"I am!" She gripped Max as tightly as she could. They held on back, even tighter. Webbing moved up Max's legs like a living thing.

"Punch it!" Finnias yelled.

"How long do you think my arms are?!" she yelled back, hysterical.

Duncan ran up and hit the webbing with the sword. It clanged off and landed in the snow. He yelped and held his hands to his chest. "Ow! Son of a bitch!"

The webbing crawled up to Shay's arm. She couldn't even try to shake it off, just hope that they didn't get pulled further in.

The web gave and they all tumbled into the snow.

"Like I said, it's time to leave."

It was Duncan's voice, but it wasn't, another layered over top of it. She looked up, shoving hair out of her eyes.

Duncan was holding the sword.

His eyes glowed a pale, frosty blue.

CHAPTER 28: HISTORY LESSON

Shay slowly climbed to her feet, feeling every ache and pain. "Dunc…?"

"Tell me you didn't," Taylor's voice shook.

"You know better than that." Emmaline swung the sword. The blade whistled and hummed through the air. The cobwebs burned away. "He didn't have very many choices, did he? You might want to take care of that, by the way."

"What?" Shay looked back to the circle. The webbing was slithering towards them. "Oh."

She balled her hand into a fist and thought about how much she'd love to drive it into Emmaline's face. Blue fire formed around her fingers, and she slammed it into the spider silk.

She jerked back, expecting it to wrap around her fist.

It screamed.

Shay slapped her hands over her ears. Fire spread across the webs, setting all of them alight. The edge of the circle vanished. Something huge and pale exploded from the circle, spiraling away into sky, too close to the color of the clouds for her to see its shape.

"That didn't look good," Finnias said.

Shay ignored him, helping Max to their feet. "Are you okay?"

Max shuddered and brushed their legs and arms, even though there was nothing on them. "I've been better. Oh, I really hate spiders. I can still feel it. What was that?"

"That was the rest of the demon, going to join the part that already escaped," Emmaline explained.

Shay ignored her, too, grabbing Max in a tight hug. It did little to ease the anxiety that spiked in her chest. "You scared the crap out of me."

"To be fair, you scare me at least three times a day." Max hugged her back.

"That's very sweet, can we get back to the part where you punch her?" Taylor asked.

"I mean, you can, if you want, but I seem to recall that was quite the problem when you did it to Finnias," Emmaline said. "Duncan invited me in, and he's allowing me to stay. He is aware that he cannot use the sword without me, and with the demon now at full strength, well, I believe you're going to need it."

"You're sounding awfully punchable right now," Shay said.

Emmaline had the audacity to smile, like they were all joking around. "Be that as it may, we do need to leave, and quickly. I assume you want a Teton Falls to return to?"

"Why can't you just—" Taylor started to say, then seemed to think better of it. "Shay, she tries anything, I'm pulling over and you're punching her out."

"Got it," Shay said.

"How about we start with an exorcism and work our way up to violence?" Max suggested. "I'm pretty sure I have a few things that would get her out of there."

"And if not, I'll drag her out," Finnias offered.

"You guys are adorable when you're being threatening, really," Emmaline said. "But I was not exaggerating when I said we are on a bit of a time crunch. Shall we?"

"Fine." Shay glared at her.

They hiked back to the road in silence. Without Duncan's chatter the only sound was the crunch of snow under their boots.

Taylor surprised Shay by breaking the silence first. "So. You possessed me for three months."

"I did," Emmaline said.

"Why?" Taylor's voice cracked.

"I was given a task, it was easier with a body, and yours was offered." Emmaline shrugged. "It was never personal, if that's what you were asking."

"Who offered?" Taylor asked. "I never agreed to it."

"To be fair, you asked me to make my presence known," Emmaline said. "And I did."

"You…" Taylor's fingers twitched like she was thinking about strangling Emmaline, Duncan and all, but she held off somehow. "You didn't answer my question. What task could they possibly want you to do? Teton Falls is in shambles because of you."

"Maybe I'm protecting you. Sometimes the cure is worse than the sickness." Emmaline's tone stayed light, but there was a dangerous undercurrent to it, a darkness in her expression that had never stained Duncan's features.

"You put people in danger, you nearly got the whole town pulled into the void, you almost killed Shay," Taylor continued.

"Are we listing everything I've done wrong or is this going to get interesting anytime soon?" Emmaline asked.

"I think that would take a while," Max said. Shay did her best not to laugh. She was afraid she wouldn't stop. Or she'd start crying.

"You're a liar and a murderer," Taylor said.

"Yes, I am both of those things," Emmaline said. "Did you ever stop and ask yourself why?"

"I don't care," Taylor snapped.

"But you will," Emmaline said. "Shay and I have already had a…heart to heart about it."

"What does that mean?" Max glanced at her.

"If someone has possession of a necromancer's heart, then they have access to the abilities they had in life," Shay explained.

"Very good, you remembered, gold star," Emmaline said. "But do you know how it works?"

"Judging by Finnias's…situation, I think I have a good idea," Max said.

"Yes, someone has to cut out their still beating heart," Emmaline explained. Shay winced, putting a hand to her chest. "Necromancers very rarely die from natural causes. Every bit of us can be useful. If someone were to take Shay's eyes, for example, holding one would give them the sight."

"Let's maybe not discuss someone carving out my eyes." Shay wanted to cover them, instinctively, but she didn't think it would be the best idea while hiking through a dense forest.

"It's true, though, and it leaves a stain on their lineage forever. Not that they usually have the chance. There are many parts of a necromancer that can be…unfortunately useful, to the right person. And those right people will pay a lot of money to get what they want. Taking a bone can make a weapon like this one." She lifted up the sword. "Or the knife that took Finnias's heart. It's the only thing that can do it. The bone of a necromancer and a specially forged blade."

"So how did you come across one?" Shay asked.

"I needed the protection," Emmaline said. "I want you to imagine, for a moment, it's the dawn of the 20th century. A young woman, spiritualist, traveler, entrepreneur, no marriage prospects, and a necromancer. How safe do you think I was?"

"I don't care," Taylor said.

"Not very safe at all," Max said.

"That was exactly what Roy Nelson thought of me," Emmaline said. "Mr. Nelson came at me with a knife, so I had no choice but to shove one in his throat."

Emmaline used her head to motion behind them and Shay looked back.

Ghosts trailed in their wake.

They were just sketchy outlines of a person, so faded and faint that they were barely visible. Four of them, as far as Shay could tell.

"I ran after that," Emmaline said. "I had a bone handled knife and a murder charge, and I wasn't going to drag Finnias into it."

"How altruistic of you," Finnias murmured.

"I am. You followed me, like you had up to that point in our lives, but others were…more successful. I killed them, too. I came here, hoping to get help from the local coven, but the knife was stolen and not long after that, well. You know the rest, I suppose."

Shay did not want to feel sorry for Emmaline. She carefully wove every true word she spoke into a dozen lies.

Still, Shay couldn't help it, there was an inkling of sympathy worming into her.

"That explains the knife, but not the sword."

"A girl has to have some secrets." Emmaline smiled. "It's quite the tale of daring escapades and a doomed romance. Probably nothing you'd be interested in."

Shay was very interested, but she could not let Emmaline know that. "Could give the abridged version."

"I stole it from an old man while he was asleep."

"I knew it would be boring," Shay said.

"I don't care about your fake sob story," Taylor said. "Or your...sword heist."

Shay wished she hadn't worded it that way, she was more interested than ever.

"Who got you out of Holt Manor?" Taylor asked. "Who wanted you to do something for them? Who...who said you could possess me?"

"I already told you, those are not questions you want answered," Emmaline said. She didn't try to disguise the dark humor in her voice. If Shay hadn't known Duncan was possessed, she would have known then.

Duncan never sounded like that. Like he was in on a horrible secret and was just waiting for a misstep before he dragged someone under the water.

"I think that's for me to decide," Taylor snapped back.

Emmaline smiled. The smile of someone opening a gift on Christmas morning, but knew exactly what it was, and it was just what she asked for. "Well, then, if that's how you really feel. I was freed, contracted, and given permission by Linda Stevens. Your mother."

Taylor punched her.

More accurately, she punched Duncan, who tumbled back into the snow, Emmaline's laughter erupting from his throat.

"Hey!" Shay got between them. Finnias got between them, throwing up an arm and stopping Taylor's next punch. "Stop it! You're only hurting Duncan!"

Max grabbed Taylor before she could tear Shay's eyes out herself and go after Emmaline with the power of sight.

"You're a bitch and a liar!" Taylor screamed at her. "I don't believe you!"

"Believe whatever you want, but I wouldn't lie about this." Emmaline staggered to her feet, scooping up the sword from the snow. Duncan's nose was bleeding and she wiped it with a sleeve. "Oh, that smarts! You're lucky you didn't break anything. Or knock his teeth out."

"If you were wearing your own face I'd knock your teeth out," Taylor snarled.

"Such animosity," Emmaline said.

"You stole three months of my life!" Taylor lunged at her and Max barely held her back. Shay stood between them, though she honestly would have rather been back at the mall. Even with Finnias helping, it seemed safer. "I hate you!"

"No one likes her, I promise," Max said. "If she wasn't using Duncan as a meat shield, I'd rip her in half. As it is, I'm still on the fence about kicking her out of his body and letting Shay rip her in half."

"Cute." Emmaline wiped more blood away. "But I think you're going to want me around, little witchling, especially since you care so much about Shay."

"Yes, I know you're being so helpful." Max finally got Taylor to stop trying to tear poor Duncan's throat out, at least. She hung lip in their grasp, shaking with fury or sadness, Shay wasn't sure. "Allegedly. I don't trust you."

"That's fine with me."

They got back to the car and stowed the sword away in the trunk, which made Shay feel a little better. Max offered to take the back seat with Emmaline, putting Shay up front.

The sun was setting, the sky a dull and angry orange. It was snowing harder than ever, thick flakes falling quickly through the beams of the headlights. Shay hoped they could get back to town without sliding, but she was starting to doubt that they would. Drifting snow bleached the road gray.

"Be safe," Finnias said before she got in the car, briefly taking her hand. "Don't trust her."

"I don't and I won't," Shay said. "I'll see you soon, Finn."

He nodded and she got in, closing the door with a thunk.

"I was hoping we'd beat the storm," Taylor muttered. The engine sputtered before it turned over with a roar. The radio blasted to life, garbled words singing through static before Taylor punched it off. "Stupid thing."

"Happening often?" Emmaline asked.

"Shut up," they all said. She shrugged and gazed out the window.

They drove out of the hills at a speed that probably wasn't entirely safe, the atmosphere tense and anxious. The moment they hit a spot with reception all of their phones dinged and buzzed. Shay dug her own out of her pocket. She'd missed a call from Jo, probably asking if they still needed help.

She was about to text her when she noticed the voice mail.

At first it was silent, and Shay wondered if Jo had accidentally called her. Her mom did that all the time.

A soft, shaky inhale.

"Shay?" Jo's voice was just barely above a whisper, and Shay jabbed at the volume button, pressing the phone hard to her ear like it would help. "I…you must be out…Arlo isn't himself. He's…I think he wants to take me to the mall. I think a lot of people are going there. Please, hurry, call me—"

The message cut off.

Shay returned the call quickly.

"What's wrong?" Max asked.

She held up a hand. She could barely hear her phone ringing over her own pulse thundering in her ears, chest so tight she thought her ribs might burst through her skin.

Voice mail picked up.

"Jo's in trouble," Shay said. Her voice sounded far away. She was back in the manor, with Jo and Max missing, and no idea if she'd be able to get them back. "We have to hurry."

"Got it." Taylor pressed harder on the gas.

Shay tried calling again.

"We're sorry," a pleasant, robotic voice told her. "But the number you are dialing is no longer in service."

Chapter 26: Radio

Shay hung up, staring at her cracked phone screen. No new notifications.

"Do you all have something to protect yourself against the nightmare?" Emmaline's voice cut through her thoughts.

"Shut up." Taylor pressed harder on the gas, the sedan moving at speeds that were probably ill advised with the snow sticking to the road, but no one told her to slow down. The radio switched on and Shay jabbed it off.

"So sorry for assuming you want to go in prepared with every bit of relevant information and assistance I can provide," Emmaline said. "Please, tell me when I'm allowed to speak to save all of you."

"We do." Max pulled out the sigil on a piece of paper they'd kept in a sachet around their neck. "It must have worked for Jo. I don't understand why Arlo wasn't able to…"

"She already had her little hooks in him, nothing would have protected him," Emmaline said. "Plus, he's probably still recovering from the ah…stint with Archibald. He was gone for weeks and he's not young, I doubt he'll ever recover fully."

"He never said anything." Shay already felt sick, but she was almost afraid if she spoke she would vomit all over Taylor's car.

"Isn't that your fault?" Taylor asked.

"I had nothing to do with that," Emmaline snapped. "Do you really think I would lower myself to help my brother's murderer?"

"Yes," Taylor said.

"Yup." Shay nodded.

"Not a doubt in my mind," Max added.

"You're all terrible people," Emmaline said. "Of course not. I...I wanted to keep him under my thumb, I wanted to twist him and control him and never give him a moment's peace. Sadly, we can't all have what we want."

"Yeah." Shay ran her thumb over stitching on her sleeve, the scars on the back of her hand. "I mean, well, you should have let me punch him."

"You destroyed him, in the end." Emmaline shrugged.

"No thanks to you."

"Plenty thanks to me."

"Sure, keep telling yourself that."

The car slid sideways with a horrible jerk. Taylor swore and pulled the wheel the other way. The car slid several yards and Taylor threw an arm across Shay like she could save her.

They plowed over the edge of the road and into the grass beyond, hitting a snowbank, the car coming to a stop so quickly Shay was thrown against her seatbelt and Taylor's arm.

They all just sat there for a moment, catching their breath.

"Is everyone okay?" Taylor asked, shakily.

"Yeah, thanks." Shay sucked in a shaky breath and let it out.

"Good, great, good. Kind of concerned the airbags didn't deploy, but…great. Good." Taylor threw the car into reverse. The tires screamed and the car strained, but didn't pull away at all. "Dammit, c'mon, you stupid piece of…"

"You, get out, help me push." Max pointed at Emmaline.

"Fine." Emmaline undid her seatbelt and got out. Even with both of them pushing and Taylor going into reverse, they didn't make any headway. Shay got out to help, mostly holding Finnias's hand so he could assist with pushing.

Taylor smacked the wheel a few times. It didn't help.

"Do you have anything we can get underneath the tires?" Max asked.

"No," Taylor said. "Nothing. Ugh. Stupid piece of crap car! We don't have time for this!"

"We'll have to hope someone is awake to give us a ride," Emmaline said.

"Fine." Taylor got out of the car, pulling out her phone. She jabbed a finger at them. "All of you stay here. Just…stay."

She walked far enough away that Shay couldn't hear her.

Shay leaned against the car and tried to breathe. Jo needed them, and they were stuck in the snow. "How far away are we from town?"

"Probably ten minutes or so," Max said.

"Too far to walk?"

Max's face crumpled, a little. "I…look, it's not far, it's going to be fine. I'm sure Taylor will get a hold of someone."

"Possibly," Emmaline said. "Or the demon has put everyone to sleep and none of her calls are going through. Who knows. Exciting, isn't it."

"How about you start walking and bring back help?" Max told her.

"No, don't do that, not unless you're going to go possess someone else," Shay said, quickly. "Could you do that, though? Go possess someone and pick us up?"

"In theory I could." Emmaline rubbed her chin. "But I wouldn't really want to risk it, in practice. For one, I have no idea how to get here by normal human means, and if the person I possessed also lacked that knowledge…"

"And Dunc has a terrible sense of direction," Shay said. She was fairly sure it was hereditary, because hers was even worse.

"And there's the problem if the demon detects me, she could control me, and no one wants that," Emmaline said. "Well, probably no one wants that. You're all quite bloodthirsty, honestly. So…best I stay here. Or go on a literal hike, if that's what you prefer."

"No, don't take my brother for a stroll." Shay glared at her. "As much as he wants to exercise more, I don't think hiking all the way back to town in a snow storm is quite what he meant."

"Yeah, better he stays here," Max agreed.

The radio turned on, so loudly she could hear it through the windows. She struggled to get the door open, reaching over to turn it off.

"Wait." Emmaline grabbed her wrist.

"Don't touch me," she said. Finnias looked ready to break Duncan's wrist, so luckily Emmaline backed off.

"Don't turn it off," Emmaline said.

"I'd really like it if we turned it off, actually." Max covered their ears. If Shay had her hands free, she would have done the same. It was loud, the static and garbled words mixing together like nails on a chalkboard.

"Wait," Emmaline said, again. "There's something…words."

"Taylor said this has been happening since you possessed her," Shay said.

"…Well, that's not great, because I certainly had no problems with it." Emmaline leaned in closer, eyes narrowed. "I can't quite make it out."

The voice didn't get clearer, only snatches of part of a word coming through, nothing that Shay could make sense of.

"It's saying to turn back," Finnias said. They all stared at him.

"You can make sense of that?" Emmaline asked. "Fascinating. It must be because I'm hearing it with these weak pathetic human ears."

"Hey, Duncan has great hearing," Shay said, not sure why she was defending Duncan's ears of all things, but she felt like she should.

"Quiet," Finnias said. He cocked his head to one side, looking a bit like Becky did when she was interested in a toy or a treat. Shay decided to keep that comparison to herself. "It's…it's a mess, but it's there. It's saying to turn back. That it's too late."

"What does that mean?" Shay asked.

The car died, the radio spluttering into silence. Without the steady rumble of the engine, the silence fell around them as heavily as the snow.

"Well, that's very ominous," Emmaline said.

"We should be able to see the town from the top of the ridge," Max said. "Maybe we should…?"

"We should go, yeah." Emmaline grabbed the keys to pop open the trunk, taking the sword. There was no sign of a ghost nearby, no glow, no sound, just the snow falling thickly around them. "Hopefully Taylor got us a ride, I don't think this thing is going anywhere, anytime soon."

They hiked up to where Taylor was, up the hill from them towards the city. Shay couldn't shake the feeling that something was following them, but every time she looked back she just saw the snow falling against the darkness of the trees.

"I think something's following us," Max said, quietly, adding fuel to the fire of her fears.

"Undoubtedly," Emmaline said. "Keep moving, try your best to stop looking over your shoulder."

Finnias walked a little too close to Shay, considering how cold it was, but she couldn't say that she minded too much.

Taylor was at the ridge already, staring down into town.

"Oh, good, I was about to go get you guys," Taylor said. "You'll want to see this."

In the snow and the quickly darkening sky, the town should have looked picturesque from a distance - every home with occupants lit up, the holiday lights downtown making it look festive.

There weren't any lights on.

Not a single one, in the entire town. No cars moving as far as Shay could see, not a single thing stirring.

And where the mall was, a dark fog concealed it entirely.

"Definitely not good," Emmaline said. "Were you able to procure us a ride?"

"Yes, but he's not happy about it," Taylor said. "Gideon will be here soon."

"I guess the sigil worked for him, at least," Max said.

"He wasn't in town, so I don't know." Taylor shrugged. "So thats probably not great. Let me just go grab my keys and—"

Emmaline held them up. "Your car died. We took the keys."

"Give me those." Taylor snatched them, rubbing her hand where it came in contact with Emmaline's. "There are still blankets in the car, we could use those, at least."

"I'll go with you," Max said. "Something feels off, none of us should be alone."

"But Shay—"

"I'm good," Shay said. "I have Finnias."

"Right." Taylor gave Finnias a doubtful look, but slowly nodded. "Let's get those blankets. It's freezing out here and it'll take Gid a bit to get to us."

"Well, just the three of us," Emmaline said after a moment. "I'm sure you have questions."

"I don't know." Shay crouched down, trying to conserve heat and get herself out of the stinging wind. It didn't really work. "Probably a million. I'm too cold and worried to think of any."

That was an understatement. She was terrified. Jo was down there, somewhere, waiting for her help, and Shay had no idea how long it had been. Her brother was possessed by a murdering thief, and she had to fight a full formed demon.

"Mm." Emmaline moved to block the wind, or at least attempt to. "You know, you don't need to worry. You're an incredibly powerful necromancer."

"Cause of the whole…fwoosh fire thing?" Shay asked.

"Your abilities were sealed for roughly twenty years, weren't they?" Emmaline asked. "The fact that you've only had them for a few weeks and you're already doing pretty incredible things…that's amazing. I don't think you quite understand what an anomaly you are."

"How do you know about the seal?" Shay asked.

"Please, I'm in your brother's head." Emmaline rolled her eyes. "Besides, your father told the Stevens. They were quite close, once, when they were young. A group of necromancers out to change the world, make a safe haven for their kind in a terrible little out of the way town, but of course that didn't work out for them, did it? Change of plans, power became more important, your father ran off…"

"They really told you about all of that?" Shay narrowed her eyes. "You're lying."

"Mm, exaggerating and filling in details, maybe," Emmaline admitted. "But the whole safe haven thing, that's completely true. Quite impossible, of course, even in this day and age there are too many people that want us dead."

"Are there still…hunters?" Shay asked, hesitantly, trying to ignore the fear in her gut. Ghosts were bad enough. She didn't know what to do against a person.

"Of course there are," Emmaline said. "And when they find out there's a powerful necromancer in Teton Falls…hm. Well. That could get messy for you, couldn't it?"

"Great," Shay murmured.

"You're welcome, by the way."

Shay stared at her. "For what?"

"For my mirror and ghost breaking your seal," Emmaline said. "You'd been having headaches, right? Terrible ones? Well, that was your powers, trying to manifest. Luckily, you ran into one of my mirrors! Broke that seal with minimal damage. You really should be thanking me."

"…A ghost dragged me across a dusty attic floor and tried to pull me into a mirror," Shay reminded her.

"See? Safe, controlled, and very little trauma! Really, I was doing you a favor."

"I don't think you know what a favor is," Shay said. She couldn't shake the feeling that something was watching her, somewhere out in the snow. It was growing darker by the moment. "Finn, you've been awfully quiet."

"I'm listening," Finnias said.

"To what?" Shay felt like something was slowly crawling up her back. Visions of necromancer hunters and deadly ghosts, lurking just out of sight, filled her head. She got back to her feet.

"Max and Taylor have been gone for a while," Emmaline said, almost conversationally. "We should really go check on them, shouldn't we?"

Shay turned back to the car, but she couldn't see it anymore.

CHAPTER 27:
WINTER WEATHER
ADVISORY

Shay steeled herself. "Let's just…make sure they're okay."

"I suppose that would be prudent, yes," Emmaline said.

Shay somehow kept herself from punching Emmaline. She wasn't sure how, considering the amount of stress pressing down on her. Reminding herself that it was Duncan and he would never say that seemed to help, a little bit. The fact that it would be ridiculous for her to punch someone while wearing mittens and a hat with a giant pompom actually got her to turn and walk towards the car without at least shoving Emmaline into a snowbank.

The snow fell so thickly she could barely make out where the road ended and the drifts began, the dark shape of the trees practically invisible, the mountains erased entirely in a haze of white.

"I don't think anyone should be driving in this," she admitted. She really hoped Gideon was okay, but she had a feeling it was going to take him a lot longer than ten minutes to reach them.

"Be careful," Finnias told her. He sounded like he was standing next to her in a quiet room, despite the howling of the wind.

There was a strange sound to it, like she could almost make out words.

Like singing.

"Do you hear that?" She stopped to listen.

"Don't listen to it," Finnias cautioned her.

"But—"

"Don't," Finnias repeated.

She nodded and started walking again. A red light glowed through the snow. It must have been the taillights to Taylor's car. Shay shielded her face with one arm and trudged forward.

Finnias grabbed her arm. "That's not the car."

"What—"

"That's a Will-O-Wisp," Finnias said. Even though he wasn't shouting, and the wind was screaming, she had no trouble hearing him. "They lead travelers off of the path to consume them. A very potent type of siphon."

The wind shrieked louder than ever. Snow formed into the shape of people and burst apart again, stinging Shay's eyes. She shielded her face again, and when she dared to lower her arm, the light was closer, and glowing the same blue as all ghosts.

"We need to go." Finnias grabbed her hand and yanked her along the road. She could barely see him. She definitely couldn't see or hear Emmaline. The wind rose to deafening volumes, attempting to tug her hat off of her hair, and all she could do was hold onto it with her free hand and trust that Finnias was leading her in the right direction. Shapes leaped out of the snow, hands and faces trying to grab her, words she couldn't understand flowing past her in hurried snatches of conversation. Her heart pounded in her chest, slamming against her ribcage like it wanted to break free.

Emmaline sword lashed out from seemingly nowhere, the edge glowing such a brilliant blue that it hurt to look at. She sliced through the strange shapes, and they blew away with a scream that trailed off into the mountains.

The wind faded until it was little more than a breeze, pushing the falling snow in front of it. She could see the car, Max and Taylor checking the trunk, and the trees behind them.

She glanced back, but there was no storm behind her, just the same snow.

"I see why the witch prefers when you don't leave home," Emmaline said. The sword stopped glowing, dull and black. "We really need to get you some hands-on training if you're going to run into some…horrible snow ghost."

"You don't know what that was?" Shay's voice was hoarse, like she'd been screaming the entire time.

"I don't know everything," Emmaline said. "But if I had to guess, whatever that was and the will-o-wisp were working together. It gets its jollies from freezing you to death and the will-o-wisp devours whatever is left. Pretty nasty work. I didn't get rid of it, so we better hope that Gideon is a fast driver."

"Right." Shay shivered, stiff with the cold and exhaustion. She limped the rest of the way to the car. Max saw her and jogged over.

"Hey, we were about to…what happened?" Max pulled off one glove and touched the spot on her neck just below her hat. She hissed when the sudden stinging hit her, jerking away, and Max's fingers came away bloody. "You have some scratches there, are you okay? If Emmaline did this—"

"I didn't," Emmaline said.

"How?" Finnias turned her head to the side. He rarely touched her of his own accord, taking her by so much surprise she just let him do it. "When did that happen?"

"There was...something in the storm." Shay glanced back again, but all she could see was snow and the highway, slowly succumbing to white. "Emmaline chased it off, but she said it'd be back...is Gideon almost here?"

"Taylor's on the phone with him." Max slung their bag off of their shoulder. "Good thing I brought a first aid kit."

"Did you bring a coffee maker, too?" Shay joked, weakly.

"It wouldn't fit next to the kitchen sink," Max said. "I'm sorry, Shay, this was my fault."

"It was not, it was mine," Finnias said. Shay didn't translate for him, too cold to play the blame game.

"We should have all come back together, that was a dumb idea."

"It was," Finnias agreed. "Nevermind, I've decided it's your fault, after all."

"Stop being silly, both of you. We can't be genre savvy all the time." Shay shrugged. Max carefully disinfected the cuts but the sting left her wanting to make noises like Becky did whenever Finnias was in the same room. She bit her lip and swallowed them down. They put some ointment on and a band-aid.

"There." They looked like they wanted to check every part of her. "I am really, really sorry."

"It's just a scratch," Shay said.

"A scratch that could have been a lot worse, I should have stayed with you, I—"

"Max." She grabbed their hands before they could really get going with the gesturing. "I'm okay. You can't be with me all the time, that's unreasonable, and there's something creepy going on with the car, of course Taylor needed someone, and we all know I'm hit or miss and she would have stolen Emmaline's sword and killed Duncan…it's fine. It's all fine. I got a few scratches but no one committed homicide or got eaten by a ghost car."

They snorted. "A ghost car?"

"A ghost car! A car ghost? A car that's been possessed by a ghost? Take your pick." She took their glove and put it on for them. When she looked back up, she couldn't read their expression at all. "What?"

"Shay, I—"

"There you are!" Taylor's voice cut through the conversation and Max stepped away so fast that Shay almost fell on her face. Headlights crested the hill, shining through the snow. "Oh, it wasn't that bad, don't be a baby. Yes, we'll all fit. You have a middle seat. Duncan might be eating for two or whatever but he's still a stick. It's fine!"

As Gideon drove closer Shay could hear Taylor's voice coming through the speakers in his car. He carefully slowed to a stop and rolled down his window. "Hey. Need a lift?"

"No, I called you out here for fun." Taylor grabbed her bag out of the trunk and slammed it closed. "Did you win?"

"I did, actually," Gideon said. "I was so focused on ghost things I couldn't even be nervous about shooting. Well? You're freezing! Get in!"

"I'll see you soon," Finnias touched Shay's shoulder, just enough to move her jacket, and was gone with a swirl of snow.

They all climbed into the car, Max insisting Taylor take shotgun and got in behind her. Shay was normally behind the driver's seat, due to her short legs, and she didn't complain this time. "Hey, Gid. Congrats on winning."

"Thanks, it was just a little local thing. Hi Max. Emmaline." Gideon nodded at her. "Can't say it's nice to see you again. Especially…considering."

"Oh, don't worry, I would never pretend to actually be your pathetic little boy toy." Emmaline squeezed in next to Shay. "Frankly, you're not my type."

"Same," Gideon said. "I'm not really into homicide. Or…ladies."

"And I'm not into men, we have some solidarity," Emmaline said.

"Wait, it was a doomed lesbian romance sword heist?" Shay asked.

"Oh, do you want to hear about it now?" Emmaline grinned and she knew she'd made a mistake.

"Do I want to know?" Gideon glanced at Taylor but focused on turning around in the slowest way possible. Shay was trying very hard to be patient, she knew they couldn't risk getting stuck a second time, but she really wanted to kick Gideon's seat and tell him a twenty-point turn was excessive.

"No," Taylor said. "No one wants to hear. It's probably all lies, anyway."

Emmaline shrugged. "Suit yourself."

"We should stop by the shop," Max said. "I have some things, but I think we need to bring a big arsenal."

"And what if the wards have been compromised?" Emmaline asked. "Do you have a plan for that?"

"Of course I do," Max scoffed. "Don't go inside. Obviously."

"…Okay, that's actually a decent plan, I'll give you that one," Emmaline admitted.

Shay was so anxious she was jittery, but eventually the heat in the car started to thaw her out, and her eyelids grew heavy despite herself. She was already exhausted, a headache already threatening to drum the inside of her skull.

"You should rest," Emmaline said, in a surprisingly gentle voice.

"Don't think I can with you sitting right there," Shay muttered. "Can you put Duncan back in the driver's seat or…or something?"

"Hmmm no," Emmaline said. "I mean, I suppose that I could, but I don't really want to."

"Charming."

"I try." Emmaline shrugged. "You know, if we worked together, I could teach you how to handle things like that. Like the things in the snow."

"You're a ghost," Shay reminded her.

"That doesn't stop you from keeping Finnias around."

"Finnias is different," Shay said.

"Agreed," Taylor said. "He never possessed someone against their will for three months. He would let Duncan take the wheel."

"Duncan is becoming a powerful necromancer in his own right," Emmaline explained. "If I let him take over, he would retain control, no matter what either of us wanted, and we can't have that if you want the sword and my knowledge, now, can we?"

"Finnias can possess him just fine," Shay said. "Maybe you suck."

"Maybe I do," Emmaline said. "My entire existence has been about control, I've never been good at giving it up, and I doubt I'll learn now."

Shay wondered what that said about her, and her own abilities. If somehow what a necromancer could do was tied deeply with their personality, with who they were, at their core. What that said about nature versus nurture.

"That doesn't change the fact that I could help you."

Shay was glad for the interruption of those thoughts. "And we're back to you being a ghost and I'm not letting you stay in a body long term."

Emmaline grinned in a way Duncan wouldn't, twisting his face into something not quite human. "And how on earth would you stop me? You have no idea what I'm capable of, and you're just stumbling along, doing your best, and messing up at every turn. Getting your brother and friends possessed, getting your witches taken, and now you've lost the closest thing you have to a mentor. I'm patient, but I don't think you can afford to be."

"Shut up," Shay said.

"What, no pun?" Emmaline asked. "No clever retort?"

"I'll clever retort your—"

"Okay, that's enough of that," Gideon said. "This is my car and I make the rules. We'll stop by Spellbound, then where are we going?"

"Where else?" Emmaline asked. "The mall, of course."

"Great, this close to Christmas?" Gideon joked, weakly. "At least it's a weekday."

They reached the edge of town, but the streetlights were off, the windows dark. The traffic lights swung back and forth, dark and dead, above an empty street.

CHAPTER 28: SEVER

Shay watched the side of the road carefully.

Buildings loomed out of the dark and snow, streetlamp poles reduced to sudden flashes in the car's headlights. The whole town looked abandoned, the dead traffic lights fluttering in the wind like heavy flags.

"It's like a ghost town," Shay said.

"Bad pun aside, yeah," Max agreed. "My parents and nana were out of town for some show, they're okay, but I can't get a hold of Leela."

Leela was Max's cool cousin, who decorated cookies for a living.

"She's probably caught up in whatever mess has befallen the town," Emmaline said.

"Or she's visiting her girlfriend and is completely fine," Shay said. "We could think on the bright side on occasion. It's okay, Max, we'll…figure this out. We'll fix it."

She had no idea how. It all felt too big, like far too much for her to handle. She couldn't even make her way through a snow storm without needing to be rescued. How could she possibly face a demon? What made her think she could do anything at all?

But the Rat King said if she wanted to keep Finnias safe and near, she had to. If she wanted to save Jo she didn't have a choice.

And the rest of the town needed her, too.

It pressed down on her like she was a garlic clove being crushed by the flat edge of a knife.

"We're almost to the house," Max said, softly. She really wished she was sitting next to them, instead of next to Emmaline. She needed their comforting presence, their faith in her.

And if she couldn't save anything, she wanted to spend a little more time with them.

"There are six of us, we should be able to figure out something," Taylor agreed. "So...um. Big spider demon. How are we going to kill it?"

"Well, I usually use a cup and a piece of paper," Shay said. "But I don't think they make them big enough."

"I say we just...smash it." Taylor hit her palm with one fist. "Squish."

"There's always the good old standby of kill it with fire," Gideon agreed.

"Could you shoot it with flaming arrows?" Shay asked. "Just...pew pew fwoosh. Like that."

Gideon considered for a moment. "Well, I don't have any lighter fluid on me, but I know Jo has some. I'll grab some from the house and we'll see about fire arrows."

"You are officially the coolest person I know now," Shay said. "Besides Max, who isn't actually in the competition. Obviously, they're another judge."

"I concur, very cool," Max said.

"Oh, well, thank you," Gideon said. "I think. I've heard you were kind of a delinquent, I'm not sure I want to be cool by your standards."

"Why does everyone say that?" Shay muttered. "Is that why you weren't going to tell me you were a medal winning archery person?"

"It's an archer, but uh, I'm pretty sure I mentioned it?" Gideon shrugged.

Shay didn't think so, she absolutely would have remembered it. Maybe she hadn't been paying attention. Or it had slipped through the cracks that were caused by the massive stress splitting her life apart. "Maybe. I don't know. It's awesome."

"That's our plan? Shoot it with…fire arrows?" Emmaline's eyebrows rose.

Shay shrugged. Out loud, it did sound stupid, but she wasn't willing to admit that. "Works in video games."

"The need to point out this plan is bad is overshadowed by my need to see fire arrows," Max said.

Emmaline sighed. "I bet on the wrong horse."

"We don't talk about horses," Shay said. She almost added that Gideon was afraid of them, but it was more of a joke than anything, and she didn't think Emmaline deserved to be in on it.

"It's hard to make a plan when we don't know what we're up against," Taylor admitted. "But I think having weapons is a good idea. Maybe not fire, but dipping the arrowheads in salt…?"

"And moon water," Max said. "We have tons in the cupboard. We'll need candles, salt, moon water…protections for everyone, of course."

"Our best course of action is to harm and distract," Emmaline said. "If we can get Shay in close enough, I think she can land the killing blow."

"It didn't work last time," Shay said.

"That's because the little coward has been hiding in a shell," Emmaline reminded her. "But that shell won't be able to contain the full might of a demon. You have a better chance than you think. The most important thing, of course, is to get my heart away from her. Without that, she can't control any ghosts. It will be miles easier to just face her rather than an entire entourage."

"I'm with her," Max said. "Every step of the way. And I'm not arguing about it."

"I had no plans to argue," Shay said.

"Our biggest problem, of course, is Finnias," Emmaline said. "Even tied to Shay, he's still a ghost without a vessel. We either need to let him possess someone or face the very real possibility that we need to sever his bond with Shay."

"No," Shay said, quickly, trying to shove away the fear that stabbed into her chest and filled every vein with lightning speed.

"I care about him just as much as you—"

"I doubt that," Shay practically snarled. She had wanted to punch Emmaline several times over the course of the night, but in that moment, she wanted to yank her out of Duncan and find out if she could throttle a ghost, anger hot on the heels of fear. "If you can even suggest—"

"I don't want to suggest it," Emmaline snapped. "But the point is, he is a liability. He will ruin any element of surprise we have, and he will get us killed."

"You're already dead," Shay snapped back.

Emmaline looked at her like she wanted to kill her, but a moment later her face smoothed over. "I am. But you aren't. And you're our best bet."

"Maybe, we don't know—"

"Not against this," Emmaline said. "Against everything that's coming."

"I don't care," Shay said.

"I care," Max said, and she stared at them. "I don't mean it like that, Shay, I just…we need to figure something out. Maybe a mirror?"

"Can we do that?" Shay asked.

"We can at least try," Max said. "We'll exhaust all of our options before we…do anything drastic. And permanent. I promise."

"Oh my god, you're all so dramatic, he can possess me," Taylor said.

"…Are you sure?" Max asked.

"Better than us all getting killed or having to listen to Emmaline throwing her brother under the bus," Taylor said. "Besides, he seems nicer than her. Duncan's never…well, he's complained, he loves to do that, but only a little."

"That's fair," Gideon said. He seemed to remember Duncan was still in the car and quickly added: "but he doesn't really complain that much."

"Liar," Shay said. "I'll talk to Finn when we get to the house."

They pulled up in front of the shop. The street was empty, dark, and deserted. They all stepped out of the car into the cold night air. Shay pulled her hat back on.

The shop usually had a few lights on, the salt lamps in the window glowing a dim orange, but it was completely dark.

"Do you want me to take a look?" Finnias asked.

"Mm, better stay here," Emmaline said. A shimmer in the air swirled the snow around her. "Oh, hello, darling! You've been keeping an eye on the house, haven't you, pet?"

Whispers that Shay couldn't quite make out filled the air around Emmaline, a hiss like a tea kettle coming up to temperature. Max stepped between her and Emmaline, almost like it was a reflex, and Shay grabbed the back of their coat.

The poltergeist had tried to kill her, more than once. She didn't want to see it, definitely didn't want to hear it.

"She says that no one has been here but an old man in a van," Emmaline said. "That…ghost hunter."

"Vic?" Shay hadn't even thought of Vic in a while. "Why was he at our house?"

"Apparently he comes by quite often, usually when no one else is home or awake," Emmaline said.

Shay shivered.

"Why would Vic come here?" Taylor asked.

"Well…it's, y'know, it's haunted," Gideon said. "The house. Shay. The whole Finnias thing. He got a lot of views on that video in the library, and he hasn't tried calling the gang back together…"

"I'll see if Sam and Meri have heard from him," Taylor said.

"I don't believe it's important right now," Emmaline said. "The house seems to be intact."

"Makes sense, Arlo and Jo were out of the house when he…" Max trailed off. "Yeah. Um. I'll do a quick perimeter check."

"I'll come," Shay volunteered. She didn't want to be around the poltergeist anymore. It made her feel sick, made the spot on her chest where it had sliced her open hurt, made her bones ache from where it had tossed her around the room.

They walked around to the back of the house.

"Looks fine from here," Max said. "I'll go in. Alone."

"What?" Shay stared at them. "No?"

"I can go in," Finnias offered.

"No." Shay shook her head. "You're safer out here, and you can't even go in without me…"

"I have the sigil and I don't have ghost touch, if anything is in there, I can clear it out," Max said. "You um…well."

"I can literally punch ghosts."

"I know," Max said, quickly. "I very much know that."

She knew she was being unreasonable, but she felt like she was going to crack. "Not alone, okay? Let's…let's go get someone—"

"I mean, I followed you back here, you might as well let me go," Gideon said, right behind her. She shrieked loud enough to wake the dead, or at least startle Finnias, and practically leaped into Max who grabbed her shoulders to steady her.

She placed a hand to her chest. Her heart beat so fast it hurt. "Oh my god. You just gave me a heart attack. I'm literally dying. We don't even have a hospital, Gideon, what are you thinking."

"I thought you heard me say I was coming with you," Gideon said. "When I talk does it just kind of sound like 'blah blah blah'?"

"No," Shay said. "I…I'm really on edge, and…and I have ADHD, and…"

"Sorry, I was trying to lighten the mood." Gideon held up his hands. "But it wasn't funny. I'll go in with Max. Is that…better?"

"Um. Yes." Shay realized they didn't really have time to argue. "Oh my god, did you leave Taylor alone with Emmaline?"

"…You better run around back to the front, yeah," Gideon said. "I'd like Duncan back unharmed, if possible."

"On it." Shay nodded. "C'mon, Finn. You're going to possess Taylor."

"I beg your pardon?" He still followed her back to the front of the house, where luckily Emmaline and Taylor were pretending that the other didn't exist, Taylor absorbed in her phone screen and Emmaline staring up at the house.

"Is it good?" Taylor asked.

"Max and Gid are getting things," Shay said.

"Get this, Vic did call Sam in," Taylor said. "He called Meri, too, but not me or Gideon. Meri told him to stuff it, at least, but she knew about Sam…That's weird, right?"

"A little, yeah." Shay was so far away from being worried about Vic that he could have been floating in the atmosphere somewhere for all she cared. He was probably after another viral video, starring her, with a black box badly edited over her face. Shay really hoped no one she knew had seen the first one from the library. Not that she had many friends outside of Max and what Duncan affectionately referred to as the boo crew. "Were you serious? About…about Finnias?"

"What other choice do we have?" Taylor shrugged. She looked more resigned than anything, but the light from her phone screen made her face strange, like she was already possessed. "Yeah, I mean, I guess that's really our only option, since we don't know what breaking the bond would do, and we don't know how, and it sounds like a terrible idea."

"I have the sword, it would make it clean," Emmaline said. "I had a plan, you know."

"I don't trust you," Shay reminded her. "You already used him once. I'm not letting it happen again."

Finnias stood close to her. "I can't…argue with your logic, I suppose. If Taylor is willing, then that might be our best course of action, but I won't be able to stay with you as easily, and if I can't protect you—"

"I'll be okay," Shay said. "Let me protect you this time, okay?"

"I…" He sighed, and to her surprise dropped his forehead onto her shoulder. "You are…you are really something, are you aware of that?"

"I get that a lot," Shay admitted, patting his back, not sure what else to do. "That I'm too much."

"Not too much," Finnias murmured. "Just enough. Be careful, and if we get separated…"

"Stay with Max?"

"Yes, please do." Finnias straightened and looked her in the eye. In life he'd had gray eyes, as a ghost they looked like newly minted coins, glowing brightly. Whatever he needed to see, he must have, because he took a step towards Taylor and disappeared.

Chapter 29: Procession

Shay paced up and down the sidewalk, glancing up at the house, trying to press her anxiety into a manageable shape.

Her foot hit a patch of snow and she slid. Finnias grabbed her before she could end up flat on her back. "Maybe you should go sit in the car."

"I can't sit," Shay said. "If I sit I'll explode."

"Really?" Finnias raised an eyebrow. At least Taylor was nearly the same height as him, it wasn't completely weird. "Explode?"

"Yes. Boom. Shay bits all over."

"That sounds messy."

"Little bit, yeah. Um. How's Taylor?"

Shay had expected Taylor would take the driver's seat, leaving Finnias as a helpless passenger like she had been for months, but so far that hadn't been the case.

"She wanted to make sure I was used to possessing her, rather than Duncan," Finnias said. "It is…different."

"Will it be okay?" She wasn't sure why she was asking, it wasn't like they had any other options. Taylor would not let Emmaline possess her, and Finnias couldn't just be floating free.

"I'll be fine," Finnias said. "I'm more worried about you."

"Don't be," she said. "Just keep Taylor safe."

"Shay—"

"I'm serious," Shay said. "This is…well, okay, it sucks. And I guess I was born to do this kind of thing. Which…also sucks. In fact, there are only about two whole things about this that don't completely suck."

Finnias smiled, slightly. It was softer and more obvious on Taylor's face than it ever was on his own. "Two whole things?"

"Well, yeah," Shay said. "Max got to be proven right, and that makes them really happy, even though they've barely gloated which is honestly so big of them."

Finnias rolled his eyes. "And the other?"

"Obviously it's meeting you." Shay's face felt warm, despite the cold. "I mean, I was trying to think of how my life would be if I hadn't had these abilities, or the seal hadn't failed, and…didn't really like it. Sure, all of this sucks but…"

But she'd met people who really cared about her because of it, she was closer to Max than ever, and she had Finnias.

"Oh." Finnias blinked, like he didn't really know how to respond.

"Yeah, sorry, that's too cheesy," Shay admitted.

"Very," Emmaline agreed from the porch and Shay's face went super nova. She hadn't realized that Emmaline could hear her. "But oddly very sweet, in a disgusting sort of way."

"No one asked you," Finnias said, loudly. He spoke more quietly to Shay. "I'm very happy I met you, too."

"Aww." She tried to shove away the mortification. She didn't care what Emmaline thought, not really, so it didn't matter.

"Gross," Emmaline said.

"Shut it, sword weirdo," Shay said.

"You'll be happy I have this in hand." Emmaline held up the sword. It seemed darker than even the deepest shadows.

A cold wind rushed past her, and the poltergeist coiled around Emmaline.

"What is it, darling?" She reached up to brush one hand against it. The low hissing started up again. "Something's coming, up the street. A procession. We should probably go inside."

"Right, okay." Shay hurried up the steps, Finnias right behind her. She unlocked the front door of the shop and let everyone inside, bringing up the rear to close the door behind her, peering through the glass onto the street.

Without the familiar streetlamps or Christmas lights it was nearly pitch black outside, only the snow reflecting the violet of the sky made anything visible.

Until the fog rolled in.

It poured down the street like a river, churning and billowing, glowing ethereal blue.

The shapes followed. Ghosts, in shades of blue, pale whites, and some of them like cut out shadows, all moving down the street like a parade. It reminded her of when Emmaline had pulled the ghosts downtown, but they were going in a different direction.

"Where are they going?" Shay whispered.

"To their new master," Emmaline said. "Delores…that demon is calling them."

"Are you mad she's taking plays from your book or…?"

"Shut up," Emmaline muttered. "Mine was much more dramatic."

The procession continued down the road, ghosts of all types mingling together. Shay thought one glanced her way and she stepped back from the door.

"What are you guys doing in here?" Max asked, quietly, from right behind her. She jumped, spinning around. They had a flashlight in their hand, and she hadn't even noticed they were there.

"Bit of a snarl with our plan," Emmaline said. "She's calling every ghost to the area. It's like, well…"

"You?" Max asked.

"Mm, yeah, like me, all over again." Emmaline shrugged. "Only I was much classier, obviously."

"Sure," Shay said. "It's like the…the night parade. The one in Japanese folklore with all the demons."

She'd been attempting to read up on ghosts in different cultures. Even asked her stepdad for help. He was a folklore professor at a university in Oregon. He'd sent her a few things and promised to get her some books for Christmas, but she hadn't been able to find anything about necromancers or ghosts the way she saw them.

Maybe necromancers were just really bad at writing things down.

Or it was dangerous, like it must have been for Robert Lichfield. His book on supernatural abilities had been so convoluted it was impossible to read, and he'd told her himself it had been a mistake.

"Normally, that would be fascinating," Max said. "Right now…not great. How do we get to the mall now?"

"Good point," Emmaline said, just as something pale slithered right over Gideon's car.

"We'll have to take a car from the back," Shay said. "One of the cars has to be there, right? It can't be like this on every street."

"You'd be surprised," Emmaline said. "I lured a lot of ghosts here."

"Unsurprising that this is all your fault, in the end," Finnias muttered.

"We all make mistakes," Emmaline said. "Or just…actions that were a good idea at the time but had unforeseen consequences. There's no point in arguing right now. Let's gather what we need and head to the back, we might get lucky."

"I don't like how you say that," Finnias said.

"With our stunning array of looks, personalities, and can-do attitude, we're sure to find a way," Emmaline imitated Duncan's inflections.

"You suck," Shay told her.

"You suck worse," a soft voice said in her ear, the poltergeist brushing past her and knocking a few things off of one of the display tables.

She shivered and stepped close to Max. "Hey uh…Delores…the demon thing…it can't control your poltergeist, right?"

"Of course not, don't be an idiot," Emmaline said. "It doesn't work like that."

"Yeah, okay, in my defense, all I know about poltergeists is the movie that Max wouldn't watch," Shay said.

"And it's German for 'noisy ghost'," Max offered, helpfully.

"They make pretty terrible company, too," Finnias offered.

In response one of the circular display racks began spinning. A few postcards flew out of their wire holders, scattering across the floor.

"You're all so rude," Emmaline said. "I ought to—"

The door rattled, loudly. Shay squeaked and stepped behind Max. The windows vibrated, the glass humming.

"I think we should probably go," Emmaline said. One of the windowpanes cracked. Shay really hoped it wasn't one of the "original to the house" windows.

They hurried into the kitchen, where Gideon was putting jars into a bag. "Hey, what's—"

"We're going out the back," Shay explained, quickly. "Ghosts out front. Lots of them."

"My archery stuff is out there," Gideon reminded her.

"Crap, I forgot about that." Shay rubbed her temple. "Um. I don't know."

She didn't want to take the time to go to Gideon's house, it was in the opposite direction. At least, she was fairly certain it was.

"It's okay, I'm pretty good at throwing, and we have no idea if it would have worked, anyway," Gideon said. "Next time?"

"...I hate that there probably will be a next time, but yeah, fire arrows will have to live another day," Shay agreed. "Okay, to the back, hopefully—"

Something slammed into the back door. Max held up a candle, the wick catching with a burst of light accompanied by the clear ring of a bell. The door stopped moving and the house stopped rattling.

"Holy crap," Shay said.

"That won't keep them away for long," Max said. "Honestly, I probably drew more attention, not less. If we're getting to a car, we need to go right now."

"On it." Gideon shouldered his bag.

They grabbed the keys from the hook next to the door and ran out into the backyard. The shoveled path to the garage had filled in with no one around to maintain it, just a slight impression in the snow. Shay stumbled through it, trying to keep her feet and look for ghosts at the same time. The garage had never felt so far away before.

Max's car was out back. They climbed in, slamming the door shut behind them. The engine took a few tries to catch, but it roared to life after a moment.

Something grabbed Shay's arm.

A face loomed out of the darkness. A white mask covered in cracks that oozed wispy shadows. Shay screamed and shook it off, grabbing the door handle. She opened the door only to immediately have it slammed in her face, more ghosts closing in on her.

Emmaline sliced through one and it howled, loud enough to rattle the tree branches above them, retreating into the mist that was leaking over the ground.

"And you called me weird for this," Emmaline muttered.

"Thank you for being weird." Shay yanked the door open and scrambled into the back seat, Emmaline right behind her and Finnias bringing up the rear. Gideon threw himself into the passenger's seat. Max pulled out of the space and peeled out into the alley.

"Wait, did we ever figure out what happens if we hit a ghost if Shay's in the car?" Gideon asked.

Something grabbed her hip, icy fingers digging into the bone. She shrieked. Finnias flung salt at her, and the ghost vanished. She put a hand where it had touched her, felt the cold radiating out from her hip.

"Ow," she gasped out.

"Are you okay?" Max glanced back.

"Just…just a shock," she said. The pain was already receding. "Didn't burst my appendix."

"That's your left side," Emmaline said. "Your appendix is on the right."

"Clearly I don't know anything about anatomy." Shay didn't see any ghosts ahead of them, at least for the moment. "What matters is I'm fine."

"Okay, I believe you," Max said. "Let me know if it gets worse. We'll head to the urgent care in Doveton, if we have to."

"Okay." Shay rubbed the spot. It was still cold, but she was pretty sure there was no permanent damage. Finnias looked like he wanted to reach over Emmaline, but refrained.

"If she drained the energy out of everything, how did your car start?" Gideon changed the subject after a few moments of silence.

"Easy," Max said. "I put the sigil on my car, right above the battery."

"Oh," Gideon said. "That's smart."

"I can get us to the mall, but after that I don't think we have much of a plan," Max said. "This is a lot of ghosts, it's worse than when…well, present company caused the first mess."

"We're stronger now," Shay reminded them. "I mean, you're awesome now, and we have Finnias and…Emmaline, I guess."

"Well, see if I save your life next time," Emmaline said.

In truth, Shay didn't feel like she had anything in hand at all. There were so many ghosts, and the only thing waiting at the end of it was a demon that she was still unsure she'd be able to do any damage to, even if she could get close enough to punch it, but with how the evening was going she doubted she'd get the chance.

"You're right," Finnias said. "Do you remember what I told you, back when we first met?"

"I'm not like other ghosts," Shay imitated him, poorly. "I'm much more aware."

Max had the decency to snort.

Finnias sighed and closed his eyes. "The other thing I told you."

"Don't worry, I know," Shay said. "I can do anything."

CHAPTER 30:
MORE CRIMES

They drove through alleyways for as long as they could, but it was only a few blocks before Max was forced to turn onto a street.

Shay didn't see any ghosts. "Clear. I think."

But the street was lined with glowing mist. When she looked up bright white lines stretched across the houses.

"Can anyone else see that?" she asked.

Gideon leaned over and looked up. "What are those lines?"

"The demon is claiming your town as its domain," Emmaline explained.

"Are you telling me that's a giant spiderweb?" Gideon cringed back from the window.

"Yes," Emmaline said. "I don't mean to alarm you, but if a normal person can see it, then we are getting dangerously close to the entire town slipping through the veil. I have a feeling you don't want that."

"Not so much." Max urged the old SUV to greater speeds. The roar of the engine echoed off of empty houses.

"She can't have taken everyone to the mall, that's a lot of people," Shay said. "They wouldn't all fit. I think. How big is Teton Falls again?"

"Twenty-thousand people," Max and Gideon answered at the same time.

"She must have taken some, but I very much doubt it was the entire town," Finnias said.

"She drew anyone with any sort of ability towards her," Emmaline said. "Whether it's a bit of the sight or just the potential for a witch."

"What about everyone else?" Gideon asked.

Emmaline shrugged. "How should I know? This is all just speculation, I have no concrete answers for you."

"This is a guess, but I think they're probably trapped in their nightmares," Finnias said, quietly.

"That sounds right to me," Max said. "What if this is a nightmare? What if the sigils didn't work after all?"

"You really think we're having the same nightmare?" Gideon asked.

"Duncan and I did," Shay said. "So…yeah, it's possible."

"Right." Gideon sighed. "Okay. Great. So we could be wandering around a nightmare realm."

"I doubt it, I would know if I was dreaming," Emmaline said.

"Are you lying?" Shay asked.

"Of course not."

Gideon slapped Max's shoulder. "Wait, pull into this parking lot!"

They were passing a strip mall, as far as Shay could see, headlights flashing off of glass store fronts.

"Okay?" Max did as Gideon told them. "Why are we…"

"Sporting goods store," Gideon pointed straight ahead to a white building with green letters that read "Cutting Edge Sports".

"Didn't you work for a cutting-edge company?" Shay asked. "What's with this town and the sharp side of a knife?"

"I'm sure Duncan would have a cutting remark about it," Gideon said. "C'mon, if we're going to do this, we should be armed."

Shay couldn't argue with that.

"What sort of weapons can you possibly find at a sporting goods store?" Emmaline sneered.

"Well, I can probably find a bow," Gideon said. "I'm not really a gun person…"

"No guns," Shay said. "They're loud and scare me."

Gideon nodded. "Fair enough."

"There should be bats at least," Max said. "It's better than nothing."

"Taylor used to play softball. She probably has a mean arm." Shay nudged Finnias, slightly.

"I suppose it wouldn't hurt," Finnias agreed.

Emmaline sighed like she thought they were complete idiots, but followed them up to the store, anyway. The glass doors were automatic, but without electricity, no amount of them standing on the pressure plate would get them to open. Max and Gideon tried to pry them open, but their straining and heaving amounted to nothing.

"Well, that was a bust, sorry guys," Gideon said.

"I have an idea," Shay said. "Clear the door, please."

"Why?" Gideon stepped back, even as he asked. "What do you—"

Shay took one of the external displays and threw it through the door.

It shattered magnificently, shards of glass scattering across the linoleum inside like beads.

"Oh my god!" Max looked like they didn't quite know what to do with their hands and ended up doing a weird little dance. "Shay! You can't just...you can't just do that!"

"That was awesome!" She probably should have felt bad about it, but it wasn't like there was anyone around to realize it was her, and they needed supplies. "Want me to do the other windows?"

"No!" Gideon and Max yelled at the same time.

"Fine, fine, be that way." Shay ducked through the door's metal frame and into the store. Despite their protests, Max was quick to follow her, turning on a flashlight.

"I can't believe you did that," they said.

"You can finally add breaking and entering to my list of crimes," Shay said. "And actual shoplifting. Smash and grab."

"Oh my god."

"I'm trying to fight a demon," she reminded them. "I get to break a few windows. It's a rule. Probably."

"She's right," Gideon said. "For every demon you have to fight, you get to smash one window."

"That's...fine, sure, that's the rule," Max said. Their flashlight roamed over the front of the store and jerked the light away when it landed on someone.

They were curled up on the floor next to one of the registers. Gideon pulled out his own light and they found a few other people. Most of them lay on the floor, a few had made it into the display camping chairs. None of them flinched when the light roamed over them.

"They're asleep," Emmaline said.

"Should we try to wake them up?" Gideon asked.

"No," Emmaline said. "Not only would it probably be nearly impossible, but they would also not exactly be helpful. Hysterical dead weight, at best."

"I'm sure they'd be more useful than you," Finnias said.

"Oh, well, I suppose I could possess one of them, but since they're just a normal person, I'd probably at the very least cause some very long-lasting trauma." Emmaline shrugged. "But hey, yeah, let's waste a bunch of time waking up random civilians, that's sure to help us."

Shay really wanted to retort with something mean and cutting, mostly about Emmaline herself being a long-lasting trauma, but decided it wasn't worth the effort.

"It's probably safer for them to stay here and asleep," Gideon reasoned. Shay wasn't sure if that was true, but she didn't have any evidence to the contrary.

"The best thing we can do for them is move quickly, defeating the demon will save everyone," Finnias said.

"Yeah, okay," Shay said. It sounded better than just abandoning them.

"All right, then. I'll go to the bows. You guys gather anything you think we might need. Some of the lanterns and flashlights might still work, and it probably wouldn't hurt to have uh…better gloves."

Shay looked at her mittens. "Okay, yeah, point taken."

Emmaline went with Gideon, Finnias followed Shay and Max to the camping gear.

It didn't take long to find much nicer gloves and Shay shoved her mittens in her pocket and pulled them on. She tried to ignore the price tag. She did not want to feel guilty. They had to step over someone to reach the flashlights.

She hoped the sleepers were okay, but she had no idea. The demon created nightmares, they were probably stuck in their own personal hells, but there wasn't much she could do. When Delores put Max to sleep, she hadn't been able to wake them up, and Duncan was out of commission.

"Holding up okay?" Max asked, quietly.

"Just…a lot of pressure," she admitted. "A lot of people counting on me. Even if they don't know it. I'm just really glad you're here."

"Of course," Max said.

"You, too, Finn."

"Don't patronize me," he said, and it made her laugh. "We'll get through this. I have utmost faith in you."

She just wished she had faith in herself.

"By the away, it's uh, nice to talk to you again, Finnias," Max said.

"I suppose," Finnias said. "Though the ah. Circumstances could be better."

"Usually, yeah," Shay said.

They raided the snap lights and flashlights, though most of the batteries were already drained. Max and Finnias each grabbed a bat and they met Gideon at the front of the store. He was holding a compound bow and several quivers of arrows.

"I'll get these covered in salt," he said. "We ready to go?"

"As ready as we'll ever be." Shay attempted to ignore the ever-growing pit in her stomach. "I hope…I hope Jo's okay. That everyone's okay."

"I'm sure she is," Max said. "We'll get her out of there, Shay, I promise."

"…Yeah." She really hoped she wasn't walking right into a trap, but she probably was. She was literally heading towards the center of a spider's web.

They prepped the arrows and the bats before they started driving again. The sky was a strange haze of green and purple above them, too bright for the hour.

The lines became more plentiful and the mist brighter the closer they got to the mall. Shay saw a few ghosts, but mostly on side streets or glowing behind shop windows. They turned a corner and things changed drastically.

Instead of streetlights, lanterns lined the streets, flames glowing blue. The buildings were shrouded in webbing. Shay fully expected an enormous spider to crawl over them, but it was completely still.

"This doesn't look like Teton Falls," Max said.

"Because it's not," Emmaline said. "We've officially crossed into her domain. Things might get…tricky."

"Sticky?" Shay asked.

"If you must."

"What do you mean—" Max had to slam on the brakes. An enormous spiderweb stretched across the street. "…Ah. That's…that's what you mean. Okay. Yup. This is fine. I love big spiderwebs. They're actually my favorite. Very Halloween aesthetic. In November. So. Who wants to turn around…?"

Shay opened her door and stepped out. The street had transformed into smooth cobblestones. It felt strange under the soles of her boots. She doubted that style of paving had ever been in Teton Falls, even back when it had been called Ravenscroft.

Finnias hurried to be at her side.

"Shay! Finnias! Get back in the car!" Max hissed at them.

"We can get through it," Shay said. "On foot. There are a lot of cars up there, I think we're better off walking."

"She's right." Emmaline got out of the car, grabbing her sword from the back. "It won't be long before your car dies, anyway."

As if on cue, the engine spluttered and cut out.

Max sighed and climbed out, Gideon following them. The street looked like it had dropped out of a Victorian novel, and they were all in jeans and modern coats.

"How far out are we?" Shay asked.

"Just a few blocks," Max said. "You really suggested walking when it could have been miles?"

"Would have been a crappy few miles," she admitted. There was a chill in the air, but it wasn't the cold of a winter night. It reminded her of the night in the governor's house, over a month before, when Emmaline pierced the veil. Shay glanced over at her, but she just looked like Duncan. Shay could usually read Duncan, but Emmaline remained a mystery to her. One she wasn't particularly invested in solving.

They started walking, moving carefully between the threads of the enormous spider web. She thought she saw movement, somewhere far above, but she didn't stick around to see what it could have been.

The town morphed the longer they walked. Buildings crowded together, tall and thin, their exteriors different colors of brick, their roofs melting into each other, like they were all jammed together from slightly different times. Some of them still had webbing that fluttered despite the lack of a breeze, as if the whole street was breathing.

She really wished she hadn't had that thought.

Something scurried across the top of her boot, and she stepped back so fast Finnias had to keep her from falling. At first, she thought it was one of the rats, but it was worse.

It was a giant pale spider, bigger than her fist.

"Nope," she said, quietly. No one had talked for so long her own voice sounded strange. "Nope I'm out. Teton Falls is done for. Bye."

"A little late for that," Emmaline whispered.

"I'm with Shay, let's go, town can fall into the void," Max whispered back.

"It's just some big spiders," Gideon said, but his voice trembled slightly, making it very obvious he was just as freaked out as the rest of them. "I had a tarantula as a kid. It was more scared of me than I was of it...all that stuff."

"Maybe be ready to shoot something," Shay said. They walked a little farther and more spiders skittered past her, each of them huge and pale with a mark like a red eye on their back.

"What was the plan again?" Max asked, voice squeaking slightly.

"Big cup," Shay said.

"Destroy her," Emmaline said at the same time.

"Don't die," Gideon added.

"Protect Shay," Finnias said.

Shay nodded. "Not our best plan but get me in close enough that I can...hopefully do something."

She felt sick with anticipation and anxiety, the two warring in her stomach, already heavy with fear.

"Protect Shay I agree with." Max grabbed her hand. "It's just, um, this feels like a trap. A really big, obvious trap."

"What was your first clue, the giant web in the sky?" Emmaline asked. "The fact that she let Jo call Shay before she was taken? Please enlighten me when you realized that this was all a set up and I'll evaluate your intelligence accordingly."

"I'm just saying, we need to be smart about this," Max said. "She's expecting us, but we have no idea what to expect."

"What, are you going to become a master of divination right here and now?" Emmaline's eyebrows rose. "Jo has an entire lineage of clairvoyant witches, and she didn't see this coming."

"I mean, we could probably start with not arguing," Shay pointed out. "Just a thought."

"Guys, shut up," Gideon said, and to Shay's surprise, they listened to him. "I thought I heard something."

They fell silent. If it was a ploy to keep them all from talking, it was definitely working. Shay was already on edge, but she listened carefully.

She didn't hear anything, but she did see something large pass over the buildings, so quickly she couldn't make out what it was.

"We are definitely not alone," she whispered.

CHAPTER 31: TWISTED

Shay kept walking, doing her best to not stare at the spot where the thing had passed. She heard the sound of footsteps behind her and whirled around, just in time to see something slink behind the haphazard buildings on the other side.

"It's fast," she warned.

"Be careful, all of you, Shay won't be the only one vulnerable to ghosts in this place," Emmaline said.

"Now you tell us," Gideon muttered.

"Just keep moving," Finnias said. "That's our best bet. I sent the poltergeist to scout, but she hasn't returned."

Shay wasn't so sure about that, but she didn't have any other ideas. They hurried along, the thing moving on either side of them, almost like it was herding them.

She caught a glimpse of it against a wall, a dark shape against pale stone. It looked too big, with too many limbs, but it was gone before she could make out any details.

"Delores wouldn't meet us out here, right?" she asked, quietly.

"I don't know," Emmaline said.

Shay wasn't quite sure why she thought Emmaline would be helpful. She tried to steel herself, ready to take down a demon right out there in the open, but it felt wrong. She knew, somehow, that the demon was at the center of everything, waiting for her prey to step into her grasp.

They hit a slightly wider part of the street. The way ahead was blocked by thick strands of webbing.

"Watch my back." Emmaline approached it. "This might take me a minute or two."

"How about a second or two," Max suggested.

She gave them a withering look before slicing at the webbing. It didn't give nearly as easily as it had in the circle, resisting the edge of the sword.

"Where is it?" Gideon asked. He had an arrow knocked to his bow, ready to draw it.

"Not sure, keeping an eye out," Shay said. She heard something, like many feet, and jerked her head towards the noise, just in time to see something crawling around the edge of the building. "Over there!"

Gideon nodded, took aim, and shot.

The arrow thudded where the thing had been a moment before, but it was already on the move, crawling quickly to the next building. Gideon drew his bow again, firing off another arrow, and another, but each one missed.

"Aren't you some kind of archery master or…?" Finnias gave him a look.

"This is a lot harder than it looks, and I've never shot with this bow," Gideon reminded him. He sighted and took another shot. The arrow landed right in front of the monster, forcing it to jerk backwards and land on the ground, right at the entrance to the open area. It rose up on four back legs, its four arms spreading wide.

It was a spider.

And a person.

Its eyes like tar pits, too many and arranged haphazardly on a face like glass, reflecting the light from the lanterns. Its thick torso was dark. Limbs that looked like they'd been stitched haphazardly on and the horrible face glowed blue.

It made no move to attack, simply watching them, eyes blinking out of sync.

"Oh, I hate this." Max pulled a salt sachet out of their bag but as they did it the spider jerked forward and they froze, holding it in front of them like a talisman. "I really hate this."

Shay took a step back, raising her fists, but she had no idea if her ability would be useful. The ghost looked manufactured in a way she'd never seen before.

"Please keep it busy," Emmaline said, calmly.

"Cut faster," Finnias snapped back.

The spider, that was all Shay could think of it as, shifted and pulled its arms in, cocking its head to one side.

"Don't provoke it," Max said, their voice thready, still holding the sachet in front of them. "Just…watch it."

Shay nodded, not daring to put her hands down, afraid the moment she did would be when it struck. The dread had a weight like a physical thing, making her too slow for her readiness to make a difference. Gideon had another arrow ready to go, the string relaxed for the moment, and Max had their candle. Finnias had a hold of one of the bats, ready to swing.

Silence, except for the shifting of the spider thing and the soft sounds of Emmaline trying to cut through the webbing behind her.

It struck without any warning.

Gideon shot an arrow, and it dodged it. Before he could nock another arrow, the spider was on top of him, knocking him flat. Max swung the sachet down, but it was knocked from their hands, salt scattering across the stone.

They held up one hand, light forming around them, and the spider grabbed the hood of their coat and tossed them back to the webbing.

She threw a punch, but it twisted around it, grabbing her arm and yanking her close, grabbing both of her wrists and slamming her down onto the street, knocking the breath from her lungs in a choked cry. Pain reverberated up her spine. The face bore down on her, the porcelain shell reflecting her terrified expression.

The face lifted.

It wasn't a face at all, but a mask. The face underneath was horribly blank except for two huge mandibles, wiggling like fingers from a too large mouth.

Shay didn't have the air to scream.

Max yelled something and light flared to life beneath her.

The mask slammed back into place and the spider grabbed her and leaped away, so far and fast that Shay was pretty sure she left her stomach behind on the ground. She was too startled to scream. It landed with a jarring thud a few yards away, the magic flaring uselessly where it had been.

"I swear I ask you to distract it for one minute—"

The spider whirled, thrusting Shay forward like a shield. For a fraction of a second all she could see was Finnias's bat swinging towards her face, but he managed to twist at just the last second, and Shay was thrown bodily into him, knocking them both to to ground. The bat clattering somewhere to the side.

Everything hurt but Shay knew she needed to move, that it was faster than anything she'd ever seen before. She looked up just in time to see it rear up above them and grabbed Finnias, dragging her to the side. A hand came down inches from Finnias's head, cracking the stone. He rolled to his feet and dragged Shay to hers.

Every part of her screamed in protest, but she had to keep moving, had to get away. Hopefully to Max, to a salt circle, though she had no idea if it would even work. Finnias ran for the bat, pulling her along behind him.

Gideon fired another arrow and Shay glanced back just in time to see the monster wrench one of the lanterns out of the ground and deflect the arrow with the pole.

"Oh, crap," Gideon said.

The lantern was thrown like a spear, hitting the general area Gideon had been in, blue flames exploding to life through the webbing.

"Gideon!" Shay couldn't see if he'd been hit, or if he was on fire, though the lack of screaming had to be a good thing.

"Let's go!" Finnias snatched the bat off of the ground and threw it at the spider, hitting it in the side.

It let out a horrible shriek, like bending metal. Finnias was already running forward, scooping up the bat again and slamming it into the thing's back. A salt circle snaked around it. It hit the side of it, little green flames sprouting along its misshapen body. It kept moving, crossing the line.

An arrow hit it from above, followed by another, and another. They drove through it, knocking it down. Shay looked up to see Gideon perched on a balcony, she had no idea how he'd even gotten up there. He shot it again and again, until its entire torso was full of arrows, its limbs writhing above it as it curled in on itself. Its shrill cries grew desperate.

"Let's put you out of your misery, shall we?" Emmaline walked over and sliced the mask in half. The body fell apart, limbs scattering before they turned into mist, fading away into the cracks of the road. "Honestly, it was one ghost, how hard could it be to defeat?"

"We're not exactly in top form," Finnias reminded her. "And there are new rules."

"That hurt," Max agreed. "You deal with this all the time?"

Shay nodded. "Yeah, it's not my favorite part of being me."

"Well, at least the way is clear." Emmaline shrugged. "Come get your arrows, Robin Hood, we aren't there yet."

"Right." Gideon grabbed the drainpipe and slid down the side of the building. Shay and Max helped him gather the arrows that they could before they kept moving.

"Well, that's going to fuel my nightmares for roughly the rest of my life," Max said. "You okay? It slammed you down hard."

"Nothing a few weeks in a comfortable bed won't fix," Shay said. She hoped. It didn't hurt to breath, her back ached. She moved her neck from side to side, but nothing felt off and she didn't hear any grating noises. "I think I'm good. Finnias broke my fall the second time, and he makes Taylor faster, stronger…"

"Yes, well." Finnias held up his bat. It was crumpled on one side. "I might have overdone it."

"Keep a hold of it, anyway," Emmaline told him. "Because we're here."

The mall came into view.

It wasn't a mall anymore.

The parking lot had transformed into a long stretch of paving stones. The mall itself was made of a pale stone in strange shapes, like the skeletons of ancient gods puzzled together. A spire pierced the green and purple sky, sharp and angular, the roofline a series of jutting stones like a spine. The entire building looked strangely organic, and even as she watched it shift slightly, miniscule changes making the shape more alien every passing minute.

Ghosts drifted past, circling the strange new building.

"That…that looks really bad," Shay said. "Worse than the town."

"I'm afraid we have little choice but to go in and face it," Emmaline said. A shimmer of air circled her. "There you are sweetheart. Were you able to get inside? No? That's all right, we'll do it now."

"Interesting that it wasn't there to help us," Finnias muttered.

"Those webs were more than just sticky strings, they're barriers," Emmaline said. "She couldn't get past them to me. So sorry if that was inconvenient to you."

"Let's just focus on getting inside," Gideon suggested.

"That's a lot of ghosts, how are we getting past them?" Max asked.

Finnias sighed. "As…much as it pains me to say this, we need to split up. Clearly, Shay, Max, and Emmaline need to get inside. Gideon and I can create a distraction."

"We can?" Gideon asked.

Shay hated the plan already. "We need everyone in there, and I'm not the only one who's vulnerable now. You can't just…hope that you can get past them without me. And if I can't take down Delores, well, kind of putting your bets on the wrong horse."

"Something I already mentioned," Emmaline muttered.

"I know you can do this." Finnias put his hands on her shoulders. It was weird looking at Taylor's face and getting a pep talk from her ghost friend. "We'll lead them into the streets and come back on the other side, we'll be right behind you, but you need to get in there as soon as you can. The longer this goes on, the less chance there is we can get everyone back."

She sighed. He was right, but she still hated it. "Okay. Fine. I'm not a fan, though. I want everyone to know that."

"You'll need more salt." Max pulled some out of their bag. "If things get dicey, make a salt circle. I can't guarantee it will work, different rules, but it should buy you a little time."

"Thanks, Max," Gideon said. "We'll meet you inside, okay?"

"...Okay," Shay exhaled, slowly, trying to find calm, but she was starting to think she'd never feel calm again. "Stay safe."

CHAPTER 32: JESTER GESTURE

Shay waited until the ghosts moved towards Gideon and Finnias, leading them back into the twisted streets of what used to be a largely vacant part of Teton Falls.

She dashed across the parking lot, Max and Emmaline close behind. Dark vines snaked over the pavement, pulsing like veins, threatening to trip her every few steps.

"This way!" Emmaline pointed with her sword to the side of the building, where Shay could just make out the entrance, framed by vines that Shay suspected weren't plants at all.

The doors were steel and glass, just like they had been before, leading into one of the department stores. Max yanked open the door for the two of them and it slammed close behind them.

Shay stopped for a moment to catch her breath before they entered the second set of doors.

"I'm hating this more and more every second," Max said.

"More than the tunnels?" Shay asked.

"Much more," Max said. "This is the worst place we've ever been."

"And it had so many strong contenders," Shay laughed, still a bit breathless. "You sure know how to show a girl a good time."

"I do my best." Max shone their flashlight into the store. Beyond the glass, it still looked like an empty department store as far as she could see. A tile path led through threadbare carpet into the dark depths of the store. Empty clothing racks cast strange, skeletal shadows, mirrored pillars glinting despite the corrosion slowly taking over their surfaces.

"Good news, I don't think anyone is working at the perfume department anymore," Shay tried to joke, but it fell flat. "Should we wait here? Finnias and Gideon have to be along soon."

"Let's move farther in, it would do us no good to linger in doorways," Emmaline said.

They stepped into the store. Eerie quiet filled every space, the sound of their boots on the tile gratingly loud. They reached where shoes must have been sold, rows of chairs still bolted to the floor.

"We can wait for them here." Emmaline looked back at the entrance, a small rectangle in the dark from where they were sitting.

Shay expected Emmaline to press on regardless. Maybe she had been human, once, after all.

Shay didn't trust the chairs and sat on the floor with her back against the end one. It was dusty, but not nearly as bad as she was expecting. Max set up the little lantern they'd stolen from the sporting goods store, lighting a tea light inside. It cast a flickering circle of yellow light.

"How long should we wait?" Max asked, quietly.

"I don't know," Emmaline admitted. "Stay here. I'm going to go check. Don't move."

She climbed to her feet and walked back towards the entrance. Duncan's frame silhouetted in the doors.

It was the first time she'd been alone with just Max in what felt like forever. "Still good?"

"Huh?" Max looked up. "Oh. Yeah. I…think so."

"Sorry," Shay said. "That was a stupid question. Fighting a giant horrible spider ghost is probably not how you wanted to spend your evening."

"I mean, generally, no, but you don't have to be sorry."

"I think I do." She sighed and curled her knees up to her chest. It wasn't nearly as cold as outside, but the lack of moving had her a little chilly. "I'm…I'm scared. This is huge, and I'm worried about everyone, and I don't really know what to do, but I know it's not just…sitting here, but what else can I do? I don't…I don't know."

"You're doing everything you can." Max took her hand. "I'm with you, okay? And we're going to get through this."

"I just feel like I keep making things worse," she admitted, in a small voice. "Like this is all my fault."

"It's not your fault."

"Kind of my fault you're here," Shay said.

"Since the only other options are being dragged here against my will or being asleep, I think I'd much rather be here with you," Max said. "We already talked about this. I'm here. No matter what. Where else would I be? Some other crappy town with no Shay? Sounds worse."

"I thought you said this was the worse place you'd ever been." Shay managed a smile.

"Oh, it is, but it'd be a million times worse without you," Max insisted. "I'm not leaving you. I promised, and I'm keeping it."

"I know," Shay said. "But talking about it and being attacked by a giant horrible ghost spider are two different things."

"Not to me." Max paused. "Okay, that came out a little weird, talking to you about how big and scary things are isn't like being attacked by spiders."

"You sure?" Shay laughed, somehow.

"I'll have you know I'm excellent at emotional vulnerability," Max said. "I'm an expert, actually. Incredibly skilled."

"Oh, wow, I had no idea I was in the presence of a master." Shay mock bowed. "What can you teach me, oh wise one?"

"Trust your friends, and yourself," Max said, sagely. "…Which is…actually advice I need to take, too. Honestly, I'm not…I get scared."

"Of…the empty creepy department store probably full of ghosts?" Shay asked. "The big spider demon thing? The town being pulled into the void? I mean, yeah, I'm freaked, too."

"Not of that," Max said. "Well, yes, that's terrifying. But um. It's a different thing."

"Yeah?" Shay scooted a little closer. "I mean, whatever it is, you know you can talk to me."

"That's the thing, it's…it's something that's really hard to talk to you about," Max admitted, and nervousness flooded Shay's gut at the thought of talks serious enough to happen in abandoned malls. "Because…because it could change things. Or ruin things. But I know that's just me making excuses because I'm scared."

"Scared of what?" Shay asked, confused.

Max held up their hand. "Um. Just. Just let me talk this out, okay? No commentary?"

She nodded.

"Great, thank you, I know that's hard for you." They let out a long, slow breath. "But…but this is…this is so big. And terrifying. And we keep ending up like this. And if I never say anything, I'll end up regretting it. Even if you already know, and even if…even if nothing changes. It's okay if nothing changes. It's wonderful, even."

Shay blinked at them, absolutely mystified and more than a little worried, but she'd promised not to make any commentary.

"Th-the truth is, um." They took another long breath and released it, shakily. "Sorry. This is. This is a lot for me, and you're probably going to laugh at me, and that's okay, just…"

"They aren't back yet." Emmaline walked into the circle of light.

Max looked like they might scream.

"Go watch for a few more minutes," Shay told her. "It hasn't been very long, and I'm worried—"

"No," Emmaline said. "I'm worried, too, but we can't let that stop us. I left them a message. They can find us. Grab your lantern, we need to get moving. If we wait much longer, we don't know what kind of problems could arise."

Shay mouthed "later" at Max and climbed to her feet. Her legs were stiff and her back hurt, but she knew Emmaline had the right idea. Unfortunately.

Max scooped up the lantern. Shay held out her hand and they took it. She couldn't feel their hand through their gloves, but she imagined their fingers were icy with anxiety. She gave their hand a squeeze and hoped it was reassuring.

The poltergeist flowed ahead of them, static like an old radio emanating off of it. They stayed on the tile path, the light from their lantern barely illuminating the carpet on either side of them. Shay had the impression of things just outside her field of vision, dark and twisted, but she didn't dare lift the lantern to confirm. Emmaline kept the flashlight trained on the floor just ahead of her.

She kept turning to the side, to ask Finnias something, to check on him, but of course, he wasn't there. It left her hollow.

Emmaline stopped. The light glittered on a massive web draped across two different perfume stalls. Shay was slightly afraid a giant spider was going to leap out of nowhere and spray some fragrance with a five in its number that smelled like scented alcohol in her face.

Nothing happened.

"Let's take a break before we find a way around," Emmaline said. "I'm going to send the poltergeist back to check on the others."

The mass drifted past Shay, tugging off her hat with a whispered "you're stupid" and a terrible little giggle. She sighed and picked up the hat, stowing it in Max's bag when they offered.

"Can't believe I got smacked around by a big spider ghost while wearing the world's largest pompom," she said. "That thing has its own zip code."

"To be fair, you fought a bunch of ghosts in a library wearing cat ears," Max reminded her. "And I had a cowboy hat."

"Guess I'd better pick out my next silly hat to get traumatized in. Maybe a jester hat with bells. Just jingle sadly into it all. And you can wear a crown." She gave a bow. "My liege, what silly jokes would thou likest to hear today?"

Max chuckled. "Why, my dear jester, as long as it's not a pun, any joke will suffice."

She gasped. "Surely you jest."

"I said take a break, not…whatever this is." Emmaline waved a hand to indicate the space between them. "You do understand the situation we're in, right?"

"Of course I do." Shay did feel bad for making terrible jokes when Finnias and Gideon were probably cornered by ghosts and Jo was still missing. She didn't know how else to cope. If she didn't say anything, if she bottled it all up inside, she was sure she'd crack.

Max nodded. "I'm just trying to keep myself from curling up into a ball and crying, honestly."

"Let's just find a way around," Emmaline turned away from the web and froze. "…Don't move."

Shay froze. She felt something move behind her, something cold, a breeze chilling the back of her neck.

Emmaline stabbed forward, so close Shay heard the blade whistle past her ear. The thing behind her let out an abrupt and high pitched scream and fell silent.

"Spider, big one," Emmaline explained. "I don't think we can wait anymore, we need to keep moving or that's going to get worse."

She'd gotten so used to Finnias watching her back, she hadn't bothered to even look around. "Yeah. Okay. Let's go."

There was no sign of the spider when she turned. She breathed in and out slowly, trying to calm down.

"Next time maybe use your words," Max said. "I was about to knock you out of Duncan."

"Please, if I was going to stab her, I would have done it hours ago," Emmaline said. "You're both annoying, but you're not that annoying."

"Thanks?" Shay wasn't sure if that was actually a compliment or not.

They wove their way around empty booths through the middle of the store. Shay thought it was much bigger than it should have been, but she knew the tile paths probably took them on a meandering route rather than straight through.

Cobwebs draped over the empty booth like sheets and more dripped from the ceiling. Shay saw movement in them and focused on the floor, trying to get through without touching any of the webs.

A pain started in her chest. She frowned and rubbed the spot, afraid for a moment that internal bleeding had started, but it didn't match the aches she already had. It felt more like a tug forward.

Something brushed past her. She bit back a scream, but it was only the poltergeist returning to its master.

"They've been captured." Emmaline's voice cracked. "Finnias was yanked out of Taylor and they...they're okay. They're alive, well...the living people are still alive, but..."

"Oh." Shay put a hand to where her chest hurt. "That's why...I can feel him."

"You can?" Max gave her a look she couldn't read.

"I was wondering...He's that way. He's far, but not too far, I think."

"Then let's go," Emmaline said. "We can't waste any more time."

"Shouldn't we form a plan or something?" Max asked. "I mean, it's just the three of us, no backup, I'm just finding out Shay has Finnias radar, what..."

"I am not waiting," Emmaline said.

"But—"

"I don't care," she said, seriously. "I would do anything for Finnias. I would kill for him. I have killed for him. Shay understands."

"Yeah." Shay understood all too well. She wanted to save Finnias, too, and if she had to murder someone to save Duncan, she had to admit that she wouldn't even hesitate.

"How about we stop bonding over murder for siblings?" Max suggested.

"Shut up, only child," Shay said. She meant for it to be a little playful, but it probably came out too snappish.

"Sorry. I'm…I'm freaking out. I'm definitely freaking out."

Max put an arm around her shoulders, and she found herself melting into their touch, just like always. "Hey, I get it, I do. I have a few people I'd murder for. I think just maybe we shouldn't be finding common ground with the homicidal ghost."

"Homicidal ghost with a sword," Emmaline said. "Probably shouldn't upset me."

"I'll take my chances," Max said.

"Me, too, because what I meant was if you hurt my brother, I will not rest until you are nothing but a curl of mist on the ground," Shay told Emmaline.

"And I wouldn't blame you at all."

They got through the booths. On the other side the department store was much worse, old mannequins dressed in cobwebs. A large spider made one of the old clothing racks spin with a horrible, long creak. A thin mist coated the ground.

They reached the store's exit.

CHAPTER 33: MALL RATS

The corridor stretched before Shay like a long, dark throat.

"Finally, our guide shows up," Emmaline said.

Shay was about to ask what she meant when she saw the glowing eyes. A shape slightly less dark than the surroundings moved. Its bones glowed with a gentle light. Its eyes gleamed like the lantern.

"Oh, it's just Beans," Shay said.

Emmaline gave her such a venomous look Shay was a little worried that she was in actual danger of being stabbed. "You named the guardian spirit Beans?"

"Yes? So?"

"Change it."

"No," she said. "Beans likes it."

She had no idea if the guardian even acknowledged that she had given it a name. It stood up and started down the corridor.

"I think it's cute," Max said. At least they were usually on her side.

"Of course you do. Fine, whatever, let's just follow it," Emmaline muttered, walking in front of them. "If it decides to bite your head off later, that's not my problem."

"It's not that bad, is it?" Shay asked Max, quietly.

"It's terrible, but very you, so it's fine," Max said.

"Wow, thanks. What were you trying to tell me earlier?" It had been at the back of her mind that Emmaline had interrupted Max at some crucial moment, but she wasn't sure how to bring it up. Changing the subject because Max said she had terrible taste seemed like as good of a way as any.

"Oh, uh." Max looked forward to where Emmaline stomped a few feet ahead of them. "Maybe when we don't have an audience?"

"What? It's just Emmaline and probably also Duncan," Shay said, trying to keep her tone light and teasing, but she still felt like she'd swallowed something hot and sparking. "If he's aware. I'm not sure, actually. Anyway, you can say anything in front of either of them, probably."

"I really, really can't. I'll die," Max said.

"Sounds serious," Shay said, trying to ignore the weird things her stomach was trying to do, like crawling out of her mouth. "Is it about murder?"

"What?" They laughed in a startled sort of way. "No. Why would you think that?"

"I don't know, maybe you wanted my help with a body, which of course you have it," Shay said. "But if they're haunting their body, I sadly cannot assist you."

"I haven't murdered anyone," Max said.

"Good, you're too pretty for jail."

"I really am."

The poltergeist blew past her again like a blast of warm wind. "You're so stupid."

"Oh, yeah, probably."

"What?" Max looked at her.

"Nothing," she said. She didn't really want to get into the poltergeist telling her she was an idiot twice in less than half an hour.

At least, she thought that was how long it had been. Time seemed condensed and stretched out at the same time, moving in strange bursts. She checked her phone but the screen stayed black. The battery must have been dead for ages.

She didn't think it would matter. They weren't really in Teton Falls at the moment. Time probably moved differently, like it had when she'd been pulled into the void. "I don't think we're in Kansas anymore."

"As long as I'm not Toto."

"Clearly the dog is Toto," Emmaline said, and Shay was slightly mortified that she'd once again overheard a private conversation. "And Shay's the scarecrow. If she only had a brain."

"Okay, tinman, maybe chill out."

"I don't want to be the cowardly lion," Max muttered. "Let's find a new metaphor. This one sucks."

"You're Dorothy, obviously," Shay said. "Click your heels and get us out of here."

"I don't think that will work. These are pretty much the opposite of ruby slippers." Max gestured to their heavy-duty boots.

"Maybe with that attitude."

"Why do you know about the Wizard of Oz, anyway?" Max asked. "And…everything else."

"The same way Finnias knows things." Emmaline sighed. "We share thoughts and memories with whoever we possess."

Shay remembered putting it a lot less tactfully when Finnias had discussed it with her. "Well, that sounds like an invasion of privacy. Sucks to be Duncan. And Taylor."

"Oh, he's fine. I do suggest we keep a little quieter from now on."

The corridor changed as they walked, from brown tile and metal wrapped store fronts to dark stone floors and white walls in the same interlocking pattern as the ones outside, studded with black doors. Shay heard whispering behind them but didn't dare open any of them up.

The pain in her chest slowly eased up. At least they were heading in the right direction, through twists and turns, going a different way every time the hallway split.

Shay was absolutely certain that the mall was not big enough to accommodate the corridor.

They walked past the atrium, with its skylights and a fountain that was much more ornate than the one she'd pushed someone into, years ago. It had a statue of three women. She realized a moment later that the women all shared a torso. They each held up a different vase, a dark liquid tricking over them and into the pool below. Spiderwebs covered the walls and draped from the ceiling like tapestries.

Like the corridor before, it was empty of anything but spiders.

"Is it weird that we haven't passed anyone?" Max whispered. "She was supposed to be pulling people and ghosts to her, right?"

"I don't know," Emmaline admitted. "She may just be luring us in."

"So definitely still a trap." Shay didn't like it. They'd been walking for far too long without encountering anyone, even with the guardian leading them.

"Oh, undoubtedly," Emmaline said. "We cannot control the where, but we can have a say in the how and when. Walking in under our own power is infinitely preferable to being dragged."

"Obviously," Max said. "But we have no idea what Delores or the demon or whatever is planning. We could be walking the exact path she wants us to."

"Do you really think the guardian—"

"Beans," Shay interjected.

"-Would lead us directly into a trap?" Emmaline ignored her.

"I have no idea," Shay admitted. "Like Max said, it's weird we haven't passed anyone."

"Perhaps it is merely avoiding every problem we may have encountered," Emmaline mused.

"Do you really believe that?" Shay asked.

"I thought you were supposed to be smart," Max said, at the same time.

Shay couldn't help but stare at them in amazement. "Max, oh my god."

"What?" Max shrugged, only looking vaguely sheepish. "I'm upset, I'm terrified, my filter is gone, I'm going to be a little mean. I could get a lot mean. We don't know what we're walking into and it's…it's scary, okay? It's terrifying. We could be walking right into her, and we wouldn't know until it's too late. And I don't like Emmaline. There. I said it. I don't like her. She tried to kill you, she possessed Taylor, and she's been really awful this whole time."

"No one is happy with this," Shay said. Emmaline made a vague noise of agreement. "We don't have much of a choice. We have to save…well, everyone. This is the only way that we can."

"Well, I think—" Emmaline started to say, but a noise had Shay holding up a hand for her to be quiet before she could finish.

A skittering sound.

"I don't think we're alone," Shay said, quietly. The sound of tiny nails against stone came from their other side, a flash of blue just ahead.

"Oh, another member of your entourage," Emmaline muttered.

"Do you know what it is?" Shay asked.

"No," Emmaline admitted to Shay's surprise. "What? I don't know everything. I've heard of it before, but only in whispers. Nothing like this. What did you even do?"

"You literally trapped me in a basement with a dirt ghost and you're asking what I did?" Shay stared at her.

"I was not responsible for that," Emmaline said. "It was already there. You riled it up. I didn't even lure you there. I offered to help and you turned me down after I was so generous to you."

"...Wait...if you didn't lure me there..." Shay frowned.

"You weren't useful anymore, Shay Shay," Emmaline said.

"You don't get to call me that."

"Oh, whatever." Emmaline waved the sword. "I'm not entirely sure on the details, but I believe it was Taylor's family. Having a powerful necromancer in the area paints a target on the town. Obviously. Since you haven't even had a month of peace since your seal fell."

Shay hated to admit she was right about the last part. "I mean. Some of that was your fault."

"Oh, I'm not arguing with you about that," Emmaline said. The skittering continued all around them. "But, it does answer the question of why no one has been around. You have help in high places."

"Or low places," Shay said.

"I still don't like it," Max muttered.

They turned and the guardian melted through a pair of large wooden doors. Faint music poured through a narrow gap. Emmaline pressed herself against it, then edged the door a open just a bit more.

"Come on," she hissed over her shoulder.

They were standing on a small balcony with a thick, ornate railing. A narrow set of stairs led down from right side.

"This isn't in the mall," Shay whispered.

"It is now," Emmaline whispered back.

Shay carefully approached the railing, keeping low to the ground and peering between the balusters.

The balcony looked down on an enormous room.

Full of people.

They danced across a black floor so polished it reflected like a dark mirror. Every one of them was dressed in spectacular evening gear in black and silver, masks covering their faces. For a moment Shay was afraid they were awake, then she saw the silver threads controlling their movements.

She couldn't be sure if that was better, nausea crawling in her throat, fear and loathing prickling at her skin.

Shay dragged her eyes away from the people. Columns rose on either side of windows made of blue stained glass, depicting things she didn't want to look at for very long. The pictures hurt her eyes. Towards the back was a dais, surrounded by a canopy of spider webs. An enormous woman languished on the throne. It took Shay a moment to realize it was Delores.

She was massively tall, and something about her face was wrong, like the bones beneath her skin had been subtly rearranged.

"There it is," Emmaline pointed, luckily not with the sword, at the dais. "The bitch is keeping my heart awfully close."

"Where?" Shay asked, then she saw it.

And wished she hadn't.

The back of the throne separated into the black curve of ribs at the top, curling inward to protect a ball of light.

"Oh," Shay said. "Are those your…?"

"Does it really matter?" Emmaline asked.

Shay supposed it didn't, but it still made her want to pat her own chest to make sure her ribs were all still intact, even though she knew, logically, that she was fine.

"Okay, so, this is awful," Max's whisper was a little squeaky. "Well. That's the situation. We know it now. What do we do?"

"We need to get in close," Emmaline said. "I'm…not sure how, if I'm being honest."

Below them the crowd switched partners all completely in sync, practically floating.

"I can't dance," Shay said. "Like, at all. Duncan made me come to this ballroom class thing once for community outreach and we were both super bad at it."

He'd forced her to go. She was starting to realize she needed to go to a lot more of the library programs, not just to support her brother, but apparently because she was living the kind of life where ballroom dancing was suddenly applicable as a necessary skill.

"Not really my type of dancing," Max admitted.

"I can," Emmaline said. "I could lead one of you, but that only gets two of us in close, and there's no guarantee that it would even work."

"Right," Shay murmured, staring over the crowd. She didn't see a flash of purple hair, but the light was strange, washing out any color but blue.

"We're not exactly dressed for it," Max pointed out. "We'd stand out like a sore thumb."

"So we need a fairy godmother," Shay said.

A weight landed on her shoulder, a hundred voices whispering in her ear. "Well, then. Allow us to play the part."

Chapter 39: Fairy Ratmother

Shay's breath caught in her throat. She had to force the air into her lungs.

Before it had been obvious it was a rat on her shoulder.

This time, it was a hand.

Everything in her screamed to not move, but she turned, slowly.

The person standing behind her was tall, thin, and clearly not alive, their skin gray. White hair cascaded over their shoulders in a tangle, surrounding a face with sharp and delicate features. Their eyes were completely black, a spot of green for a pupil. They extended a hand to her, encased in a black glove with silver claws.

"Shay O'Brannon, we are pleased to finally make your acquaintance properly." Their layered voices seemed strange, coming from one source. Despite the external appearance, it was still the Rat King.

She took in other details. The interlocking silver loops embroidered to look like tangled tails of rats embroidered on their black evening jacket, the movement in their hair, a ghostly rat crawling out of the tangles and peering over their shoulder at her. Everything about them was unsettling, from the way the oil slick eyes were trained on her, the sharp smile that was just a little too wide, and the way the silver threads moved ever so subtly across their shoulders.

"Rat King." She found her voice and accepted the hand up. She didn't have time to offend them. Their hand didn't feel like there was anything close to flesh and bone beneath the fabric. Her fingers shook and she quickly tucked her hands into her pockets. "You look…"

"We are united, for a time," the Rat King said. "In our assistance."

She frowned. "I thought you couldn't help."

"We can bring you to your destination," they offered. "That is all we can provide."

"Shay…" Max put a hand on her shoulder, the opposite of the one that Rat King had touched. She realized her entire body was shaking.

"There is no need to be afraid, little mouse," the Rat King said, and the nickname made her skin crawl. "Even in this shape. You belong to us, and we always take care of what is ours."

Her stomach twisted.

Emmaline stepped in front of her, sword held out. The Rat King moved the point away, their expression more annoyed than afraid. "We could unravel what little there is left of you, Emmaline Woodard. It would be wise of you to not anger us."

"We can't trust it," Emmaline said. "Let's just run through the crowd, cause a big distraction, and I'll stab it."

"With this?" the Rat King seemed amused, still holding the tip of the blade. "The blade is not what it once was, and neither are you. It is not what you should be counting on."

"I bet it could kill you," Emmaline said, lunging forward, but they exploded into smoke and reformed behind her, grabbing her by the back of the neck, fingers glowing. Shay made a noise and stumbled forward, not sure if she could do anything, but it was Duncan they were holding onto. They let go and Emmaline stumbled forward, rubbing her neck.

"Do you want to save your brother, Emmaline Woodard?" the Rat King hissed, like whispers coming from every direction. "Have I not assisted you this far? Given you all that you need? That sword has one remaining purpose, and one only. To cut off the source of her power. Without it, the nightmare weaver will be merely a thing to be destroyed."

They gestured to the throne. Shay checked to make sure Delores hadn't noticed them, but she seemed focused on her dance.

Emmaline blanched. "You can't possibly mean—"

"What else could we possibly mean?" Their smile didn't change at all.

"That would leave me with nothing," Emmaline protested. "Less than nothing. I'd be a shade, a death loop."

"You could always follow in your brother's footsteps and latch on to a necromancer as he has." The Rat King clearly did not care at all. "Let him lead you, for once."

"Who on earth would do that for me?" Emmaline gripped the sword hilt so tightly the bone creaked.

"You tore the veil to retrieve it and you failed," they said. "That is how the one you called Archibald slipped from your grasp. Why you requested the alliance with Shay O'Brannon."

"I knew it," Max muttered, and Shay glanced at them, but they were staring at Emmaline with something like pity.

"Maybe the sword can't kill her, but it can weaken her, enough for Shay to deliver the final blow," Emmaline said, quickly, like she was searching for any other solution. Shay couldn't blame her, and despite herself, she pitied her. "How do we plan to get in close?"

"The plan you came up with, Emmaline Woodard. We will go with the crowd."

Shay looked down and she was wearing a coat similar to the Rat King's over a button up shirt and soft white pants tucked into black boots that came up to her knees. Max and Emmaline were dressed similarly, though their coats were a plain dark blue. They both wore masks of molded silver.

"Fairy rat mother," Shay said, for lack of anything else to say.

"It is merely an illusion, do not think too hard about it, Shay O'Brannon, or it will not hold up," the Rat King told her. "I will be your partner, for we have much to discuss."

"But—" Shay looked at Max.

"You can't dance, anyway, by your own admission," Emmaline reminded her. "Shay, if you can distract her, I can get a sword through her. Then you should be able to finish the job. Can you do that?"

"I'm very distracting," Shay admitted. "I think so."

At least the entire plan didn't come down to just her.

"Can you give us a minute?" Max asked. The Rat King spread their hands and nodded, and Max nodded back. They took Shay's wrist and pulled her back towards the doors. She was very sure that Emmaline and the Rat King could still hear everything they were saying, but at least they had the illusion of privacy. "This is insane. Like. An absolutely terrible plan. You know that, right? We can figure something else out."

"This whole situation is insane," Shay reminded them. "We're inside the mall, right now, and it looks like this."

"…Okay, yeah, point," Max said. "But I'm serious, if you want, we can figure out another way. Just say the word."

"What, and ruin your dream dance with Duncan?" Shay joked, weakly. "Well, Duncan's body."

"Yeah, gross, I'd rather dance with the Rat King."

"I will not let you do that," Shay said, no room for levity in her voice.

"I know." Max tugged a hand through their hair, making it stand on end.

She reached up and touched their cheek, just under the mask. "I appreciate it, but we don't have time. We have to save our friends. And like, the town, I guess."

"If we have to." Max took her hand. "Hey um. About earlier, I was trying to tell you…well, when this is over, I'll tell you, okay? Don't let me chicken out. Even if Emmaline is standing right there."

"Okay?" Shay felt something weird and fluttery in her stomach. There had never really been anything Max couldn't just tell her. She might not ever find out what it was. The plan was flimsy at best, and she had no idea if the Rat King honestly thought she could kill Delores, or if she was a lamb being sent to the slaughter. The words tumbled out of her. "Hey, um. I love you, you know that, but…I love you."

At least she said it.

"I love you, too." Max kissed her forehead. "We'll get through this. We've watched, like, fifty period dramas with Nana. We got this."

She smiled. If that was what it took to get them to muddle through it, then she supposed it would have to do. "Yeah, we do."

She turned back. The Rat King held an arm out to her, and she hesitantly placed her hand in the crook of their elbow. Something moved under their sleeve, and it didn't feel like an arm. She swallowed down her revulsion and allowed them to lead her down the stairs.

"You should know I have no idea how to dance," Shay said.

"We will lead."

"Oh, well, that's reassuring."

They reached the dance floor.

They twirled her around. She did her best to move her feet in time with the Rat King's. It was like a dream. Or a nightmare. Surrounded by people moving in the exact same way, suspended by silver threads glinting in the blue light. Their faces were covered by round porcelain masks. There were no eye holes and barely any features, trimmed with lace like webbing and held in place with black ribbons. They made Shay think of the spider they'd fought in the street. She shuddered, looking away.

"Do not focus too hard on what is around us, or you will see it for what it is," they murmured.

She didn't want to look at them, but there was nothing else to look at. Luckily, the mask blocked her peripheral vision. She didn't want to see where they actually were. She had a feeling it was not nearly as grand as Delores wanted them to think it was.

"Knock her throne over, if you can," the Rat King said, very quietly, next to her ear.

"I don't know if you've noticed, but I'm not even five feet tall, and that thing is huge," Shay said.

They chuckled, slowly. "We are very aware, Shay."

She stared at them. "What's with the familiarity? You always used my full name before."

"O'Brannon is a name you use, but even you do not consider it your true name," they said. "We know who your father is, but we do not speak his name. And you are ours. So we no longer need to be so formal."

"I don't belong to anyone."

Their grip tightened on her hand and at her waist. Not hard enough to hurt, more of a warning. "You are young and mortal and foolish, so we will not take offense this time. No one belongs wholly to themselves, Shay. No one. Parts of you will always be under the stewardship of others. Part of you belongs to Jocelyn Johnson. Another part to Geraldine Johnson even though she has passed. To your parents, your brother, to your Finnias Woodard, to your Max Patel. And without us, you would not be here, so you are ours. You cannot change this, and you should not want to. Without us, you would belong to the thing you call a demon, and you would be lost."

"Isn't she a demon?" Shay glanced up at the dais.

"She is what you call a siphon. Not a pale imitation, as the ones you have faced, but an ancient one. Something that has been devouring souls for centuries."

"Is that what you are?"

"Do not presume to know what we are," they hissed in her ear, the voices low and deadly. "We are not like that thing on the throne. We are much older. We are much more. We have always been over you necromancers. And you are very lucky that we want you alive."

Shay tried to keep her breathing even, as the Rat King could surely feel her pulse fluttering under their fingers. "Why?"

"You summoned us, Shay," the Rat King said, quietly. She wanted to freeze, to think about what they'd just said, but they kept dragging her along.

"No, I didn't."

Even as she said it, she doubted the truth of her own words.

"Did you not?" they regarded her carefully through their mask. "Then how were we there? Why would we arrive to save you? You summoned us, Shay. You freed us. We will not forget this."

"But I didn't mean—"

"Your intentions are not on trial," the Rat King said. "You summoned us. We gave you your life. That is enough."

They smiled. Their teeth were too sharp. The expression all wrong.

"Be very careful, Shay, because we are the only ones who will not kill you," their voices were very quiet. "Be grateful, that we have claimed you as ours. Others would not find you a marvel. They would merely devour you without a second thought."

"A marvel?" Shay didn't know what else to ask, what else she could say.

"You are the most interesting necromancer we have ever come across, and you do not know the extent of your ability," the Rat King said. "You do not even realize what you are doing. You are changing things."

"Things are supposed to change—"

"No." The word was harsh, guttural. "We do not change. Ghosts do not change. The one you called Finnias should not be changing and yet he is. He changes more every day, and he should not. It is not possible. And yet, you have done it."

"Oh." What could she say to that? To any of it? She'd had no idea. She just thought that Finnias was especially aware in spite of his missing memories, or maybe because of them. His death had been so sudden and traumatic, it was the perfect recipe for a self-aware ghost.

She'd thought he was just warming up to her. Not that he was changing. Not that he was becoming someone new. He was a person, once, she thought that meant he was a person still.

She didn't know what it could possibly mean. About what she could do. About what she was.

"We have shaken you."

"I'll get over it." She would have to. They were nearly to the dais, and Delores noticed something was wrong, sitting up on her throne.

They pulled her in close again, too close, their breath warm on her neck and ear. "We have done all we can for you, Shay. The rest is in your hands. We believe you are capable of this. You must stop her, by any means necessary. Otherwise, your town will be lost. Remember the price for failure. We will not kill you, but we will take what is owed."

"But no pressure, right?" she asked.

They laughed, a hundred tinkling sounds from every side. "Good luck."

They spun her away from them, towards the dias. She felt the illusion of her dress drop, the mask falling away from her face, replaced by her glasses. She leapt up onto the dias with the motion, it was luckily only a few steps above the dance floor or she never would have made it.

"Hey, Lori," she said. Delores went from standing to sitting with a blink. "Can I have this dance?"

CHAPTER 35: PUPPETEER

Shay immediately regretted saying anything.

Delores's towered over her, even with her back hunched. Her dress shifted and bulged, the seams ripping to make way for a second set of arms. Her face looked like it had been painted onto a torn and fraying mask.

"One more for the party," Delores said.

"You keep saying that, but I'm worth at least two," Shay said.

"A lamb to the slaughter, then, if you prefer." Her voice echoed, layered and almost mechanical, a buzzing sound making every word flat.

"I'm a really mean lamb." Shay was really starting to think that maybe she should have come up with a better plan than distracting a massive, ancient siphon to see if Emmaline stabbing her in the back with a sword that had been stuck in a tree for a century worked. "More of a goat, really."

"It was a mistake, coming here." Delores ignored her, moving her fingers like she was playing some massive, invisible stringed instrument. "I know every one of your nightmares."

"You and everyone who works at Spellbound, you're not special." Shay tried to keep her own tone light, to hide her fear, but it reached up and gripped the inside of her ribcage. Her bravado crumbled around her, and she desperately scrambled to shore it up. She tightened her hands into fists, to be ready to punch, but also to hide how much she was shaking.

Emmaline climbed onto the dais behind Delores, Max next to her, a candle in their hands. She glanced back and wished she hadn't. The dancing had stopped, the dancers facing the stage, their faces rendered blank by their masks.

Delores didn't say anything, just kept moving her fingers, the tiniest hint of silver made Shay realize she was moving nearly invisible threads, plucking at them like harp strings.

The dais cracked, the tiles turning dull and brittle. The cushion of the throne sunk into the seat, the back cracking, only held together by a festoon of spiderwebs that dripped from the mold spreading black across the ceiling.

Black ooze bubbled up from the cracks like a festering wound. A huge, clawed hand erupted from the center, slapping down onto the tile with a wet slap. Shay stepped back and her heel hit the edge of the dais.

A person pulled themselves up from the dais, the cracks spreading, the ooze dribbling over the edge, staining the bottom of Shay's shoes. She tried to control her breathing, to keep calm, but it came in gasping little shudders no matter how hard she tried, the fear trying to drown her from inside her lungs.

Archibald.

He was in a form she'd seen a few times, gray skin pulled taut over too large of bones, tattered clothes stained, a black and crackling void instead of a face.

"He tried to control me, once," Delores somehow injected delight into her stilted words, fingers moving quicker. "Let's see how he enjoys it."

Archibald lurched forward in time to her plucking at the strings. He reached for Shay, and she had no choice but to jump down from the dais.

The dancers formed a ring around her, staring at her with their blank masks. She tried to move farther back but they pushed her towards Archibald. He stepped down from the stage, rot following him, mold skittering up the dancer's clothes, voluminous skirts shedding cloth like dead petals. One of the masks cracked and blackened.

Archibald lunged and she ducked under his swipe. He grabbed her wrist with his free hand. Her sleeve fell apart at the seams, his fingers molding around her arm like putty.

She slammed her free hand into his torso.

Blue fire burned away the gray and the rot. When it was done Archibald was standing in front of her, gently holding her wrist, her sleeve intact once again. He let her go and straightened his vest, giving her a brief, tight smile.

"Thank you," he said, voice distant and echoing. "Goodbye, Shay. Tell Finnias…well. Tell him I'm sorry."

A shimmer of light, so bright she had to look away.

He had vanished when she looked back. All of the rot and devastation he'd wrought swiftly mended itself.

The demon snarled, her fingers contorting on the strings. Shay straightened, trying to catch her breath, trying to be ready for whatever came next.

She'd had a lot of nightmares.

The point of the sword appeared in the center of the demon's chest. Delores stared down at it.

Nothing happened. Shay didn't even dare to move, waiting for whatever change the sword would bring.

Delores grabbed the blade and yanked it fully through her chest, throwing it onto the floor. The metal rang against the tile.

The hole left by the sword closed up. Delores's head snapped around to face Emmaline, who stumbled back from her.

"Pathetic." The word was practically unintelligible, a garbled sound from a mouth not made for human speech. The body twisted around to follow the head and she advanced.

"Duncan!" Shay ran to the dais, but the dancers reached out to grab her. She slapped at them, reaching for the sword, forgotten on the tile.

Max stepped forward and a salt circle formed around them, and Emmaline before Delores reached them. The salt deflecting her lunge, forcing her to the side. She growled and twisted again, plucking at the invisible strings.

Shay heard it before she turned, her heart in her throat.

The crowd parted.

On the other side of the ballroom was the first siphon she'd ever fought.

A huge, pale monstrosity with black spikes jutting out of its back, its legs fused together into a long, whipping tail. Its eyes were twin points of blue fire, mouth a round hole full of serrated teeth.

A ragged, gasping sound filled her ears and it took a moment to realize it was her own breathing.

She clenched her teeth, curled her hands into fists, nails stinging her palms, dredging up every scrap of courage she could. "C'mon asshole! I beat you once, I'll do it again!"

It was too breathy, too scared.

The siphon screamed and she flinched back, hard. It moved, faster than anything should have been able to, barreling straight towards her.

She couldn't get the fire to appear around her fists.

She dodged at the last second, long claws scoring the tiles where she'd just been standing. She slid away and it twisted towards her, slashing at her again. She had to hit the ground to avoid being sliced to ribbons, rolling quickly to one side, claws coming down directly in front of her face.

"Hey!" Max yelled and the siphon spun to face them.

They had left the dais, standing with a candle held high. The flame roared above the wick, the same gold as Max's magic. The siphon charged at them. Another circle of light appeared around them, forcing the siphon back.

Emmaline helped Shay to her feet. "You took care of that thing easily the first time.

Shay shook her head. "I can't get my fire to appear."

"You're letting her control the narrative," Emmaline said. "Simply don't let her."

"Oh, yeah, I'll just not let her turn my whole freaking life into a nightmare even though that's literally her thing and we're directly in her domain," Shay said. "Sounds easy. What great advice."

"It told you that you're a powerful necromancer," Emmaline said. "Now act like it."

The siphon clawed at the edge of the circle, green sparks flying from where it tried to touch the barrier around Max.

Each strike rang out like a bell, wearing the line away. Max thrust the candle in its face, but the flame burned low, and Max looked exhausted. The claws gouged into the tile right outside of the circle.

Shay's self-preservation instincts went up in smoke.

"Hey ugly!" she screamed, so loud her throat hurt. The siphon whirled to face her. "I'm over here!"

It charged her and she barely dodged in time.

The next swipe sliced into her shoulder, all the way to the bone. Blood fountained down the front of her jacket, and she choked, the pain hitting her in all of its intensity a moment later, wrapping her up and squeezing tightly.

If she was going down, she was going down swinging. She wouldn't let it hurt anyone else, and she would protect Max with her dying breath, if she had to.

She punched the siphon in the side.

It made a horrible noise, like wet paper tearing, and exploded into fire and dust.

She sat down and it was like waking up. There was no tear in her jacket and there wasn't any blood on her shirt. Her shoulder ached, but like she had smacked it against a door frame, not like she'd just been cut open. It took a moment for her brain to catch up, she could still feel the claws against her bones.

Max knelt in front of her. She hadn't even seen them move. They pulled her jacket open to check her shoulder and practically slumped with relief. "Oh thank god. You're okay. You're okay."

"I'm okay," she agreed, not really believing it herself. The pain had been so real, she could still feel the hot wet blood dripping down her fingers.

A thread wrapped around Max's wrist.

They both stared at it.

Max's hands jerked forward and closed around her throat.

It was so sudden he couldn't do anything but let them shove her over, holding her down. The pain and lack of oxygen kicked her survival instincts into gear and she struggled, but it was too late. Max had size and strength on their side, there was no way she was going to get them off her before she ran out of air without hurting them.

All she could see was Max's face, drained of color, their eyes wide and terrified. "Shay, I'm so sorry, I'm not, I can't, no—"

The sound of steel through the air and Max slumped over, releasing her. Shay breathed in, deep, and coughed when the air hit her bruised throat. She sat up, expecting to find the worst, but Emmaline had just sliced through the threads controlling them.

"C'mon, Shay, get it together," Emmaline said. "She's coming."

The demon stepped off of the dais, dragging herself forward by one set of arms, the other set furiously playing the strings.

"I'm about to punch you," Shay warned Emmaline.

"Save it for her."

The poltergeist slammed into the demon from behind, sending her sprawling. Emmaline dashed forward, stabbing at the nightmare.

The nightmare's fingers twitched, yanking someone into her path.

Finnias.

The sword hit him in the chest. He looked alive, for the moment. Blood dribbled over his lips, and he touched the spot where the sword had hit, right below his heart.

Emmaline screamed.

It wasn't a scream Duncan could have made. It sounded almost like an animal, wild and broken. She let go of the sword and backed up, her hands to her face, making that horrible noise. Finnias fell to his knees. He pulled the sword out and blood darkened his vest to black. The sword clattered on the tile.

Shay clambered to her feet too slow to help, running towards them but it was too late. She hadn't been able to help at all. "Finnias!"

He looked up at her, young and scared.

He was dead. He had been for a century.

This was a nightmare. One that belonged to her and Emmaline.

They would never get close if this kept up. She'd had a lot of nightmares the last few months, and things would only get worse.

She needed to end it, now.

The strings.

She grabbed forward, ignoring Finnias and Emmaline, ignored how it burned in her hand. Blue fire raced down the length of the blade and she ran towards the demon.

She sliced through the complicated webbing. It went up in flames and the nightmare screamed, high and long and loud. Shay dropped the sword and slapped her hands over her ears and stumbled back, but the sound swelled in volume, shaking the windows, dust raining from the ceiling.

The living people dropped to the ground.

Ghosts surged over them in a blue wave.

Chapter 36: Popular

Shay put her fists up, but she was already tired, and there were a lot of ghosts. Her right hand was black from holding the sword, spreading across her fingers and the back of her hand.

Taylor stepped in front of her, throwing salt at the first ghost, making it reel back with a shriek.

"Holy crap." Shay stared at her.

"Hey, sorry, she had me a bit tied up," Taylor explained. "Yanked Finnias right out of me, which wasn't fun. Gideon is posted up."

"What does that—" Shay started to say. An arrow passed through a ghost next to her, disrupting its energies so violently that it fell apart into a fine mist. She looked up to see Gideon on a balcony above them. He saluted her with an arrow before he nocked it. "Oh, yeah. Posted up. Got it."

She punched at a ghost when it got too close, some formless thing with a face like a child's clay project. Max's candle flared to new life, burning ghosts into hollow shadows and forcing the rest into retreat. The demon reeled back with a shriek.

"Go get Finnias!" Taylor told her.

Shay nodded and ran to him. He was back to being blue, the blood was gone, but he was just sitting there. Emmaline hovered close by, the sword on the ground a few feet away.

"I don't know what to do," she confessed. "Without my abilities I can't…I can't do anything."

"You can keep that thing busy. I'll wake him up." Shay had no idea if she could do anything, either, but she had to try. She was vaguely aware of the poltergeist slamming into the demon's face, but she couldn't pay attention to it.

She couldn't lose Finnias.

"Hey, Finn?" she tried, quietly. No response at all, he kept staring at the floor, reflected in tiles slowly losing their luster.

She went to touch him. The cold burned before she even made contact and she snatched her hand away.

It took a moment to steel herself long enough to touch his cheek using the side of her hand. Her fingers were already black, it probably couldn't get much worse. "Hey, c'mon, Finn. We don't have time for this."

She turned his head, so he was looking at her. He blinked a few times. "Shay?"

"Hey, there he is," she said, her voice shaking. She'd never considered losing Finnias before, but the thought of him not being there terrified her. It had only been a few weeks, but she didn't want to get used to not having him around.

Awareness snapped back into his eyes, and he sat up completely. "What happened? Where are we?"

He was on his feet and pulling her up to hers with a hand that wasn't nearly as cold as it had been a moment before. Relief overwhelmed fear, if only for a moment, and without his help she wasn't sure she would have been able to stand.

"Thank god," Emmaline said, quietly.

"Okay, so, about where we are…"

The demon screamed.

She had all but shed the last vestiges of Delores, becoming the bulbous and horrific monster that Shay had faced a month before in the circle. Her body dragged behind her far too many arms. The hands were long fingers, nails dark and ragged, gouging the tiles. The eyes on her arms were open, red rimmed and pale. The only trace left of Delores was the ragged mask of a face.

"Oh, I see." Finnias yanked Shay behind him. "How do you always manage to get us into these situations?"

"I can't help it, I'm very popular!"

Another scream and the demon charged at them, so heavy she cracked the tiles. Shay ran, Finnias's hand still in hers, so he was able to pull her out of the way when the demon slammed into the wall right where she had been a moment before. The windows shattered, scattering blue glass like ice. She was close enough Shay tried to punch her, but another ghost reared up in front of her, burning away in her flames.

The demon laughed, a throaty deep chuckle that rose in volume and octaves until it was a shriek, shaking dust from the rafters. Ghosts formed a ring around her. Emmaline was on the other side, slashing at them, but there were so many she would get overwhelmed quickly, and Shay was pretty sure the sword wouldn't last for much longer, the blade already seemed shorter, the edge ragged and rusted.

"I can't get close as long as she can use that." Shay pointed to the throne. "We need to knock it over."

"Got it." Finnias ran with her to the dais. He was up it in a flash, helping her scramble up.

With Archibald gone the throne was whole again. The webbing had burned away, leaving the ribs completely exposed, part of a skull still attached to the top, the bottom jaw and teeth missing.

Shay didn't want to think about it too hard.

Someone touched her shoulder, and she whirled around. Max held up their free hand. "Just me. We're knocking this thing over?"

Shay nodded. "Let's break stuff."

Finnias grabbed her hand and shoved against the throne. She helped, though she doubted between the three of them she was doing much. It was a solid piece of furniture and impossibly heavy, sitting sturdily on clawed feet.

Shay glanced back, hoping to call for help. Emmaline was busy, her and the poltergeist tag teaming against the demon and her legion of ghosts. Gideon was shooting arrows as fast as he could, but he would run out before too long. Ghosts swarmed up the stairs and he ducked back into the hallway.

Taylor ran up to the dais and helped to shove, too. The chair rocked back on two feet and crashed down onto its back.

"Oh, that was very loud," Taylor muttered.

Shay glanced back. The demon rushed forward, dragging herself forward, all the eyes on her arms trained on them.

"Get the heart!" Max instructed her, throwing down a satchel, a salt line spreading around the front of the dais, but Shay doubted it would hold for long. Emmaline slashed at her side and the demon slammed a hand down towards her, but Emmaline dodged back. Still, Shay knew that Duncan was not very athletic, and ghost powers or not he wouldn't last forever.

Finnias dragged her towards the back of the chair. The ribs had cracked, the skull rolled away with a clatter.

The heart sat amidst the broken, blackened bones, glowing slightly. Shay's hands shook as she scooped it up. It seemed smaller than she thought it would be, encased in something like ice. "Well, that's definitely not a metaphor."

"How do we destroy it?" Finnias asked.

"How would I know?" Shay asked. "I could throw it or…crush it? Or maybe we could use it? Max could?"

"I don't think we have the time," Finnias said.

"Could you use your abilities? Your fire stuff?" Taylor suggested.

"I don't know," Shay admitted. She hated to admit that she didn't want to destroy it. Without it, Emmaline would be reduced to nothing. Maybe Shay didn't really care for her, she certainly didn't want to join her or to help her with her plans, but could she really be responsible for basically killing Finnias's sister all over again?

She knew Emmaline was a bad person. That she wouldn't hesitate to do just about anything to get what she wanted. She was ambitious, cruel, and unpleasant.

But she was clearly present, clearly still a person, just like Finnias, and could Shay really be her judge, jury, and executioner?

A small voice whispered that she hadn't worried about that with Archibald, and he'd been present, too.

"What are you waiting for?" Taylor practically shrieked.

"Right." Shay didn't have any other choice. She held the heart and let the fire surround it, the blue flames covering the heart.

She was suddenly hyper aware of exactly how to use the heart. How even as a necromancer herself she could harness the abilities that Emmaline wielded in life, controlling every ghost in the room. They all stood to attention. She didn't need to see it to know exactly what they were doing.

Any power in the world could be at her fingertips, if she chose it. If she just used it.

Finnias stood ramrod straight, waiting for her orders.

She dropped the heart like she had been burned. Dizziness washed over her and she staggered back, right into Finnias.

"What happened?" Taylor asked.

"...I can't...I don't have the ability," Shay said. Logically, she knew it was better if she did try to use it, tried to control the ghosts, but the thought made her feel physically ill. "I don't want to touch it again."

"Okay, we'll figure something else out." Taylor grabbed a piece of wood that had broken off from the chair at an angle, ending in a sharp point. She used both hands to slam it down on the heart, but the wood blunted without doing any damage at all. "Dammit! We don't have time for this!"

"Whatever you're doing make it quick!" Max yelled over their shoulder. Ghosts swarmed the salt line, and she knew that they couldn't have much energy left, not after everything.

Shay didn't know what to do. The ghosts were upon them, the demon right behind them, wearing down Emmaline who had a useless sword and a poltergeist that was more annoying than doing any actual harm. Her friends were all hurt and exhausted, and it wouldn't take long for them to be completely overwhelmed.

And she still couldn't even fathom using the heart, her thoughts turning away from the idea like curdling milk.

"I'll distract her," Shay said. "She really hates me, should be easy. If you can get the heart out of here, maybe..."

"Maybe what?" Taylor asked.

"Dunno, haven't thought that far," Shay admitted. "Get out, okay? I'm trusting you."

Taylor nodded, grim faced and pale, grimy with blood near her hairline. Shay had no idea how badly it had gone when they were captured. She imagined not well. She scooped up the heart. "I can do that."

"You are not leaving me here," Max told her.

"Wouldn't have anyone else with me," Shay said, more sincerely than she'd ever meant anything in her life.

They took her hand.

The four of them ran into a sea of ghosts. They clawed and grabbed at her. She hit away the most insistent, Finnias fielded off the rest, by her side as always. If Taylor could get out of the mall with the heart, it had to count for something, it had to at least make things easier.

"Hey! Big and ugly!" Shay yelled, waving her arms.

The demon whirled on her. She didn't look like Delores at all anymore, her face a scarred mess. The mass of eyes on her arms rolled in Shay's direction. She gestured with several of her hands and the ghosts swarmed towards Shay and Max, scrabbling over each other. Max threw down a salt circle, but Shay knew it wouldn't last long.

Max seemed to know, too, pulling her into a hug. She hid her face against their shoulder. They wouldn't get a chance to tell her what they wanted to, and it was all her fault.

She'd never get to tell them what they meant to her.

The ghosts never hit them.

Shay looked up after a minute and all of the ghosts were frozen in place around them. Emmaline held the sword above the heart, the tip an inch away from its surface. She looked torn, her hand shaking so badly that the blade wavered in her hand. "Make one more move and I'll stab it.

"You need that," the demon's voice was much worse than it had been, nothing human remained in it, just a flat growling sound that barely formed words.

"Maybe," Emmaline said. "I won't be me without it, but maybe I've been me for a little too long."

"Come work with me, Emmaline. We can do amazing things together." The demon beckoned her closer with several hands, sibilant voice nearly a purr. "You could be my most powerful general. I would allow you to keep the heart, to lead armies, topple nations, whatever you would like."

"You know, I'm really starting to understand Shay," Emmaline said. "No thanks."

She stabbed down.

CHAPTER 37:
OVER

The sword hit the heart with an explosion of energy.

It blew away the salt circle around Shay and Max. All the other ghosts disappeared, vanishing like smoke.

Shay grabbed Finnias's hand, just to be safe. His fingers curled tightly around hers.

The blade cracked, light leaking through the black metal. What was left of it flaked apart, the pieces turning to sand before they reached the floor. The sand scattered across the cracked and dull tiles, the sound loud in the sudden silence. Soon all that was left in Duncan's hand was the bone of the handle. A moment later, it disintegrated between his fingers.

Silence.

The demon screamed, long and wordless and horrible, charging forward, heading straight for them.

Shay shoved Max back. A massive hand reached for her and she smacked it way. The entire limb burned away. The demon kept coming at her and she kept hitting it, over and over again. For a moment she thought it wasn't going to work.

But without Delores, the demon was just a big, ugly siphon.

Fire wreathed it and it shrank in on itself. It shed great parts of itself, burning up to nothing in seconds. It covered its scarred face with its many hands, yanking at its matted hair even as that disintegrated into sparks and dust.

Shay gave it one final punch.

The demon shrieked one last time, loud and echoing.

All that remained was Delores, the actual ghost, all in faded blues, her shawl around her shoulders, her cigarette holder in one hand.

She smiled, briefly, mouthed a thank you, and turned away. A bright light flashed, and Shay threw an arm up over her eyes. When she lowered it, nothing remained, not even the scent of tobacco.

They stood in a department store. The tiles were still cracked, mannequins lay askew. Everything was filthy with dust and cobwebs, but there were no visible spiders. Stale and close air closed in around them.

Shay sneezed.

"Is it over?" Max asked, quietly.

She turned to face them and stumbled, badly, a wave of dizziness washing over her. "I hope so. I have nothing left in the tank."

"That was…a lot," they said. "Are you okay?"

"I think so?" She looked up at them. She thought she should have felt triumphant, or at least happy, but she just felt empty. Hollowed out. "I…she's gone. Just…just like that."

She didn't know if she was talking about the demon, Delores, or Emmaline. Maybe it was all three.

She'd succeeded, but it didn't feel like a victory at all.

"I'm tired, and you're tired, and there's…a lot to unpack here, but we should probably do it outside, or better yet, back at home," Duncan said from behind her.

She turned to him. He looked exhausted, a bruise forming on his cheek and his hair styling had not held up at all. He was covered in dust, Shay wasn't sure when the finery from the Rat King had vanished, but he was back in his normal clothes. "Hey, donuts. Whole dozen?"

"Whole dozen, more or less," Duncan said. "I feel like crap, think I sprained like six things and have a million bruises, but yeah. All me."

"And…Emmaline?" Shay asked. "Is she…?"

"I don't know," Duncan admitted. "Things went black and when I opened my eyes she was gone. I think…she's not coming back. Um. I think Gid and Tay are finding Jo and Arlo, but uh…yeah, we have enough bad rumors, we should go."

"We have rumors?" Shay asked but let Duncan usher her towards the door. "Since when?"

"The last town meeting was wild," Duncan said. "I'd suggest you come to them, but I think you might hit someone, and then I'd have a whole slew of other problems that I really don't want to deal with."

They left through a different set of doors than the ones they'd entered through. It had been night when they entered, but at some point the sun had risen, flooding the world with gray light through a thick layer of clouds. It was snowing, gently. Cars filled the parking lot, not strictly adhering to the lines. It would take forever to sort out.

But the ghosts were gone, and beyond the lot the town looked completely normal, strip malls and apartment buildings.

Teton Falls felt safe and very quiet.

"You…wanted to talk to me?" Shay asked, taking Max's hand. It still felt like everything was slipping by too fast.

She couldn't really believe it was over. She looked back at the mall, half expecting it to be the same strange structure, or crawling with spiders. But it was the same reddish-brown brick it had always been, snow piling on the roof and the remains of the old neon signs that hadn't been lit in years.

"It can wait," Max said.

"You got thrown around a lot, I remember that part." Duncan tilted Shay's head from side to side and she had no choice but to let him do it. "No weird sounds. Does anything feel broken?"

"No," she said. "I don't think so. What's the difference between a bad bruise and a break?"

"Have you never broken a bone?" Duncan made her lift her arms. It seemed excessive, but she was so glad he was there she found she didn't really mind that much. "Trust me. You know. It's the difference between 'oof owchy' and 'I think I'm going to puke now'."

"Okay, yeah, no puking, I think," Shay said. "What about you? You were possessed by…um…"

Finnias stared at the snow. She gently pushed Duncan away and walked over to him, her boots crunching in the fresh snow. Duncan let her go without a word.

"Hey." She slipped her hand through the crook of his elbow, linking their arms together.

"Hi." He didn't look at her.

"How are you…that's dumb, this is dumb."

"Sometimes you are." He finally glanced at her.

"Thanks, appreciate that." She looked down at where she could see her arm through his. "I'm glad you're here. Still here. I…I really…"

It was over.

She'd won, in all the important ways. She'd done everything she'd really set out to do. The town was safe, she'd saved her friends, the demon was gone, and Finnias was with her. Right next to her.

So she didn't know why she was crying. Why it felt like everything terrible and awful had been squeezed into her chest and up into her throat.

Finnias faced her, she wasn't sure when he'd unlinked their arms and moved, but his hands were on her shoulders. "I…I'm okay, Shay. I'm here. Everything is fine."

"I couldn't stop her, not in time," Shay admitted, her voice choked and small. "I couldn't do it alone, and Emmaline, and I…"

"She was an awful person," Finnias reminded her.

"Maybe, but…but she was still your sister, and…" Shay was interrupted by a sob that felt like it was tearing her chest in two.

"It's okay." Finnias pulled her close. It was cold, and he was freezing but she couldn't find it in her to care, burying her face against the right side of his chest. Sobbing hurt, like it was coming from deep down at the bottom of her ribs and she was ripping it out, but she couldn't stop for a while.

When she finally could talk again, her voice was even smaller, even more choked. "I couldn't do it. I couldn't save everyone. I'm supposed to save everyone."

"You can't always save everyone," Finnias said, quietly. "You can't put that on yourself. None of this is your fault. You did everything you could. It's all right, Shay."

"But…"

"I…I still don't remember her," Finnias admitted. "And I haven't forgiven her, for the things she's done. For how much she hurt you. I don't know if I ever will, and maybe that's terrible but…"

"That's not the point," Shay said, quietly.

"I know," Finnias said. "I know it's not. But…in the end, she made that choice. And…it's okay. It really is."

It didn't feel any easier. She took a step back and looked up at Finnias. He had a soft smile on his face, maybe a little sad.

The Rat King claimed she was changing him.

It scared her. Everything felt too big, and she knew that even if she'd destroyed a demon, even if Emmaline was gone, nothing was really over. The Stevens were still going to cause problems, and Emmaline had warned her about the hunters. If there wasn't already, killing a demon would definitely paint a target on the town.

"There's um. There's still so much we need to talk about." She sniffed and wiped at her face with the knitted cuff of her sleeve. "And we need to prepare, and—"

"Not right now." Max stepped up behind her. "We can worry about that later, okay? For now, let's just…get back to the house."

She nodded, sniffing again.

"…Also we need to go because I think I left my car in the middle of the street," Max said.

That made her laugh, wetly, but she felt a little better. "Wow, who's the real law breaker here?"

"Still you." Max gave her a quick hug, just a squeeze, but she felt a little better.

Jo hugged her, next, and Shay was so relieved to see her that she almost started crying again.

"I can't believe…you really just…" Jo sighed. "I'm sorry I left you to deal with this on your own. Again!"

"And that I'm the reason she wasn't there," Arlo added.

"Not your fault," Shay said against her shoulder. "And I wasn't alone. I had a lot of help. Always do."

"Always will," Max said.

"Still…" Jo sighed. "That's it, we're redoing every ward on the house, we are doing a full cleansing, nothing is getting overlooked. This is not happening again."

"Okay," Shay said. "Sure."

"This is all lovely, and I'm glad we're all okay, but can we go home now?" Duncan asked. "I am exhausted and Shay's practically falling over, and we should really get out of here before more people in there or out here wake up because I do not want to explain even a little bit of this."

"Fair," Arlo said.

Shay ended up next to Duncan for the walk, by his design.

"It's not your fault," he said.

"Kinda…feels like it is," she said. "If I was a little faster, and stronger…I don't know."

"It's not your fault," Duncan repeated, firmly. "We were just…cleaning up a mess. It sucks that we had to, it's absolute crap that it was a mess to begin with, but…we were just the janitors of this story."

"Janitors are the unsung heroes of the world," Shay said.

"Oh, absolutely," Duncan said. "But just…you can't beat yourself up about it, okay?"

"Yeah."

"Yeah?"

"I'll do my best," Shay said.

"Good, now be proud, you saved the world," Duncan said. "Or at least the uh…east side of Teton Falls. Lots more than most people save."

"Yeah, I guess so," Shay said. It didn't feel like she'd done much, but the snow continued to fall, the world turned a little brighter.

She saw Beans, standing on the corner, smaller than ever, the sunlight shining through it. It bowed its head to her, turned, and walked away.

CHAPTER 38: MOSSES AND LICHENS

Shay lay in bed under her blanket, tapping away at a crappy phone game that relied too much on ads.

She hadn't talked much.

She knew, deep down, that there was absolutely nothing for her to mourn. Emmaline had tried to kill her, more than once. She'd done terrible things and, in the end, she'd made the decision. She'd died over a hundred years ago, and nothing Shay did now would change that.

The facts didn't really help.

At least the darkness had receded slowly from her palm until it was a smudge like charcoal. She didn't know if it would ever fully go away.

A cold hand reached into her blankets and grabbed her wrist, the blankets yanked back a moment later. "Hey!"

"That's it," Finnias said. "I'm not letting you mope about this anymore."

"I'm not moping," she insisted, knowing she was lying.

"How long have you been under that blanket?" Finnias asked.

She checked her phone. At some point, it had turned into early afternoon. "...Yeah I don't know why I looked at the time, I have no idea. I gotta work tonight. I'll get up."

"How long since you replied to a message from Max?"

She pulled down her notifications and winced. Their last message was from the day before, letting her know that they would be there for her. "Okay, yeah, you got a point there. I'll invite them over, right now."

"Good," Finnias said. "You might want to...take care of yourself, first."

She looked down at her days old pajamas and tried to pull a hand through her hair. "...Okay, yeah, you have a point, I'll give them a time. They're punctual."

And she missed them, she realized, feeling a little guilty that it had taken her a few days to realize that.

"They are," Finnias agreed. "I suppose it's one of their good qualities."

"Oh, shut up, you love them, too."

"No."

"Yes you do, don't be shy, it's okay." She grinned at them, feeling more like herself than she had for a while. Teasing Finnias felt normal, and for the first time in days, she didn't feel very guilty about things being normal. "You love them. And me."

"The last one I'll accept."

"Aww Finn!" She grabbed him in a hug. An indignant sound escaped him. "I wuv you, too."

"Go shower, even I can smell you, and I'm dead."

"Wow, Finn, that's rude," Shay said. "Here I am, showing my love and appreciation for you, and all you can say is that I stink?"

"Yes. Go away."

"Fine." She crawled off of the bed and hopped in the shower. She hated that Finnias was right, and she felt a lot better once she was clean.

She stared at the fogged-up mirror probably longer than necessary. She could just see her own reflection in blocks of color.

It would be all she saw.

She drew a heart in the steam and left the bathroom.

By the time Max got there she was feeling a little nervous, but at least she was in fresh pajamas with her hair braided.

They knocked on her door frame and she was up and grabbing them in a hug before she even really thought about it.

"I'm sorry," she said.

"Nothing to be sorry for," Max said.

She leaned back and looked up at them. She thought maybe something should have changed, in the days that had passed, but Max looked the same as always - perfect brown skin, tousled hair, and their lovely dark eyes. She felt better just having them there, and part of her never wanted to let go. To just attach herself like some sort of barnacle.

"Nah, I do," she said, after staring a moment too long. "I've been a real butt."

"All that matters to me is that you're feeling better," Max said. "But I have missed you, a lot."

"I missed you, too," she said. She glanced back, but Finnias had left the room at some point while she had her face pressed against Max. "Just wanted to make sure…anyway, I just…it's dumb, she was already dead, but she's gone and…I don't know. I needed a little bit of time, I guess."

"It's not dumb, you—"

"But!" Shay interrupted them. "I don't want to talk about it. Or her. Or any of it. Come to my big, beautiful window seat and chat with me. How is Max. What is happening with them. Is Nana doing well?"

"She's puttering around as always." Max let her lead them to the window seat, sitting down next to her. Sun streamed in through the window, slanted and weak. Snow covered everything, sparkling in the small break between the clouds. November had shifted into the cold grip of December while she'd been hiding away. "And I'm okay, just…work. Same old. We made the news."

"We did?"

"Yeah, mysterious break in to local sporting shop," Max said. "It was so hard to keep a straight face."

Shay laughed, feeling something untangle in her chest. "That's hilarious. All that, and I get on the news for throwing something through a window. That sounds right, though. Definitely sounds like me."

"Definitely." Max laughed, too. "How has everyone here been?"

"Donuts is back to his usual frosting covered self," Shay said. "Jo and Arlo seem fine. I think they all just want to forget it happened, you know?"

"Yeah, I get that," Max said. "I think…everyone just wants to forget. Pretend it all was a bad dream."

"Just a long nightmare," Shay agreed. "So uh. You said you had something to tell me, back in the mall? And…then I kinda shut you out, and I'm really sorry about that, but you can tell me now, if you want."

"Oh! Uh, I don't know," Max said. "It all feels a little stupid after…all that, I guess. I mean, I feel stupid, that it's taken me so long to say anything, but I guess…all that made me realize that you have to say things that are important to you."

"Definitely," Shay said. "So…I'm not supposed to let you out of it. Past Max was very clear on that. Spill the beans."

"Okay, but they're my beans—"

"Spill them all over."

"Really not loving this metaphor," Max laughed, despite what they said. "Yeah. Okay. Um. I had a whole speech prepared. I don't remember it. The last few months…a lot has changed. Not all of it bad. I mean, we've made some cool friends, and you live in a cool house now. And…I feel like we're closer."

"I feel like that, too," Shay said, glad they were on the same page for that, at least. "I mean, you've been my best friend forever and you always will be but…I don't know. Feels different, I guess. In a good way."

"Definitely," Max said. "Um, so, I don't know if…more change is good."

Shay's heart thudded painfully in her chest. "What do you mean?"

"I mean I am messing this up, so bad," Max said. "Because nothing has to change, that's not what I meant. I'm being stupid. You asked me…last week? Was that only last week? Anyway, you asked who I had a crush on."

"Yeah?" Shay felt like she'd swallowed an entire energy drink in one go and it was fizzing between her bones. She really didn't want to hear about Max's mystery crush, not after everything. She would probably die. But they were her best friend, she'd said so, and she vowed to just be happy for them, no matter her own feelings. Max deserved the world. "Did you finally work up the courage to confess?"

"Oh my god." Max stared at her. "You really have no idea."

"No idea of what?" Shay was going to combust if they didn't get to the point and just tell her so she could cry for a few hours, later, when she was alone.

"It's you."

It took a moment for it to sink in. "…It's…me?"

"Yeah, it's—"

"You said I knew them really well!" She stared at them.

"I uh…thought you knew?" Max gave her their most sheepish look to date. "And I was trying to be cute?"

"You're always cute!"

"You are, too," Max said. "So…so yeah. It's you. It's always going to be you. I love you. I'm in love with you. I think I always have been. And…and it's okay, if you don't return those feelings, I just—"

"Max." She grabbed their face, smooshing their cheeks. "Stop."

"Shtop?" The word came out slightly garbled.

"Stop talking," Shay said. "You're telling me that for the past week and…whatever, I don't know what day it is, I've been jealous of myself?"

Max's expression shifted from horrified to like they might laugh. "Shay…"

"I mean, of course I'm in love with you, too!" Shay let go of their face. Her own was hot, her heart pounding against her ribs, and the bubbly feeling filled up every part of her.

Max hugged her, tightly. She hugged them back, hard enough to probably hurt their ribs, but they didn't make any complaints. They kissed her temple and leaned back. "You really do?"

"Of course I do." Shay had never meant anything more. "I can't even picture my life without you, I never want to, and…and okay it took me a while to figure out, because I had a head full of rocks. Just chock full. They don't even move. Covered in moss and lichen and other green things."

"That's okay," Max said.

She grinned. "Because you lichen me?"

"I lichen you the moss out of anyone."

"Oh, you can't do that to me, that's practically proposing," Shay joked, her voice shaking.

Max laughed, and it was a little shaky, too. "I'm just...so happy right now. I didn't think I'd ever tell you. I was perfectly happy being friends with you, but I just...I like this."

"Me, too." Shay knew they needed to define their new "this", but she was perfectly content to just lean against their shoulder for the moment.

They sat like that, for a while, not really saying much, just being in each other's presence.

"Oh, crap, I told Jo I'd help her with something," Max said.

"She can deal."

"It will take two seconds. Will you really be that sad if I leave for two seconds?" Max asked.

She pouted at them. "Yes. Broken hearted. Might not ever recover. You know I close tonight, right? I only have so much time with you."

She'd agreed to work a few hours that evening. An agreement she regretted.

They stood up and kissed the top of her head. "I know. But...you have someone you need to talk to, too."

Finnias was sitting in the chair next to her bed.

"You're right, I do," she said. "But when you get back..."

"I'll be right back," Max promised.

They closed the door behind them.

Shay crossed the room and sat on the bed, right across from Finnias. "Hey, um. You heard...all of that?"

"It's a little hard not to," Finnias said.

"Are you…upset?" Shay couldn't quite tell what his expression was.

"No," he said. "I…I don't know. It doesn't matter, does it? I'm not…alive. Sometimes, it's like I forget, and then something changes, and I'm reminded all over again. That it's something I'm incapable of."

"Maybe not," Shay said. "I mean…I think you are, capable, that is. It hasn't been that long, but…I feel like you've changed a lot since we first met. And since you first came here."

"Have I?" Finnias asked. "Or do you just think that?"

"I know it," she said. She hadn't repeated what the Rat King told her, about how she was making things change, and everyone had been giving her space for days, so she hadn't had to confront it.

They were quiet for a moment, then Finnias reached over laid his hand over hers. "Maybe you're right. Before, I don't know that I would have cared."

"Now?" Shay asked.

"Now, I'm just…very glad you're doing better," he said, quietly.

"Yeah." She turned over her hand so she could hold his. "I think no matter what happens, it's going to be okay."

"Yes," Finnias said. "Eventually, it will be."

CHAPTER 39: FAVOR

"**W**hat about kissing?"

"You kiss me all the time," Shay told them.

Max laughed. "I meant on the lips."

The two of them sat on Shay's bed, shoulder to shoulder, leaning against the headboard. Max had burst back into the room saying they needed to talk about boundaries. She'd laughed, at first, but she was glad they were having the conversation.

"Mouth to mouth resuscitation doesn't require a license, but if you don't have one, I am within my rights to sue you," Shay said.

"Wow, what do you know, I'm licensed in CPR and First Aid, looks like we have it covered."

Shay looked at Max, wondering what it would be like to kiss them. Probably nice. Probably more than nice. Her face was getting warm, and she had to look back at her ugly bedspread. "Slow?"

"However slow you need," Max said, like they'd said to several things already.

Shay was pretty sure they had the patience of a saint. "So…I'm fine with girlfriend, obviously. All girl here. Girl and friend and girlfriend."

"So fast," Max teased her. "A girlfriend. Already."

"We've known each other for sixteen years, I would call that glacial," Shay said.

"Okay, yeah, point made."

"Anyway, what about you?" Shay asked. "Obviously I'm not going to use a gendered term. But I don't want to use something dumb that you hate."

"There are a lot of dumb terms that I hate, yes. I'm very judgmental," Max said. "How about partner?"

"I like it." Shay grinned. "Kind of mysterious. Makes us sound like detectives. Or cowhands. Or space rangers."

Max laughed.

"I think that's about everything, right?" she asked.

"I think so," they agreed. "Besides, we have time."

"That was a very short serious conversation, I'm so proud of our communication skills," Shay said. "One more thing, though, and this is a big one. Finnias."

"No," Finnias said from the window seat.

"We're talking about you, not at you!"

"No," he repeated.

"Too bad!" she thought about throwing a pillow at him, but it would just hit the window behind him. "He's not going anywhere, I'm going to make sure of it. Is that okay? Because this is my one real deal breaker."

Finnias looked absolutely shocked, which made it worth it, even as her stomach squirmed. They'd just started, and she could end things so quickly.

"I know," Max said. "You're a package deal, and I respect that."

"Good." Shay's insides relaxed. "We are."

"You are," Max agreed. "Kind of like how I have to put up with you and Duncan being a package deal and tag teaming against me."

"To be fair, we tag team him sometimes, he probably just thinks it's within his rights to get even," Shay said.

"He's wrong, of course. That being said, my other deal breaker is you cannot tag team against me with Duncan. I'll cry."

"I would never," Max promised.

"Well, good." Shay nudged their foot with her own. It was still a little strange to her, but in a good way that made her feel giddy.

Max checked their phone. "I think I've used up all of your pre-work time."

"Yeah," she sighed. Jo said the shop had become busier than ever but had tried to give her as much space as she needed. Shay didn't know if their money problems were over, but Arlo said they did get paid for the mall job, and he'd sold probably a thousand protection sachets, each one with the sigil inside. Jo didn't think they'd need the design anymore, but that it was probably better to be safe than sorry. "Gonna stick around?"

"Of course," Max said. "I'll be up here, though. I figured out where you keep your candy stash and I want to ruin your high scores in all of your games."

"I suppose I'll allow it, you being my partner and all, otherwise I'd have to kick you out," Shay joked. They both knew she really only kept a candy stash for Max.

"Aww, I love you, too." Max kissed her cheek, keeping their promise to take it slow. "Have a good evening at work."

"Gross yuck."

They laughed. "Good luck at work."

"That's better." Shay hopped off of the bed and went to close the curtains. It wasn't very late, but the sky was already dull orange as the sun drew close to the horizon, a few of the streetlights flickered on.

Work ended up being just as busy as Jo warned her, right up until she flipped the sign over to closed. Shay set about sweeping the shop and turning off the lamps that they didn't need on during the night, just a few in the windows. Jo said it was important that they always appear welcoming. She didn't say to who, but Shay wasn't going to argue with her boss.

"Did you mean what you said?" Finnias asked.

"I've said a lot of things today," Shay said. "If it was 'have a nice day', then no. I've never meant it. Not once."

Finnias sighed. "You know what I meant."

"Yeah, I do." She swept between the bookshelves. "And I did. If they'd had a problem…well, it sure would have been awkward, but…you're important to me."

"And literally stuck to you."

"That, too," Shay said. "But I don't want you to have to worry about that. I want you to be my awkward third wheel forever and ever."

Finnias's expression went flat. "Wow. Thank you."

"You're welcome." She grinned at him. "It's not actually awkward. I care about you, too. I like having you around. I want you here with me, and I always mean that. So…yeah. That's it."

"…Well, I like being around you, too," Finnias said, after a moment. "Of all the people I could be haunting, I'm glad it's you."

"Aww Finn."

"I'm not saying it again." He seemed almost embarrassed.

"I know, I appreciate the one time I got to hear it very much," Shay said. "I love you, too. I know I said it earlier, but I was being annoying, so this is a sincere I love you."

"Yes, fine."

She finished sweeping and emptied the dustpan into the garbage before tying it off so she could take it out back, it was full of receipts and a few drink cups.

Something skittered past the garbage can.

She stepped back in alarm. The scratch of claws on hardwood filled the closed shop. Finnias stood in front of her.

"We are not here to harm," the Rat King said from behind her and she whirled around. They looked at her in amusement, holding up their hands. They were dressed exactly as they had been in the mall, the silver loops on their jacket moving subtly in the dim light. "Hello, Shay. We are glad you were successful."

"Yeah," Shay said. "…Thanks. For…for the help."

"And now the siphon is gone and we can begin our true business." They sat down on the stool behind the counter like it was a throne. They ran their claws over the wooden countertop. "A favor is owed."

Shay really wished she still had the broom in her hands, if only for something to hold onto. Her nails bit into her palms, but she didn't dare relax. "And if I refuse?"

"Then your life is forfeit to us," they said, like they were commenting on the weather. Like they might yawn at any moment. "But we believe that our goals converge, Shay. We have one task for you. Are you ready to receive it?"

What choice did she really have? Finnias gave her a warning look, but all she could do was shrug in response.

"I'm ready," she said, swallowing down the trepidation in her throat.

"Good." The Rat King smiled sharply, leaning forward. "We require you to retrieve Finnias's heart."

Acknowledgements

Three books is an exciting milestone, and I never could have made it here without all of the help I received along the way. As always I want to start with a huge thank you to my beta readers, Brooklyn and Jennifer, who got me through the many drafts this book went through and still being excited like it was the first time they were reading it.

To Cindy, for being an amazing friend and giving me ideas that would scare her.

Carmilla, of course, for her continued support and the incredible cover.

My writing groups for letting me share out of context quotes.

To Cloaked Press, for continuing to believe in these books and publishing them!

And of course, to you, dear reader! Without you none of this would be possible, and I truly thank you for reading all three books from the bottom of my heart.

Please don't forget to leave a review, and join me for book 4: Heart of the Matter!

About the Author

A. Lawrence is a nonbinary writer living in the PNW with their cat and hundreds of ideas. They hold a BA in English and spend most of their time either writing or drawing. They enjoy walks through cemeteries and spending time in the woods.